My Ground Trilogy

Joseph Torra

Also by Joseph Torra

Fiction

What's So Funny
Call Me Waiter
They Say
The Bystander's Scrapbook

Poetry

domino sessions
Watteau Sky
Sixteen Paintings
August Letter to My Wife and Daughters
Keep Watching the Sky
Duck Tour: The Movie
After the Chinese
Time Being

Praise for Joseph Torra's Fiction

The Bystander's Scrapbook:

"Torra's novel is . . . highly powerful . . . A moving and elegant book [that] illuminates the complexity behind America's image as the 'cradle of democracy' and 'land of the free.' - Kirkus UK

They Say

"Reads like a string of interviews delivered in broken English. That gives it a documentary-style authenticity — a good way to juice up the tale of a struggling Italian-American family in Boston . . . Torra's characters speak in an almost poetic cadence . . ." - Boston Magazine

Call Me Waiter

"Torra writes wonderfully about work . . . There are two kinds of writers, those who want to imitate literature, and those who want to imitate life, and the second kind are better, Torra's in that second category." - Daisy Fried

My Ground Trilogy

"How often can you claim to have bumped into an unprepossessing novel that makes you beg 'tell me more?' " – The Boston Book Review

"This is the genuine article. It's dirty and prickly, quirky and poetic, everything writing ought to be." - Geoff Nicholson

"In its understated way, GAS STATION is a celebration of artistic truth, not as something to put on a pedestal, but as a necessity, inextricably entwined with life and hope." – Los Angeles Times

"His deadpan tone leads to touches of humour and pathos, while his highly compressed prose at times achieves the intensity of poetry." – Observer

"[In MY GROUND], he offers a jumbled text that cuts awkwardly back and forth in time and reads like the Benjy section of Faulkner's The Sound and the Fury, cut with Sylia Plath's The Bell Jar. The result is a stunning portrait of a mentally damaged, pathetic, lonely woman. Absolutely brilliant." - Gay Times

"Torra's writing is accurate, beautiful, and most importantly simple. . . . he doesn't hyperrealize the characters or setting. He's an anachronism, the unHemingway, writing the great American novel of lost innocence except that Torra realizes there isn't and never was any innocence to regain." – The Poker

My Ground Trilogy
PFP, INC
publisher@pfppublishing.com
144 Tenney Street
Georgetown, MA 01833

PFP Edition, August 2012
Printed in the United States of America
© Joseph Torra 1996, 2000, 2001, 2011

First PFP Edition © 2012
ISBN-10 0983313903
ISBN-13 9780983313908

Reprint:
Gas Station
previously published Zoland Books Cambridge, MA 1996
Tony Luongo
previously published Victor Gollancz London, UK 2000
My Ground
previously published Victor Gollancz London, UK 2001

My Ground Trilogy

Foreword

My wife has always given me my best lines. It was Angela, back in the days before kids, and spending an afternoon idling in a bookshop was nothing unusual, who came across a slim paperback with a red and blue neon cover: *Gas Station*, by Joseph Torra, published by Zoland Books of Cambridge, Massachusetts. It must have been 1997, and *Books Etc* on Charing Cross Road wasn't a bad place to find what you didn't know you were looking for. I'd worked my way through Angela's Raymond Carver collection; I was looking after David Gates at work; Victor Gollancz had always had something of a reputation for fresh voices. Incredibly, no one had picked up the UK rights. I managed to buy not only *Gas Station*, but also the other two titles contained in this volume, and a fourth book from Joe: *The Bystander's Scrapbook*. The reviews were generally outstanding; the sales ho-hum, but by today's standards pretty respectable.

A decade or so on, and it still puzzles me that simply writing about the huge expanse of this thing called life isn't, somehow, quite enough. There's no real high concept in Joe's books — just the sadness, the beauty and the things that raise a smile from everyday life, from people's lives. Dipping back into these books now, *Gas Station* is slower, but every bit as beautifully drawn as I remember. *Tony Luongo* is a fast, furious and exhilarating trip through the voracious life of its eponymous vacuum-cleaner salesman. Like all of Joe's books, it's pure, sexy, funny and full of moments of astonishing sadness and beauty. I wouldn't envy the task of a young editor sitting in a publishing meeting today, proposing a novel without punctuation — but that's a misnomer really. You won't find a greater page-turner without punctuation; it means that *Luongo* (as it was originally known), is kind of literally unputdownable. Joe knew what he was doing on that score. *My Ground* comes from an even darker place, and still haunts after all these years. But what I remember most is the clarity and precision and the wonderful flow of Joe's writing. A world rendered so pure on the page. Like Raymond Carver, every word has been thought through; not a word is wasted. You are what you are, and where you come from . . .

Books Etc became *Borders*, which became *TK Maxx*, which sells brassy handbags and end of line fashion. Next door is Charing Cross Road's first Mexican restaurant. In publishing Victor Gollancz became a fantasy and science fiction imprint. I got shunted over to non-fiction. It's true: Don DeLillo and Paul Auster probably wouldn't get a deal if they were starting out today. One of the low points of this last decade was failing to secure a UK deal for Joe for *Call Me Waiter* — the greatest book about working in a restaurant you'll ever read. But for now, if you haven't read the three books that make up this loosely connected trilogy, you're in for a real treat. It's a bit like not having watched *The Wire* . . . A renowned literary events organizer here in the UK once told me, "The problem you have with Joseph Torra, is that he's ten years ahead of his time." Well, that was nearly a decade ago . . .

Ian Preece, UK Editor
London, April 2011

Author's Introduction

I wrote the three novels in My Ground Trilogy by ear. In each instance, I heard a voice that had a story to tell. I had in mind William Carlos Williams's ideas on the importance of writing in American speech. Moreover, I believed in Williams's view that the local is universal. These books tell the stories of three working-class, Boston area people — each of whom is trying to crawl out from under.

Joseph Torra
April 2011

Gas Station

Joseph Torra

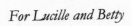

For Lucille and Betty

I'M BURNING TRASH piece by piece tossing take-out coffee cups, crumpled sandwich paper, paper bags, pizza boxes, donut boxes, this morning's *Record American* into the rusty fifty-gallon drum holes punched through sides for ventilation. Cigarette butts I glean and smoke stirring the black-smoke paper fire. It smells back here where Countess is chained up all day her shits sit various stages of decay. Stacks of burned-out engines, transmissions and rear-ends exude sludgy streams of stale motor oil, transmission and rear-end fluids. Nothing smells foul as rear-end fluid. The labyrinth drains into a wide puddle inches thick black muck hottest days reeks like death. Keep an eye out says he'll break my legs catches me smoking he'll smack me around a bit, yell a hell of a lot, but won't come back here too lazy he'll holler haven't heard the hose bell ring no one at the pumps. What's the best gas I ask something stupid what do you mean what's the best gas Jenney's the best gas I know Jenney's the best gas what's the best Jenney gas, regular or premium? Premium he shouts premium's the best gas that's why it costs more. Regular's 28 and 9/10th cents per gallon premium 32 9/10th cents four cents a gallon better. Blue 1965 Chevy Impala just out of the showroom new lines for the Impala not so square as the '64 more streamlined, sleek, this one with one of those new vinyl tops at first look like convertible tops but it's hard what's the point for looks. Sporty car for old Mr. Woods just retired paid cash orders his usual five gallons I start to pump the old man washes the windshield looks the car over says too much of a loss soon as you buy a new car his one concrete reason to dismiss something now cars beginning to come equipped with seat belts he won't use 'em because he read of an

1

accident a car caught fire the driver unable to unfasten the seat belt burned to death now he uses that as an excuse to dismiss seat belts. Never actually looked *under* a brand-new car put the gas nozzle automatic low down on my hands and knees spotless shiny configuration of undercarriage. The gas tank is cool to touch, the spotless tailpipe burns my fingertips, up front a gleaming oil pan and red-orange engine block, black transmission hospital clean eventually to be rust grease and grime myriad of leaky valves, seals, gaskets, hoses, fuel lines brake lines water lines slowly manifest with time. He's yelling I forgot the gas already gone over ten gallons what the hell are you doing I wanted to see what it looks like under there what do you think it looks like under there. Mr. Woods insists paying the difference my father won't hear of it turns on me soon as Mr. Woods leaves yelling how much I just cost him got to learn to pay attention this is a business.

FREDDY GOLAR AND "Red" Duncan blasting a pint between them long two-and-three-bubble sips wash down with cold Pepsi thick twisty rolled glass bottles I stock in the machine. They cough and ooch it doesn't take them ten minutes finish and commence to hoedown Red slapping air bass on broomstick Freddy air violin fiddling. Red's "Red" because Red's wavy shiny red hair orange-freckle-ridden complexion when he drinks his face burns bright red his eyes flame. Red's big and solid with muscular tattooed arms fit from years working in the tunnels down from Prince Edward Island with his brothers James and Joe digging the Callahan Tunnel James dies in a tunnel fire someone lights a cigarette where they shouldn't. Joe tells stories of his days digging the tunnels Red never does Red's singing laughing Freddy puts his fiddle down combs his thick white hair over his face nearly reaches his mouth dancing in circles clapping his hands. Don't know how old Freddy is married forty years no children now he's drunk tells me again about overseas in the service he fought with a crazy Italian soldier who grabbed hard hold of his balls twisted his scrotum around his leg and made him sterile. His wife calls calls again third call he goes. Red's only getting started won't see him after tonight for a week or longer out on a tear lives in the house behind the station with Joe and their mother. There's always someone hanging around the station picking up a little work as a gofer or cleaning cars on the side or having a good time like Freddy and Red. I bum cigarettes off them company helps pass the time my father trusts me alone with the station at night he's at the dog track playing cards maybe with a woman.

FEW MECHANICS MASTERS Lenny Barns no master. Lanky Lenny mug shot eyes greased hair combed back pointed pockmarked face chain-smoking Camels grabs me by my ears says like two loving cup handles pulls my head down between his legs wrap your lips around it it'll only take me a few seconds never sure whether he really means it he's got the most beautiful red-haired wife. Tortures Countess when the old man's not around ties things around her head laughs at her struggling to free herself grabs the shotgun from the compressor room loads it chases me into the garage hide behind a stack of tires sudden BLAST concrete fragments fall on my head. Says he was a mechanic for Connie Kalitta national drag racing champ the Zona brothers tell me Lenny never knew Connie Kalitta. Lenny quits shortly after the fire I'm home and Michael Mackey from down the street with ten brothers and sisters screaming the gas station blew up and he's got half his brothers and sisters with him and they're hollering the gas station blew up. Lenny's smoking while pumping gas blown back in the initial blast knocked off

3

his feet shouts to Doctor Bagsarian who's still sitting in the burning car get out and the doctor gets out and away in the nick of time. For days everybody talks about the fire the station closes for several days the *Mercury* runs articles front-page photo Lenny sitting at our kitchen table Lenny tells the story how it blew tossed him the fuck back like a bug same story he tells the newspaperman or me or customers or anyone who will listen fervor like he really enjoys what happened and telling the story over and over changes slightly more polish and drama each telling. The *Mercury* photo sitting dazed at our kitchen table face and hands bandaged, eyes awry, double shots of whiskey Lenny.

OAK STREET'S A connector street allows Malden and Melrose traffic access to Interstate 93 and Route 28. Before this is a gas station it's a variety store old-timers remember cigarettes eight cents a pack. In 1949 huge holes are dug for gasoline storage tanks, new piping and a pump island installed, an outside pit's dug down where a mechanic climbs automobiles driven over him. The two-car garage out back's soon built woodstove heat during winter and wet weather now only used for storage then a one-car garage is attached to the office a lift installed pit outside filled in. Still later another one-car garage added onto the first space limitations won't allow the garages next to each other but one in front of the other long garage two years ago my father with the help of Bill Gleason gets a second lift installed in newer back half of the garage so when it's busy we can keep several jobs going at once. There are houses on each side of the property in which the Wiggins, De Franco, Hart and Maynard families live though the Maynard family's only old Clyde who's eighty-seven and his younger brother Ralph who's eighty both retired railroad workers still wearing their engineer's caps. Traffic's light on Oak Street except during morning and afternoon rush not busy enough to sustain good gas business most gas customers regulars from neighborhood. My father's ignored by the Jenney Company because of the company's obligation to the higher-volume stations at the same time they're not around as often with their noses in his business as they are at big-volume places which my father says is fine. Look closely discern uneven patchwork various building sections first garage red brick is melded with stucco office structure second garage concrete blocks makeshift fit to red brick first garage outside the building painted white with red trim big blue JENNEY letters above office picture window. Over the years learn cars and faces people who drive by tired bleary eyed morning traffic stream late afternoon early evening yawn return. Imagine spacious houses, quiet green lawn shrubbery streets in Melrose, children who own their own skis eat dinners of beef gravy potatoes desserts day's events discussed over oversized glasses of milk. Families of Saturday morning drive by, skis attached to roof racks winter, summer's beach chairs and coolers towing boats and campers to Newfound Lake New Hampshire or Bar Harbor Maine. Country Squire wood-grain station wagons, new blue four-doors.

BLIZZARD OF '68 midnight plow all evening drive home old '48 Willy's Jeep plow piston breaks plow stuck down turn around head back to the station if we can make it fix it in the morning. Snow swarms through headlights' view, rolls over top of the plow in waves little truck grinds forward a tank the old man says. Turn off the Fellsway up Oak can we make the hill lucky not to burn out motor or transmission four wheels spinning broken tire chains slapping into the station lot sleep in the garage, rubber-tire beds, fender guards for blankets. Morning

5

snow drifts five six feet high across the station lot still snowing radio stations on storm emergency Blackie fixes the plow piston I shovel two-feet-wide strip around pump island, another two feet away from the building, my father plows one long pile into bigger piles ten feet high front and rear of the station. Interstate 93 closed blocked hundreds of cars abandoned must be cleared for plow trucks most of the abandoned cars are locked we have to struggle with a coat hanger to get the doors open Blackie and I returning to the station in the tow truck with a car on the boom my father's broken English over the radio WBZ emergency hotline tella de people no locka de cars whenday leavem onnada highway we laugh out loud tella de people no locka de cars Blackie mocks. We tow twenty-four hours straight thirty-three cars in the lot nowhere to put more my father charges twenty-five for the tow fifteen a day storage some argue too much but want their cars back and pay.

PINUPS IN THE compressor room a blond sitting in a wicker chair holding an ice-cream cone, pig-tailed brunette woman in cheerleader skirt and socks looks like Sally Field think she is Sally Field I watch *Gidget* can't tell. Calendar out back by the tire machine courtesy Riverside Auto Parts redheaded woman with large breasts who burned two black spots where her nipples should be hangs here the whole year. George arrives with coffee and donuts shows us a magazine pictures of woman having sex with a pig look at that curly little tail Joe says laughing Tommy and George tell me look closely that's how it's done son, that's how it's done. Pig looks a bit like Annie they laugh George says hasn't stopped you Joe Tommy you neither. One night working alone Annie comes in for gas in the front seat Billy Coniglio from my seventh-grade class next day at school ask him he goes out with her isn't she old so what. George says

Annie ain't pretty but ain't she pretty fat.

SIX-FIFTEEN A.M. he wakes me wash and dress stop on the way Town Line Donuts buzzing with city workers, cops, Freddy from Freddy's Sunoco. All the guys crazy for Willa and Cookie's two daughters Willa and Cookie own the Town Line their two daughters a few years older I never keep my mind on what I'm ordering. Sometimes I get two honey-dipped with coffee today a bacon and egg sandwich takes a little longer she has to make it over the grill short hemline on the uniform she leans over the grill to flip the egg she's got legs all the way up to her ass Freddy says to me I nod my head yes but doesn't everyone? We open at seven before I eat turn on the pumps and compressor, bring out the tires in the little B. F. Goodrich tire stands, jacks, windshield wiper center, roll out the hose for the bell. Two bites into my sandwich someone pulls in for gas or leaves a car for work morning's busiest time my father's already barking out orders for me Blackie figures out what parts we need for various jobs the old man off for several hours chasing them while I work the pumps Blackie takes it all apart. In between gas customers hang out and talk with Blackie lets me smoke his cigarettes he's got a 1955 Chevy Bel Air red and white cherry clean showroom stock a biker rode with the Disciples his wife looks like a pinup girl made him quit biking though once after he quit and sold his bike she saw him riding down the Revere Beach Parkway at the head of a pack with a girl on his back. Blackie has a brother Billy and the Zona brothers kind of famous locally since Billy owned a fuel dragster raced for two seasons at New England Dragway placed third in finals once now it's in need of much work sits rusting in the garage at Billy's parents' house. The fastest I ever went in a car was in Billy's '54 Ford Skyline with pearl green paint job full-blown 312 V-8 Billy rebuilt from a wrecked '56 Ford Interstate 93 130 miles an hour pinned to my black leather bucket seat Billy ripping madly through those gears. The old man's back 10:30 after coffee I help Blackie with an exhaust system a '58 Pontiac Chieftain later I sit in a '59 Caddy with the huge tail fins up on the lift await Blackie's instructions to pump the brake pedal so he can bleed the brake cylinders. Long minutes up here stare out at rows of tires in storage to my right and long row fan belts and radiator hoses hanging to my left. I turn on the car radio 'RKO or 'BZ Beatles maybe Gerry and the Pacemakers Roy Orbison "Pretty Woman." I think about Willa and Cookie's daughters my dick hardens Blackie shouts shut the fucking radio I can't hear him when he tells me to pump. By noon most of the work finished my father goes out for subs I take a meatball Blackie's a fussy eater roast beef cooked on the grill with mayonnaise when we get pizza he takes his cheese and pepperoni off eats with sauce only I put his cheese and pepperoni on top of my slices. Old man naps after lunch pulls the tow truck around back sleeps in there Blackie finishes up the last of his work then pulls his '55 Chevy into the garage lets me grease it and change the oil. We turn the radio up and smoke Blackie listens to 1950s music his friend Phil who drives a '63 green Corvette Stingray says that was music you could really make a broad to. Temperature's climbing kids I know from school walk up to the pond for swim Blackie and Phil check out the girls whistle and catcall. Wow Phil says Phil always says wow Angela Gambini passes by in her red bikini — wow — slowly and emphatically — W-A-O-U-W. Three o'clock work's finished old man's out getting iced coffees all the kids parading down the hill from the pond to catch the bus. Tonight we eat here my mother brings supper around 4:30 after Blackie leaves, a loaf of Vienna bread two pots separately wrapped in kitchen towels one for each of us sausage vinegar peppers fried potatoes still steaming from the kitchen ten minutes away the old man drinks ice water I drink Pepsi ice cold. He leaves around 6:00 got some errands to run says he'll be back in time to close at 9:00 and he always is.

MY FATHER'S NERVOUS new Registry officer's here to make sure the station's ready for the upcoming inspection season and if so drop off the little boxes of gold — inspection stickers. Johnny the MDC cop who hangs around the station drinking coffee talking about pussy with the guys says the new Registry cop's a real prick Registry cops got the easiest job in the world no need for them to be such assholes. Larry the old Registry officer's been transferred this new guy sweats fat his black hair's parted on the side greased thick into a wave he's short and round in blue and gray Registry uniform he inflates more than wears. The old man offers him two bottles of expensive Scotch Larry used to like but he refuses doesn't drink says if the old man wants to do him something he can always throw him a little something so he might take the wife out for a dinner the old man on the defensive fumbles to remove cash from his pocket officer tells him it can wait until the next time. The officer checks that the big white headlight board is clean unobstructed and in its place at the end of the garage and it is I painted it myself along with the thick yellow strip on the floor to help drivers guide themselves in. He quizzes Blackie tries to trick him up with his questions contradicts some things Blackie says watches Blackie jack up the front end of a car check for wheel play possible loose ball joint or faulty tie-rod end. They talk allowances of eighths-of-inches play, headlights, brake lights, directional lights, horns, wipers, brakes, tire-tread depths and the officer seems pleased enough leaves the stickers says he might check back during inspection time to see how things are

9

going. The old man after he leaves can you believe that son of a bitch a little something so he can take his wife for dinner?

PHONE CALL FROM the State Police car out of gas on Interstate 93 when we arrive the trooper takes my father aside tells him the guy out of gas has no money his license plate's from Tennessee they're running a check on him. In the meantime the old man tells me to gas him up I grab the five gallon can out of the back of the tow truck empty its contents into the gas tank of the man's old Plymouth station wagon. The police find no reason to detain him a matter of how the guy can pay for the gas he looks dazed his eyes glazed like he hasn't slept in days he's got a watch takes it off shows it to the old man the old man says follow us back to the station just off the next exit we'll fill your car up and figure something out. At the station I fill him up ask where he's from Tennessee my father asks how he ended up stranded with no money he was supposed to get work in Maine and it fell through he was on his way back to Tennessee. Blackie and I are amused listening to my father and this man from Tennessee converse my father's Italian broken English and this guy's rebel accent so thick talks so low every time he says anything have to ask him to repeat what he said and he and my father misunderstanding what the other one says by the time their verbal exchange is finished the conclusion each has arrived at is completely wrong. One thing we all understand is that the man hasn't eaten since yesterday when he had three donuts my father takes twenty bucks out of the cash register gives it to him leave the watch when you get to where you're going mail the money we'll mail back the watch. My father thinks the watch is worth some money when the man leaves he puts it in the locked drawer where he keeps the inspection stickers remains there years each time I see it I see the

10

Tennessean's beaten face, bad teeth, tattered clothes and glassy eyes.

ALWAYS SOME KIND of payoff he's doing a favor for someone or someone's doing a favor for him. Always a license or permit or stretch of road you can bargain for my father's the stretch of Interstate 93 from the Medford/Somerville line north to the intersection with 128. His friend Tom Riordan secured him that stretch of towing rights my father does more favors for Tom than anybody else. Tom was a member of the state House of Representatives now has an official job on the state payroll perpetually deals a hand my father's ever eager to grab so my father has rights to all the road service and towing work on three and a half to four miles of Interstate 93 through the favor system and bringing expensive whiskey and beer to the State Police barracks once every month. He drags me along with him so I can carry the cases of booze up the barracks stairs he acts like an ass with the troopers thinks he's just one of the guys retells the same story the time he was servicing a car up on 93 and a speeding passing car tore the open door off of Trooper Lopez's cruiser and the car never stopped. We leave the booze and for the next several weeks the towing business booms then slowly trails off until someone spies the tow truck from Sonny's Mobil towing our stretch of road then the old man goes out buys more cases expensive booze and beer and we make our pilgrimage to the barracks again.

GO DOWN THE Jew's and get me some cream he says handing me a dollar bill every day drinks cream for his bad stomach every day cream and Maalox cream and Maalox. He won't go into Harry's store claims one time Harry overcharged him for something every time I go into Harry's Harry tells me *his* version of the story. Most people in the neighborhood call Harry Harry the Jew and his store Harry the Jew's I call him Harry and the store Harry's he's a friendly man wise in ways knows locals don't like him call him Harry the Jew he has an IF I CAN'T TAKE IT WITH ME I'M NOT GOING sign up brown and curling around the edges feeds right in with my father's belief that Jews are money misers but that sign means more about living than money says Harry. Harry used to sell and repair bicycles now with all the department stores around it's been years since anyone bought a new bike from Harry and he's still got a couple of dusty fat-tired bulky boys' bikes you don't see much anymore with all the new streamlined stingrays and ten-speeds. Harry still fixes a few bikes, sells some milk, cigarettes or candy but if the store wasn't the downstairs part of his house I don't think he could afford to stay open though he's not really open usually he's upstairs when I enter a little bell rings up there in a minute or two Harry's footsteps descend the creaky wooden stairs, never in any hurry Harry with the cigar stub in his mouth wearing baggy brown pants, white wrinkled shirt and ill-fitting tie, old gray button-down wool sweater, balding scruffy gray head of hair, thick eyeglasses I try to look him in the eye but the round brown balls blur says my father never liked him no one else in the neighborhood either he can't understand treats everyone fairly always has I tell Harry people are funny that way Harry says it's closed minds. Usually I get a Ring Ding or Devil Dogs with the change eat them on the walk back to the station the old man glugs down half the carton of cream puts the rest in the Pepsi machine which doubles as a refrigerator sits back down at his desk belches for a few minutes holding his stomach and groaning in pain, looking at me for sympathy with his green eyes, his hair thinning, midafternoon five o'clock shadow, blue uniform shirtsleeves rolled up

12

above the elbow revealing thin hairy arms, mole on the inside of his left forearm like a big period at the end of a tattoo that reads MAMMA TU SOFFERTO PER MI. How much did he charge you for the cream he asks and I tell him and he shakes his head you could get it for five cents less anywhere else.

SATURDAY SEASON'S FIRST snowstorm predicted for Sunday everyone looking to get their snow tires put on Joe and I change tires nine hours straight stopping only for a quick sub around noon. Not allowed to use the power wrench when we change tires my father says they strip the lugs which they don't we do it all by hand with lug wrenches by the end of the day my arms ache. Some snow tires already mounted on rims we loosen the lug nuts, jack up the rear end of the car, spin the lugs off, remove the tire and replace it with the snow tread, spin the lugs back on snug, drop the car back down, tighten the lugs, pop the hubcap on and we're through. Other snow tires aren't mounted on rims so when we get the summer tires off we must remove them from their rims on a machine bolted to the concrete floor. The machine holds the tire tight while I get under the lip of the tire with a bar turn the bar round 'til the tire lip's off do the same to the bottom then put the snow tread on reversing the procedure. Sometimes I have trouble mounting a snow tire since over the summer its rubber has dried or gone out of shape being stored incorrectly in someone's garage or basement floor. Then I spray it with rubber lube really bend and bang the bar to get the tire mounted and if I can't get it to inflate and seal properly around the rim which often happens with brand-new tires or tires that haven't been stored properly, I place an air belt around it which inflates squeezes the tire from the center more banging and pulling it will catch if not I call Blackie over he bangs and readjusts the belt swears Jesus

13

Fucking Christ or come on you motherfucker bangs and eventually the tire catches. We bang and jack 'em up and let the jack down by end of day how many sets snow tires. My father gives us a wad of cash to split more than a hundred dollars at two dollars per set of tires four dollars if they're not mounted over fifty dollars each first time the old man's ever paid me for a day's work must have won big at the track.

THE AMBULANCE DEPARTS siren wails as we arrive State Police have closed off the lane, red, orange, blue, pink colored lights flash and swirl from police cruisers, tow truck and road flares, a light show in the dark into which my father and I rush turning the colors of our faces and blue uniforms yellows orange crazy pinks purple. Scratchy voices blare from police radios Volkswagen Bug's run into a concrete bridge pillar front half of the Volkswagen wrapped around the pillar cars and trucks ripping by in the other lanes inside on the driver's side floor lone penny loafer caught in gnarled metal pool of blood on floor front seat dashboard splattered I can't breathe my father yells let's get going back to the tow truck dig hooks and chains out from the wooden red box first push the Volkswagen off from the pillar too wrecked to tow from the rear but we can't push Volkswagen off it's infused with the pillar so down on my back under the Volkswagen with flashlight look for a place to hook so we can first pull the car off the pillar with the truck then hook it and tow it away from its demolished front. I ask a trooper if the driver's dead says he was still alive when they took him away finally get the car off of the pillar then get it winched from the front a car pulls up a woman climbs out of the passenger side hysterical shrill-screams that's my son's car that's my son's car that's my son's car. The officers approach her and guide her back that's my son's car she's back in the car

14

with the windows closed I can hear her glass-muffled screams that's my son's car. Every day I go out back look into the Volkswagen various color stages blood early bright red to livery brown I dream I try the penny loafer on looks very big but fits fine I'm working but it isn't really at the station my friend Jerry Hastings is here to inspect the wreck after school the driver's alive and after several months of intense recovery and therapy appears one afternoon to pay the bill on the Volkswagen and sign release papers for us to junk the totaled vehicle. It's been weeks since I've looked inside but when Spadafora the junk man comes to tow it away one last look tarry brown blood-stains shards of broken glass penny loafer tangled in twisted metal that's my son's car.

TINY'S GOT THE best flattop haircut works for my father during the fifties big bruiser-type guy but gentle and quiet works Saturdays now a day or two during the week if busy he's got cancer a hole in his throat covered by a white cotton band-age scratchy voice a great effort for him to talk clumsy often drops things smokes Luckies though he shouldn't smoke with his cancer drinks ice-cold bottles Pepsi down five or six gulps huge lunches of steak bombs veal cutlet subs large French fries the old man buys lunch for the crew says Tiny could put him out of business. Tiny punctures a hole in the radiator replacing a water pump on a '60 Plymouth Belvedere hands me a quarter go down the Jew's buy a bunch of Juicy Fruit gum when Harry comes down he tells me *his* version I say people are funny that way Tiny and I chew up several packs of Juicy Fruit which he plugs the radiator hole with don't say anything to the old man I won't. My father looks at the clock says take Countess up to the pond for a bath wants to get rid of me hear him on the phone today talking low making some kind of plans been a long, slow,

15

hot day many pond visitors packing up or already gone strange silent humdrum heat-haze brush Countess her day's clumps loose hair let go her collar she dives straight in swims a large sweeping circle returns right back to me drenched shakes water off soaks me lather her up with shampoo back she goes take off my Oak St. Jenney shirt socks and shoes go in with blue jeans water's still clear cool swim out sandy bottom copper-yellow late afternoon sun hue slants ten or twelve feet below. Countess excited swims near too close get my arms scratched by her dog-paddling claws slowly tread water in the middle of the pond onshore lifeguards turn over the rowboat pull in bar-rel markers late sun orange-gold band head to toe to bottom sand.

JOE AND RED alternate their drinking so one of them takes care of their mother. Red returns home from a weeklong bend-er Joe's been dry about two weeks hanging around making some cash polishing cars last couple of days says he's thirsting for a cool one he talks about it for a few days sonny I'm thirst-ing for a cool one then disappears for three days returns sick for the rest of the week his ulcer. Sometimes he goes out with Annie but not really going out they just go somewhere and fuck like Annie and George though George takes her out some-where in his Oldsmobile 98 the pond at night they do it there. Joe takes her out to the rear garage the old man keeps pad-locked cars in storage they do it inside one of the cars. Tommy swears he and Annie haven't done it Joe and George say he has Tommy says they shouldn't kid around like that 'cause if his wife ever catches wind she'll have his balls. They sound dis-gusted when they talk about Annie like they don't like her or like fucking her. She's kind of heavy bad facial skin stories I hear she really likes getting it sometimes I think of her when I masturbate doesn't work out. Joe only goes with her if he's drinking sober swears he'll never go near her again neither Joe nor Red ever married Joe talks a lot about a Puerto Rican woman Maria he was in love with worked as a maintenance man at Boston College she's a cleaning woman in one of the dorms how they do it in a broom closet hear students walking by in the hall tiniest prettiest little quiffer he illustrates with his fingers delicate oblong shape one hot day both drenched with sweat in the broom closet I wonder whatever happened to my Maria. Joe says Tommy's definitely fucking Annie but doesn't want anyone to know. Tommy works three nights a week sometimes Saturdays during the day he works at a parts store fancies himself a mechanic mostly pumps gas his friend George hangs out with him sometimes Tommy'll do some minor work like a tune-up uses Chilton auto repair manuals to make sure he's got plugs and points set right timing mark correctly marked sure sign says Blackie of someone who doesn't know what the fuck they're doing's when they use a manual for something simple as a tune-up. Tommy's a dark, big, roly-poly guy eats three and four donuts at a time with Pepsi old man says he steals laziest guy who's ever worked for him. Tommy moves slow does little when I'm hanging around has me pump gas unless it's a woman driver 'cause now so many of them are wearing miniskirts all of the guys, Tommy, Joe, Blackie, George, Phil, even my father, rush out to the pump island to wash the windshield whenever a woman pulls in race among themselves see who gets there first only time Tommy's in any hurry. Tommy says true sign of a guy hasn't got a fucking clue about broads says I love you when he's fucking one.

SCHOOL'S OUT HE'S waiting for me out front in the tow truck no time for a cigarette Jerry Hastings hands me off a couple which I pocket and hop in the truck. Everyone comes at the last minute for inspection folks who've been holding back they know something's wrong with their cars we write lots of rejection stickers pick up much repair work the last week of the season. I help Blackie in the garage checking registration numbers, brake lights and directionals, scraping old stickers off, replacing taillight bulbs, headlights, flasher fuses. Traffic's backing up on the street waiting line old man's out there directing whistling broken English yelling to folks bring it arounda put it ovah deer hey pull it uppa pull it uppa. Those rejected argue a ball joint isn't loose or a bald tire's legal, but nobody wins an argument with my father. Anyone gives Blackie a hard time he calls the old man who pulls out the book shoves it in faces goes on like this for hours until around 7:00 when Blackie leaves. My mother brings big bowls macaroni meatballs and sausages. Around 7:30 he takes off okay with me I've got homework to do which I half-do between the trickle of gas customers and assorted visitors. A '64 Ford comes in and pulls up to the air pump on the side of the building. The driver gets out takes the hose off the lever but I don't hear any air pumping. I look out the door 'round the corner he picks up the hose I've startled him looks like he's been nosing around out back. Got a tire gauge he asks one right on the pump I tell him oh yeah didn't see it he checks the air on his left front tire thanks me leaves the hose on the ground backs out and drives away. Two years every day at school Kathy Quinlan tells me she sees my father the night before at her house what's he doing at her house visiting her mother? Don't see her much since I've been in high school he's probably down Wonderland chasing the dogs he was penciling around the race form while he ate. Around quarter to nine Annie pulls in with her 1965 red Ford Mustang convertible glows under huge overhead pump island lights. Fill it up I remain in the rear hold off washing her windshield avoid

18

conversation with her only takes three gallons backs up throws gas over the bumper and my pants. Wash the bumper with water collect money aren't you going to do my windshield? Oh sure I forgot grab the squeegee start on passenger side over to her side anybody around? Freddy Golar was here earlier. Joe too. George? No haven't seen George probably tomorrow night when Tommy works. Thanks sweetie she says leaves in a flash peels out her tires faint hint of rubber smell in air.

WORKING UNDER CARS winter snow and ice forms under wheel wells, on bumpers, in corners of chassis and frames. Once a car's up on the lift starts melting rain of ice-cold drops down my back on my head all day long every day for months cold water soaking my hair slush down my neck into my eyes. Joe's drunk singing "Prince Edward Island" the old man heads out for lunch returns two large pizzas one pepperoni the other sausage Blackie takes the cheese, pepperoni, and sausage off and gives it to me. The old man tries to get Joe to eat a slice of pizza into the Pepsi machine Joe pulls out last can of beer from his six-pack. John the postman comes to collect for the number — John's numbers racket brings him more money than his mailman job the old man's been playing a number given to him by my grandfather in a dream always says things like Grandpa came to me in a dream last night told me play this number or that horse. Blackie plays the same number every day for years a dime a day he's hit three or four times. If I want to play a number I've got to do it through Joe the old man would flip if he found out I'm gambling but Joe's been drinking all morning too drunk and silly to communicate with. My father says this is what happens with Joe soon as he works a few days cleaned and polished a few cars, he's got some money in his pocket and off he goes. Joe leaves when his beer's gone won't see him for a week or so rest of afternoon is slow the old man takes off, Blackie does a little maintenance work on the tow truck. I'm sitting in the office listening to WRKO, watching the clock hands slip second by second, minute by minute away on the old dirty illuminated B. F. Goodrich clock. An occasional gas customer, Beatles on the radio, fierce battle in Viet Nam, where is Viet Nam how do you say it right, kids returning from the pond dripping swimsuits and hair, who needs a dime for the bus.

MY FATHER GRABS Countess by her collar left hand a crowbar raised in his right says now get the fuck out of here the Jehovah's Witness guy turns and flees reaches the curb opposite side of the street turns and glares my father stands this side of the street crowbar in one hand Countess in the other stay the fuck out of here now. He comes around to pass out literature friendly anyone ever wonder what a Jehovah's Witness is everyone says no my father not interested then Red says yeah I've wondered what a Jehovah's Witness is the man proceeds to take Red aside very seriously talks about what being a Jehovah's Witness means Red listens nods yeah after five minutes the old man says okay that's enough but the man's persistent and Red's acting goofy looks at me and Blackie grins the old man says okay we've got work to do but the man continues standing over Red who's in a chair finally the old man says look we're not interested in Jehovah's Witnesses we're Catholic. I've never seen him go to church but every now and then Father Everheart gasses up corners my father in the office asks us to leave and with the old man down on his knees without an argument Father Everheart hears his confession. For a few moments the man's determined states that Red wants to hear the word the old man says he's only kidding he doesn't want to be a fucking

20

Jehovah's Witness Red looks up says yes I do I do want to be a Jehovah's Witness the old man says c'mon now Red enough is enough tells the guy get off my property the Jehovah's Witness says you can't stop me from spreading the word oh no my father wants to know gets the crowbar and Countess chases the Jehovah's Witness off. What are Jehovah's Witnesses I ask no one seems to know Red says they're pretty fucking weird though they don't eat meat and stuff like that but are they Christians. No they're not Christians my father says more like Jews.

"UNDER THE BOARDWALK" the Drifters? heat waves lift off station lot's asphalt my father off somewhere Blackie doesn't work Mondays during summer, Countess curled up in a cool corner of the garage too hot for her behind the station afternoon sun beats down back there. I rinse my head in the water trough my T-shirt cut off at the shoulders drenched with water and sweat haven't had a gas customer for over an hour watch the clock slow motion. Distant sirens closer make their way up the hill flash of ambulance and fire trucks pass I saw them turn in to the pond the lady in the '65 Plymouth Valiant says as I wash her windshield no sooner she pulls out first kids start trickling down from the pond excited someone just drowned a girl. No not a girl it's a boy it's one of the kids from Harris Park not one of the kids from Harris Park it's one of the Mackey kids not the Mackey kids I said hi to them this morning when they walked by Frankie the second oldest thirteen cramps not cramps tangled in weeds off Pickerel Rock. Pickerel Rock other side of the pond no swimming allowed out of sight of lifeguards ten-foot-high rock kids dive off. Several people drown there over the years Frankie Mackey hit his head on the rock diving his brothers jump in try pushing him up Maureen the oldest stands on the rock has his hands in hers for minutes but can't pull him out too steep and the water's too deep all the time Frankie's out cold Shorty Monahan says right before Frankie dives he takes off his Saint Christopher's medal gives it to his brother Michael says here take my Saint Christopher's medal for me in case something happens. Shorty says all the Mackeys are going crazy up there Michael's screaming Frankie Frankie Frankie places the Saint Christopher's medal around Frankie's neck when they have him onshore ambulance drivers have to walk halfway around the pond with their equipment and stretcher 'cause there's no road for the ambulance and when they get there Frankie's already dead they try to revive him but can't so they put him on the stretcher and at a trot take him out followed by all the screaming Mackeys and other by-standers he'll be okay once they get him to the hospital but everyone knows he's dead Shorty says. Drowning's in the newspaper and locals are outraged asking why kids are allowed to swim there and I saw Mrs. Mackey and Mr. Mackey drive by our house the morning of the funeral in the black limousine looking straight ahead dazed. The weather's hot for a couple of days foot traffic to the pond is light though Shorty Monahan still swims every day stops to talk says he still can't believe it how Frankie removed his Saint Christopher's medal gives it to his brother Michael take my Saint Christopher's medal in case something happens.

I'M WEARING MY green Quaker State motor oil cap big an-niversary sale eight years old just learned to pump gas Joe dressed as a clown hands balloons out to kids when he needs more fills them up with a big tank Al Moran the mechanic goes to the tank breathes in gas talks funny high pitched cartoon voice. A huge mechanical cowboy robot out on sidewalk waves at drivers as they pass red white and blue flags flap everywhere in wind above the pump island strung out across the station lot on rope. Tire promotion dozens of tires strewn around the lot in multicolor ribboned B. F. Goodrich stands we're giving away drinking glasses with every purchase of five gallons or more sales representatives from Jenney and B. F. Goodrich walk around smiling and talking with customers. Bill Gleason from Jenney's a large man with white hair and red face always happy in various stages of drunkenness does many favors for my father like getting Jenney to paint the station before the big sale my father brings him home and my mother cooks for him he loves Italian food my mother runs around the kitchen in a simple blue and white check dress and her cooking apron, long straight brown hair brushed back in a ponytail, cooks and serves them pasta pizza soups and Bill eats one course after another all the time drinking whiskey and water telling my mother what an amazing woman she is getting up wrapping his arms around her thin five-foot-tall frame kisses her on the cheek how my father doesn't know how much of a good thing he's got she turns red my father sits smiles like it's entertainment. My sister laughs at his antics Bill squeezes her cheeks bella bella bella she pulls away turns to me motions turning her index finger to her head she thinks he's crazy. Bill eats and eats when he's finished into the cabinet for anisette a couple of glasses of anisette before he and my father leave wraps his bearlike arms around my mother again kisses her what an amazing woman you are running around making jokes everyone's laughing at inside the office has a shot of whiskey. Gilbert Jones B. F. Goodrich representative is a short balding white-haired man wears plaid sport jackets skinny bowties white shoes smokes long menthol cigarettes when he lights one and takes that first drag his nostrils flair for some reason he reminds me of someone who's from the south though I don't know an-

yone from the south. Gilbert Jones buzzes around talks to customers explains specifics of new tire treads on B. F. Goodrich
tires why they are superior to all others why now's the time to
buy prices never this low again. The anniversary sale goes on
for three days each one of the days my mother brings huge pots
of macaroni meatballs and sausages for everyone to eat for
lunch. My father wins a portable black and white television for
selling so many tires a photographer from the *Mercury* comes to
take his photograph as he is presented the television by Gilbert
Jones from B. F. Goodrich which the *Mercury* runs on the fifth
page in their "Goings On About the Town" section my father
still thin, hair thinning, smiling, bow-tied Gilbert Jones to my
father's right in his green plaid sport coat which is black and
white in the photo smiling as he hands my father the television
and Al Moran standing on my father's left flattop haircut. Al
Moran whose brother dies in an automobile accident on Interstate 93 driving north in the southbound lane runs straight into
a tractor-trailer truck. My father frames the photo hangs it on
the office wall next to the framed scratchy black and white
photo of him on a hunting trip biting into one end of a foot-
long submarine sandwich his friend Vinny Larusso biting the
other between them hangs a big gutted dead deer Vinny shot
inside cavity held wide open with heavy sticks.

MORNINGS PASS QUICKLY afternoons, if business is slow,
drag. My father's at Rockingham catch a couple races Blackie's
gone out for a couple of beers I listen to the radio, smoke cigarettes, wait on gas customers in the desk drawer girlie magazines. In the compressor room pinups takes a while interrupted
by gas customers wait a minute until my dick softens before I
go out the customer leaves back in start over. Delays don't
bother me pleasurably prolong help pass the time leave the

door open a crack see anyone driving in convinced the dark-haired woman with pigtails in pinup *not* Sally Field. Woman in pinups prettier than woman in magazines where people have sex skinnier acne nudist magazines don't entice bunch of naked people playing volleyball or tennis or eating barbecue puts me off they're older wrinkly but look to be enjoying themselves. I cum wipe with a rag roll it up place bottom of oil-and grime-soaked rag bin laundry company picks up each week replaces dirty orange-pink rags with bright clean pressed stack of rags, imagine someone at laundry company unfolding my cum-laced rag. Cold bottle of Pepsi, cigarette, check clock how much time killed.

TWO WEEKS AFTER half of Malden Square burns down my father takes me to the shoe store in Malden Square first pair work shoes real black steel-toe mechanic's shoes my feet finally big enough. The day of the fire droves of sirens every direction customer says Malden Square's burning down climb to roof of station in distance tips of flames waves of rising black smoke. Next day local television news shows reels of buildings burning front page *Record American* runs a half page color photo old Strand Theatre ablaze. First chance see damage myself shoe store my father buys work shoes from didn't get touched had the wind not died down when it did the fire would have swallowed up the entire square. Up the stairs we climb third floor three-floor red-brick building amid a whole block three-and-four-story red-bricks three blocks away from last block the fire destroyed. Burned out gutted buildings still stand windows boarded yellow ribbon fences run lengths of blocks keep out danger signs every twenty or thirty feet. The Strand Theatre and one of the old factories long since closed collapsed all's left piles red bricks and burned-black timbers twisted wreckage of the Strand Theatre marquee. Little shoe store not like most shoe stores with fancy displays woman who owns the place my father knows buys work shoes here for years sizes me up you've got small feet. I want to know about the fire she obliges with minute-by-minute account what happens day of fire points out you can still smell smoke and I do describes how she first hears the old Parker Building's burning on Pleasant Street a little while later fire spreads down the block soon news the Strand Theatre's burning and finally she closes the store to investigate the Strand Theatre is fully engulfed in flames wind blowing firemen being called from neighboring cities to help contain spreading flames within the block but by early afternoon windblown flames ignite other buildings and blocks other side of the square the building her store's in out of danger she returns opens up again within an hour another block succumbs others in her building growing restless around three in the afternoon black smoke permeates hallways and shops fire burning its way closer and closer then the fireman came up and told us all to leave the building. Then the firemen came up and told us all to leave the building. Something about the way she delivers that line the sounds of her words as if she's in a play then the firemen came up and told us all to leave the building same way Lenny Barns and his story of the gas station fire over time retelling the story so it sounds better with each telling then the firemen came up and told us all to leave the building. Everyone in the building evacuates but the wind's lessening fire's coming under control only a few blocks from the shoe store by early evening her building's out of danger. At home in bed new black work shoes on floor can't sleep can't wait to wear my shoes to the station tomorrow, turn her words over. Days, weeks, months her words in my mind my mouth mouthing the sentence then the firemen came up and told us all to leave the building.

26

BLACKIE REPAIRS FOREIGN cars more of them around these days extra business most local mechanics don't own metric tools or know anything about Volkswagens or Triumphs or Fiats popular with long-haired college students from Harvard and Tufts. Blackie's pulling the engine from an MG Midget help him slide it over and away from the car methodically proceed to dismantle it. I remove intake and exhaust manifolds hoses and anything hanging loose Blackie points out gunked-up rocker arm assembly from oil not being changed enough that's why the engine spun a bearing in the first place. He takes off the rocker arm assembly unbolts the head bolts we lift off the head valves are beat Blackie wonders how the number three fired at all raise the engine block higher in the air with the pulley I remove the oil pan Blackie lets me unbolt the crankcase bolts which hold the piston rod bearings wrapped around the crankcase at number three cylinder bearing cap fragments of spun bearing fall into my hands I knew it Blackie says. Remove bearing caps, pop the rods up, pull the pistons out number three piston's leaking piston rings are shot so it goes until we've a complete dismantled engine rocker arm assembly, lifters, pistons, rods, crankcase valves intake manifold exhaust manifold belts hoses water pump fan timing chain carburetor block head hundreds nuts and bolts strewn over the garage floor. I organize parts nuts and bolts into boxes so we can find them when time to put it back together after the head's rebuilt with new valves and the crankcase ground down new rings replaced heads of pistons wire-brushed and buffed I spend a half day scraping gunk off other parts sanding down gasket areas so new gaskets hold tight without leaks. Blackie knows all the ins and outs be careful not to overbore the block or the pistons won't fit back right and lube new bearings with STP before you replace 'em to avoid metal to metal friction when the engine's all back together and started and use the torque wrench every key nut and bolt from crankcase bearings to head bolts has torque specification must be tightened exactly to specification with the torque wrench effortlessly one task to another occasionally stuck Blackie swears come on you motherfucker or Jesus fucking Christ until he works it through. I'm smoking Blackie's Pall Malls radio tuned to Blackie's oldies station in between shop-talk Blackie talks about girls and parties when he was a biker and his old '49 Ford if he had a dime for every time he got laid in that car. Moment of fate rebuilt engine's lowered back into a car, buttoned up to its transmission, exhaust system, bolted down to the motor mounts — hoses, belts, fuel lines, water lines and linkages connected up and Blackie instructs me get in and turn it over. They never start on first turn usually the distributor's not in quite right timing's off or the carburetor needs adjusting once a Triumph Spitfire did turn right over and we couldn't believe it but ten minutes running seized up and a half day fiddling Blackie says the engine's got to come out again turns out parts store sent the wrong bearings even though they fit when he placed them in and bolted them down but once the engine started they gave in so he begins the procedure over again my father fights to get the parts store guys to admit it was their fault and assume the cost of tearing the engine apart a second time. When it's all done listening to it run hard to believe that fucker was sitting on the floor in a thousand pieces two days ago Blackie says purring like a fucking kitten now.

PARTS STORE BONANZA discount oil filters my father buys them up runs a special lube oil and filter lowest price around regular and new customers take advantage. I know all our regular customers by name, quickest way to find out where strangers get their cars serviced is look on the inside driver's door thin sticker name of service center date of last service performed, odometer reading, services performed. I tear them off replace with new interesting how long people go between oil changes should be every two thousand miles most go way beyond and many don't change the oil filter when they change the oil Blackie says like washing your face with dirty water because the filter's where all grime from the oil system ends up so clean oil runs through a dirty filter. Oil filters must be tightened by hand if tightened too tight gaskets strip and leak and if an oil filter hasn't been changed in a long time it's extremely difficult to remove must use a tool that's a handle with a belt band attached wrap the belt band around the filter tighten it up then turn the handle. Sometimes they still won't budge Blackie says last Mickey Mouse mechanic put it on too tight he takes a long screwdriver with a hammer bangs it straight through dirty oil splatters everywhere including my hair once the filter's drained turn the big screwdriver the filter turns off with it. Several weeks lube oil and filter business booms big sign out front LUBE OIL AND FILTER BONANZA. When the first of the BONANZA cars returns with a leaky filter my father blames me put it on too tight stripped the gaskets but first thing I learn about replacing an oil filter is to tighten it by hand so we replace it and when more cars return Blackie begins to suspect the filters faulty over half the cars come back with leaks and my father calls other stations same problems he calls Sammy at the parts store Sammy I've got news for you your BONANZA KAPUTZ!

POUR LAST OF the hot chocolate from red and black plaid thermos brought by my mother into red plastic cup. Lukewarm. Two degrees outside wind gusts who knows how cold dressed in layers take off outer coat inside between customers. Mittens do fine but hard to make change or write credit card slip take them off put in jacket pockets my hands dried and cracked. No one out tonight Oak Street like a quiet country road smoke seven cigarettes masturbate maybe Joe'll come down what's going on with Annie she likes George really wants to date you Tommy says to him George has a nine-inch dick this is what she wants George says grabbing himself Joe says she's really good and likes to get it. George says she's too ugly Tommy says it's not the face you fuck but the fuck you face. Fiercest rain or snowstorm or coldest day of year's when people decide they need their oil or tire pressure checked driving rain down a quart put one in the lady says 55¢ 65¢ or 90¢. 65¢. I put it in she pays me a dime short I say you're a dime short she says 55¢ for the oil I put in the 65¢ 'cause that's what you said I told you 55¢ she insists and I'm standing in downpour getting drenched my father comes out what's going on I tell him he takes a dime out his pocket gives it to her says here's your goddamn dime don't come back keeping the kid out here in pouring rain. Hydraulic systems art forms in themselves jack up a '62 Cadillac four door bumper jack lifts whole half car all because a little piston and petroleum mix in a valve and ring-sealed unit. Floor jacks smaller for jacking one quarter of the car up least safe of jacks, bumper jacks have safety bolts steadier easier for a car to slip off a floor jack especially if either the car or the floor jack is bumped. Lots of guys have stories about the time the jack slipped my father knows a guy killed under a car in a jack accident if you're going to get under a car for long you jack it up and onto jack stands. On the pumps the numbers tumble click-clocking the amount of gas pumped the amount of cash owed. Every six months an official comes around tests the pumps makes certain amount of gas pumped is consistent with amount owed otherwise what would prevent gas sellers from fixing

30

pump mechanisms to their own advantage. At the same time a sample of regular and premium is taken sent to a lab tested to make certain 87 octane actually 87 octane and the 90 octane 90 octane. The new pumps sleeker and angular old ones taller thinner and round at the top. We're one of the last to get new chrome pumps I polish every two weeks old pumps peeling faded metal paint red. We pump 500 to 1,000 gallons of gas a day barely pays the rent real profits from repair work and inspection time or special events like tire or battery sales. My father gives my mother $100 a week some days we make more than that in repairs alone he loses a lot at the track some months he's behind on bills even when it's busy. I love the smell of gasoline instant I begin to pump first delicious waves tickle and burn my nostrils swear I could drink it.

I MAKE DIME phone calls for a nickel Blackie shows me to how drop a nickel in the hole and just when it falls through the mechanism it clicks right then pop the coin return button with the palm of my hand a dial tone. Timing's everything. Months of practice I don't believe it can be done except Blackie does it all the time finally I get a dial tone a dozen more tries before I do it again then every fourth time every second now any time on any pay phone for a nickel I can call. Blackie knows these little tricks drives a standard can shift through all four gears without using a clutch in the tow truck watch him gently push his way through all four never a hint of a gear grinding. I've tried several times no luck afraid of transmission damage, my father says it can't be done he's seen Blackie do it insists it damages the transmission Blackie says you don't know the first thing about transmissions and he doesn't. My father can't make phone calls for a nickel tried many times when he needs to make a phone call he has me or Blackie get a dial tone for him.

31

The guys at the parts store like to give my father a hard time they know he's hotheaded stubborn and won't order his parts from Gus Sammy's partner because Gus always screws up orders so he calls asks for Sammy even when Gus answers sometimes Gus lets the phone sit on the counter doesn't tell Sammy my father says he can hear them all talking and he starts whistling into the phone yelling S-A-M-M-Y everyone at the parts store gets a laugh listening. I'm not aware of my father's accent until I hear him converse with others and realize they have a difficult time understanding him he shouts into the phone I got a business to run and this is not funny Gus comes out *I'g abusin ta run and isa no fungus* or he orders me to *take-a de fron ties offa da blue Buke and balanca.* We're out on Interstate 93 south near the 128 intersection heavy traffic whips dangerously close by pick a '61 Chevy Impala up by the front end ready to tow away a car pulls up behind us horn blowing a guy gets out passenger side yells stop. His '61 Chevy Impala's out of gas he's got a can full my father says that's fine but still going to have to pay him for the tow 'cause we were called by the State Police already have the car on back of tow truck but the guy says no way he's going to pay he left a note in the window that he was out of gas and the State Police had no right to call my father who says yes they do you can't abandon a car in the breakdown lane says so on all the signs on the entry ramps but the man insists my father let the car down off the tow truck boom my father says not until you pay $15 for the tow guy says you haven't towed it anywhere soon as it's up on the boom it's a tow and even if it wasn't you have to pay for the road service guy says he didn't call for road service my father says pay for the tow now or we'll tow it and once it's in the station I'll charge you a day's storage charge guy says I order you to put the car down now my father says no way I'll see you at the station the guy threatens to sue you'll be walking to your lawyer's office. The man offers to pay $10 my father says okay the man pays the ten I let the car down off the boom unhook the chains and free the '61 Chevy. We're getting in the tow truck the guy's pouring gas into his car yells now I know what highway robbery is my father says now I know what an asshole is in the tow truck he adds if the guy wasn't such an asshole he would have told him $10 right from the start.

BLACKIE STANDS OVER his '55 Chevy, hood open, large Styrofoam cup full of coffee in left hand, freshly lit Pall Mall in right, stares into that 283 quietly humming red rag hangs out right rear pocket of his blue uniform pants, open-end wrench sticks out the left. Someone always drops by with half dozen and coffee mine small cream extra sugar Blackie large regular my father small regular Joe black no sugar Tommy large milk George small cream no sugar Floyd large black with sugar. Floyd works Sundays and Saturdays if it's busy on Saturdays he gets a ride from his girlfriend but on Sundays my father picks him up takes him home after closing. Floyd doesn't have a license alcoholic my father makes me ring the bell at the beat-up three-decker Floyd lives in in Chelsea. He doesn't answer means he's been drinking down the street to a pay phone my father rings him after several minutes Floyd picks up the phone I'm always fearful he won't means I've got to pull the Sunday shift. Floyd's a short solid man with marble green eyes, greased back dark hair, sideburns and a long bone-carved nose which has a bump from being broken he got into trouble when younger spent time in jail but my father says you can trust Floyd though he makes mistakes and has accidents drops the charge card machine on glass desktop or pours a quart of oil into someone's radiator. The guy who works Sundays before Floyd sells his own oil out the trunk of his car my father can't figure out why he doesn't sell oil on Sundays finally gets on to the guy and fires him. Except on busiest days there's time to take ten have a honey dipped coffee and cigarette and in the process we end up standing around looking at and discussing a car — Phil's Corvette, George's big black brand-new Oldsmobile 98, Joe's brand-new 1965 Chevy Impala red with black vinyl roof red interior two-door 283 V-8 Tommy's green '62 Buick Tommy will only own Buicks, Billy Zona's '54 Ford coupe, Blackie's '55 Chevy Bel Air. Blackie's forever fiddling with that 283 runs so perfectly strain to hear it like an anti-sound. I do legwork when my father and I plow, most driveways straightforward a few have some bends the plow can't get at I'm out there with a shovel then ring doorbells to collect money he remains warm and dry in the old Willys. Ten dollars a driveway plow a dozen or so every storm works out for the old man because the storms bring school cancellations he gets me for the day. I think my father's been with Annie too, something about the way they're talking, kind of flirting, she brings coffee in the afternoons even though she knows George isn't here hangs out in the office talks with my father. Blackie loses tools a lot swears where the fuck did I put that usually a wrench or pair of pliers finds in his back pocket or under some parts he's removed and placed down somewhere. It's real cold road service calls people with dead batteries need a jump battery charger runs all day line of batteries waiting to be recharged. I don't like working with batteries acid forms around the cables and posts burns layers of skin on my hands a guy who got battery acid in his eyes went blind. My father does work free for Tom Riordan who needs a jump my father rushes right over to his house no matter how many calls are ahead we plow Tom Riordan's driveway for nothing my father says he can't put a dollar value on all the favors Tom's done for him. I'm carrying a battery by a battery strap which holds the battery by its posts one end slips off battery falls to ground narrowly missing my foot it could have crushed a corner breaks makes terrible mess acid burns a stain on the hot top.

GREASING A CAR rainy or snowy days water drips everywhere down my back reach with my hand to find grease fittings upper ball joints then lower ball joints two fittings on the tie-rod assembly one on the driveshaft. I squeeze too much grease into a fitting blob of grease lands on my shoulder wipe the glob off with a rag. If a car's front end's not greased frequently ball joints or tie-rods will dry out causing metal-to-metal friction. 1962 Ford Falcon we tow from Interstate 93 tie-rod assembly snapped right front tire caves in Falcon skids across three lanes and down a steep embankment. Traffic's light my father says if it happened during rush hour there'd be a major pileup. Johnny Whittier can't use his arms polio when he was a kid a contraption on his 1964 Ford Galaxie 500 allows him to drive and steer with his feet, he places his right foot into a wheel on the floor to steer while he controls gas and brake with his left foot. Electrical system switches — wipers, horn, lights — transmission shifting, opening and closing doors are all worked with his feet and knees. In 1958 he buys a brand-new Ford and a mechanic at Ford rigs Johnny's first car it's never quite right things break down frequently and his accessibility to the electrical system switches is limited. Blackie studies the job the Ford mechanic did so when Johnny buys another new car Blackie does a better job designing and building the special assembly than people at Ford. Several weeks Blackie works on Johnny's new Ford, takes trips back and forth to machine shops for parts and pieces he's designed to be made to specifications. There's only a half a dozen cars like Johnny's in the country I watch him drive arms and hands by his sides, fingers limply folded into palms, legs and knees turning and bumping, starting and stopping, wants a

Pepsi I hold under his chin the bottle while he sips through a straw he has lunch with us after I'm finished with my sub cut his up into small pieces and feed him his ham and cheese. Johnny runs the concession stand at the pond winters in Florida his girlfriend actually does most of the work and he oversees she's younger than he is though Johnny's a fuckhound Joe says he's got a second woman on the side I wonder how Johnny fucks must be on his back with her on top greasing his '64 Ford is tricky because of all the extra fittings in the special assembly he stands around watches over me points with his forehead you missed one there.

BILL GLEASON DRINKS Little Nicks at the kitchen table finishes his second bowl of macaroni what a fantastic cook my mother smiles fries veal cutlets at the stove serves them with fresh tomato sauce and salad from greens I pick from the garden. Mamma mia Bill says kisses tips of his fingers like he thinks Italians do you've outdone yourself again my father tells my sister get Bill another bottle of beer she says no he raises his eyebrows and his voice what did I just tell you and she goes to the refrigerator brings Bill his beer he reaches for her cheek bella donna she pulls away my father grinds his jaw gives her a look of rage she settles down. He turns to Bill what about the paint job Bill throws his fork down mamma mia do you have to start now I told you don't worry you're going to getta da paint mimics my father my father doesn't own the gas station he's a proprietor responsible for regular maintenance while services like painting are performed by the Jenney Company but Jenney neglects us low gas volume outside paint's peeling and yellowing. Bill tells my father before the end of summer he'll have a fresh coat of paint on the walls relax you worry too much his face turns redder the more he eats and drinks he's already half drunk when he arrives near suppertime which means he's looking for my father to take him home for food. After he eats he helps himself to the liqueur cabinet pours large amounts of anisette into his black coffee another terrific meal is he being good to you oh I guess so her shy smile most of the time well he better be and if not you let me know and I'll straighten him out.

MY FATHER'S FEET stink awful during the summer sitting on his ass leaning back on his hands holding a tire stable with his two feet Blackie's on the creeper working on the wheel bearings backs himself out from under the car says get the fuck away from me with those things he can smell my father's feet through his shoes. Sometimes in the afternoon my father sits in the office, removes his shoes and socks, places his feet directly in front of the fan to cool them you could clear Fenway Park with those things Joe says. I pull the tow truck to the side of the building and wash it when I'm through Blackie hands me keys to his Chevy lets me move it over give it a wash. The old man's finally letting me drive again and allows me to drive to and from home in the tow truck a few months ago I'm moving a black 1963 Ford Galaxie away from the pumps racing the engine by accident I pop the automatic into reverse lay down some rubber right there tearing into it damn near run over the old man out of the way just in time swears and screams waves his arms I jam the brake screeching halt. He's pissed for days says I can't drive again until I have a license which is still two years away but Blackie still lets me move cars when the old man's out and when I run errands with Joe he lets me drive his car a few days ago I was moving the tow truck when the old man pulls in sees me not a word. First time I ever drive I'm ten grounded a bad report card he brings me to the station to pump gas on Saturdays comes home for supper with a car on the back of the tow truck to be towed to Spadafora's Junk in Malden before dinner he and my mother are arguing over money he hasn't been giving her enough. My sister and I are fighting at dinner we're kicking each other under table he and my mother eating in silence I let out a belch at my sister he swings a backhander across the table catches me on the side of the face says we eat and shut up inside of my cheek cut against my teeth taste blood in the tomato sauce start to cry but choke down my tears don't you start crying now. After supper I go to my room he sticks his head in come with me to drop a car off in Malden put on my shoes he's waiting for me in the truck. I know where all the gears are and how to use the clutch he's been promising to let me drive I sit in the truck when it's parked practice going through the gears. Spadafora's Junk yard is acres big row upon row of junk cars stacks of fenders rear ends engine blocks tires rims radiators bumpers doors long rows of shelves with windshields and windows a towering crane that can pick a car up and with one sweep transfer it to the crusher on the other side of the yard. Inside the office my father's talking to Spaddy wearing same grimed blue overalls every time I see him Jane's Fortune in the seventh he says to my father I'm telling you the dog can't miss all the time short cigar stub clenched between his teeth. Back in the tow truck he drives in the opposite direction where are we going to run an errand turning onto the Revere Beach Parkway follow it around Bell Circle slow down as we approach Wonderland take a right into the parking lot I'm going to be about fifteen minutes wait in the truck departing in a hurry and trotting across the parkway through the entrance gate. The windows are rolled down and I can smell the ocean and see the roller coaster off in the distance at Revere Beach suddenly voracious roar of a crowd coming from behind the high fence man's voice over loudspeaker can't make out his words. Rub my tongue against the fresh cut inside my mouth get out of the truck walk across the parkway can't see over the fence look through narrow space between fence slats lots of bright lights and green another great crowd-roar loudspeaker voice and there goes Swifty. Seems like an hour before he returns drives to the far side of the lot which is vacant stops asks you ready I want to know for what he says to drive. The truck lurches forward then stalls I let the clutch out too quickly slow he shouts let the clutch out slow three or four more times before I'm able to move forward shift it into second now I push the clutch in pull the shifter toward second gears grind second second he yells screech to a halt it goes on this way several more attempts until I'm able to take off and shift properly into second gain enough speed shift it into third around the vast parking lot about ten minutes until he has me stop and back in the driver's seat he drives out of the parking lot toward home don't say anything to your mother about coming here. He does wash his feet regularly don't know why they're so rank his white socks permanently stained mustard yellow no matter how much my mother bleaches them.

CHRISTMAS EVE DAY people won't schedule any regular maintenance work only emergency Mrs. Bowlan's '60 Plymouth wagon exhaust system clamp snaps Fellsway Shopping Center parking lot three quarters of the exhaust system on the ground I'm under the Plymouth with wire a pair of wire cutters ice and slush my back is soaked tie up the exhaust best I can drive the wagon to the station replace the clamp back the car out of the garage the oil pan catches the corner of the lift not fully down tears a small hole in the oil pan oil leaks all over a gallon of the black stuff garage floor puddles the old man shouts soon as he finds out Blackie saves me says it's his fault he thought the lift was down told me to back it out brand-new oil pan's expensive from the Plymouth dealer my father calls Spaddy at Spadafora's Junk they have one cheap he's still pissed because he has to take the time to go pick it up and he can't get to tending his annual office party sets a little bar up strings some lights everyone gets offered a drink there's eggnog he mixes with whiskey only a few takers in the morning the mailman and Mr. Laporta who drinks a lot his face red smell it on his breath it's only nine-thirty in the morning happy holidays drinks a healthy shot down Freddy Golar staggers in at eleven several belts toasts everyone asks my father won't you have one with me but my father doesn't drink first Christmas we haven't sold Christmas trees out of the station first week of December my father and I drive up Route 1 towards the New Hampshire border meet the truck packed full with trees down from Maine driver follows us to the station drops off the trees my father pays him cash each year sell fewer and fewer trees last year lose money too many people buy artificial trees this year he bought one too.

IF YOU CAN beat me you can eat me read the bumper sticker of a woman who used to hang out at the White Tower restaurant drove a 1957 Corvette convertible full-blown engine no one ever did beat her Blackie says that Corvette was so fucking fast Phil wants to know what ever happened to that spoiled little rich bitch. The White Tower on Broadway Somerville's a burger joint hangout for rodders and bikers Blackie says now it's mostly kids he hardly knows any of them. During the fifties there was much street drag racing Blackie and Phil remember a stretch of road on Route 2 near Concord measured off for a quarter of a mile late Saturday nights anyone who's anybody is there to race cars and bikes get laid and there's a flagman in the middle of the road waving the official start they race through the night down to final two the winner floats through the next week honors of being reigning champion can get any girl he wants except during that period of time none could beat this woman in the 1957 Corvette convertible W-A-O-U-W Phil says could that fucking Corvette fly W-A-O-U-W was she a looker too. Blackie says she married a guy with more money than her father had lives somewhere in suburbs has kids and gets a new Cadillac every two years. Phil comes in late morning puffy half-mast eyes he's been out the night before drinking and partying with a woman you should have heard this broad screaming reenacts details of his date last night parking at the Sheepfold she was just dying for it and you should have heard this broad screaming give it to me give it to me I had to roll up the fucking windows. The Sheepfold on Route 28's part of the Middle-sex Fells Reservation woods long time ago farmers grazed sheep and cattle there now it's used as a picnic area by day at night couples go parking once my friends and I go there find used discarded condoms on the ground. Phil's old to be parking he's old as Blackie and Tommy and Blackie and Tommy have kids. Phil still lives with his parents doesn't work not sure where his money comes from hangs around drives his Corvette to the beach or to clubs like Sammy's Patio down Revere Beach where he and Blackie know everyone. Blackie knows the woman Phil's talking about says I remember those screams well that's why they call her Screaming Laura. Man you ain't kidding one fucking bit Phil says, W-A-O-U-W.

HARD TO KEEP the men's room clean everybody uses it all day women's room around the side of the building keep locked gets little use clean it once a week wash the floor, sink, mirror and toilet it's already clean. Sometimes George or Tommy or Joe uses the women's room with Annie door locks from the inside tight in there not too tight for blow jobs though George fucked Annie in there standing up I can't imagine George so tall Annie short. Men's room's inside the office clean every day floor gets dirty sink and toilet too. He walks down Oak Street in the morning up Oak Street in the evening, a tall husky man with a slight limp special black leather shoes one sole and heel thicker than the other wears a suit and tie carries a briefcase works in town somewhere every morning asks to use the bathroom spends ten minutes in there stinks up the office something awful. He's polite opens the window closes the door behind him thanks us much relieved though lately my father gives him the key to the ladies' room asks him to go out there. Periodically the Jenney Company sends inspectors around to check on service in stations the inspectors gas up use the bathrooms note how friendly service is and the overall cleanliness of the station. My father's won several little plaques for clean rest rooms he hangs on their walls. One night someone breaks in through the men's bathroom window steals some cash and tools my father believes it's someone who knows the station where the money and tools are maybe the Valiant brothers who live behind the station next to Joe and Red they're the only ones capable of such a thing Joe says they steal cars and shoplift. A friend of my father's has this beautiful one-year-old German shepherd he can't keep so we take her as a watchdog, her real name's Countess my father calls her Condess so we call her Condess until one day my father's friend comes in and when he sees her he calls her Countess Countess I ask yes Countess. We have bathroom windows barred and since we've had Countess around there haven't been any more break-ins though one night my father's getting ready to close a guy walks in out of nowhere holds my father up at pistol point makes off with several hundred dollars cash while Countess is asleep out back.

I'M WEARING KNEE-HIGH rubber boots standing in smelly black sludge dropped Mrs. Amerault's keys down the grate in the garage floor, if I move abruptly sludge slips down into my boots bend over work muck with my hands feeling for keys. More muck I turn over worse the smell can't find the keys but several wrenches screwdrivers and pliers fallen through the grate over the years. An hour in the abyss can't take the smell any longer Blackie pulls me out my father's angry calls Mrs. Amerault she's upset because her house keys are on the chain my father assures her they're lost in the drainage grate no one will find them. He drives to her house in Melrose for her spare set when they're both back at the station shows her the drainage grate you don't have to worry no one will find them down there but she's not pleased. Mrs. Amerault's a serious woman doesn't smile much she's got short, wire-curly gray-blue hair, a grayish complexion and sharp blue eyes. She's a schoolteacher lives with another woman who's a schoolteacher Blackie says they're not the kind of women who like men — when she leaves my father lectures me my mind's always someplace else when will I learn to pay attention. Blackie calls me Floyd the second it's the kind of thing Floyd would do my stomach's unsettled from the sickly smell sludge turning over my hands and feet stained black scrub them with a scrub brush days before they're back to normal. People get angry when gas prices rise two cents per gallon they complain to my father who explains prices are dictated from the Jenney Company and everyone else's gas prices have gone up but they believe he's trying to pull a fast one on them go down the street Freddy's Sunoco he says up three cents a gallon there. Hard to keep the station warm in winter soon as the garage door's open heat gets sucked outside leave the garage door open a second too long he yells close the door what do you think I'm heating Oak Street. When a car's running inside the garage during winter we attach a rubber exhaust hose to the tailpipe and run it out a hole in the garage door from outside exhaust fumes pour out colder the temperatures denser the exhaust fumes. My father records how much gas pumped how much remains in main tanks and once a week we check the level with a long wooden pole with inches marked off, drop the pole down into the tanks measure the depth x amount of inches on the pole equals x amount gallons in the tanks. Most customers order gas in dollars' worth or a fill but old timers tend to order in gallons, usually five or ten like the old days. By the way he walks into the garage asks if they can get their car inspected I know something's different about him. He's thin with red unkempt hair and beard wears short shorts and a pair of rubber thongs emphasizes the $s's$ when he says can we get an insspection ssticker Blackie and my father look at each other smile bring the car in the guy walks out yells Lawrence, Lawrence, the man says to bring the car in. Lawrence drives the Volvo in Blackie guides him he's a quiet man can't tell if he pronounces his $s's$ way the other guy does, he stands and watches proceedings seemingly amused and skeptical at the same time. The first guy's friendly asks Blackie questions what are you checking when you lift the car up ball joints and tie-rod ends. I've heard about queers and once at Jimmy's Cleaners I saw a magazine called *Hot Rods* men doing all sorts of things together after looking at it awhile I got an erection like seeing women do things with each other arouses I wonder do these two guys like photos of women with women or men with women some folks like it all Blackie says people who like it both ways are bisexual Tommy says Doris Day is bisexual I don't believe it. Their car passes inspection I lick the inspection sticker place it on the windshield Blackie says to the first guy okay Sunshine that'll be a buck the guy pays, backs out, once they leave the lot my father walks around the garage on his tip-

44

toes mocks the red haired guy says oh Lawrence, oh Lawrence. I tell Tommy and George about the guys Tommy says in the service they had one of those fruits in their squad he and the other guys hid parts of his uniform and locked him outside at night in his underwear until finally the guy got discharged everyone knew something was up with that fruit he never wanted to go pussy hunting with the rest of the guys. George says more of those types around the more pussy there is for guys like us.

THE PHONE RINGS middle of the night it's a tow call he asks the usual questions — is the car locked or unlocked, is it north or south of Roosevelt Circle, is there a police cruiser at the scene? During school vacations he wakes me to go with him he's bought a second tow truck though there's barely enough business for the first he's taken out a loan for the new one which is four years old. It's a long boxy truck with a big cab and an oversized boom on the back, bigger than the old truck capable of towing tractor trailers though we don't tow tractor trailers my father says there are many truck companies in the area he can pick up extra jobs the truck will pay for itself and more. Tom Riordan's secretary writes a business letter Oak Street Jenney has a new tow truck capable of towing up to x amount of tons available twenty-four hours a day mail them out to all the truck companies in the area weeks anxiously await but not one response. Blackie says truck companies have their own tow trucks told my father before my father bought the new truck but my father bought it anyhow Tom Riordan secured a second towing plate and towing plates are hard to come by only so many allotted cost thousands of dollars you have to know someone in order to obtain one. Tom tells my father take advantage of having another towing plate if business doesn't work out sell the truck and the plate which he can turn a profit on.

45

Several months the large blue wrecker sits outside unused until my father puts the truck up for sale several months later someone from one of the truck companies makes an offer my father refuses. Another month passes no takers my father calls the man at the truck company back this time the guy offers him less than the first offer my father grudgingly accepts then sells the towing plate for several thousand dollars but he's lost money having the truck around all these months. If it's a school night he goes on tow calls alone an hour or so later returns he's not a good sleeper spends the night on the living room sofa smoking until it's time to open the station then throughout the day he's tired and irritable sleeps through the afternoon in the tow truck or on a bed of tires in the garage where's your father people ask gassing up sleeping I tell them he didn't get much sleep last night. Christmas dinner just finished the antipasto my mother's about to drop raviolis into boiling water phone rings State Police need a tow truck on the Route 28 overpass where it crosses over Interstate 93. My father says he doesn't tow Route 28 but they need him anyway there's another tow truck on the scene a black 1964 Oldsmobile 98's seesawing precariously over the guardrail it'll take two trucks to get it off. The Olds teeters back and forth over the guardrail rocking like it might slide off and fall straight down onto busy Interstate 93 below. The police block lanes off on 93 direct traffic around in case but there's a line of cars parked in the breakdown lane their occupants stand outside watching the proceedings. Each time the wind picks up the Olds begins to rock people start wows and ahhs and my father says it's fucking Christmas don't they have anything else to do state trooper says people love a catastrophe. My father and Phil from Phil's Tow debate the safest way to get the black Olds off the guardrail, if they lift it the wrong way the weight shifts it goes over the side and cables on the truck winches won't hold it. The Oldsmobile's driver is a priest came around the turn too fast spun out flipped over and landed up on the guardrail. He's an elderly man with a bad toupee who gets out of the cruiser so drunk he can barely walk the trooper rushes over I thought I told you to stay in the cruiser the priest points to the car tries to talk but too drunk the trooper takes him by the arm and leads him back to the cruiser. My father and Phil agree to hook the Oldsmobile on each of its sides, line the trucks up at a certain angle and simultaneously pull. They hook their cables and we wait for more police cruisers to arrive so they can close off a small stretch of Route 28 before and after the bridge and close off a bigger stretch of Route 93 below. Finally several local police cruisers from Medford and Stoneham clear away observers from the breakdown lane, close the other stretches of road, my father and Phil signal each other go and the black Oldsmobile comes flying off of the guardrail smash lands on four wheels in the middle of Route 28. The priest gets out of the cruiser again staggers towards the Olds as if he's going to get in and drive away but the trooper walks him back to the cruiser. All four of the tires on the Olds are flat so my father lifts up its rear end with his truck and Phil slides the dolly under the rear wheels so he can tow it from the front. Back home I'm biting into the raviolis I recount the story black Oldsmobile seesawing back and forth over the main highway phone rings State Police barracks brought the priest to his parish going to try to keep the incident quiet, Phil agrees not to charge the priest for the tow my father says if it's okay with Phil it's okay with me. The priest has a record driving drunk the church anxious not to have the accident go public anyone else would be in jail right now my father says biting into his raviolis.

A. J. TERANI TRADES in his Cadillac every two years his second wife's much younger than he though he talks about his grandchildren from his first wife. He likes two-door coupes currently a 1965 red Eldorado convertible with a white top owns a construction company his charge card reads A.J. Terani Construction Joe says that he's a mob man. Mr. Terani's the most impeccably groomed man I know thick wavy silver hair neatly cut and combed wears expensive sport coats and suits my father says those Italian shoes can't be found under a hundred dollars a pair. Twelve months a year he sports a tan his skin's tough and leathery his second wife's always tanned too her skin I taste in dreams. He wears several big rings and a gold watch manicures his nails notice when he signs his charge slip — clean, shiny, trimmed. A. J. Terani never actually signs his name but two swirling loops that are supposed to be his initials. His young wife has long red hair sometimes teased up wears short skirts long lovely legs her cleavage take my time washing the windshield steal quick glimpses she usually wears sunglasses not sure she's noticing me noticing her. Once or twice a year he has the oil changed on his Cadillac people who trade cars in every two years do little regular maintenance won't own vehicles long enough for regular maintenance to pay off. A. J. Terani's an associate of Tom Riordan my father says he's well connected whenever we're on the highway and there's construction going on most trucks bulldozers and steamrollers have the name A. J. Terani Construction painted on the doors. How many trucks does Mr. Terani own I ask he's got more trucks and money than he'll ever know what to do with. Phil says that A. J. Terani's second wife was a stripper he remembers seeing her strip years ago at a club downtown this was before he went into the service but how can you forget a body like that.

WATER TROUGH LIKE in western movies during fights

men get punched into horses drink from we use mostly washing our hands reach into tin can of gelatinous mechanic's soap
cool squish scoop lather hands and bottom of arms remove
grease from most recent job rinse off in trough three quarters
full. The old man only allows us to dump and refill it two or
three times a day after several washings the water's sickly gray
hot days when he's not around we refill it often Blackie and I
stick our heads in cool off. Lenny holds my head down in the
water until I'm panicking swallowing water breathing it up my
nose. Working under cars held up by a floor jack use the jack
stands my father warns fuck the jack stands Lenny says. I use
the trough look for tire leaks overinflate the tire submerge it in
the trough, turn slowly keep close eye out for that first trace of
bubbles indicates location of a puncture. Tires with tubes make
more work 'cause I've got to break the tire down from the rim
on the machine remove the tube fill it with air and check it in
the trough and if the leak's repairable rough up the puncture
area with sandpaper spread glue torch the glue until it bubbles
blow it out then press on a patch. More and more tires are
tubeless repair them with a plug and glue hard to believe a little
rubber plug and glue can repair a tire puncture so the tire holds
a car's weight though sometimes they don't my father doesn't
like these new tubeless tires Billy Lipo owns Lipo Trucking gasses up here says he'll never use tubeless tires in his trucks. I
don't know why Billy Lipo calls his company Lipo Trucking it's
really only a dump truck and steamroller they haul around on a
trailer mostly they do driveway hot top work. Some days never
end sit restlessly in the office watch the clock listen to the radio
the old man's off somewhere Blackie's out back working on his
car reread the *Record American* study the entertainment section
ads for the clubs downtown girls girls girls what can it mean no
cover charge.

GAS FUMES WAFT into my nostrils squeeze the nozzle hear gas rise up the hose swish of it through the nozzle. Summertime gas through the nozzle's metal cool in winter warm. Tumblers click dollars and cents gallons and tenths. How many more gallons will I pump in my lifetime hundreds of thousands of gallons I'll be here a while. Hon Annie asks will you pull my car around fill it up her Mustang's got a V-8, automatic chrome stick floor shift, leather bucket seats I back it up to the premium pump how does she maneuver around in here when she's with a guy Billy Coniglio at school says they do it in the car not much you can do with bucket seats and shifter between backseat's small and tight. Annie pays me thanks hon leaves Joe says be nice to Annie you never know what might happen. Dollars and gallons tumble to closing time read the multi-digit figure under the dollar and gallon digits on each pump, subtract that number from previous day's closing figure determine exactly   how many gallons-to-the-tenth pumped on that pump that day — multiply that figure times the amount per gallon to find how much should be in the gas cash roll minus the twenty dollars started out with at the beginning of the day. We don't ring each gas sale up whoever works the pumps carries a cash roll with him, usually it balances within fifty cents at the end of the day sometimes when Tommy works we're short a ten or twenty. My hands constantly reek gasoline skin's perpetually dried, cracked, dirty white. I've a nozzle on automatic for a fill kicks back gas splashes my eyes on fire multiple washings of cool water. If my father tows a car and no one claims it after sixty days my father legally inherits the vehicle. Joe gets the most destitute car spit-shined inside and out showroom new. My father does whatever work's needed to get the car running, repairs any small dents scratches and trimming, puts it out front on the lot with a for sale sign. It sells. If he's got floating cash

50

my father'll buy a used car when he comes across a good deal and with little work except for a good cleaning he turns a good buck selling it. This 1956 Ford Customline Victoria, black with red interior sharpest car he's ever had, he likes it too been driving it around with his repair plate shiny and ready for a for sale sign for two weeks but hasn't put the sign on it yet. Can we keep it no it's a two-door we need a four-door for a family car but he'll get stuck on the car and keep it today after school it's gone and for a good price. Freddy Golar drives straight into our fence with his 1962 Ford Falcon Christ he says stumbling out the passenger door I didn't think I was that close. Not much damage to the chain-link fence but the left side of his front quarter panel's scratched. Sonny he says hands me the keys will ya move it for me and I do. He's on about something I'm telling ya it's a disgrace yelling into my father's ear Freddy not today I'm not in the mood. He's not in the mood he says to me, Sonny I seen two world wars served in one of 'em and he's not in the mood. Freddy leave the kid alone he's got work to do go out and help Blackie with that exhaust system if you've nothing to do. I can hear them in the office the old man yells Freddy leave me the fuck alone a few moments later Freddy's out pestering us, boys I've been through two world wars and Blackie's about to light the acetylene torch so he can cut through an old exhaust system Freddy if you don't want your ass singed you better be out of my way too. Freddy grumbles then back in the office shouts I don't have to take this shit at my father and leaves. It takes him five minutes to get his car started and drive off the lot with all his starts and stops. Blackie puts his goggles on hands me a pair I put them on hold up the end of an exhaust system he's cutting through. Blackie's careful wearing goggles and taking precautions Lenny never does I get a tiny chip rusty exhaust metal in my eye like stuck with a pin try washing it out my father takes me to the hospital the doctor

51

drops different colored liquids in my eye removes the metal chip washes my eye out over and over wear a patch rest of the day tiny painful wound pesters for days always wear goggles working on exhaust systems goggled Blackie says freshly lit Pall Mall hangs out his mouth torch in his hand working the rusty metal exhaust pipe shades of blue and blaze orange the torch cuts through muffler and tailpipe fall into my arms.

HIDE MY CIGARETTES in Blackie's toolbox he smokes filterless Pall Malls I prefer Marlboros but buy Pall Malls so my father doesn't get suspicious seeing Marlboros in Blackie's toolbox. Joe and Red smoke Camels my favorite filterless, during summer Red rolls a fresh pack upper sleeve of his white T-shirt, stands arms folded in blue jeans, pointed boots, greased back red hair, on-deck Camel placed behind his right ear like he's carved from marble. Girls have always loved Red Joe says Red's got a big monster a sight to behold with all that red hair brother James who burned to death in the tunnel fire was the shy one but Red's never had any problem with the ladies. Red helps Joe with cleanings and polishings most of the time Red just hangs out, the house they live in is paid for all they must do is take care of the upkeep and their mother. Red removes a half pint from his right rear pocket breaks the seal unscrews the cap and in three attempts empties its contents. That stuff will kill him says Joe who can't drink hard stuff an ulcer but finishes a case of beer in a half-day and Joe probably all of 120 pounds. There's an old friend of George's just moved up from the south living in a little automobile trailer the old man lets him park behind the station for a week. He's a scary looking guy-short, dark, blackhead-embedded facial skin, dirty greased back black hair, sunken mouth from false teeth and in the middle of conversation he'll pop his upper choppers out and make an ugly face. Calls me stupid little guinea prick but gives me cigarettes whenever I ask says he'll buy beer for me appear at his trailer now parked behind a junkyard on Riverside Ave. He's got a six-pack of Private Stock malt liquor. I'm smashed halfway through my second he starts getting close to me, grabs my dick push his hand away stop what's wrong don't you like sex yeah but not with men. Have you ever done it with a man no have you ever done it with a woman no then how do I know whether I like men or women. He's got a point but if I did want to do it with a man it certainly wouldn't be him he rubs my dick again push him away backs me into a corner of the tiny trailer's kitchenette pushes his body against mine moves to kiss me turn my head away and with all my strength manage to sidestep him knocking over my half-filled beer at the same time. I'll be real gentle he says I'll like it moves towards me again better get the fuck out of here grab my jacket he grabs my shoulder don't go I'll stop head for the trailer door he says keep this between us we don't want my father to find out I've been drinking. I'm afraid to tell anyone wonder if George knows about his friend for weeks the image of that wild-eyed foul-breathed creep coming after me.

SEWELL D. FRANK SPEAKS in soft mumbles I say pardon me and what after he says something. He's a dull quirky man an engineer at MIT I'm not sure what MIT is but Tommy says it's a college for people who are smart but don't have a lick of common sense. Blackie says Mr. Frank's one of those geniuses whose head's in the clouds, incapable of everyday kind of thinking. Mr. Frank's odd looking, medium build, mid-forties, bald, wears glasses, pale complexion, thin lips and flat nose, twice a week purchases ten gallons of gas and has me check *everything* under the hood including his oil, transmission fluid, brake fluid, radiator water, battery water, belts and hoses. I don't understand why he needs to check all of this stuff it's only been three days since he was last here stands guard over me as I dip the dipstick, show him on the stick full to the line, same with the transmission fluid and when I pop the top of the master cylinder he looks in to see the brake fluid's full then the radiator and battery and if one of the battery cylinders is down a fraction of an inch of water he has me top it off then watches me check belts and hoses for tightness. A radiator hose should be solid rubber to the touch too dry it should be replaced before it cracks and leaks. I complain to Blackie why does Mr. Frank make me check all that stuff every time there's no way a hose or a radiator can go bad that quickly and if the oil's right up there one day it'll surely be up there three days later if Mr. Frank has only driven a hundred miles. Mr. Frank's one of those peculiar people he says engineers tend to be like that spend their lives studying all that cause and effect stuff in the rain I go around with a tire gauge check the tire pressure never once has one of his tires been below 28 pounds. Servicing Mr. Frank's 1961 De Soto with the two-tiered grille and shark-nose taillights he shadows me in the garage watching every move with his car up on the lift making certain I don't miss any grease fittings or that I put enough grease in all of them. Can you put a little more grease in that lower left ball joint I squeeze the grease gun hard grease comes shooting out from the fitting I nail him with a glob of grease sorry he backs away takes a rag wipes the top of his bald head but it doesn't stop him moments later he's right next to me breathing down my neck. Sewell D. Frank what kind of name is Sewell D. Frank I ask my father and Blackie says it's a pretty fucking stupid name my father says it's Jewish.

NO SOONER MY hair falls over my ears he hands me a buck

go to Jimmy's cut your hair. Jimmy's barbershop is two blocks up and down a side street his shop's located on the first floor of a three-story tenement. Jimmy's open two afternoons and Saturdays he's got a fulltime job cutting hair at a hospital on the other days two guys ahead of me good to kill some time get a break new *Playboy* calendar up in the bathroom and girlie magazines top of the toilet tank I don't have to go to the bathroom enough time to check out all twelve months on the calendar July 1967 my favorite. My father's cousin Lucy lives upstairs from Jimmy's in one of the apartments sees me going into the barbershop come up when you're through for a sandwich or dish of macaroni. Lucy and her husband Al always in the kitchen on the phone rings all day they're writing figures and initials on their notepaper, names of horses in the fourth, how to play today's trifecta, who's up who's down. Not sure Lucy's really my father's cousin Lucy's family and my father's family are commadre, somewhere between family and close friend. My father's on the phone with Lucy and Al at least once a day and often hangs out up there drinking coffee and smoking cigarettes it's a small apartment, cramped rooms, low ceilings, during summer dreadfully hot few windows poor ventilation humclick of kitchen window fan does little to alleviate. Hottest days cars overheat several times per day drivers clank onto the station lot steam shooting out from under the hood never touch the radiator cap until the engine's off and the cooling system has a chance to cool down or it can blow and spray scalding hot water my father's right arm scarred from a radiator cap that blew just below his tattoo in Italian reads MOTHER YOU SUFFER FOR ME. First snow means snow tire sales and service, rainy days mean electrical problems, cold weather brings dead batteries, hot days spew faulty cooling systems I'm sure of these things season to season.

PARTS STORE'S STUFFY smell rubber, metals, petroleum products and assorted chemicals. Long busy counters lined with thousand-page books listing hundreds of thousands of parts, parts men with phones pressed between their ears and shoulders flip through myriad grime-bemarked pages with dirty fingers, numbers, years, makes and models narrow down one particular part and its corresponding part number. Phone conversations of makes and models, Starfire or 88, was a 1962 you said, two-door or four-door, V-6 or V-8, automatic or standard transmission, I don't see it listed let me check another book. There's good money to be made in parts, my father charges list, buys at a considerable discount and won't install parts purchased elsewhere — you don't bring your own food into a restaurant. The woman who works in the sub shop next to the parts store looks a little like my mother olive skin small frame straight dark brown hair she keeps in a ponytail large brown eyes protruding nose I think she and my father have a thing for each other. Yesterday he sold the '62 Volkswagen Beetle's been sitting out front five months for sale, someone walks in off the street how much my father says $400 without making a counteroffer the man says he'll take it and returns in an hour with cash. My father picks up the car for nothing it needs a clutch that costs $40. He's gone all day today I'm sure he's at the track that cash burning a hole in his pocket. In the morning when we open up someone has to scoop last night's piles of Countess's shit strewn all over the garage floor. Using the little broom and shovel from one pile to the next don't know how one dog can shit so much doesn't matter when we feed her morning noon or evening she shits around the clock and turd duty's tough first thing in the morning my breakfast is waiting in the office. I love the radio but my father wants to listen to WBZ for local news and traffic in the morning, later in the day he's off somewhere I listen to WRKO Beatles Stones Who. Blackie likes the oldies station plays music from the fifties Chuck Berry and Little Richard Blackie says that was rock and roll not that noisy crap I listen to can't understand the words what does he make of Little Richard womp bomp baluma awomp bam boom? My father likes sports baseball basketball hockey baseball's his first choice nothing so boring as listening to a baseball game on the radio. He listens to radio talk shows at night tunes into "Sports Talk" followed by Larry Glick I can't believe how stupid some of the callers who mumble and when Larry asks what's your point they don't have an answer must call just to hear themselves talk. He looks up at the clock and starts fidgeting. I wait on a gas customer he makes a phone call ends abruptly as I enter the office then within a few minutes hands me the gas cash roll he's got to go see someone about a used car disappears until closing time. I switch to WRKO, smoke, drink cold Pepsis, new girlie magazine in the desk drawer. During the summer bathe Countess every week she gets filthy around the station, she loves her baths stretches her back out her head raised in the air brush out all her excess hair, hose her down, lather her up, rinse her off, then do it all again when I'm finished she runs off and rolls around in some grime. I take her up to the pond and bathe her there after hours they don't want me washing my dog where people swim tonight look at the new girlie magazine George dropped off. When I first looked at nude photographs of women in magazines I believed the images painted or fabricated somehow.

BUSINESS IS SLOW sweep the lot a light breeze blows neat little piles I make. Keep an eye out for stray screws or sharp pieces of metal endlessly coming to rest on the ground always something you can be doing my father says I take my time when I'm through there's a pump island to paint or the back corner of the garage to clean where stuff's piling up from various jobs — old engine heads, tire rims, an intake manifold from a 283 Chevy engine, a radiator, wheel drums, carburetors, all usable with a little work enough potential value saved them from the trash. I notice him eyeballing the pile this morning at the pumps soon as one car pulls in there's a run of others. I put the broom aside seven or eight customers in a row several at once. I handle at least two at a time, the key is the car's positioning so I can use both pumps at once get one fill started wash the windshield quickly get second car started first car's still filling wash the windshield on the second and it goes smoothly until someone wants only a dollar's worth and another wants me to check under the hood but I keep the line moving. You're a young boy to be doing all of this yourself I'll be thirteen. Resume sweeping he's in the office drinking heavy cream penciling the racetrack section of the *Record American* on the phone with Vito soon he'll barrel off to Rockingham in Vito's Caddy. Vito owns part of a racing horse my father's talking buying in with him my mother doesn't like the idea won't stop him if he's determined. I finish sweeping he says got some things to do be back later help Blackie if he needs me or organize the pile out in the far corner of the garage calls Vito be there in a couple of minutes. Light a cigarette switch the radio station Blackie's tuning a '62 Chevy Impala that smooth straight six won't need me except to turn the ignition when he sets the distributor cam high lobe to adjust points and condenser. Then he starts taking apart the engine he's rebuilding from a '61 Volkswagen go down the Jew's and get us some Devil Dogs and milk. Devil Dogs and milk, ice-cold milk, Blackie's favorite things to eat and drink. He takes a buck out of his wallet and I walk down to Harry's buy Devil Dogs and a quart of milk Harry your father doesn't like me but I never did anything to your

58

father warm afternoon light passing through greeny-dull store-front window illuminates him hands out to his sides palms open I tell you I just don't understand people.

NEVER WITHOUT A cut or abrasion on one or both of my hands try to loosen a generator nut wrench slips my knuckle comes down hard on edge of the generator pulley bloody gash my right knuckle wash it bandage it impossible to keep clean though it doesn't get infected Blackie says dirt and grease heal by sealing an open wound that's why mechanics never get infections with all the great cuts and abrasions they receive that swell turn different colors blue and grime black scabs. Rusty exhaust systems are dangerous layers paper-thin sharp old metal can cut right through bone Freddy at Freddy's Sunoco's lost the tip of his middle finger. During winter my hands always cracked gaping open cracks on my knuckles bleed the more I wash my hands the worse they get sometimes use lotion Tommy says only a woman would use lotion on her hands but even with lotion the cracks remain until the weather warms. Blackie's torching through the exhaust manifold pipe on an Olds 98 I'm holding up the back, one hand on the tailpipe one on the muffler, shift my weight let go the muffler one second suddenly the bracket gives way whole exhaust system comes crashing down in the middle of the garage floor Blackie and I run out from under narrowly missing blows to the head Jesus Fucking Christ Blackie says reaching down for the torch fallen on the floor still blowing fire shuts it off. My father and I are out on road service four degrees above zero he cuts his hand on the under edge of a car's hood hardly notices until back into the tow truck after jump-starting the car in the heat of the cab blood fountains forth from my father's left palm gashed open and deep cold froze the blood and it didn't thaw until the heat of the cab the emergency room they stitch him up. I rub lotion into tender sore open knuckle cracks they burn and bleed until spring.

SQUIRRELS AND BIRDS live in the small stand of trees back of the station where a little hill rises to backyards of Gaston Street houses. Let Countess off the chain she runs around sniffing out discarded tires oilcans a shopping carriage rusting on its side. She never shits where I want her to no matter when I feed her she shits right around her house where we keep her chained and in the garage and office at night. Light a smoke, walk into the thick foliage unseen, sit down on the overturned carriage. Countess sniffs around takes short pisses on different things Mrs. Terani gassed up this morning her blue Thunderbird convertible miniskirt bathing suit top, tanned, freckled, long thick red hair bound by a bandanna rest blows behind her when she drives her breasts concealed so slightly beneath her black swimsuit top don't care if she is watching me watch her from behind her sunglasses work the squeegee back and forth. I rub it she rushes up jumps on me my father's calling. Blackie says Mrs. Terani has a pool in her backyard once he went to start her car she was sunbathing by the pool in a bikini looking like goddess oil gleaming in the sun. I chain Countess she immediately shits next to her house where the hell were you out back letting the dog run around. Someone's driven in with a flat tire and he wants me to fix it. In the old days he says he worked hard but my father's adept at doing as little as possible, the only thing he gets enthused about is a tow call. He lives for the telephone to ring with a call from the State Police then gets all excited barking out orders get Mr. Lampry's wagon in for a grease and oil while I'm gone runs full tilt to the tow truck like an ambulance driver tears out of the lot orange and red lights flashing and turning drives wildly beeping the horn for people to get out of his way yelling don't you see these lights as if he's going to a life or death struggle when often a car's out of gas or a flat tire. I jack up the car and remove the left front tire fill it with air and place it in the water trough bubbles up through water tire's picked up what looks to be a roofing nail I remove plug the tire and place it back on the car. There's something nauseating about the smell of air blown through rubber whether I'm pumping air into a tire or letting air out. I plunge my hands into the can of gelatinous goo of mechanic's soap think Mrs. Terani leave them submerged squeezing goo between my fingers.

HE'S SEEING THE woman who works in the sub shop next to the parts store where he's been hanging out drinking coffee and smoking fine with Blackie and me because he's out of our way at the station. We get our morning coffee and donuts at Town Line Donuts but he changes to the shop next door to the parts store ten minutes out of the way donuts taste old I now know for sure the way his mood elevates when he's in there making little jokes teasing she yawns what are you yawning for didn't you sleep last night all the while his wide smile not enough not enough she answers. When my mother catches him with my fifth-grade schoolmate's mother she throws him out for two months and he lives in a rooming house in Malden. I see him nearly every day he picks me up after school or at home on Saturday mornings asks how's your mother doing complains how unhappy he is the woman who owns the rooming house is so cheap he pleads with her turn up the heat. Back at home kisses my mother before going to work in the morning and when he arrives home at night, this goes on for a few months. He goes bankrupt the first time he runs the gas station during the 1950s he's only in America three years when he takes over the business in 1952. I'm only around for an afternoon once a week elementary school a big thing just to pump gas he gambles every penny away she catches him trying to cash in savings bonds put away for me and my sister he owes a lot of money the phone's ringing men are looking for him hangs up the phone unnerved. He files for bankruptcy my mother can't take the gambling he's got to move out and does for a month takes me and my sister for rides and ice cream cries he wants to come home we cry and back home plead with her take him back she does. Several years later the Jenney Company contacts him again two recent proprietors failed to make the station go if he's interested they'll help him get the station back. He's driving cab and on Saturdays takes me with him with a little kid in the front seat he gets better tips talk with business-men in suits with briefcases on their way to the airport for places like Atlanta and San Francisco and Germany they tip my father and sometimes me too. He's not earning enough driving cab, days are long, too long for one who's already had a taste of having others work for him so he takes the station again — they kick off with a huge grand opening complete with my fa-ther's usual special event fanfare mechanical man out front, flags, clowns, free glassware with a fill-up, balloons for kids and all his old customers turn out. Why does he choose women who look like my mother this new one's younger than my mother divorced has a daughter he's always particular about how much heat and electricity we waste. During the winter he's constantly on me about keeping the garage door openings and closings to a minimum, at night he puts lights on one at a time, first he switches on the Jenney sign which is illuminated from within, some kind of red, white and blue plastic exterior with the word JENNEY in red. The old sign was made of wood, letters hand painted, lit from lights on the outside. Years of pestering the Jenney Company and taking Bill Gleason home for dinner lead to the new sign. Ours is the last station in the city with an old wooden sign and old-fashioned narrow gas pumps. Along with the Jenney sign pump lights light up directly behind the glass on the pump so you can see the tumblers and know the amount. The new pumps have the tumbler light and a light that illuminates the regular and premium letters on top of the pump, and above the pump is-land are two big fluorescent lamps which light the pump island area and much of the station yard. As soon as it's dark first of these lights goes on. They take several minutes to warm up and reach maximum potential. He never turns the second island light on but if he's not going to be around I turn them both on brightens up the yard makes the place look like it's got some life. The office light's on when it's dark and the garage is kept dark whenever it's not in use. I get my father's old uniforms when he and the mechanics switch over to new every year so I wear short baggy pants squeezed tight around the waistline by a belt and an oversized faded blue shirt with my father's name on it. During summer I wear a T-shirt and jeans though he insists I wear the full uniform T-shirt and jeans look sloppy. All afternoon my mouth waters thoughts of pepper and egg sandwiches my mother has promised for supper. Now that I'm eating I'm put off too much olive oil's seeped through thick crusty pieces of bread, the paper wrap, and lunch bag she brought it in. Halfway through the first sandwich feel slightly nauseous out back of the garage where Countess is sleeping give the sandwiches to her she chomps them up and swallows with aggressive methodical mouth and throat movements. Nausea passes I'm hungry and the old man's off for the night nothing to eat I'm hoping that one of the guys will come around get me a sub. My mother's idea of dessert is fruit and the pear she put in the bag got soaked by the olive oil from the pepper and egg sandwiches. The phone rings a woman's voice from the sub shop when do I expect him back closing time. I thought he was with her must be at the dog track saw him with Wonderland schedule this afternoon. I smoke three cigarettes in a row and my nausea returns in the bathroom I'm going to throw up but only dry heave.

MOST PAY CASH a few use credit cards means I have to go into the office run the card through fill out the slip bring it back to the customer to sign with their copy and bring the merchant copy back into the office. At the end of the week list every credit transaction by hand on a Jenney Company form which I forward to the Jenney Company. Jenney's a small company there aren't any Jenney stations outside New England rumor is they'll merge with a bigger company. We give credit to some long standing regular customers and friends who pay by the month or sometimes not records are kept in a small metal file box slips for private accounts many long overdue folks for one reason or another never return to pay their bills. Danny Walsh and my father play cards together still lives a few blocks away hasn't been in for over a year he and his wife have lots of kids little money drink heavily Danny doesn't keep jobs. He's into my father for six months of gas and repairs on his beat up old Pontiac wagon held together by wire and string Blackie says. Danny stops attending card games and coming to the station, we see him around town he looks the other way why not ask him for the money my father says Danny wouldn't have it. We haven't seen Lou Gioisa the bread man for two years. Lou delivers bread for one of the South Medford bakeries, working on his truck's tough too big too high to use the lift use a jack I change the oil on my back on a creeper grease the fittings with an old-fashioned hand-pump grease gun. Lou's in over his head with the bookies owes people all over the city in South Medford Jimmy's Cleaners has a sign in the window reads LOU OWES ME TOO. One thing I never see is a bottom line.

Don't know how much he brings in for sure but during inspection time Blackie's flat out, Joe, Floyd, Tiny, Me and Tommy at different times flat out too. The money for the inspection sticker is clear profit sometimes we inspect hundreds of cars a week and all the revenue from extra repair work adds up. There are weeks he makes a thousand dollars but he overspends at the track or card games, buys a new tow truck, gives Johnny Calderone six hundred bucks a year and a half ago doesn't hear from him since. Johnny's an old biker friend of Blackie's hangs around the station doesn't have a job but rides an impeccable full dressed Harley lives with his girlfriend Denise every time I see her I beat off for days her blond teased-up hair and tight black jeans high-heeled shoes black fishnet stockings skimpy summertime tops get hard watching her wrap her hair up in a kerchief, put her motorcycle helmet on and climb up onto the back of that full dresser sitting legs apart, high heels on the footrests, slender white arms wrapped around Johnny's big belly. Johnny's a short powerful guy shaved head big gold earring tattooed arms like tree trunks. Johnny's got a friend who's a horse trainer in the know about races at Suffolk and Rockingham gives Johnny tips Johnny and my father end up with several impressive winnings at the track one day he's got a tip borrows three hundred from my father my father puts up three hundred of his own Johnny's off to Suffolk and that's the last time anyone's heard from Johnny. Word is he ripped off several others same way same day Blackie thinks he left the state says Johnny would steal from his own mother. I don't get paid for my time at the station but when I'm sixteen I can have a car and he'll take care of the expenses. My first car's an old Ford a '49 stripped and engineless parked for several months in the back of the station I'm ten years old spend hours behind the steering wheel driving listen to the radio make up my own songs stop for gas my father laughs says I gas up a lot. One day

the car's sent off to the junkyard he says there'll be another second's a '59 Volkswagen needs an engine and a paint job Blackie and I rebuild the engine Blackie gives it a bad paint job fire
engine red I drive it around the station lot for two weeks then
my father sells it for $250 says we'll find another one before I
get my license. It's best when people pay cash paperwork's easier more people pay cash the more money my father can keep
off the books. The bookkeeper is a man who looks like Bob
Hope his nose is pickled red from drink he has a high-pitched
nasally voice, wears striped sport coats and bright bow ties,
you're doing all right he assures my father you 're doing all
right.

HOW MUCH DOES he spend at the track or on his women
gives my mother $75 per week to run the house she's been tell-
ing him she needs more he ups it to a hundred. He says he's
going to play cards with Tom Riordan who picks him up but
Tom doesn't play cards he's got a summer house on a little lake
in Marlborough an hour away I think they go there with wom-
en. Not one of my father's women but Tom's women there are
two a black one and white one Tommy says they're Tom
Riordan's regulars and the black one's really something tits out
to here he illustrates with his hands. Tom Riordan's married to
a beautiful blond woman who has a well-paying state job but
rarely goes to work some kind of secretarial thing Joe and
Tommy say that his wife's had a boyfriend for years she and
Tom have an understanding when Tom was running for politi-
cal office it wouldn't have been okay if he was divorced the
marriage became a sort of business arrangement. Tom's not a
state representative any longer but he's worth considerable
money one of the grandest homes in Medford new cars summer house in Marlborough winter home in Florida and last

winter my father went to Florida with Tom for a week's vacation took the two women with them my father worships Tom Tom always picks up the bills costs my father little my mother trusts Tom that's why she didn't say much about my father going to Florida with him he told her he was going to help Tom paint the Florida house. Tom's switched on like he never stopped being a politician perpetual smile scrubbed clean round face hair cut once a week nice blazers ties and well-shined shoes comes to the house the night they are leaving picks up my father and his baggage don't worry I'll keep an eye on him assures my mother. My mother finds out about the woman in the sub shop drives up to the woman's house walks through the front door my father sitting at the kitchen table claims he's there to collect for plowing she puts him out calls a lawyer the lawyer tells her she's got grounds for divorce my father's got a small cot for a week sleeps in the back of the garage picks me up for work at the house asks how's your mother is she still talking with the lawyer suddenly the lawyer's gone he's back in the house not seeing the woman in the sub shop but tonight he's with Tom and Tom 's women.

NEEDLE-DICK-THE-Bug-Fucker Tommy calls me any smaller he says I'd have to take it out of my pants with a pair of needle-nose pliers. Compared with other kids in showers during gym class don't seem to have too much more or less Tommy says you can't tell soft. I've never seen one hard except the guys in magazines huge ones I'll bet you don't even hit five inches hard Tommy says how much you want to bet are you going to show me no but I'll show Joe he says five bucks. I go into the bathroom with the new *Playboy* look at the centerfold spread beautiful brunette lounging poolside nervous half hard start to pump it swells want to bring myself off big as it gets call Joe who comes with the ruler places it alongside my you've got a hunk of meat tells Tommy Tommy refuses to pay George and Joe put the squeeze on Tommy pulls five out of his wallet throws it at me here you little prick remember it's not what you got but how you use it and I'm not talking about using it with your hand. Joe says you ought to be putting that thing to use Red and Freddy Golar drive in in Freddy's black Ford Falcon Freddy's so drunk I don't know how he drove them here in one piece. They've got a pint Freddy's shouting Red's eyes and face blaze Tommy throws them out before they get too comfortable. Tommy no trouble no trouble Red repeats but Freddy's loud yelling at Tommy a lot of nerve you got putting me out I won't have it. Tommy says get the fuck out of here and Freddy and Red stagger back out to the Ford Falcon, take a few swigs from the pint in the front seat, then in slow motion Freddy backs up, turns an about-face and drives away. Tommy says they'll be lucky if they don't kill someone or themselves. At home in bed I stroke myself the woman in the *Playboy* lying on her stomach on a chaise lounge, right leg up in the air toes pointing to heaven, water beads on her smooth ass glistening in the sun well tanned except white inside her bikini lines. When he first opens the station my father works for a year by himself seven days a week twelve hours a day. He's not much of a mechanic more of a wire and tape man Blackie calls him Mick the Mouse Take the Easy Way Out. I'm removing a starter nearly electrocute myself forget to disconnect the battery screwdriver strikes live juice starter wire. Blackie gets frustrated but stays cool my father would have thrown a fit over me removing a starter without first disconnecting the battery Blackie says I buy you books and send you to school and nothing happens. My mind endlessly drifts don't hear everything folks say Blackie removing belts from a '60 Mercury says get me a 3/8-inch open end I walk to the toolbox can't remember I'm thinking about going up to the pond with Countess later in the afternoon swimming my shadow in late afternoon clear water light. Three-eighths-inch open end he says voice raised he sees me pause in front of the box. Lots of times thinking about women I'm afraid I'm masturbating too much when I'm in confession Father Everheart grills me about touching myself wants to know do I think about girls and what is it I think about I tell him simple lies when he comes in for gas I'm afraid he might recognize me. My father forever strips nuts and bolts tightening too much or turning the wrong direction pulls on an oil filter so hard with the filter wrench it slips and pokes a hole in the radiator. Blackie keeps him out of the garage as much as possible says that guy could fuck up a wet dream.

MUSIC'S ELECTRIC WILD rhythms and sounds long-haired music Blackie and Phil call it can't understand the words how the hell could you get laid to it if rock and roll's for anything Phil says it's for getting laid. My friend Jerry Hastings has all the latest albums the other day at school we skipped two classes went to his house and listened to music Jerry plays electric guitar and he's teaching me. Jimi Hendrix this morning on the radio Blackie climbs out the trunk of a Rambler he's doing electrical work in shut that fucking shit off. Phil says give him "In the Still of the Night" I strip a bolt tightening down a valve cover gasket hope it won't leak start the engine it leaks Blackie finds a self-threading bolt close enough to the original size bolts it in for me be careful with a self-threading bolt he says go get us a cigarette Pall Mall unfiltered so strong straightens me up an inch when I inhale. Phil fidgets with the radio Chuck Berry "Maybellene" leave it there Blackie says can't do any better than Chuck. Why can't you be true Blackie shouts takes a long drag on his Pall Mall twists a bit with his ass sticking out.

There's trouble at home his beautiful wife drinks he gets home from work she's drunk they fight my father tells him you've got to pour that booze down the sink in front of her and put your foot down he does and things are quieter now. I need to get out and have some fun he says throwing his cigarette down stomps on it and climbs back into the little brown Rambler's trunk singing why can't you be true? I fantasize I'm alone with Blackie's wife she takes me to bed my first hot radiator cap blasts off doused with hot water blisters on my chest. I thought the radiator had cooled enough when will I learn to pay attention my father wants to know. Late in the afternoon beach is already deserted undress down to my blue jeans Countess rushes in makes one of her hard striding circles swim out to the middle of the pond tread water keep Countess and her dog-paddling claws at a distance. Cool water soothes the blisters on my chest could masturbate out here no one around hard to keep myself afloat with one hand.

THE POLICE FIND the stolen Chrysler New Yorker parked in the back garage my father's taken to the police station for questioning. Al D'Amato's paying my father to store the cars under arrest part of a stolen car ring tells the police my father has no knowledge cars he's been storing are stolen. Two cars out back nearly a year 1961 Lincoln and a 1962 Chrysler New Yorker three weeks ago Al removes the Lincoln so the police find only a Chrysler. Local papers feature the story on page one it makes page four in the *Record American* several dozen under arrest my father's name is saved from the *Record American's* story but the *Daily Mercury* mentions that one of the stolen cars was recovered at my father's station. My father's called to be a witness at the trial customers and folks around town are talking all about it stolen cars have been found at several area garages and junkyards the owners of which to a person claim ignorance. Al D'Amato's described by the media as one of their ringleaders testifies on the stand my father had no knowledge that the cars he's been paying him to store are stolen. Manny Cabral owns the big junkyard in Malden where seven cars are found Blackie says Cabral Junk's where cars are stripped for parts then put to the cruncher. Other cars marked for out-of-state sales are re-painted in Manny's body shop so Manny is indicted too when it's his turn to testify as a witness my father claims all along that he had no idea the cars were stolen and over past couple of years he's stored several cars for Al and never had a problem. Customers question me they question my father he tells them the story of how he thought he was storing cars for people who were going out of state or the country they accept the story or if they don't believe him they don't let on they don't. Several months pass between the time police find the stolen Chrysler and the beginning of the trial by now it's as if it happened in another life my father's talking to his lawyer and Tom Riordan who've been giving him advice the trial lasts for two weeks the stolen car ring is in the newspapers again seven of the twelve men on trial are convicted. Some customers including Mrs. Amerault have not been in since it was first reported that the stolen Chrysler had been discovered at the station. Three of the seven men convicted end up with jail sentences Al D'Amato receives seven to ten but will probably be out in four. After the trial my father's quiet and lethargic weeks of mooning around orders wrong parts and mixes up the lunch orders I'm not sure where he's been going his racetrack friends call for him so he's not with them.

FLICK OF THE compressor switch first thing in the morning *varoom* kicks in runs about fifteen minutes shuts off until we use the lift or power tools or the grease gun which run off the compressor. Early in the morning the compressor's noises annoying by the end of the day I stop noticing. It's not that he hits me much anymore though he's still capable of lashing out with a backhander when I least expect it, but it's the way he'll nag on about my mind always being somewhere else how next time I'll crack you over the head. During winter kids skate on the pond after school on Saturdays walk by woolen hats and gloves skates over shoulders my father won't allow me to skate on the pond I wouldn't anyway breaking through ice into the cold depths. Countess tries to go out on the ice slips her legs fly out from under her three girls a few feet from shore watch boys play hockey vying for the boys' attention one of them looks over at me awkward in my blue uniform pants and dirty jacket call Countess and leave. I see her several times now walking up Oak Street on her way to or from the pond tight wet blue bathing suit cut deep into her ass cheeks. The lift has a safety mechanism in case the compressor should suddenly shut down while a car's in the air so the car won't come crashing down. I wash the front windshield the rear window if in the mood or not in a hurry and offer to check under the hood which is checking the oil radiator water battery water then I have them start the engine if the car has an automatic transmission because for reasons I can't understand the engine has to be running to check the automatic transmission fluid. Automatic transmissions are at least twice the size of standard transmissions because a standard transmission is very simple gears just gears that fit one into the other. Automatic transmissions have gears and all sorts of valves and seals myriad intricate inner workings most garages won't even work on automatic transmissions send customers to automatic transmission specialists. My father never worked on automatic transmissions until Blackie though Blackie's not comfortable working on them he does. He has an instinct for finding his way, that's where you separate the R & R men who remove and replace from the real mechanic like Blackie never afraid to take on a job he's never done before first time he rebuilds an automatic transmission follows repair manual gently finding his way says key thing is understanding the nature of what's at hand. No carburetor rear end front end transmission or electrical problem he can't fix. I like it raining because we don't have to wash the windshields or offer to check under the hood.

HARDLY A DAY passes someone doesn't wander in jacket over shoulder this one out of breath from the trek up Oak Street from Interstate 93 where he left his fuel-less car parked in the breakdown lane. He doesn't want to leave the five-dollar deposit on the gas can no deposit no gas can my father hears him giving me a hard time charges in from the garage what's the problem he doesn't want to leave the deposit no deposit no gas can. The man grudgingly digs into his wallet removes a five I fill the old round dented red with yellow letters FUEL can. Before the deposit policy several folks return to their cars on the highway and just take off now they must return for the deposit fill up at the same time stupidest thing anyone can do is run out of gas my father says. The State Police stop traffic middle lane of the interstate rows of flares cruiser lights whirling car's out of gas I'm pouring two gallons from the can *air-ear-whack* of cars and trucks speeding by in the other lanes my father shouts hurry up from where he's bullshitting with one of the troopers. Blackie's doing an engine job pile of parts for me to scrape and clean spend the afternoon between gas customers listen to the radio stand over cleaning sink in the garage scraping stuck gasket bits and wire-brushing grime-ridden parts make sure you get all the carbon off the top of those pistons Blackie says. I know all the parts, know where they go, but can never reassemble and make it all run.

SATURDAY NIGHT MY fourteenth birthday Joe buys me a six-pack pours me a cold one into a Styrofoam cup hands it to me happy fourteenth little man. I guzzle the contents in a few swallows slow down he says you've got all night it's going to be longer than you think Tommy adds I ask what's up Joe smiles tonight young one you become a man. Annie's agreed to breaking me in it's the guys' birthday gift to me I'll be first among all my friends Annie's not my first choice but I can't tell them that Tommy'll say something like beggars shouldn't be choosers and he's right. I press for details when how Joe says be patient and when she arrives later he'll give me a signal I'm to go out back in the big tow truck she'll come along later don't worry trust my instincts Tommy says tonight you're going to get reamed steamed and dry-cleaned. What time is she coming will I need a rubber a hundred-per-minute scenarios what might happen in the truck alone with Annie. What should I say to her Tommy says I'm not out there for a fucking debate I'm out there to fuck Joe says everything will be fine Annie knows what she's doing Tommy says better your dick than mine. Annie arrives says hello walks over gives me a quick kiss on the lips happy birthday she says and looks prettier than I remember sweet taste of her lipstick really not as fat as I thought Joe offers her a beer she accepts we stand awkward small talk car rolls in over the bell hose ding-ding Tommy says for me to go out and take it I tell him he's the one getting paid tonight it's my birthday

74

calls me ungrateful little prick on his way out. More small talk I get the signal grab my cup of beer walk out back there's been much rain past few days the petroleum-muck puddle is high lay some boards down over it and as I traverse them they sink into the mush cause a thick *squisshh* sound. It's humid and the smell is rank between the muck puddle and Countess's shit piles so I close the windows in the tow truck sip my beer in fear that I'm not going to be able to get it up or she gets pregnant. Tommy's given me a rubber with instructions on how to use it afraid I'll go soft when trying to put it on. In a few minutes she walks around the building maneuvering the planks squish into the muck-puddle opens the door slide over honey with a smile. Sit in silence a few seconds like an hour don't be nervous everything's going to be fine leans over kisses me softly on the lips her tongue pushes deep into my mouth I give my tongue back don't know when to stop pulls hers back I assume that's enough. Then she leans over and kisses me with her tongue again and I reach up inside her top for her breasts full round softer than imagined underneath her breasts her belly rests over her jeans because of the way she's sitting. I start to rub her breasts slowly I read in men's magazines how a woman likes to be seduced slowly have her breasts fondled her cunt gently licked and how to control oneself not cum too quickly. Her nipples are large and hard like tollhouse cookies can hear Joe say squeeze one between my fingers ooch she jumps back easy she says easy hon sorry. Reach down between her legs can't get anywhere her thighs are large her jeans tight she reaches down unbuttons her pants sits up off the seat pulls them off I do the same each of us in our underpants I lift up her T-shirt hold it up move down to lick and suck her breasts she's rubbing the back of my head. I make a motion to go down on her she stops me says don't she's having her friend sit up straight confused can she have sex she says it'll be fine it's near the end she just

75

has to remove her pad reaches down into my underwear rubs my cock and balls I begin to stiffen and she goes down gets me fully erect working it up and down with her mouth. Now she sits up removes her panties I take the rubber from my shirt pocket I won't need it she reaches down to remove her pad when she does it makes a squishing noise of planks going into the muck-puddle rolls down the window tosses it out lays back down on the bench with her legs spread. I climb onto her but can't find my way in she reaches down takes it in her hand guides me at first it doesn't want to go then suddenly I'm inside pumping for all I'm worth ready to cum within a minute so I slow myself down so she'll enjoy it too don't cum too early pump slowly enough suck on her breasts and swap long tongue kisses suddenly Tommy's voice a banging on the side of the truck how the hell you doing in there. Tommy get the fuck out of here you asshole Annie shouts I hear Joe yelling for him leave us alone what an asshole you ain't kidding Annie says now I'm beginning to soften my cock slips out she stops it with her hand pumps down low near my balls until I'm hard pumping again if I wore a watch know how long I'm going so I can cum can't hold back as I'm cumming see the image of the woman fucking the pig in George's magazine. I shift and moan into a long kiss with her all I want is to lie back try to keep my softening dick inside her keep pumping until she's satisfied she says it's okay she's all set I ask her if she came too she says never ask a woman that. We dress ourselves in steam window silent darkness odor of the muck-puddle and Countess's shits hot August night sweat and beer breath mixes with sex smells cum blood and cunt. I'm worried I did her all right you were pretty good she says really yes. She's first out I follow we walk the planks the muck swells up and over them *squishlup* each of our steps. My eyes are sensitive to the bright office lights I'm feeling tipsy from the beers a little sick to my stomach Joe fills all our beer

76

cups Annie finishes up says gotta go walks over kisses me before she leaves the guys want to know how it went I tell them everything I can recall Joe says sounds like I did just fine. I thank them all Tommy says don't thank me thank George only reason Annie consented was they got George to agree to take her out again if she did me she just can't get enough of that huge thing swinging between his legs. Because it's my birthday I don't have to be home until eleven it's not yet nine I walk looking for my friends to tell them everything but they're not around the usual haunts home early parents out go upstairs fill the bathtub with warm water dried bloodstains on the bottom of my T-shirt can't put it in the hamper my mother will see it and ask questions roll it into a ball put in a paper bag I place in the bottom of the trash barrel outside. Back upstairs dried blood specks on my shriveled cock and on the inside of my left thigh I slide into the full warm tub submerged to my neck.

LET'S TAKE A ride I want to talk I'm in trouble must be something I've done at school sometimes Mr. D'Evani my math teacher comes in tells him I need to concentrate more I'm goofing off but he's nervous if he's pissed he'd show it I hop in the Jeep he drives to the pond road halfway around pulls over and shuts the engine. Tom Riordan's been talking about a state job for him might come up in the not so distant future I'll be a senior next year and then graduating if he sells the business he can make a little money for all his years of work there and have a chance to work a job where he can wear a clean shirt and have a retirement plan 'cause he's not getting any younger and there's no retirement plan with the station but he knows I might want the station and if I do want the station he won't sell and when I finish school I can come on with him though who knows what will happen since there's talk that the Jenney Oil Company's being taken over by the Cities Service Company otherwise known as Citgo. Don't know what to say he's never talked to me this serious before I have no idea he's thinking about all of this stuff I fantasize about running the station someday but when would it be my station and no longer his? Last Sunday at Jerry Hastings's house listen to new records Hendrix and Cream and Velvet Underground Jerry plugs in his electric guitar cranks up the volume in paisley bell-bottoms Nehru shirt shaking his long blond hair wails. I imagine being at the station the rest of my life all the long hot afternoon days of summer and cold wet snowy slush-down-my-back mornings of winter the pump tumblers clicking away endless gallons and dollars and cents out there something's stirring like bottom-of-the-barrel burning trash. I don't really want the gas station but I'm scared as hell where I'll end up though I might get drafted and have to go to Viet Nam Jerry says he's not going even if he's drafted he wants to start a band and without the station on my back I'll have more time to practice. What does my mother think I ask she thinks I should sell the station so we'll have some money to retire with otherwise who knows what will happen. He's fidgeting with his hands and fingers looking down at his lap and won't make eye contact with me hoping I'm certain that I don't want the station and I don't. Are you sure yes I'm sure. He stares out his window at the pond then looks down at his hands still fidgeting well then if you're sure you don't want it because if you do want it I won't sell.

HE'S LESS AND less interested in the station, business declines if Blackie can get some help from the bank he's going to buy my father out. Countess is gone all morning last time I saw

78

her she was sleeping her usual spot back of the garage Blackie saw her drinking from her water bowl about ten. After lunch I walk up to the pond nose around surrounding woods' roads empty beer cans a used condom pair of women's underwear no sign of her back up Oak Street to the heights down Fulton Street cut back across Brackett past Jimmy the barber clippers and comb in hand standing at his barber chair man sitting in the chair several waiting anyone seen Countess no. Up to Cousin Lucy's apartment she's on the phone her full-volume shouts I had that damn trifecta in my apron and the son of a bitch tripped in the stretch. She hasn't seen Countess all day commands a good view of the neighborhood from her kitchen window late afternoon my father returns from the track he's worried calls the pound maybe she was picked up by the dog-catcher no. I make another sweep of the pond one of the life-guards is securing the lifeboat says he saw her around sometime during the day but isn't sure when. I walk back down Oak to the Fellsway and Route 28 sound of cars and trucks whipping past on Interstate 93, alert neighborhood folks coming in for gas or walking past close the station at nine my father says that maybe someone stole her she is a full-blooded German shep-herd on the way home we cruise the neighborhood once more. This morning bring the oil and window washer stuff to the pumps, take out the jacks, tire displays, windshield wiper dis-play, air hose. Flick on the compressor *varoom* steady drumming MDC police cruiser pulls into the yard Johnny the MDC cop gets out Countess's choke collar in his hand says someone jog-ging around the pond this morning found her dead on one of the trails the officer isn't certain but it looks like she's been poi-soned. Poisoned who would poison her oh there are a lot of sick folks out there Johnny says we can have an autopsy done to know for sure but my father will have to pay he says no. A van rolls in across the hose who would poison the dog thoughts of Countess dead and stiff through the night what pains she might have suffered swallow hard my choking throat eyes tearing fill up the van into the office run the charge card through my father sits back in his swivel chair shakes his disbelieving head at Blackie says feel like lost a son.

Tony Luongo

Joseph Torra

For William Corbett

Three weeks is the longest I ever went without taking a shit it was in boot camp the first time I went away from home graduating high school in June September I joined in the Voke I took carpentry and could've found work as an apprentice but in the Marines I could go someplace far away like Korea and I knew I'd never see Korea from Somerville I loved basic training but being away from home the change of food hard exercise and officers up and down your ass every second I couldn't shit I didn't worry at first 'cause I'd gone a week without shitting before but when it started getting near two weeks the cramping got real bad and I couldn't eat I went to see the doctor who said it was almost impossible to go three weeks but since I was a little kid it was nothing to go two or three days and I could remember times when it was a week or more though it never went this long he gave me some stuff syrup to drink and said it would clean me right out I took it for three days nothing happened the cramping got so bad I could barely stand and thought I would wash out of basic training then finally at the end of the third week after nights doubled over from the cramps and long days I never thought I would live to the see end of we were out in the field on drills it was pouring rain they had us crawling around in mud that's the only reason nobody knew I shit myself the way I did I couldn't control it it poured like a fountain I just laid there on the ground it flowed and flowed suddenly the sergeant was over me screaming to get moving so I got up and ran down a gully and pretended to fall into a stream so I could get my pants washed up if anyone knew what happened I would have been tossed out it was the strangest feeling on the muddy ground thinking every last bit of my insides was oozing out of me not being able to move until it ran its course when I graduated boot camp Ma and my sisters and brother Peter came down to see the ceremony Ma carried a dish of macaroni and meatballs on the plane she said if I could only eat her food I'd go to the bathroom better I wasn't away that long but it was the first time Ma looked old hunched over tired squinting to see behind her glasses the recruits went crazy for Gina I wouldn't let any of those animals near her and made her button her blouse Peter always quiet didn't want nothing to do with the barracks and mess tours like most boys his age and Josie hiding behind her glasses tending to Ma talked about Frank in prison when they visited him they brought food the prisoners loved Ma's cooking in boot camp I got into the discipline yes sir no sir push-ups running and those motherfucking drill sergeants up your ass I'd be proud if a son of mine wanted to serve I learned respect from Ma telling us to always be respectful to elders and I called elders by Mr. or Mrs. or Sir or Mam and at work the guys called me an ass-kiss 'cause I called the division managers by Mr. Santisi or Mr. Fournier instead of their first names like everyone else but it wasn't ass kissing they were my boss and older than me other recruits didn't like the regiment of training or the drill sergeants and when the sergeant came yelling and banging in the middle of the night we had to stand next to our bunks at attention waiting to be inspected God help the guy who left something out of place they never could nail me for anything my mother thought if she

could only talk to the general or something they might let me
get stationed close to Boston if they knew she needed me nearby being the oldest son which I wasn't but Frank was in jail first
I went to California then we got shipped to Korea a few of the
companies went to Vietnam but no one had even heard of it
yet from then on I had it made I was with a construction company we did maintenance work around the base every month
we went out to the field for drills I was there for sixteen
months Ma was different when I got back from Korea she lost
the sight in her right eye said if that's what God wants then
that's what she wants I saw relatives and they wanted to hear
about Korea and the Marines but it wore off then I found a job
at Pratt's retail store Central Square Cambridge in the display
department I missed Korea it was the first time in my life I was
on my own I mostly kept to myself in free time went out to
strip bars to see these shows with girls putting snakes and bottles and whatever else up inside them I drank a lot and when I
was horny I got a blowjob for pennies those girls let you come
all over their faces then I would get rice somewhere fried rice I
love fucking fried rice I got the biggest order and staggered
back to the base eating the rice leaving a trail of it behind for
pennies they let you come all over their face and the personnel
manager at Pratt's said they needed someone who could do nit-
ty-gritty construction work for the display people so I spent my
days measuring spaces and building little wooden constructions
and then Joe Letto and Celeste King decorated over them with
women's purses or men's shirts or the latest model vacuum
cleaner I wanted to move out of Ma's apartment Frank moved
back in there the girls were sharing a room and Frank Peter and
me had to share a room this guy named Danny Kelly who
worked in the shoe department was looking for a roommate so
I moved into the second floor of a three story on Porter Street
and walked to work in less than five minutes I always wanted to

do Celeste but never had the chance when I first started at Pratt's she was dating Bill Nardella the division manager of the paint department who was just going through a divorce there was something about her got me wild she knew it too the tease wearing those mini-skirts and wasn't ashamed to climb a ladder or bend over digging for something in the display room I told her on no uncertain terms she smiled not on your best day Danny Kelly was probably the best friend I ever had we lived together for two years Danny was kind of wild he liked to drink and smoke pot he got it on with guys and chicks I never had much money 'cause I was on a salary in the display department it wasn't very good but the benefits were and I tried to give my mother any extra cash I could to help keep her going Gina graduated and got a job at an insurance company downtown Peter quit school and got a job working at Schrafts Candy Company in Sullivan Square so they were helping with some money Frank was living with a woman in Everett then they had a fight one night and he beat her up and the cops in Everett were looking for him so he moved back in with Ma the hardest thing was to give money to Ma and make sure Frank didn't get his hands on it everything went to gambling Frank had only the clothes on his back when he lived with a chick he didn't pay no rent he was supposed to be looking for a job 'cause he was on parole but mostly he hung around his usual haunts like Pal Joey's on the hill the job at Pratt's was working out for me I liked display and got to work all over the store and there were some hot chicks working in those departments in a few months I started fucking this young one in the candy department she was a little screwy a few of the guys had already been at her including Bill Nardella while he was dating Celeste but Celeste never knew and this chick she did Danny and me not at once but we were both in bed with her and she took Danny first and then me I'm not sure she was even legal age she said she was eighteen man did she know what she was doing I wanted them all young ones old ones May Sullivan the division manager of women's was in her early fifties and she was so sexy I told her I'd marry her any time she'd have me but she said she would never marry again she did her playing outside the store one of those people who can keep themselves from shitting where they eat at that time everyone was smoking pot it made me dizzy and sick to my stomach it was no good for me in bed it made me go limp and all scared but people said it was great for sex but the thing about sex for me I never have a problem just getting to it I believe it's what everybody's always thinking about anyway I don't care who they are or where they are if you're working you think of sex if you're driving down the street and you see a chick you feel that fire and it's only then it can be quenched it's pure in a way and I never needed drugs for it I'd rather fuck sober than drunk and then all the guys started growing their hair long I didn't but in a year it was like the Corps was a strange part of the past that I wasn't sure happened though Ma kept my letters and there was still my color portrait in dress blues sitting on her mantle I only remembered images a girl putting a snake up her cunt being down on my belly in the mud shitting my insides out one night Danny brought this chick home and we both did her while we were getting it on he made a move for me it was the first time and I didn't know what to do but to my surprise the chick dug it so I got into it too then the next day I felt fucked up like there was something wrong I couldn't talk to Danny for a few days finally I told him how I felt he said there was nothing wrong with any of it I told him about Frank and me how Frank used to make me do him when I was a kid but I didn't think Frank did any guys no more it was just kind of being young and exploring different things I tried to keep myself in shape being in the Marines I got built up for the first time in my life my arms got so

87

big from all those push-ups I must have done a million all you had to do as look at that sergeant the wrong way and you were doing fifty so I did push-ups I ran after coming back I stopped drinking as much as I did in Korea Frank liked to tear one on once in a while then all hell broke loose Pa was the great drinker when we were kids Ma would march us into whatever bar he was in Frank Gina me Peter Ma pregnant with Josie I wore Frank's hand-me-down clothes the shoes were so worn out my toes stuck through she said she wanted to embarrass him in front of his friends so he would be ashamed and come home but it never worked when he finally came home he roughed her up I don't remember a time when there was money we lived on macaroni and bread except on Sundays Pa hit Peter who needed glasses but Pa wouldn't pay for them and something was wrong with his hearing too we all knew at school the nurse sent notices home that he failed the hearing test Pa said he was stupid and when he was drunk he told Peter things like I should have flushed you down the toilet when you were born I get so sick now if I drink too much but once I have a couple I don't stop I'll go all night but with me I never needed it like Pa did and the stuff makes me happy not mean 'cause Peter was the kindest kid who wouldn't hurt a bug besides Ma he got the worse from Pa Pa if he loved anything besides the bottle he loved Sunday dinners and Ma every Sunday made her gravy with all the sausages and meatballs and pork I remember once or twice when we all sat around the table at our old Marshall Street apartment and ate Sunday dinner together Ma and Pa Frank me Gina and Peter this was before Josie was born and Pa didn't drink too much and Ma was happy and Frank was still a boy in junior high but before she left Pa he was usually never around or when he was it was late in the day or after we went to bed he came home drunk wanting Ma to boil him some fresh macaroni and make sure the gravy was hot they gave us so much food in the Marines no matter where we were even in the field the cooks laid it on heavy steak and eggs for breakfast pancakes huge lunches and dinners of steaks and roasts and chickens I was always hungry all I could ever think about in Korea was getting my off time and getting blowjobs and fried rice it was so hard to jerk off one thing about the military for all the good is you get no privacy Ma put up with a lot from Pa drinking and sometimes whoring even the occasional beatings but two weeks after Gina turned twelve I remember 'cause Gina was starting to grow tits she kept us home from school one day and after Frank and Pa left she pulled out a suitcase she had been hiding in the basement which was already full of clothes and marched us to South Station we took a train to New York City this woman who spoke no English and her four children aged fifteen thirteen twelve and ten Frank had just quit school and had a job at A & P Supermarket and she left him behind with Pa Ma found us a room above a bakery in an Italian neighborhood and she applied for welfare but it didn't come for a while the owners of the bakery this husband and wife felt bad for us and gave us day-old bread we ate nothing but day-old bread and milk though there were times back at home when that's all we ate the doctor said that's why Josie had rickets and took cod liver oil finally Ma got on welfare and somehow the welfare people got in touch with Ma's sister Lena in Boston and a while after we were on welfare my aunt and Frank took a train and found us in New York City they wanted to bring us back but Ma was afraid Pa would kill her like he threatened he would if she left him Frank and my aunt brought articles from the newspapers with a photo of Pa and the headlines about where did Anna Luongo and her children disappear to a picture of Pa acting all sad saying his heart was broke and he would die without his family Ma couldn't believe it when I told her in Italian what it said in the articles she didn't want to

89

go home but my aunt had legal papers told Ma all she had to do was sign them and Pa could never go near her again for two days Ma kept saying she would never go back but then finally she signed the papers and we went home to Boston and Ma went on welfare and never saw Pa again only once did he see us after that it was a Sunday afternoon he took us to the North End we ate spaghetti and walked around the feast but then Pa started drinking and kept drinking and didn't get us home 'til after midnight so Ma wouldn't let him take us out ever again he died a year later Ma wouldn't even go to his funeral none of us did except Frank I'll never get over how we had to be on welfare I swore when I was a kid that when I grew up I would take care of everybody so nobody would need nothing it wasn't that we needed all that much it was the idea we were on welfare Ma said sometimes she wished she stayed in Italy 'cause there was no welfare there everyone took care of everybody I loved it when we lived in New York City and roamed Times Square looking in porno shops and movie houses until the cops or a bouncer chased me off everywhere was guys chicks and sex I mean that's what they're there for one thing no bullshit like let's go for a drink or to the movies or out to dinner where everybody's on the make anyway you go to a restaurant you see this hot chick sitting at a table you get a sexy waitress and what do you think you think I'd do her in a second the chicks think the same thing when a good looking waiter walks up to a table some chick sitting there for dinner's thinking how she'd do him it's crazy what it does to you in New York City I couldn't get privacy in the little apartment me and Peter slept on a mattress on the floor in the front room Ma and the girls slept in a bed in the one bed- room I got myself worked up in Times Square had to wait 'til the middle of the night when I was sure that Peter was sleeping I sat in the old torn chair Ma sat in during the day and did it there so when Frank and my aunt came to bring us home I missed New York City in Boston Frank took me down-town where it was kind of like Times Square people were on the make and there were porno stores theaters and strip joints he got me into a movie that's the first time I saw a porno movie this black and white thing all guys in the theater jerking off Frank too that's what everyone comes here for he said so once I realized no one was paying attention to me any way I jerked off too being on welfare once a month we had to go to the wel-fare office we got a box of food mostly stuff we didn't eat the coffee was weak we didn't like peanut butter but there was things like lard and milk we laughed going through the box at the macaroni and cheese and canned beef stew Ma put it away in case there was another depression it was after Pa died Frank started getting into more serious trouble he broke into a furni-ture store and got caught the owner didn't press charges so the police let him go but when he robbed the Sunoco gas station at the foot of Broadway they sent him to reform school in Billeri-ca everybody said Frank was pretty stupid to rob a gas station in his own neighborhood I was the first one in the family to finish high school we had a party Ma cooked a great dinner and invited relatives most of them told me that now I was the one who had to take care of the family it was up to me I could have made more as a carpenter's apprentice and lived home but there wasn't any room if I joined the service I could send mon-ey home when Frank was arrested for robbery a second time they sent him to Concord prison for three years he was never the same after that time he spent in Concord what I liked most about the Corps was the discipline that's what helped me so much in my life on my job at Pratt's Mr. Sanford the personnel manager said I was a model employee I was never out sick or late in all my years there display was easy compared with the Marines didn't have to be in until eight got a twenty-minute coffee break in the morning a forty-five minute lunch then another twenty-minute coffee break in the afternoon and with all the standing around bullshitting with everyone especially the ladies on the first-floor lingerie and all the nude mannequins so many jokes you can make so when you got down to it I was only actually working about five or six hours a day with nobody up my ass and all these beautiful chicks from sixteen to sixty I got out at five with Saturdays and Sundays off Sundays I went to Ma's and brought her money she cooked a gravy and we all ate together except Frank he only showed up at Ma's if he needed a bed he usually had a girlfriend Ma's was his last choice I always believed the most important thing you can do with your family is eat together and that's part of the problem with families these days everybody is so busy nobody has meals together any more all you hear about is fast food take-out now people eat in their cars I went over once or twice during the week to check on Josie see how she was doing in school or make sure Gina wasn't wearing her skirts too short or smearing too much make-up on her face sometimes I would bring Chinese food but the only thing Ma liked was spare ribs so I always got an extra order just for her this will be my dinner she said and she could eat every rib down to the bone mostly she liked to cook and eat her own food pasta-fagioli or roasted chicken usually Friday and Saturday nights I went down the Zone alone watched a movie and a strip show the girl in the candy department went a little loony taking drugs emptying the nitro-tanks for filling kiddy balloons to get high she took a liking to me but I stopped getting on with her she still came on to me and asked about Danny and one day she told me that she and Danny were still getting it on and Danny told her a few things about him and me and she wanted to get it on with the three of us that's the first time there was a real rift between me and Danny 'cause he never told me he was still doing her he had no right to tell her about what happened with him and me and that chick it's not that I didn't like what happened sex is sex I don't care who you are if you're a guy and you're blindfolded someone starts sucking your dick it will get hard it doesn't matter if it's a guy or a chick but Danny talking about me and him to somebody else like that pissed me off I told him and he said I always took this stuff too serious and he'd been thinking about us making it together again just the two of us together I didn't like the idea but I tried it one night after we went to the Zone when we got home it was good but it didn't feel the same way as when the chick was there I was thinking maybe I was queer Danny said it was just sex don't think about it so much then he started seeing this chick who worked in the catalogue department but she wouldn't let the two of us do her at once but she told Danny she would do one of us while the other watched so that's what we did but then she started showing up at our apartment in the middle of the night acting crazy she was missing work and got fired the last time I saw her was a couple of years later late one night on Mass. Ave. in the center meridian wandering aimless high on pills she didn't recognize me she came from a rich family in Hamilton once she was in a mental hospital for a while she had a horse and the riding clothes I wanted her to dress up and use that crop on me but she wouldn't go for it when Pa was in a good mood he played the mandolin and sang one night after he came home drunk and started playing Ma told him to stop 'cause he'd wake everybody up he smashed his mandolin to pieces on the kitchen floor sometimes he gave us all a penny he said he picked from a penny tree in the yard then once Gina and Peter went to the window where Pa was sweeping in the yard they asked him could they have a penny off of the tree and Pa walked over to the window threw the broom at them and cut Gina above the eye she still has a little scar she's a beautiful girl my sister but he gave her this scar the Asian chicks were small their cunts tiny they don't have much hair on their bodies but they could take it all when I was doing Joyce in ladies' make-up she blew me but she wouldn't let me do anything I had to lean back on the bed then she would blow me if I tried to rub her tits or hair she would push my hand away she didn't want me to touch her while she was doing me I met her mother and she was a looker too both blondes with tight bodies and Joyce told me that she and her mother used to go out together and pick up guys they wouldn't do them together wolfing her mother called it that's a little fucked up if you ask me then she started fucking Mr. Aria the controller and dropped me he was a good looking guy Mr. Aria quiet type but he was fooling around with more chicks in the store than anybody when I was a kid in winter we sledded down Winter Hill on cardboard boxes we couldn't afford no sleds and when we got home Ma made hot chocolate told us stories when she was a girl her mother sent her to the baker's for bread and before she left her mother spit on the ground and told her to hurry because if the spit dried up before she got back it meant that something terrible was going to happen to her when Frank did what he did to Gina Gina hit him over the head with a rolling pin so hard it took twenty stitches he never went near her again I told him if he did I'd kill him she was coming out of the shower he pulled her towel off saying how nice she was looking all grown up I never talked with him about what happened when we were young but I thought about it it wasn't right but I was young Frank was my big brother I idolized him then it was before he started getting into trouble after I got back from the Marines one night he was trying to get money off Ma I was there and told him to leave her alone and quit bleeding her and he told me to keep out of it and called me a few names but I think he knew that since I was in the Marines I was able to handle myself because I called him out and he backed down but it upset Ma to see us fighting she said it was her fault and sometimes she thought maybe she should never had us Frank hit his girlfriends he only dated women who liked getting hit he said all he needed to do was talk to a chick for a few minutes he could tell whether she liked it rough he took as much money from them as he could Gina said he was doing a few odd jobs for a local gang I asked her what kind of jobs she said she didn't know when I asked Frank about it he said I was crazy the day Bobby Kennedy was shot I got my five-year pin at Pratt's during one of the monthly store-wide meetings held in the furniture department I always loved the Kennedys and if John wasn't killed like he was a lot of the stuff that happened in the sixties I don't think would happen I loved the storewide meetings the girls were wearing mini-skirts and sat with their legs crossed on the plush sofas and Mr. Sullivan the store manager made a little speech some jokes and announced the next big promotion talked up the profit-sharing plan which Pratt's was famous for then he handed out pins and Henry Bell was retiring from furniture he had thirty years in with over a hundred thousand in his profit-sharing there was a party at the Adam Bronk House restaurant before I was married I always went to the parties it was a good time to get to know the chicks better by the end of the night married or single folks were dancing drunk cheek to cheek and kissing in the dark corners someone was always retiring or receiving a service pin they said the best job to have at Pratt's was big-ticket salesman these were the guys who sold the major appliances washers dryers stoves and refrigerators they worked on straight commission the best of them made more money than anyone in the store except for the manager they were always fighting over sales and customers they would stand at the bottom of the escalator yelling out at the people coming down washer or dryer today each trying to get to the customer first the manager was called in to break up arguments over who stole whose customer it was like entertainment and if there was some kind of fiasco it didn't take long for the word to get around the store and if you could you went down to catch the excitement the management liked keeping the guys at each other's throats to keep their teeth sharp pity the browser when one of them put the hook into you there was no way out sometimes people would buy something just to be free of it then call and cancel when they got home when I had my yearly personnel visit with Mr. Sanford and he told me again that I was the model employee I mentioned that I might like to switch over to sales at sometime in the future he seemed amused and said that he thought I was perfect in display I mentioned that I might like to sell big-ticket items many people would like to sell big ticket but it wasn't for everyone he said and there were people waiting to get into big-ticket from other departments besides those guys would eat me alive I told him I'd like to be considered anyway working with Celeste got me so horny once she said she'd have drinks with me and after a few we made out she said she dug me but knew I was only after one thing and both of us being in the same department it wouldn't work but she wore those short skirts and tight blouses then she cut off her long hair which I didn't like at first but then I got used to it and thought it was sexy everyone said Joe Letto was queer the way he dressed in colorful suits and shoes he got his nails manicured and colored his hair red brown and talked a little like a chick but he denied it all the years we worked together I never saw him with a girlfriend he was funny liked to joke around and talk about sex like me he listened to my stories always said something funny back he was about fifty when I met him told me about when he was growing up rich and how when he was a boy he had to dress in a suit for dinner they had a butler and a maid he never really knew his parents 'cause he was raised by a nanny Joe said he didn't really have to work even though there was less money than there used to be he just did it to keep busy when I told him stories about growing up poor he said that he wished he had my mother and that family meant different things to different people I think family is the most important thing in life it was my mother keeping us together as safe as she could what saved us except for Frank but there are guys like Frank who come from rich families too so who knows only thing I do know is as long as I remember I couldn't think of too much else besides sex I mean at some point no matter what I was doing or who I was with or where my mind wandered before long it was back to sex I knew that someone had to keep the family together and if it wasn't for the Marines I'm not sure I would have had the discipline to do it maybe Frank would have been a different guy if he joined the Marines when he quit school but things just happened the way they did when I first laid eyes on Audry she had on a pair of tight jeans and a halter-top it was one of those sweltering days she just started working in the marking room upstairs in the warehouse and it didn't have no air conditioner it's where every single piece of merchandise that came into the store was inventoried given a merchandise number and price tag on my way to coffee break I got sidetracked when I saw her tight ass and bareback Lillian the veteran of the marking room knew me like a book and said it didn't take me long when I went in nosing around she introduced us and I asked Audry did she fool around and she said it all depended I asked on what she said I'm not sure it's any of your business Lillian laughed and said she's got your number already meantime I was dating Laura Murphy who was probably the love of my life she worked part-time in customer service and was going to college she was smart Laura was her father owned Murphy's Funeral home on Broadway they had money and I always felt one of the reasons me and Laura didn't work out was she thought I was beneath her she dumped me for a guy who just started law school after a year that we were going out the greatest sex I ever had was with Laura we used to fuck in the morning in the afternoon and night hot days in that Porter Street apartment sweat pouring off us soaking the sheets she always said no one ever did her like I did her and that she loved me and would always love me but it just couldn't work out between us it crushed me I couldn't eat or sleep I had to take tonic to shit once a week it went on for weeks I couldn't jerk off I lost weight at work everybody asked was I all right and the problem with the store was everyone knew your business it bothered me knowing they all knew Laura dumped me I confided a lot in Joe Letto he was a friend through it and in all the years we worked together I never saw him go out with anyone after work for drinks or go to any of the parties but two different nights he took me out after work and we went for some food and a drink and he let me talk and said he was sorry to hear it and it must be very painful Joe always said that love is a misunderstanding between two fools and even though he knew it he took the bait every time that's why they made bars and we went to the Napoleon Club which I heard of but never been inside of there were mostly guys about Joe's age or older and real young dudes there was this big piano bar and everyone sat around drinking Martinis and Manhattans singing songs from shows and movies I was uncomfortable at first but after three quick bourbon and cokes I was singing I'm a yankee doodle dandy arm in arm with a group of old queers swaying back and forth with them all of us heartbroken one way or another one loved someone that didn't love him one loved someone who loved him but was married Joe never mentioned anything about those nights again and I didn't neither but he helped me through a rough time and I'll never forget him he was the one who told me to keep putting the bug in Mr. Lentine and Mr. Sanford's ears about getting out of display and working out on the sales floor they said I had a great personality I would be good at it so I told the display manager he was surprised but if he could help me he would the next year when I had my annual meeting with Mr. Sanford I asked him again about going out on the sales floor he said you are really serious about this aren't you and I told him I was that's why I kept telling him every time I saw him he said give it a little time he'd look into things then somehow the guys in major appliances got wind of my intentions and started needling me saying things like so you want to play with the big boys but I didn't pay them any mind Ma was living with Peter and the girls Peter was working the overnight shift at Schrafts it was for the best he quit school he had a hard time there in a special class but they liked him at the factory and they loved Gina at the insurance company she got a raise almost right away Josie said she wanted to be a nurse so she was in the state college Gina Peter and me paid for her books and tuition and in her spare time she took care of Ma who was proud that Josie was in college and said it was hard to believe girls in college but it was good Josie was smart 'cause God didn't give her much to look at and her chances of finding a husband were not too good in time I got over Laura but I never forgot her whenever I thought of her over the years I got this drooping sensation in my stomach that must be what love is when you can't stop thinking of someone and all you want to do is be with them fucking sweating and swallowing each other but maybe that's only sex not love where do you separate the two if being of one self can also be of the other and the other being of one self can also be of two this is the kind of stuff Danny would say when he was smoking pot I thought it was a bunch of crap there was love and there was sex sometimes you had sex with someone you loved Danny also liked to watch television when he was high he said it made everything more intense but that shit just made me scared and hungry in the middle of fucking on it I lost my train of thought it's hard to say how much Pa's beating on

Peter had to do with Peter being slow Ma said she blamed Pa for Peter's problems but Peter was always slow slow to learn how to talk and when he talked he talked funny when Pa was drunk and beat Peter up Ma tried to help but Pa hit her too if I did anything I got smacked Frank was big enough to take on Pa but he never did he said it wasn't right to hit your father but it was all right for a father to hit his kids Frank kept magazines under his mattress he let me look at them when he wanted me to do him it was all right what him and me did he said between brothers we needed to know what it was like I never swallowed he tried to get me to I just spit it out into the rag he kept beside his bed he called it his goo-rag always keep a goo-rag near your bed he said the girls liked Frank the worse he treated them the more they liked him I never understood it but this buddy of mine in the Marines used to say the same thing once you tell them you love them you lose no matter who the chick is the worse you treat her the better she likes you but I loved chicks and never wanted to treat them bad Frank said that's why my heart was always getting broken I never saw Frank's heart get broken when the welfare lady came to our New York apartment we didn't have a real bath so we had lice in our hair she gave Ma a shampoo and we spent a day with Ma scrubbing our heads over the cold water kitchen sink with water she warmed on the two-burner stove Ma cried 'cause she felt so ashamed the lady must think she was a bad mother from then on I always had this thing about bugs in my hair and being clean so I took at least two showers a day and spent a lot of time in front of the mirror pushing my hair aside with my hands looking for the little things never found one since that time in New York and Ma said this life you give me God you must be testing me and in New York she first said to me I was her boy who would make her proud so she wouldn't have to live her life in disgrace and I always remembered that for a while Audry and me played

100

cat and mouse she knew I was after her but she kept her distance finally one day I got her to have coffee with me we made small talk my usual questions like do you fool around and all that didn't amuse her and when our time was up I said so we going to get together or what and she said thanks but it wasn't a good time she just got over a relationship and not interested in dating anyone from the store I kept after her while screwing around with a couple of different chicks Joe Letto said it was possible that I could wear it out so I should slow down Audry was kind of plain with long brown hair and no make-up but she had a great body and knew how to wear clothes to show it at work she hung out with people from the marking room and never went out after work or to work parties Danny decided he was going to California and gave his notice at Pratt's he was going to see the west so Peter moved in with me and it gave the girls and Ma more room at the apartment I talked with Peter about sex but he didn't seem interested don't you like girls I said oh yeah he liked girls but he got embarrassed one night I took him to the Zone I thought he was still a virgin he said he wasn't and did it twice with a girl from Schrafts he didn't like the Zone and wanted to go I got him into a bar even though he was under age but he ran out when one of the strippers spread her pussy in front of him when he had a few drinks he could get angry and start saying things about Pa how it wasn't right the way he treated everybody I knew it wasn't right but that was in the past you couldn't do anything about changing it his face turned red his eyes flared behind his thick glasses poor Peter I always hoped he would find a woman who would take care of him but I knew he might always need one of us I missed Danny 'cause with Peter it was more like home again we went to see Ma and the girls on Sunday for macaroni and at least another night during the week Peter went over on other nights too I started my day off with sit-ups and push-ups and still counted

out like we did in the Marines staying in shape chicks seemed to
dig me but whenever I took a shower strands of hair gathered
at the drain at first I hoped it was something temporary but in
time I knew just like Pa I was going bald Frank had a thick
head of dark hair he got from Ma's side like the girls and Peter
had curly red hair we don't know where that came from but Ma
said there were red-headed cousins in Italy my hair was always
thin and I was afraid I was the one to get the bald genes from
Pa he was bald except for a narrow strip on each side of his
scalp when Ma brought us to roust him out of some bar I
found him by spotting the bald head shining in the bar-room
lights then he would get so mad to see us all there he would
tear up the house when he got home and yell and scream in the
middle of the night for months Audry teased me acted friendly
and smiled a lot when I did my social rounds around the store
in display there was a lot of time in between things when there
wasn't much to do I wandered the store talking with everybody
tried to time my coffee breaks around Audry's but she always
sat at a busy table in the coffee shop so I could never get her
alone the marking room people worked different hours I knew
she took the Mass. Ave. bus and lived in Arlington Heights but
she got off a half hour before me I liked hanging out at strip
bars mostly I could sip a drink for over an hour and I never
talked with any of the girls more than a drink or two 'cause it
could get costly there was this beautiful young black chick used
to work the clubs I always liked watching her show she had the
tightest body I've ever seen from standing she could lean backwards all the way until she put her hands out flat on the floor
and walk upside down like a crab with a gorgeous shaved purple lip pussy she got to recognize me and hit me up for drinks
if she knew I had the cash she called herself Sugar wouldn't tell
me her real name if I bought her a second drink she might let
me touch her pussy under the table that clit of hers stood up

rock hard I can still feel it between my fingers and think of it when I jerk off it took forever to get over Laura but a chick like Sugar helped things start to come alive again I could eat drink jerk off shit and this new chick who worked in the coffee shop was looking real good she was tall and for some reason wore wigs no matter when I was with her she always had a blond wig on she liked to fuck and party a lot she had pretty blue eyes soft skin Sandy from Alabama had a real strong accent I couldn't understand her half the time she said her last job in Alabama was a chicken chaser she was the one who chased the chickens around the coop and put them in a sack for the butchers we went out for a few drinks and ended up fucking all night at my apartment she lived with her aunt on Summer Street turns out she was married her husband was in jail in Alabama she had a kid and her husband's parents had the kid she drank every drop of cum and even licked it off of her hands when she did me then I found out she was fucking Billy Grimes in maintenance I liked Billy but he was a little sleazy the last night I dropped her off she blew me right in front of her aunt's house on Summer Street with cars passing by and people walking on the sidewalk after that I put an end to it who knows who else she was doing but she didn't stay very long anyway and moved back to Alabama I still had the hots for Audry and just when I thought she was never going to have anything to do with me one day I was sitting on the parking lot wall eating a sandwich and she came out said hello lit up a smoke and sat down next to me it was the first time in almost a year since she had coffee with me alone we made some small talk and finally I said look let's cut through the crap Audry you know I'm crazy about you why won't you go out with me and she said you haven't asked me yet I told her I sure had asked her she said asking someone if they want to fool around is not the same as asking them out and she had a point in time I got real good at display there was

nothing I couldn't build big or small Joe Letto had a real flair for dressing and we won awards like division of the month and employees of the month but I still wanted to get out on the sales floor with the big-ticket guys they were the ones who made the real money and all of them wore nice suits and owned houses and drove fancy cars and Nick Luciano had a boat and Tony Deluca had a horse and Mike Cordano had a beautiful house with a built in pool and Charlie Fresno made a lot but he was divorced and spent every penny paying alimony and gambling it doesn't matter how much I make he said I never have anything I knew no matter how long I worked in display even with raises I couldn't make as much as those guys and be able to take care of my family right ever since we were kids I tried to talk Frank out of the stupid things we could be walking down the street and Frank suddenly decided that he was going to climb the side of a building and start climbing if a car was left running Frank hopped in and drove off one time we went to a jewelry store when I wanted to buy Ma a bracelet from all of us on her birthday while the salesman showed me different things Frank stole a bunch of rings I never saw him do it when we left he pulled the stuff out of his pocket he told me they were for one of the neighborhood girls who was my age he was making out with her and feeling her up he told me that she wanted to make out with me too one day we were alone in her yard she said that she would show me her pee thing if I would show her mine I was just starting to get hair and all scared but I did anyway she ran into her house and told her mother her mother told Ma who beat me with a broomstick like she did the time she caught me looking under the table when I was little trying to see up the dresses of my aunts I thought women had a penis and the only difference between us was that women had tits Ma pulled me out from under there hitting me with the broomstick saying I was dirty Ma did her best but sometimes during the
104

week things got real lean she made soup out of a bone or spaghetti with garlic and oil and that's what we lived on I did good in school but I liked working with my hands especially with wood I liked the feel of all the different grains and texture when I first took woodworking in junior high and built a wooden matchbox to hang on the wall mine was better than anyone in the class Ma hung it in the kitchen old Mr. Peck the junior high woodworking teacher said I could take woodworking in the Voke instead of going to the regular high school I loved those shop weeks in high school 'cause no matter what you were doing you had some space around you in regular classes having to sit in one place all day drove me crazy my mind wandered different girls in my class then I'd get a hard-on and pull my shirt out because you never knew when a teacher would call you up to the blackboard I didn't want to get caught with a boner in high school we took our regular classes with high school kids I hated regular classes but I could check out the girls in shop it was only guys Mr. Nunziato was the shop teacher a lot of the guys goofed off he was always breaking up some kind of fight for the most part I didn't get into any trouble Mr. Nunziato said I was a natural with my hands if I stuck with it I'd do good for my graduation project I made Ma a dresser out of oak and surprised her with it she cried that I could make it out of my own two hands when we were kids and Frank first started getting me to do him I was curious because I was feeling these strange things down there too I don't remember how old I was but he guided me and told me to put it in my mouth and suck it at first I sucked it too hard easy he said when he came in my mouth it scared the shit out me I had no idea what it was and spit it all over it only happened for a few months then I told him no more there was a guy who washed out of basic training the guys said was queer I didn't know him good Frank couldn't be queer he was just a little

105

fucked up he always had a girlfriend but nothing would surprise me about Frank who knows it was not too long after I stopped with Frank I started jerking off after the day Audry came out to the parking lot to talk to me we finally went out for Chinese food in Chinatown she loved Chinese food too I thought that was a good sign she drank a beer and I had bourbon and cokes by the end of the second one I started to feel it and warm up Audry was cool not in a beatnik way but with her feelings you had a hard time telling what she was thinking but we talked a lot that night and got along good most of the talk was about work and gossip then she said one of the reasons she didn't like to go out with anyone she worked with was you end up talking about work all the time so we made a vow not to talk about work and I told her a little bit about the Corps and she laughed 'cause her ex-husband was a lifer in the army a sergeant and that got her talking about her marriage she wasn't married long the dude was real strange and old fashioned never let them see each other naked Audry could never change in front of him they only had sex in the dark and he didn't go for nothing but getting on and off after two years she left him there was a lot of problems going on with them he wanted to have kids and she wasn't getting pregnant he smacked her a few times and that was the final straw after dinner we went to a bar downtown for another drink by then I was telling her I was burning for her she said she wasn't a one night stand and she knew all I was looking for was sex so why didn't I go have it with someone else I tried to get her to come home with me she wouldn't in front of her house we went into a liplock that must have lasted twenty minutes when we were finished she let out this loud sigh like an engine releasing all the pressure I could feel her trembling in my arms we made out for a while and I started feeling her up her breasts were so perfect and hard after a few minutes grunting and groaning in the car she said come up why don't you just come up and I did we never left each other after that it seemed natural to be together I loved taking drives especially alone it was one of the only things I know calms me down I never drove until I was in the Marines so when I got home and settled at Pratt's I bought myself a used car when I was feeling anxious or nervous I just took a long ride it happened a lot at night 'cause I had trouble sleeping I could sleep for three or four hours then wake up my mind would race around so anxious I'd go out and take a walk when I was a kid many nights I went out in the middle of the night nobody ever knew I was gone there's something about how quiet the night is like the dark and the electric lights are like a man and woman right after sex when they lay there in the quiet and it's still sometimes Audry and me took long rides after we got married but a lot of times I went alone up to New Hampshire turned around and drove back it gave me time to think and was better than tossing and turning in bed with my mind running after dinner at Ma's on Sunday in the summer I drove down to Cape Cod and got out of the car to look at the ocean at night it was incredible if there was a good moon or a lot of stars the ocean just pounding in I stood there for a few minutes then turned around and drove back to the Porter Street apartment if I got horny I could just jerk off as I drove down the highway it was easier than you think with no cars on the road in the middle of the night I just kept a goo-rag under the seat strange being out on the highway doing yourself at sixty miles an hour I knew a chick who used to do herself on the road in daylight she'd wear a short summer dress with no panties when truckers drove by she'd flash them and finger her pussy for them one night when we were at her place doing it she ran out into the hall of her apartment building and started fingering herself on top of the stairs I had to drag her back in crazy thing was she never could come when she was having sex with me she said she never came with any guy she could only come when she was doing herself she was one of those clingy chicks I met her through Danny she was a friend of one of his girlfriends when I wanted to break it off with her she made a lot of crazy scenes and kept calling the apartment and sending long letters she was religious too wanted me to go to church on Sundays I guess you have to believe in God otherwise what do you believe in that doesn't mean that I go along with everything about the church and rules I liked the smell of incense and lighting candles all the colors inside the church and praying when Ma took us to the Italian mass in the North End all the old Italian widows wearing black saying the mass along with the priest in Italian smell of garlic from the old ladies' breaths some of them did their own kind of voodoo when I had a stomach ache my mother would sing the worms away making weird sounds and moving her hands over my stomach once I had a bad ear ache my mother's friend Filomena brought over some fresh breast milk in a tiny bottle she got from her daughter Ma dropped some in my ear and sang these songs Filomena said it worked better if the nipple is in the ear and the milk was fresh squeezed when Audry was pregnant her tits got milky I could gently squeeze her nipple and milk would come out she liked it when I did her pregnant said she was real horny for a few months we did it a lot and her whole body changed her pussy got wider and her tits swelled up over her belly which grew by the day she didn't like it if I sucked too much on her nipples she didn't think it was right that I should get off on sucking out the milk it didn't bother me at all but then after little Tony she wouldn't let me near her for about three months and after that even when she did sex was never the same between us Audry didn't get into doing it the way she did before the baby she liked to leave the television on for light and sometimes when I was doing her I could see her watching the screen out of the corner of her eye

108

it bothered me but I never said nothing by the time Gina was pregnant I knew she married a loser she married him too quick after four months going with him he was one of the managers in the insurance company and made good money but he had a kid and a wife to support from another marriage he treated Gina like shit from the beginning I don't know why she wanted a guy like that I tried to talk some sense into her she wouldn't listen it was her life she said after the baby came he started hitting her she didn't have to tell us but I knew when she wasn't coming around much anymore and stopped calling I dropped by her place one night she had black and blues on her arms I made her pack right then and took her and the baby to Ma's he came there a little while later I stood on the porch and told him I'd beat him to death if he came near the house but Gina went back to him and left him again a few times before he finally took off with a young chick to California she quit her job because she couldn't face the people there so I moved her and the baby in with Ma that first week Audry and me were together we had an intense seven days and night I dug her and maybe even loved her but she wanted some kind of commitment from me when I told her I wasn't ready for a commitment she said she wouldn't see me any more she didn't want to be another one of the chicks on my list even though I told her she was more than that so we didn't see each other for a week and avoided each other at work then one night I came home from work there was a card from her in the mail and it said I do my thing you do your thing and if by chance we find each other it's beautiful I'll always remember it that was really important to me I still have that card I called her and we saw each other that night and stayed together a few weeks later Audry gave her notice at Pratt's to take a job at Tags in Porter Square we didn't want to be part of the gossip circle of the store since we were living together and people did talk the day she started at Tags she told me she was pregnant which blew my mind 'cause I thought she was on the pill she said she was on the pill but went off it for a short time 'cause her doctor told her to she wanted to know what we should do there was nothing we could do but get married she said she could get an abortion but there's no way that was ok with me she was worried that I would feel trapped I told her I didn't though deep inside I did but I loved Audry our sex was great and when we were together we talked about everything and it felt real easy and right I knew I wanted to get married and have kids some day but I was afraid to 'cause it would mean a lot of changes if I married Audry I could never do another woman again never how the fuck is someone supposed to only have sex with one person for the rest of their lives that's what I wanted to know I had been at Pratt's long enough that I had a little money built up in my profit sharing that I could borrow against it wasn't much but with that I put a small deposit down on a beat-up three-decker on Broadway in East Somerville with Audry pregnant I didn't want her to work though she said she would I believe some in all of this new women's liberation but I wanted my wife at home with the children I wasn't against women working or anything and even at the store there were lady managers coming in who just graduated college black managers too hey more power to them then they starting to give commission sales jobs to these chicks who were only working there a short time I told Mr. Sanford I was with the store for eight years and for three I was asking to go out on the floor and sell big ticket I should have a chance too but all I'm saying is if a woman's going to marry and have children her place is in the home that was always ok with Audry for the most part she's really old fashioned later when I got into sales she always had my suits laid out for me in the morning and my shoes shined the house on Broadway needed a lot of work Audry and me moved in on the top floor my mother and

110

the girls and Peter moved in on the second floor and I rented out the first floor to a nice Mexican couple the wife worked at the store she was hot too and before I met Audry or she met her husband once Carmen and me made out when I drove her home from having drinks but nothing ever came of it and we never said anything to each other after she moved in they paid their rent on time and I let Ma and Peter and the girls live free they just had to pay the utilities and I started fixing the place up in my spare time tearing down walls replacing windows refinishing floors replacing and hanging doors plastering ceilings painting it never ended day in and day out but once I was out on the sales floor I wasn't able to use my hands any more so I liked doing that kind of work at home with Ma and the family taken care of Frank was living with a woman in East Boston but was beginning to hound me to throw the people in the first floor out so he could move in with her but I wouldn't Gina's girl was already walking when I was starting in the vacuum-cleaner department where Mr. Sanford said I would have to prove myself before I could consider working with the big boys in major appliances I always thought when I fell in love with the right woman that it would be easy to not fool around but after Audry and me were together for a while and then after little Tony came we had a lot less sex before Tony came it was pretty good but Audry was on the conservative side I was always trying to do different things and she mostly just liked me to eat her and get on top which was fine some of the time but Christ those chicks in Korea some of the things they could do I never dreamed of and I thought I'd seen it all but Audry didn't like to talk much about that kind of sex let alone do it after little Tony there seemed to be no time he was up all night or part of the night or she was tired or something but I still jerked off I liked jerking off in the shower best but it was hard to find time and privacy and little Tony was up crying during the night or sick sometimes I would take a drive but Audry didn't like it when I went out in the middle of the night within two months I was the top salesman in the vacuum cleaner department there were three of us me and Bernie Cohen and Faith Cameron Bernie was the strangest dude he had been working in vacuum cleaners for twenty years never moved on like most to major appliances or televisions or furniture those guys would eat me alive he said he made a decent living was never top man but never bottom man he was a little spaced out and a lot of the guys made fun of him he had some kind of weird thing going on where he would fall asleep in the middle of the day everyone who had been working in the store for a while had their Bernie stories how once he fell a-sleep leaning on an upright vacuum in the middle of the sales floor or the morning he was late and someone spotted him in the parking lot asleep at the steering wheel of his car there were a number of times I remember him falling asleep in the bathroom he used to say Tony I'm going to the bathroom in case I'm not back in ten minutes check on me and I would and he'd be asleep on the toilet Faith was hot and I always wanted to do her but she was seeing the manager of hardware who was married she was five or six years older than me and worked in the customer service department until they decided to put women out on the big-ticket sales floor we start-ed in vacuum cleaners about the same time she had a great body big tits and it's not that I'm a tit man I like them every shape and size but she had beautiful tits and real nice legs and could wear them short skirts even though she was a little older she was a tough cookie on the sales floor and gave Bernie a run for his money I never took a coffee break though I had to be off the floor for lunch or dinner but I was back in my posi-tion on the minute I was allowed and I concentrated on noth-ing but selling I treated every customer with the same enthusi-asm it didn't matter whether they were just looking or there to

112

buy I would often pick up people that Bernie had let go because he didn't think they were interested and then I would sell them it drove Bernie crazy and the guys in major appliances picked up on it 'cause I was breaking records for sales in the department and they started harassing me that was when I really started learning the art of needling with those guys they were masters all they did was needle each other and try to psyche the other guy out and they enjoyed their arguments in front of customers so they started coming around and watching me with customers or when they saw me ring up another sale they'd pass through and say nice another one pretty soon you'll be down with the big boys I told them you better believe I wanted in and had every intention of working in major appliances in vacuums I started making more money than I ever had before in one week I could make what I was making in two weeks in display just from selling vacuums so I started putting half my earnings in a savings account every week and the rest was enough to keep up the household but I was restless I loved Audry and little Tony and when I got home from work Audry had dinner ready and I could play with little Tony and Ma was downstairs with the girls and Peter and I never saw Ma so happy she could finally take it easy and get the rest she deserved some days when Faith wore her short skirts and her heels to work she'd drive me crazy and all I could think of was doing her and I would have to block it out of my mind so I could concentrate on selling but I couldn't wait to get home and do Audry but sometimes she wasn't in the mood or little Tony would be restless and I would go into the bathroom and jerk off thinking of Faith once I made the mistake of telling Audry that I still jerked off and she got all mad and jealous like and said that was an insult to her I said that everybody masturbates and she said that she didn't but I'm not sure if I believed her so I had to keep it to myself and be careful around the house most

113

of the time I did it in the basement where I hid some magazines Jimmy out on the loading dock gave me Audry was so
jealous that she drove me crazy she said she knew how I was at
the store and my reputation and all so I stopped going out after
work for drinks and I didn't go to any more store parties I told
Audry she should just go with me to the parties if she didn't
trust me but she said that she didn't want to go and if I wanted
to go I should but I knew she didn't mean it I could tell by now
it was clear I was going bald and with the standing around
most of the day in the vacuum-cleaner department I wasn't getting much exercise at work and Audry always cooked a big meal
when I got home when I had a dinner hour on an evening shift
I drove home and she fed me Ma taught her how to make a real
gravy and meatballs so on Sundays we all ate together I was
eating a lot and putting on weight between the job and the pro-
jects around the house I stopped doing my push-ups and sit-
ups and for the first time I didn't feel like I was looking good
anymore Audry said she thought I was handsome as ever and
every morning she shined my shoes put my suit out for me and
after only a year they put me and Faith in major appliances and
it turned that division upside down because Faith was the first
time they had a woman work in major appliances in the Cambridge store and here's this nice looking chick among a pack of
wolves which kind of made the move over a little easier for me
since I was at least a guy but the guys worked to keep us new
ones out of the pack Ma was always a screamer she screamed at
us kids when we were causing a fuss she screamed at my father
she screamed at God and called upon the apostles and all the
saints like they were right there overhead but when she started
losing her sight she got quieter this is the way God wants it first
he gave me your father and then he takes away my eyes he must
be testing me she said in Italian Ma never learned much English
she was able to say a few words here and there from hearing it

around but if you spoke to her in English she could not understand though Frank and Gina said that she understood a lot more than we thought she did maybe she did when Audry's youngest sister came to stay with us and she heard her swearing and talking back to me and Audry she said she never heard such disrespect Sue just turned nineteen and was having trouble at home so Audry's mother and sisters thought maybe some time north would help her get it together she was a little tease walking around the apartment in a t-shirt with panties and no bra she knew she was getting me hot I could tell by the way she sat and looked at me and walked through the room she was picking up on me picking up on her she didn't look anything like Audry except for that tight body perfect ass nice firm on the small side tits her face was different and she was a natural blonde she got from her father she and Audry had different fathers I never knew Sue's father and I never knew Audry's father neither he was out of the picture by the time we met but I couldn't stand Audry's mother if ever there was a cunt she did everything she could to control her daughters and really fucked up Audry and how she saw men because her mother hated men and was always trashing men she was married and divorced three fucking times and of course it was always the guy's fault she didn't trust anybody and that must be where Audry got her thing about trust always being suspicious and jealous I guess I'm an excitable guy it's only when other people point it out that I'm aware I wave my hands and move my body when I'm talking my voice gets louder and more excited when I was selling I used this to my advantage in vacuum cleaners I would gather a crowd around me by throwing down dirt and cigarette butts and anything else that would catch someone's eye and demonstrating the new canister with the beater bar and I would point out the trash on the floor vibrating in its path it beats it sweeps it gets out the deep down dirt I told them and to show

how strong the new plastic canister was I jumped up and down on the canister several times with all my weight and I'm a hundred and eighty pounds I'd say and sometimes someone who had no intention of buying a vacuum cleaner that day bought one and bought top-of-the-line selling one unit was a good day's pay in commission I was selling two and three a day with service policies which we had to sell one of the conditions of staying in big-ticket sales was having to sell top-of-the line and sell service policies when they advertised a vacuum cleaner for eighty-nine dollars we were not supposed to sell any of them too many in one month or not enough service policies sold in one month and you were on the carpet with the division manager two months in a row you were on the carpet with the hard line manager I never sold the advertised items and I sold service policies I started selling double and triple service policies when I was in major appliances all the guys got on my back about it because they said I was making them all look bad one time we were at a regional sales meeting for people who worked vacuum cleaners in all the stores in eastern Massachusetts and I gave a demonstration of how I start getting a crowd gathered and once I got their attention I went through all the steps and the final thing from the first bit of dirt I threw on the floor to jumping up and down on the canister was always letting some lady vacuum the stuff up herself so after all my work there was a regular person like everyone else in the circle vacuuming up the mess and smiling and I'd be waving my arms around to the other people with my voice in a fever pitch saying look at that how easy it is what a machine and it never failed I always sold at least one I figured I was only going to make the big money if I didn't wait for the customers to come to me all the salesmen in the audience cheered and gave me a standing ovation after I was finished and when I got into major appliances I kept my cool and never got into any of the fighting

116

no matter how hard they tried to piss me off I had my temper but was more likely going to yell at home when me and Audry were in a fight or I was arguing with Frank after the couple on the first floor moved out I decided to put a wall up in a big room and make two smaller bedrooms and Frank was over hounding me about taking the apartment he had a job at the Winter Hill Tavern as a cook and was keeping away from gambling and he wanted to move in there with his girlfriend who was a waitress at the tavern and said he would pay his rent on time and when I told him no we got into an argument he said I never gave a shit about him I told him he treated me and the rest of the family like shit ever since I could remember Ma came down crying with Gina and Audry and little Tony too Frank said in front of them my own brother would leave me out on the street and I got so fucking mad I took a sledge hammer and knocked down the wall I just finished building Audry was afraid I was going to have a heart attack 'cause I was screaming and turning red all out of breath but I didn't stop until every bit of that wall was down a month's work down the toilet the house needed so much work outside and in no matter where I was working it seemed there was too much to do I worked nights after work and mornings if I had an evening shift at the store and on my days off even Sundays except I took a couple of hours off for dinner so all I was doing was working and coming home to the house and there was always a problem like the toilet was backed up or ceilings were leaking in the rain or the electrical system would fail 'cause it had to be updated no matter how many times I told everyone not to use all the things at once they still used too many things and finally Gina would turn on her hairdryer and blow a circuit and I blew my top it was great to see little Tony growing but Audry seemed sad and said she wanted to have another baby so she got pregnant with Johnny by the time Johnny came everything seemed to be at its worst with the house all the work I did you could hardly notice I finally let Frank move in the first floor which was the only finished apartment for the first few months he paid his rent on time but in a matter of a few weeks he was having huge fights with his girlfriend they both worked nights and drank after work and didn't get home until one or two in the morning they would argue and keep us all up she would yell out things like I hate your fucking guts and he would call her a bitch and a cunt I tried to talk with him he said keep out of it one night he started hitting her I went down there and told him if it happened again I would call the cops and I meant it that's when he ended up fighting with her out in the street and took out his pistol and shot it in the air it made a hole over the front door the hole was there forever I went down out of my mind we fought in the street I wasn't in the shape I was when I got back from the Marines but I was crazy enough with anger that nothing Frank did could stop me I ran down and beat the shit out of him I beat him bloody and his girlfriend was screaming at me to stop and by now Ma and the girls and Audry too all screaming the cops carne and took Frank down the station and confiscated his gun they took me too we spent a couple of hours at the station and since no one wanted to press charges they charged Frank with shooting a gun or something and if he pleaded guilty they reduced it so he got probation he begged me not to put him out he had no place to go and his girlfriend moved out so he could only pay me half the rent I let him stay on the condition that if he violated his probation he was out and he said ok Audry didn't like Frank and she told me right out there was something about him that gave her the creeps and I have to agree even though he is my brother Frank's a fucked-up dude Audry's mother and sisters kept hounding her to take the kids and go down and visit but Audry came up with different excuses why she couldn't go but the real reason was

118

she didn't trust me and she didn't want to leave me alone for any length of time she watched me like a hawk if I didn't go home for lunch she asked who I ate lunch with and one day a week when I worked evening shift a bunch of us went out for supper across the street Iagos or for Chinese food it drove her crazy if any of the girls from the store went along and though Audry never came right out and asked me to the point about anything she had a way of questioning in this slow and round-about way to find out exactly where I went out on errands or who I spent time with at work I had no friends since Danny moved out to San Francisco and I didn't hear from him no more at work I still flirted with all the chicks I could but I drew the line and didn't go out after work with anyone and didn't fool around since Audry and me had been together I was either at the store home doing work on the house or out getting supplies I needed for the house work Audry was busy with little Tony and Johnny and shit before you know it Johnny is five and already starting school at the store I was mostly first or second in sales every month I sold the most top-of-the-line merchandise which meant commission and a spiff a spiff was a bonus sometimes twenty or thirty dollars on top of the commission I had the highest service policy sales in the region the managers loved me and the guys hated me by now there had been so much fighting in major appliances over customers that a timer bell was put in each one of us got five minutes on the point when the bell went off the next in line got the point for five minutes and so on and made the amount of customers distributed better but I still outsold everyone most of the time the guys made remarks about me living in Somerville in a three-decker house and my beat-up car when I drove it into the ground and bought a little Japanese thing it gave them something to rib me about they drove Caddies and Rivieras and big Oldsmobiles and always wanted to know what I was doing with all my money maybe hoarding it away not spending it on a house or car that's for sure but when I was at work I never lost it I concentrated on nothing but selling sure there were chicks around and that could distract me especially at that time in Cambridge all these hippie chicks coming into the store no bras and mini-skirts I had all I could do to keep it in my pants and when Audry took her first visit down to see her mother and sisters she took the boys with her and one of the nights I decided to go out by myself to the Zone and went to a movie and a bar to watch some shows like I used to do before I was married and in one of the joints there was a gorgeous young blonde and I spent over a hundred dollars buying her drinks and she rubbed me and said she sometimes saw guys on her off hours let me tell you that was the fucking test but I went home and jerked off about five times and when Audry got back she seemed anxious for me to do her so I did and we had great sex but over the next couple of weeks we argued a lot because in her way of being kind of passive she was trying to find out my every move during her trip if she caught wind that I went to the Zone it would have really made trouble we talked on the phone every day she was away and even then I could sense her on the other end trying to figure things out when me and her were having sex Audry never liked giving me head even when she did and it wasn't very often it was obvious that she wasn't into it so it kind of ruined it for me I always asked the girls in the bars the same questions like how long they'd been a stripper and where did she come from how old was she did her parents know what she did 'cause I think of that sometimes if I had a daughter what would I do if she was doing this and I always was interested in people and finding out about how they think and why they think that way I liked the shops in the Zone best all the books and magazines shelves of vibrators and dildos and double-ended dildos it's another world I always asked Audry was there anything special she would like me to do to her but she didn't like to talk about those things she'd think I went crazy if I ever tried to use a vibrator or a dildo on her Frank's new girlfriend loved it when he pulled out his box of toys he had something for every hole he said that was the same girlfriend he used to piss on they used to go into the shower and turn the shower on and then Frank would piss on her and she would get off he said she loved it shit I couldn't even get Audry to blow me and Frank's pissing on chicks in the shower downstairs when I was having the house done over with aluminum siding Frank got in way over his head with the bookies he borrowed from a loanshark to pay the bookies figuring he could gamble his way out of it but it got worse and he needed ten thousand dollars fast he said I was his only hope or he was going to be in serious trouble with some bad people I gave him the ten thousand then threw the workers off of the job they only finished three sides of the house with the yellow siding but I left the fourth side which was the one you could see from both streets 'cause it was a corner house unfinished with the old tarpaper shingling to serve as a daily reminder to Frank Audry pleaded with me to finish the job but I left it and Frank stopped paying rent again but was being friendly and had some movies he wanted me to see they were mostly orgy movies with everyone fucking and sucking each other Audry thought it was all disgusting but later that night she wanted me to do her and she told me that when she was bringing some trash down she could see part of the movie screen in Frank's apartment because the kitchen door was part open and she watched for a few minutes and it got her real hot we did it two or three times that night I thought we made a breakthrough but the next day it was like it never happened when I brought it up she hushed me up and said she didn't want to talk about that stuff with the kids around the boys were great and good kids too little Tony was the goofy and noisy one and Johnny was the quiet one I never went in for sports and that stuff but I figure you should do that with your sons so I took them both to the sporting goods store and bought new gloves and bats and balls a few times we went over to Foss Park and hit the ball around but I wasn't too good at it and the boys didn't seem to be all that interested I took them to Fenway Park to see the Red Sox play Johnny liked it ok but Tony didn't I never watched sports like most guys mostly I didn't watch much television it wasn't that I didn't like it but I was always doing something Audry had it on all the time she watched those soap operas in the afternoon it was the same old stuff who was doing who just like at the store the only one who wasn't doing anybody was me except for Audry and that was only once in a while even though Audry denied it she only did it to make me happy most of the time she never even got off but at least she didn't fake it that would have been worse Ma belonged to one of the religious societies in the North End so we always went to the feast from the time we were little kids and I used to take Ma and Audry and the boys on Sundays during the summer the boys enjoyed it and ran around the streets and Ma sat in with all her old lady friends from her religious society most of them widows wearing all black Audry and me went around and ate I loved the quahogs raw but it made Audry sick the sight of those things sitting there on the shell I would throw down a buck and suck back a handful each of them like the pussy of Venus and we always got sausage and pepper sandwiches and Italian ice when we were kids Frank and me carried the blanket behind the statue of the saint in the parade people would pin bills right on to the statue and the parade would stop while they lifted up a cute little girl to pin a dollar bill on the statue of Saint Anthony and the blanket was so you could toss change into it from the sidewalk or above where people hung out windows Frank would steal change from the blanket when no one was looking one day he made ten dollars there were always some hot looking chicks running around and Audry would get pissed when she'd catch me checking one out and she'd want to go home then we'd get into a fight driving on the way home and I'd threaten to drive the car off the road with everybody in it and Audry said that was a nice thing to say in front of the boys the thing about Audry was she really hated going out of the house she made me the grocery list and I did the shopping she had no friends though I didn't neither but even when I wanted to go out to the beach or the zoo or somewhere she never wanted to go and lots of times she would say why don't I take the boys and go and sometimes me and the boys would go out alone Audry liked to do the housework and watch television mostly and besides that she talked to her sisters and her mother in North Carolina on the phone the phone bill was through the roof most of the time but it was her only thing she really spent money on so I didn't say much about it except if she talked too much when I was home because it drove me crazy the gossip and shit and which one of her sisters was breaking up with who it would go on and on finally I would tell her get off the phone and talk with her family when I was at work when I got my ten-year pin I was the top salesman in major appliances and the number one salesman in big-ticket throughout the district of eight stores and I never let up so that year in and year out eve-ryone knew I would come out on top the fight now was for who would be behind me in second I made more money than I ever dreamed of but I was starting to get bored while I could sell top-of-the-line and service policies in my sleep it was taking more energy out of me 'cause I had to fight my boredom I was bored at home the boys were growing and had their own friends and Audry and me seemed to disagree about anything if the sun was shining and I said nice day she would say no it isn't

123

and it just got to be this constant kind of bickering even though I loved her more than I could love any other woman she had my children and was a great mother a great wife and would never refuse sex but it's not that she wouldn't refuse sex but that she wasn't really into it Josie got married to a great guy who was an accountant and Peter moved out and got his own place in Medford and Gina was seeing this guy off and on but he was a loser and it wasn't working out but her daughter Maria was as beautiful as she was and smart too Frank had stopped paying any rent for a couple of years so I carried the nut on the whole house but I bought it cheap and as the years passed it seemed like less and less so I was still able to save a lot of money and looking to pay off the house completely they had to make me take my vacations at Pratt's I had so much built up so when I took time off I mostly stayed home and worked on the house Audry never wanted to do much sometimes in the summer we might go to the beach or I'd take the boys over the Foss Park pool but Audry would stay home one thing I can say about her she kept the place immaculate Ma would be proud if she could only see 'cause Ma always said that any woman who couldn't keep her house clean was not a woman you wanted to be married to but mostly during that time she sat at the front window all day and we checked in on her the boys would always visit her but she sat quiet by the window it was the strangest thing for me watching Ma get old and quiet said she was waiting for her time God was going to call her soon she would be ready she was still healthy and except for her eyes the doctor told her she had a long time to go before she was ready to go to God but she said she knew that God did what he wanted to do not what the doctor said and she wanted to be ready when it was time on Sundays we walked her to church she never missed one Sunday at mass I took communion with her when we were young and when she took to sitting at the window all day she had her rosary beads in her hand and said the rosary in Italian when me and Audry did talk about going away somewhere she only wanted to go visit her family in North Carolina there was no way I was going down and stay with her mother and sisters for a week I told her she could go herself and sometimes she did it was fine for me I got a little time alone at home and snuck out to the Zone for an evening but no matter how close I came and how much I flirted I always stopped short of fooling around I wanted to go to New York City for a vacation that was the last place she would go but one time after I hounded her and then got real quiet for a long time after she said she would go with me it was the first time we were together without the boys we left them with Gina for the weekend and stayed at a nice hotel but we didn't do a fucking thing because Audry wouldn't leave the room she was afraid we would get mugged and said we shouldn't go out walking the streets of New York if we didn't know our way around I wanted to go out and have dinner and walk through Times Square I mean just the energy in that city it's all sex it's the only place I've ever been where I get a hard- on just walking down the street so we got room service the first night and the second night I told Audry that I wasn't staying in the room again and we had a fight so I just went out myself and had a ball they got live sex shows and people come out and fuck right in front of you I went to peep shows and live shows and porn shops and talked with strangers on the street it was like this high I didn't get back until six in the morning Audry was up and had our bags packed we left and fought the whole ride back to Boston somehow that trip to New York was when things really started going bad for us of all my family members I worried about Peter the most he was always lost even though he had his own apartment in Medford he spent a lot of his spare time at Ma's and she cooked for him and sent him home with food amazing Ma the way she could still find her way around the kitchen and cook being blind Peter wanted more than anything to get married but I knew it would take a special girl to marry Peter he wasn't the best looking guy and wore his glasses and a hearing aid and speech defect because he was hard of hearing he was a tall guy with curly red hair gentle like a little kid except if he drank so he didn't drink too much once and a while if he got too drunk he'd show up at Ma's and start yelling about how bad his life was I had to calm him down and drive him home he cried sometimes and said I don't know what it's like to be alone I have Audry and the boys he'll always be alone and never have a family who would want him I told him marriage isn't all it's supposed to be and if I had to do it over as much as I love Audry and the boys I would stay single and he should stay single he's not missing as much as he thinks there was plenty of whoring he could do if he quit feeling sorry for himself sex had nothing to do with how you look it had to do with your attitude some of the most ugly chicks can be sexier than the prettiest chicks if you ask me and there would be plenty of chicks who might be interested in him in the meantime he could always pay for it there was nothing wrong with that but he believed that kind of thing wasn't right there was something to what he said that was true about having a wife and kids because as hard as it was having kids no matter how it changed everything with me and Audry that connection I had with the boys was hard to describe but not like anything else little Tony was heavy and we tried to keep an eye on his eating 'cause he always ate too much if you didn't stop him or he would go into the cabinet and eat a box of cookies so we had to be on him as he grew older Johnny was kind of fragile he never slept good many nights he woke up crying and I would sit in the rocking chair in the living room with him on my lap and rock him for hours until he finally fell asleep sometimes we slept there all night and he was just the

126

opposite of little Tony once he started getting older he never wanted to eat he looked so skinny and we had to struggle with him all the time to get him to eat he was anxious and nervous and twitched his eyes which the doctor said was a nervous habit but they were good boys never got into trouble and did what I told them to do I sent them to St. Ann's because I think the sister schools give them more discipline though now a lot of the teachers aren't sisters any more but they still give them the religion and the discipline which I think is important for kids with all the stuff going on around with drugs and protest too many of those kids had never been away from home and they ran around and criticized this country this is the greatest country in the world why do you think everyone wants to come here from other countries if these kids don't like it they should go to China or Russia and smarten up fucking fast when they end up working the fields all fucking day for a meal and a bed it's not I'm against the long hair and the chicks burning their bras more power to them sex and love you got it but you can't just decide you're gonna change the world overnight and expect it to happen I mean what the fuck you can do anything you want I started out with nothing and one of my dreams was always to have my own business so as I got more bored at the store and was able to save money I started looking around at different things I guess one of the things I always thought would be a good thing to invest in was a pizza shop it's good money a pizza cost a quarter to make and you sold it for four dollars and I figured the boys could work after school and that kind of thing but a lot of the guys at work said I was crazy to do something like that I would make less than I do now and work more hours seven days a week Audry said that whatever I thought was best was ok with her I had enough built up in my profit sharing and savings to do it I looked at a few places and they were pretty dumpy it would use up all of our savings to do it and if it didn't work I'd be stuck 'cause there's no way to guarantee I could get my Pratt's job back and Angelo Russo from hardware left Pratt's after twenty years and moved his whole family out to California to open a pizza shop out there and did fabulous and came in the store a year later on a visit looking tanned and said it was the best thing he ever did and the week he got back to California he dropped dead from a heart attack so that kind of scared me a little I took a huge life insurance policy in case something should happen to me the house would get paid off and Audry and the boys and Ma would be ok they made me take a medical exam it was the first time since I was in the Marines 'cause I never went to the doctor if I had a cold or a stomach bug or something I just let it work itself I knew after my five-year pin when I never called in sick that no matter how long I stayed at the store I wasn't going to call in sick when I had the physical they told me I had to get exercise and lose weight I gained thirty pounds since I left the Marines and being a short guy it looked even worse but I let myself go and I didn't eat right sometimes if I couldn't sleep I'd boil macaroni in the middle of the night and eat a bowl and go back to bed I loved ice cream and could sit down and eat a quart like nothing but the doctor told me if I didn't watch it I was going to be right on target for a heart attack so I went on this diet and Audry helped me and cooked all this diet stuff I ate a lot of salads and chicken and had to stop eating ice cream and cut down on the macaroni they said I had to stop drinking Pepsi 'cause I drank about six or ten cans a day sometimes so I switched over to sugar-free stuff and it tasted like shit at first but after a while I got used to it I started doing sit-ups and push-ups again it took a while but I started to lose some pounds I wanted to lose the thirty that I gained after six months I lost twenty Audry said I was looking good and for a while we started having more sex it was easier without the big belly underneath me I had more energy and felt

128

like a new man and the chicks at the store were all saying I was looking good the only thing was most of the hair was gone from the top of my head it made me feel real awkward about myself when I lost the weight I had to buy some new suits 'cause the others were too big then I bought another new Toyota which cost twice as much as the first one I bought but I was feeling good and not as bored as I was at work and I finally had the last side of the house sided and the three front porches done over after all the years most of the work was done Christ where the time goes I can't tell little Tony was already in his first year of high school the sex thing with Audry didn't last too long she was jealous that chicks in the store found me attractive and after a while we were back to our bickering deep down I knew that she would just as soon we sell the house pack up and move to North Carolina 'cause a couple of times she said that there was no place to get a good pizza any where down there it would be a great place for me to open up a business the last fucking place I would move would be North Carolina but her family always came to visit us and parked themselves in the apartment for as long as they wanted that bitch mother of hers and the little tease sister I don't know which one of them went through more guys all they did was sit around smoke cigarettes drink coffee and gossip they couldn't stand me one bit so I made sure if I could I made them uncomfortable as I could without pissing Audry off too much it wouldn't bother me if they never came back again after all the work and money I put into the house all they did was try to get Audry to move down there as time wore on they didn't care if it was with me or without me once when her little sister was staying with us she said she was in the basement bringing down trash Frank cornered her and forced himself on her she whacked him hard 'cause he had a mark on his cheek he said she came on to him and when he tried to push her away she hit him I believed

Audry's sister though I wouldn't put coming on to Frank past her I lost my cherry 'cause of Frank I was twelve and he used to do his girlfriend at her house her parents   weren't home during the day and one day Frank brought me along his girlfriend had a younger sister who was fourteen when Frank and his girlfriend went into the bedroom me and the sister were on the couch she asked me did I want to make out and we did it didn't take long 'cause she knew what she was doing she made me pull out and not come inside her years later Frank told me he was doing the little sister too after that it was a couple of years before I had sex and it was because of Frank again he fixed me up with some friend of one of his girlfriends who liked the idea of doing it with a young kid she was eighteen man did she go to town she left claw marks on my back later I used to see her around town she was a waitress at Sandy's Diner on Mass. Ave. she had a couple of kids but I think she got divorced her old man got hooked on drugs but it's the sex thing I can never figure out it's the first thing I think of when I wake up and the last thing I think of before I'm sleeping if I'm lucky I dream about it too in the course of any day at the store between the chicks who worked there and female customers I could have fucked morning noon and night and not been satisfied I wasn't getting much at home even if Audry wanted it was always the same way me eating her then getting on top I wanted to mix it up use some toys watch some flicks but Audry wouldn't and when she did go down on me she did this gagging thing like she couldn't keep it in there it's not that I was so big I wasn't it was a reflex as soon as she'd put the head in she'd start to gag and that was a turnoff but a lot of the people in the store were having a good time I had to be the only one not in on it there was Jane De Pasqulae a recent college graduate tall dark long legs and big tits who within a month of being in her position in ladies' fashions went right to the top and started fooling around with Mr. Mur-

130

phy the store manager and by the end of the year Jane was promoted over many more qualified people to manage the television and stereo department and May Sullivan of ladies' fashions was fooling around with Eddie Arziano the manager of automotive who was married and May never fooled around in the store before and all the younger kids were doing each other Brian Walsh the new kid in vacuums which merged with sewing machines who was married with two kids was fooling around with Diane Di Martino she worked part-time in draperies and linens who was married with three kids on and on and everybody but me I just jerked off whenever I could and flirted my ass off but you get pretty fucking tired of window-shopping Audry would be all over my ass about who I was hanging out with at work even if I wanted to fool around it would be impossible the way she kept tabs on me but she knew I flirted said I know you Tony and I know what you're capable of sometimes I used to want to just go out and do it to get back at her sometimes I would just want to do it because I wanted to do it why shouldn't people be able to take advantage of the greatest thing God gave us I could never understand but to me even if you're married if you want to have sex with someone else and they know you're married and they're just into it for the sex why not let the flame burn it's not cheating it's just sex I mean if Audry wanted to have one of those marriages it would be ok with me but she never would I wouldn't mind knowing Audry was doing some other guy as long as she loved me and things were the same way they were at home shit they'd probably be better we'd probably have more sex hey I wouldn't mind watching her or joining in there's nothing wrong with three-ways and foursomes but Audry was too hung up about that stuff I guess we all have some kind of fucked-up feelings because even though I like the idea of doing those things with Audry she's the mother of my kids so that kind of makes it a little weird but

131

how do you put a gauge on all that stuff who's to say what's normal when Craig started working at the store part-time that Christmas season he was a floater and worked in any department that needed help except for the big-ticket departments only straight commission people worked there but he worked in sporting goods a lot which was right next to major appliances and the guys made jokes about him being a sissy and a member of Joe Letto's church he was a sweet kid but something a little wild about his eyes one day Ned Logue from hardware called him a ballerina in front of him and I could tell the kid's feelings were hurt he turned red and ran into the stock room I told Ned to back off and he said oh sure Luongo I've had your number all along Ned was getting back at me there was a blonde that worked in the office and her and Ned used to fool around sometimes I was doing her at the same time and Ned wanted her all for himself she told me that Ned told her that Danny and me used to get it on but there's no way Ned could have known about me and Danny so Craig got kind of friendly with me and I got to know him a little bit he was a frail kid feminine too but cute in an odd sort of way dirty blond hair and blue eyes after the Christmas season he stayed on in the shoe department working a few nights a week I saw less of him because shoes was upstairs but one night when Audry and the boys were on vacation it must have been February because it was during a freezing spell he was out in front of the bus stop when I was pulling out of the parking lot and I pulled over and picked him up he lived in Dorchester and said he didn't want to put me out but I told him it was no problem besides it was zero outside and quarter of ten at night I thought he'd have to get home he couldn't be more than seventeen but he asked me did I want to go out for a drink and he took me to this place in the South End called The Other Side believe you me it was dimly lit with candles and there were queers and guys in drag and

132

couples clutching in the corner shadows everyone on the make transsexuals and transvestites the guys that weren't in drag were dressed in jeans and black sweaters and leather caps and Craig knew everyone and introduced me around I couldn't believe it it was like nothing I'd seen yet and I'd been in the Marines and traveled to the Orient some of the queens were young young as my little Tony and it was hard to believe they weren't real chicks but some of them were kind of pitiful the older dudes with holes in their stockings bad make-up jobs and beat-up wigs me and Craig sat down in one of the corner booths he told me a little about his home situation his mother was dead his father was a severe alcoholic and when he was drunk he beat-up on Craig and his sister and brother Craig had spent some time on the run and lived in a half-way house he moved back home when he got the job at Pratt's and was going to take some kind of test so he could get his high-school diploma 'cause he dropped out when he went on the run but he was a good student when he was young but for a while he was either staying with friends or sometimes on the street he was on pro-bation and that was why he had the job and moved back in with his father he was driving in a car with someone who had drugs they both got arrested and since it was his first offense he only got probation we talked for hours I told him about my growing up and Audry and the boys the joint seemed to be open all night and I didn't get home until four in the morning the phone was ringing when I was coming through the front door Audry was hysterical wanting to know where I'd been and saying how worried she was she called my mother Ma said I never came home from work she called the store and it was closed and she was getting ready to call the police I told her at the last minute I decided to go out for drinks with a few of the guys at work and because I was sleepy from the drinks I stopped at Mr. Donuts for a coffee and a donut donuts are one

of my weaknesses and before I went on my diet I would sometimes stop at Mr. Donuts and pick up a half dozen and eat
them while taking a drive but anyway I told her the coffee woke
me up and I didn't want to go home to an empty house 'cause I
missed her and the boys so I decided to take a ride and before I
knew it I was at the New Hampshire border and on the way
back I ran out of gas 'cause I forgot to check the tank I was out
there for a long time it was below zero when finally a trooper
came up and took me to a place open all night so I could get a
can of gas and so that's why I was getting home so late she believed me though later she found ways to work in questions
about the night to try and trick me into a mistake in my story
but there was a code with most of the guys at work if you said
you were out with them you were and I told Ma next time
Audry called when she was away don't tell her anything Ma got
more frail and lost her appetite if it's one thing she always had
was a good appetite we started having to beg her to eat and I
wanted to take her to the doctor for a check-up but she would-
n't go she said she was ready to go and when God wanted her
she wanted to be there by then Josie had her first kid a boy and
Gina's Maria was already in junior high school Peter met this
woman who worked at Schrafts who was kind of odd old fashioned looking like she lived in the forties or something she was
quiet and older than him and still lived with her mother and
father in Roxbury and in a few months they got married they
were the strangest couple don't get me wrong I love him and I
took her in as my own by Jesus she was bigger than he was and
had a mustache and I was best man and Frank was an usher
and Josie and her daughter and Gina were bridesmaids and we
got the Italian American Hall on Broadway and had a great party with a band I drank too much wine and got a little wild and
led a dance around the hall waving my napkin with my shirt off
except the bow-tie and Audry got all pissed and said I made a
134

fool of myself but I had a great time besides Audry wouldn't dance with me anyway and then on Sundays Peter brought his wife Teresa over for dinner she reminded me of a nun and I couldn't imagine doing her that's saying something for me but she loved Peter he loved her and that's what counts they were trying to have a baby but it wasn't happening for some reason so they were going to the doctors for check-ups the doctors said Teresa was a little old even though she was still able to get pregnant the odds were not good Peter took it real bad he started drinking and getting into arguments with her Teresa called me on the phone and I had to go over and calm him down one time it happened she had a bruise on her face and that's when I found out he was hitting her which was so fucked up because Peter was really so gentle he was the last guy I think that would hit his wife but when he drank he had no control I shook him up some and told him if it happened again he was going to deal with me he started on one of his pity me things how bad it's been for him everyone always made fun of him and Pa hated him now he wasn't going to be able to have kids then before you know it Teresa got pregnant forty-four years old and delivered a healthy girl they named Anna after Ma I must say most babies are cute no matter what but Anna was an ugly baby with this oversized head everyone was nice about it though and said how cute she was Frank's cigarette beer and grocery money came from his various girlfriends as old and fat as Frank got he always had a good looking girlfriend to live with and take care of the bills I got tired of trying to get money out of him what's a few hundred a month to me he said I had plenty the house was almost paid for and Gina didn't pay rent why should he I told him Gina took care of Ma and she paid her utilities if Frank didn't gamble he would have done ok he was a good cook they liked him at the Winter Hill Tavern and paid him good I remember a guy in the Marines same thing it was cards with him though Frank it was more dogs and horses and the sports games Frank loved to watch sports if you had a bet on the game he said it made it special somehow but this guy in the Marines most of the guys would be out looking for pussy he was at the card game and always owed money soon as our pay came in every month all of his went to everybody in the company who he owed they say it's a disease gambling I never took to it when I was young Frank took me to the dog track with him he tried to show me how to handicap and all that I just looked at the dogs and chose the one I liked I did as good as Frank with all his arithmetic and figuring things out in his little notebook and that would piss him off most of the time we just lost so by the time Frank was a teenager he was already los-ing a lot of money every week it's a hard habit to break I tried to teach the boys the rights and wrongs of things they see Frank and know about his gambling they know how something like that can ruin your life they heard stories about Pa from Ma and me and Gina and Josie little Tony had trouble in school he was a slow learner his report cards were never good mostly Cs and Ds but he got good marks for effort Johnny got As almost all the time what a fit he threw when he got a B I loved the boys more than anything it's funny how when you have kids everything changes I worried about things I never worried about before and it got me to thinking more about myself and the things about myself I wouldn't want the boys to know like some of the sex stuff and hanging out down the Zone but eve-rybody has different sides to themselves and the boys were only human too and would have their own things but there were things about myself I didn't want to see in the boys and I wor-ried about them being around Frank a lot him being so crazy I never appreciated Ma more as when those boys were growing up and I re-alized how much work she had to do alone to keep the family together and deal with Pa and all his shit beating up on her and never having any money around how much she loved us and made sure we had food in our stomach and understood right from wrong and respect for certain things that's what I tried to teach the boys and mostly we got along good only sometimes when I lost my temper and yelled they got upset I never hit them but sometimes if they were driving me crazy I'd yell and threaten to burn the house down or something like that Audry would interfere and then me and her would start arguing I guess I yelled a lot around the house and that wasn't too good for the boys but everybody makes mistakes raising their kids there's no perfect way to do it I don't care who you are when Craig started missing shifts at work and not calling in or anything I heard they gave him a warning and then the week he got fired I talked with him and he said things were real bad at home and his father had been drinking a lot and hitting everybody sometimes he didn't come in because he was afraid to leave the house 'cause there was no one there to protect his brother and sister from the father but I lost touch with him after that and often wondered what happened to him that was the summer me and Audry actually split up for a few weeks she went to North Carolina with the boys and I flew down there to get them back when I first realized they left for the airport I drove down there like a maniac and left my car out front of a terminal and ran all over the airport trying to find the next plane to North Carolina when I got back the car was towed and I owed three hundred for storage when I got down to North Carolina I paid a hundred bucks just to get a taxi to her mother's place all I had was an address and we had a big scene in front of her mother's house 'cause Audry wouldn't come out and talk to me her mother told me from the porch I had to get off her property and little Tony and Johnny were in the upstairs window looking out and I threatened her mother I would kill her and the rest of her family if she didn't let me talk to

Audry and kept me from my boys and that bitch called the cops on me and they threatened to arrest me if I didn't leave so that night I sent a telegram from my hotel to the house to Audry it said I do my thing you do your thing and if by chance we find each other it's beautiful and Audry called me at the hotel and said she was sorry for everything that happened but things were unbearable for her in the house I didn't know how hard it was to live with me I was always yelling and making threats and trying to make rules for everybody and everybody outside thought I was such a great guy but they should see me at home her words made me really angry I wanted to just go nuts having to hear that I wasn't nearly the great husband and father I thought I was on one hand and thinking Audry was full of shit and brainwashed by her mother and sisters on the other but who was the one working his ass off all these years making the money and working on the house so that now it was worth something why was I all of a sudden such an asshole all these years and she never said nothing before she said she loved me but ever since Ma died and I turned forty she said it was just getting worse Ma died in her sleep but in the end we never thought it would come for she kept sleeping longer and longer every day until she was sleeping over twenty hours a day eating like a bird and shrinking away to nothing there were days when she was in extreme pain and Gina would beg me to call the doctor and Ma calling from her bed in the room yelling in Italian don't call the doctor Ma made me promise to leave it to God and go when he wanted her that she lived her years and did everything she was going to do and now it was up to God in his hands she didn't want to go to the hospital and get hooked up to those electronic machines that keep you alive so I kept my promise even though there were times when Gina and Josie Peter and even Frank were fighting with me about how to care for Ma she should be in a hospital or nursing home call the doctor but I gave my word to Ma and I kept it to the end one morning Gina went in and Ma was cold her body stiff Ma got her wish but Gina said it wasn't fair that we all had to sit around and watch her die for two years I had a nice headstone carved for her and buried in her own grave just the way she asked me to and not with Pa who was at a nearby cemetery and I went to Ma's cemetery every Sunday morning and brought flowers sometimes I brought the boys but Audry never went she said she didn't like cemeteries her family was going to get cremated when they die I told her if she died before me there was no way I was going to have her cremated she was going to have a church funeral and be buried with me in a proper grave with a headstone so Audry stayed in North Carolina she said she loved me and didn't want the marriage to break up but she needed a little time and I had to give her space I was worried about the boys and couldn't stand the idea that they were with her but they were having a good time and one of Audry's sisters had horses and the boys were learning to ride I had all I could do to not go down there kill Audry and her whole fucking family and take the boys back home with me but I wasn't on my turf down there and knew that the cops meant business so I went back home and played it cool at work none of the guys knew what was going on except that I had to do my own clothes and shoes and laundry and cooking and cleaning I talked to Audry every day and told her I wanted her to come home she said she wasn't ready yet and one night I was working at the store and got a call near closing time from Craig who said he was sorry to bother me but he had nowhere to turn his father had thrown him out he was in a bad way could I come down to The Other Side and meet him so after work I drove down the South End and when I got to the bar I couldn't find him at first I was about to leave when I heard him call my name and I turned to see him in the same corner table we sat in the

first time we were there but he was in drag and that's what
threw me off I guess I should have figured it out in the first
place I mean I knew he was queer and all but he never said anything about being a dresser he had on make-up but his face was
bruised and there was dry blood on his lips he didn't have a wig
on just his own blond hair with these long fake diamond earrings and this long evening dress and heels I was uncomfortable at first but once I relaxed it was ok shit everybody in the
place was ok no reason I shouldn't be he thanked me for coming it was really nice of me and he always knew I was someone
special I ordered a bourbon and coke and drink for him though
he was slurring his words and I could tell he must have already
had a lot he told me his father came home drunk just when he
was getting ready to leave the house and when his father saw
him in the dress he went crazy beat him up bad then threw him
out for good there was still blood trickling from his nose he
had a lump over his eye he looked at me and said I don't know
what to do I feel like there's nothing left for me I said there was
always things you could do but first he had to get on his feet
and get a job and a place to live we finished our drinks and I
took him to the Howard Johnson's Motor Lodge and got him a
room for the night he could barely walk by the time we got to
the room being on heels drunk so I helped him undress first I
took off his shoes and earrings then his necklace and the long
white gloves I leaned him up on his side unzipped him then
pulled his dress down over his shoulders to his waist then over
his ankles I saw him in the bra and pantyhose and realized I
was digging it and I wanted him so I went to the bathroom to
get a grip of myself and soaked a washcloth to wipe down my
face then his face and got the dried-up blood and smeared
make-up off he also had a cut on his lip I remember that's
when I realized how close men and women really are and how
with a little bit of imagining there wasn't much different in the

way a boy or a girl looked except how they wore their hair and made up their skin and dressed it was only naked that the differences were obvious but in the face it was closest I saw him then as a chick the exact way he would have looked if he was a chick and he leaned his head back on the pillow and made a content sound like mmmmmmmm and looked at me and lifted his head to kiss me and I kissed him on the lips then he shoved his tongue down my throat and was all over me it was like nothing I ever knew in my life we went at it for hours I lost count of how many times finally about three in the morning I knew I better get home so I gave him some money to get him through a few days and told him I wanted to help him but only call me at work and I went home Audry had called the house all night I told her I went out to Chinatown then for a long drive 'cause I was missing her so much and feeling so down and she said Tony if I find out you're lying it's over but then she said she thought it over a long time and didn't want to let the marriage go that easy we should give it another try but some things were going to have to change the idea that she had the boys down there still made me crazy and when she said she was going to be home soon I told her I couldn't wait and how much I missed her and the boys and I was nothing without them I couldn't sleep the rest of the night the next morning on the way to work I left early and drove to the Howard Johnson's Motor Lodge but Craig was already gone I couldn't stop thinking of him and what I had done with him the night before sometimes I just told myself it never happened in time I think I could convince myself I felt sick inside in a strange sort of way because after all Craig was only a few years older than little Tony and I couldn't help but think that I was really fucked up that was the first time in my life I really felt guilty and fucked up no matter what I did in my life or what other people did my attitude was always whatever turns you on and I believed that too what difference did it make anyway whether it was a chick or a guy it was the first time ever I fooled around with anyone else on Audry not to say I would have fucked a thousand times under the right circumstances but the circumstances were never right before I couldn't get my mind off him all day I couldn't eat or concentrate on my work the guys teased what was wrong today when I got out of work I went home and called Audry she was coming home in a couple of days and then I went down to The Other Side to see if he was there but didn't recognize anyone so I went down the Zone and started drinking bourbon and cokes and watching some strip shows but my mind was on him when the girls came around looking for some company I gave them all the cold shoulder later I went back down The Other Side and he still wasn't there but a friend of his this black kid who was really beautiful in drag and wore a blond wig said Craig was supposed to meet him that afternoon but never showed and he was beginning to worry something was wrong so we went out driving around looking for Craig and that's when I found out he was on drugs again and his mother wasn't dead his parents were divorced and she lived in California and I was asking myself what the fuck I was doing in the middle of all of this when Craig's friend pointed him out getting out of a car he was in full dress the same outfit he wore the night before and the car drove away and we pulled over to the curb when he recognized us he got in the back seat and we drove to The Other Side he seemed drunk again but by then I knew it must be drugs I never knew anybody on the hard drugs before he was slow in his talking but acting more girlish than ever at the bar we had a couple of drinks and I asked him did he have a place to stay he said no I asked him where would he go he said he'd find a bed someplace so I got another room for the night and I didn't mean to because I went looking for him in the first place to tell him that what happened was fine but it couldn't happen again and my family came first I couldn't put anything at risk and now we were back in a room together all over each other and this time we spent the night he did things even the chicks in Korea never did there wasn't one part of my body he didn't know how to touch right I was crazy for it and I fucked him so hard the flesh on my cock got raw and when Audry got back it still had some marks but we didn't have sex for a couple of days after so it worked out ok when I was a kid one Sunday at mass the priest made a sermon about this guy who lived all alone who never went to church he had no friends or family when he died and they went into his room in the cheap rooming house all they found besides his few clothes and things were boxes full of dirty magazines of the most evil kind and it got me real hard listening to him talk and how he said of the most evil kind and I remember how wrong it must be to get a boner in church I couldn't stop thinking about what must be in all those dirty magazines in Frank's magazines there was mostly naked girls and sometimes naked girls doing things with guys once I had to stay home from school with the flu and Ma was working at the time at the Converse Factory and I was home alone and I beat off so many times with Frank's magazines my dick got raw then too and I couldn't touch it for over a week it scabbed up that was the same priest who said mass at Ma's funeral only then he looked so old I thought he might die before the mass was done I thought that they let priests retire but who knows there was hardly anyone at Ma's funeral the church felt empty and she was all shriveled up and tinier than ever in the casket it was like yesterday she was up and around shouting at us in Italian to clean up for dinner or clean up our mess or clean up for bed or clean up so we could go out and find Pa there's no doubt that Pa was a rat but he was still my father no matter how bad he was and you have to show a little respect no matter what Peter used to get all worked up when Pa even got mentioned but Peter had it worse than anybody except Ma of course Pa never hit me I remember him hitting Frank sometimes and when Frank got older he stopped hitting him but it was Peter Pa hated mostly if he didn't hit Ma he hit Peter after Peter's little girl was born he started drinking a little more and roughed up Teresa who called the police one time and they took Peter down the station Peter called me and I had to go down to the station with Teresa and the police wanted her to sign this thing where she could press charges but she said she didn't want to press charges she just wanted Peter to stop hitting her then he would be good for a while then out of the blue I'd get a call from Teresa Peter was drinking and I'd have to go over and smooth things out I don't know what Peter wanted he had a wife and child and had a pension at the factory and made decent money but when he had a few drinks he started feeling sorry for himself saying things like he was a loser and a freak usually I got him calmed down and into bed he slept it off when Audry got back from North Carolina I couldn't think of anything but Craig but I told him I couldn't see him any more I cared for him and wanted to help him get back on his feet but my family came first and what happened couldn't happen again I thought it for the best that we stay out of touch but if he needed to call me he should only call me at the store and never at home my feelings went back and forth between this huge guilt that somehow I'd gone against my vows to Audry and after years of staying true to her I strayed and worse I strayed with a boy not much older than my son of course Craig was street-wise and years beyond little Tony that way but it was still wrong what I did even though in my heart I believed that sex is sex and two people can love each other and have sex with other people and shit you could even love more than one person I mean I loved Audry when she got back from North Carolina but I was obsessed with this kid I stopped eating and shitting Audry wasn't ready to just jump into bed after we had been apart and that was ok with me 'cause I wasn't feeling like it anyway I wasn't jerking off and even when I thought of Craig I thought of holding him and taking care of him not having sex with him I couldn't think straight it worked to my advantage because Audry thought I was all messed up 'cause of us almost breaking up and the problems we were having I truly wanted to get back on track with the marriage at first I had a hard time looking the boys in the eye because I felt such guilt and I took everyone out for supper and we went to the Burlington Mall and the boys and Audry shopped all day and Audry and I had late night heart to heart talks about how she was feeling and that she loved me but I was very hard to love and over the years I'd grown distant and all I cared about was work and being the number one salesman and with all the work on the house and the time I spent doing things for my brothers and sisters and Ma it didn't leave that much time for us or time for me with the boys I half listened quietly and was I not thinking about Craig I would have really got pissed after all everything I did I did for Audry and the boys I wanted to give them what I never had I never wanted them to want for anything and they never did there was always plenty of food in the house and Audry never had to go chasing me out of some bar I was always home when I wasn't at work and it wasn't easy working as hard at the store as I did and keeping up with all the work the house needed over the years but I shook my head like I agreed with Audry and in a way I guess she was right about some things but I couldn't get my mind off him that night Audry and me went to bed and we made real hard love straight ahead just me on top but I was ramming her hard and she liked it in between telling me to go easy and when she fell asleep I laid there in bed with my eyes wide open fighting the urge to go out and look for him instead I just laid there and about three in the morning I knew I wasn't

145

going to get to sleep I tapped Audry and told her that I was going out for a drive she said I love you and be careful as I left and I drove up to New Hampshire but instead of turning around I kept driving and the time it was getting light I could see the mountains off in the distance but I couldn't remember a thing since I'd passed my usual exit then turned around at the next one and speeded home Audry and the boys were having breakfast and I told them about my drive and how beautiful the mountains were and how next summer we would all take a vacation up there I never saw the White Mountains before and they were only two hours away I drove into work wondering how I would get through the day so tired but I had one of my best days of the season by now Mr. Sanford was gone and replaced by Ms. Hollingsworth as personnel manager and in our annual meeting she said that she thought I would make a good division manager had I ever given it any thought in fact I had but only years ago now I would have to take a cut in pay to be a division manager it was said I made more money than anybody in the store except for the store manager she said she would think it might be nice after all these years to get out of the pressure of working straight commission but I'd rather work on straight commission it was kind of like working for yourself a division manager got a salary and had to work extra hours and all that sure it looked good you were a division manager and you got to carry around a clipboard but who needed it I didn't hear from Craig and me and Audry were doing ok I had to either block Craig out of my mind or I did nothing but think of him some days I thought that I was in love with him other days I just felt so guilty for what I did that was the year we took the vacation to Disney in Florida and Gina and Maria came too we had a great time it was the best time we all had together ever we stayed at this big hotel and it was the first real vacation I took in my life since being out of the Marines I mean when I got out

146

of the Marines I didn't work for a while but it wasn't really a vacation I was looking for work and all the years since working at Pratt's every time I had time off I worked on the house and having the time off down in Florida got me thinking about my own business again I wasn't getting any younger and I had some good money built up in profit sharing and a big savings account over the years the property in Somerville started going up and I had the house paid off so we were sitting pretty good I didn't want to spend the next twenty years at Pratt's there had to be more so when we got back I started looking around again but there was mostly just pizza shops and breakfast joints and that didn't seem right for me then one day I got a call from Craig again it was strange because it was just long enough since I heard from him before that I was starting to feel like maybe it never even happened and since Florida I was eating again and shitting again regular and even getting five or six hours of sleep a night Audry and me were getting it on once in a while 'cause for the longest time the first thing when I opened my eyes in the morning would be to get this sinking feeling in my stomach thinking of him and then when he called I had that feeling all over again I told him it wouldn't be good to see him and that it was best we let everything go he said don't you think about what we had and I told him I did I thought it was beautiful but it was what it was and he said he had nowhere else to turn but if that's what I really meant that was ok I gave in and told him I would meet him after work I called Audry and told her I was going out for drinks with the guys I could tell by the tone of her voice that she suspected something this was the first time since she got back from North Carolina I was going out she asked me who was going and I told her and she asked me where we were going I told her I wasn't sure but I'd be home early I met Craig down The Other Side and he looked real bad he wasn't in drag but just jeans and a t-shirt worn-out sneakers

and no socks he was dirty and it was the first time I ever noticed he had a beard and there was stubble he looked older and
real high said he was on the street again and admitted he was
strung out but he said he was going into the clinic and going to
clean his act up this time but he needed some money if I could
lend him some as he promised he'd pay it back 'cause soon as
he was clean he was going to get a job and go to college part-
time at night but I didn't want to give him anything if he was
going to spend it on drugs I made him swear to me that he
wouldn't use the money for dope and he swore he said there
was a friend he could live with if he could come up with some
rent money it would be easier after he got out of the clinic to
get back on his feet if he had a place to go to but I only had
about fifty bucks on me and the banks were closed until the
next day so on the way to work the next morning I took out
five hundred bucks and on my lunch break went to meet him in
Harvard Square it was easy for me to get at the money without
Audry knowing 'cause I handled all the money Audry never
knew how much was in the savings or the checking account I
kept the bank book and paid all the bills Audry hated doing
that stuff and could never balance the books otherwise there
was no way I could give the money to Craig but I did and like
the night before he tried to kiss me but I held him off even
though I was tempted and wanted him I told him to call if he
needed anything 'cause I believed in him he was a smart kid and
could do anything in the world he wanted he said I was the only one in his shitty life who really cared for him and he would
always remember me I didn't hear from him after that for a
while but I started thinking about him again it even got to my
work 'cause that month for the first time in ten years as a
big-ticket salesman and being number one I was third and
Mike Cordano who was second behind me all those years got
first I knew why I slipped I lost my concentration and started

148

taking long coffee breaks and daydreaming the guys at work called it middle-age crisis I didn't really understand what all that shit meant except that I was bald and a lot heavier I still felt like I was twenty-one but it didn't even bother me that I was third and the next month I was second and for the first time in six years I didn't win the annual Easy Payment Plan promotion award and one day the division manager took me aside and asked me was everything all right I told him yes he said if I needed to talk to anyone I could talk to him we went back a lot of years we did I always respected Mr. Zizzo most of the guys hated him he seemed like a hard-ass but that was just his job he was the kind of guy that on his days off went to lectures on history and stuff and liked to read but at work he was always on our backs if we were selling too much advertised product and not enough service policies and saying old Mrs. Howe from the stationery department could outsell us he liked to keep us at each other so he would do a lot of baiting one guy against the other only Faith wasn't a guy and over the years everybody respected her 'cause she pretty much did as well as any of the guys and didn't let anything get to her she took long coffee breaks and lunches but when she latched on to a customer she didn't let go until she sold top-of-the-line I think the ladies trusted buying from her 'cause they figured she knew more about things like washers and dryers and stoves being a chick at that time Frank was living with a new girlfriend who had a daughter who was seventeen built like a dream he told me he was doing her too and the mother knew and it was ok with the mother I thought that was really fucked up and I told him so I never told Frank about Craig I never told anyone about Craig and that made it hard 'cause there was no one I could talk to about it to try and figure things out I didn't know what I really wanted I mean how could I be realistic and think there was anything in the future for us it was crazy and I was a sick fuck

149

when I took a look around me I felt even worse with my brother Frank doing his girlfriend's daughter and Peter still drinking beating up on Teresa and even my little Tony suffered 'cause kids have a way of picking up on things even if you don't think they do but he was getting bigger and bigger and the school doctor sent home a note we should help him eat better and get him on a diet we tried Audry cooked special things for him and he didn't seem to eat much at home but Audry would find empty bags of candy chips and cupcakes hidden in his room he wasn't doing good at school they said it wasn't that he was stupid but he didn't concentrate too good I tried talking to him and for a while we went on a diet together we both lost weight but I had this kind of double life part of me was where I should be with my home and family and part of me wanted to be somewhere else a day didn't go by without thinking about Craig and where he was and why didn't he call to let me know how things were working out because he promised he would sometimes fighting off the temptation to go out and look for him between me and Audry it seemed like the same old bickering like for almost twenty years we were together we got to really hate each other as much as we loved each other and I loved her a lot then I started looking around for some kind of business of my own again I went to seminars and went to the library and the lady helped me get books out on small businesses I was ready to make the move as soon as the right thing came along there were so many different kinds of things I almost bought a van so I could start a business picking people up at the grocery market and taking them home then there were the sales things 'cause being good at sales a lot of the franchises said I would do real good with products you could sell from your house then I thought maybe I could get a real-estate license and start my own agency but nothing seemed right one Sunday I went to this convention in Boston with all these different franchise people and there was this soft ice cream franchise you could open six months a year and make enough to close the other half of the year so I almost bought a place that was already in operation it was in Lawrence and one Sunday afternoon after dinner I took the whole family up there and everybody seemed excited except Audry who thought Lawrence was far away to have a business we might have to sell the house and move closer Audry had wanted for a long time to move out into the suburbs but I had lived all my life in Somerville and after all the years of working on the house and finally having it in shape it was all paid for I got to feeling that I wouldn't leave the house ever but Audry would leave in a second she wanted more than anything a single family somewhere and Gina could take care of herself she was an office manager and making good money there was only Frank and after all the years of beating me for the rent I should let him fend for himself but there was something about the house that held me there and I could always see Ma sitting at the window and remember carrying little Tony up the stairs from the hospital after he was born that it was the only real home I ever had so it was hard to think of giving it up besides the suburbs were so quiet and nothing ever seemed to be going on there were so many kinds of different people in Somerville and Broadway was a main street so there was a lot of cars and trucks and people on foot all hours of the day and night you could hear people and engines and horns and sirens you get used to knowing something is going on out there that's why I loved New York City so much all that kind of energy I still can't believe old Ma packed us kids up got us there and we ended up safe so many things could have gone wrong the day Ma sent Gina out for some dry beans at the market which was just next door to the downstairs baker and Gina went the wrong way and didn't come back we couldn't find her and for a couple of hours it was the worst feeling I remember really understanding how huge that city is how it could just eat you up and finally some-one found Gina crying on a street corner ten blocks away and they called the cops we had already talked with the neighbor-hood cop and they brought Gina back in a squad car Ma was hysteric screaming and cursing praising God and all the saints she lit candles and said novenas every day for months after that when I was young I loved church and for a while I wanted to be a priest Ma said she always thought I would be a good priest I loved the candles and the smell of the incense I became an altar boy and learned some of the Latin I remember standing up next to the altar on Sunday mornings with all the lit candles and the music on the organ blaring loud and Ma sitting in the front row tears in her eyes seeing me and I loved when I was the one who got to ring the bells there was a married couple who used to sit in the front row every eight-thirty mass and she was pretty and I used to think about her a lot when I jerked off so I got to look forward to eight-thirty mass and seeing her there every Sunday morning then when Father Leonard started hearing all the altar boys' confession he started asking stuff about my thoughts and did I touch myself what did I think about when I touched myself I never told him about the lady in the front row at the eight-thirty mass but I did say that I lied so I hoped that would cover it later Skipper Capraro told me that Father Leonard gave him a blow job in the confessional and told him if he ever told anybody he would go to hell for sure I figured Father Leonard was doing himself in the confessional when he asked people all those questions but hey everybody jerks off and priests know it and the nuns know it too but they say a lot of nuns get it on with each other you would think they might get it on with the priests but the priests they say get it on with each other or have a mistress but there was something about Sunday mornings at church and the rituals you need those kinds of things to help bring life into some kind of balance even though I mostly stopped going to church especially after Ma died but I always respected the church and priests and nuns too there's something special about those kinds of people who have a calling but how the fuck are you supposed to go without sex no one can you can put a guy in the seminary but you can't stop him from jerking off I always tried to give the boys as much privacy as possible when I was a kid I had none and I was always trying to figure out how to be alone so that I could jerk off without someone around the house I told Audry to always make sure she gave the boys as much privacy as possible so that they didn't have to worry about that stuff one time Audry found some magazines in little Tony's room when she was looking for food I told her leave them it was normal for little Tony to be doing that kind of thing she wanted to take the magazines and throw them away but I wouldn't let her besides if we threw them away little Tony would know that we knew and were going through his things it would be embarrassing for him little Tony already had a kind of complex about that stuff being overweight he didn't have a girlfriend and didn't go to his high-school dances or proms I figured he could at least find one of the fat girls at school he didn't take to other things at school like sports or clubs Johnny was interested in science and math and didn't have no trouble with girls being interested in him but he wasn't all that interested in them it was like he'd rather have his nose in a book I don't know where all that came from I don't know of anyone in the family who was ever book smart Johnny was a first I think if we had sent the boys to regular high school little Tony would have done even worse than he did and might have got into more trouble it wasn't serious stuff but little Tony seemed to be sometimes in the wrong place at the wrong time like one day when he was younger we got a call from one of the sisters she said little Tony started a fire in a wastepaper basket I had to go up the school and talk to the mother superior little Tony said it wasn't him that lit the fire it was someone else but he didn't want to say who but the mother superior said that Sister Gloria whoever knew for sure it was little Tony I had to punish him it was hard to punish little Tony 'cause if you made him stay in it was ok with him he hardly ever went out anyway mostly he watched television and ate snacks so we took television away from him for a month but it only lasted a week the poor kid maybe he didn't light the fire when they accused him of carving the words cunt and prick into the wooden desktop he said it wasn't him it was there one day after public school kids took catechism class in the room it's hard not to believe your kid when they look you right in the eye and say they didn't do something I knew he was having a hard time it's tough for kids trying to figure things out and he seen some fucked-up things at home with Frank living there all the years and even me when I lost my temper but no matter what I always told the boys I love you no matter how messed up things must seem to them at certain times with Audry and me having problems they should always remember that I loved them and I would do anything for them when I finally got a call from Craig it was almost as if what happened with me and him was some kind of dream and I couldn't remember was it last night or last year or five years I thought of him less and less but I still found myself when my guard was down remembering how I felt during that sex we had and wondering was he ok imagining where he might be and did he ever think of me he said he was doing good and thought of me a lot but didn't call 'cause he knew I wanted to stay away but he wanted to let me know he was doing ok and soon would be taking the test to get his high school diploma he was working at a hardware store downtown but he just lost his job 'cause business was slow so instead of laying him off so he could at least collect they fired him for some stu-

154

pid reason now he was out of work again but looking and he wondered if I might like to meet him for coffee and as easy as if someone from the store just asked did I want to go for coffee I said yes and the next day I had to work an evening shift so I left a little early and met him he didn't look too good but he said he was staying off drugs since he got out of the clinic he only slipped once or twice and a few times he was going to go get some he thought of me and what I did for him and it helped him stay strong so I gave him a couple of hundred dollars and drove him to his father's house in Dorchester 'cause he moved back in with his family he leaned over and kissed me and the little fuck took my breath away right there I had all I could do to hold myself back those old feelings about him came back to me I told him it couldn't happen again but for days after that all I could think of was him and it was during the time when I started looking for a business again so the next time he called me I met him the next day which was my day off and I told Audry I was driving down to Fall River to look at a pizza place and we spent the day in a motel by then I knew I was helpless when it came to Craig I would do anything for the next couple of months it went like that once or twice a week I would tell Audry I was going to look at a business someplace and I would meet Craig sometimes we would just get a room and sometimes we would go out to The Other Side for drinks sometimes when I picked him up he was dressed and other times he wasn't it's strange how after a while he seemed to be Craig to me whether he was dressed like a chick or a guy funny thing when he was dressed like a chick it brought out his manly side you noticed more his boy's beard or muscled hands and when he was just a guy he looked more like a chick his skin was soft and his face looked girly and every time we met I gave him money fifty here a hundred there he didn't seem to be using drugs and passed his test so he got his diploma and as soon as he got a job he was going to go to college part-time and after all the years of Audry knowing my every move I had the perfect alibi with the business thing and I was amazed at how easy it was to do it and to have this other life Audry's sisters and mother kept sending her real estate flyers and business listings and telling her how much better we could do with our money down there so she was always kind of relieved when I got home from one of my visits to a business for sale and said it was lousy for one reason or another she was secretly hoping I would get discouraged and consider moving down to North Carolina the only cousin I kept in touch with lived up in Tewksbury Leo grew up in Somerville but he bought three acres of land and was growing his own food and had chickens and went out every morning to gather eggs and milk his goats they had no television and Leo was real strict with his kids like after school they always had plenty of chores to do they weren't allowed to hang out with other kids he said it was a crazy world and he was going to keep his kids away from all that evil stuff he was a religious guy too always telling me Tony you have to read the Bible it's all there and Jesus can save me too and I should move out there and get out of the rat race I lived in there was no meaning to it but the last place I could live in is the country milking goats and cutting firewood no fucking way besides I told him he needed to give his kids some freedom if he didn't he would be sorry 'cause you can't build a wall around yourself it'll crack no doubt about it kids need to be kids that was part of Craig's problem he never had a chance to be a kid and if there's one thing I gave my boys it was space and time to be kids and not put a lot of pressure on them no one's perfect as a parent but one rule of thumb for me was to think about how I felt when I was a kid when you put yourself in a kid's place sometimes it helps and things just went on like that with me and Craig I figured out he was still using drugs but I still

156

gave him money I always made him promise he wouldn't buy
drugs but I knew he would so when we were together I tried to
get him to eat we would go to Chinatown and I'd order a lot of
food he just sat and picked at a chicken wing for an hour I
would force him to eat some rice and vegetables he was so
skinny his bones were showing through his flesh I had the
waiter wrap the leftovers and wherever I dropped him off he
walked away holding a brown bag full of food I wondered did
he just throw it in a trash can after I drove away then I didn't
hear from him for a few weeks and I got real worried it was
strange because I didn't just care about helping him any more
now I wanted to be with him it wasn't just the sex sometimes
we didn't even have sex though even when he was real high he
tried to give me a blow job but I wouldn't let him it got kind of
sad and the more I wanted to be with him the worse I felt
about myself that I was able to just be another person when I
walked into my home and saw Audry and the boys they would
ask what was it like and I would make up some laundry or pizza
shop and how if it only had better parking I might have been
interested and things were pretty good between me and Audry
at that time that's what was really strange 'cause we were getting
along talking better though we long since stopped fucking regular except on our anniversary or birthday though sometimes she
jerked me off but she never wanted me just to do her with my
hand or mouth she just did the hand job thing out of some
sense of duty but it was good and I must say she had a strong
wrist and got the job done at work I was just not into it any
more when you lose your concentration you just can't do your
best it was a year since I'd been number one Faith had become
top salesman in major appliances and all the guys walked
around the store with their tails between their legs when the
monthly figures were posted I thought it was great more power
to her then they started talking about putting more chicks in

157

major appliances since Faith did so well and all the guys started getting uptight and about that time the economy was slowing the stocks were down and my profit sharing was getting less and less I was thinking that if I didn't do something soon I would never have enough to buy a business there was this building right across the street from my house for sale it used to be a hair dressing shop for years it was cheap and the right size for an ice cream stand up and down Broadway there was not one ice cream stand in the summer people either had to wait for when the ice cream man came around or drive someplace everybody said I was crazy that I'd lose my shirt but I figured it out how much it would cost to fix the place up then how much I might bring in a day for the six months we were open and I wouldn't have to pay too much for help 'cause I could work it myself and the boys could help and Audry too the house was paid for so we didn't have a lot of expenses no one knew how much I had in the savings account but it was a lot more than Audry ever figured and I could get the place up and running with only investing my profit sharing from twenty years at the store Frank wanted in right away and asked to be a partner but there was no way I would do it because Frank had no money I wouldn't be partners with him anyway then I figured out that he was only looking to have a place he could run a gambling business I was used to Frank it could have been any of my brothers and sisters who had something wrong with them and needed to be taken care of the girls had done great Josie was the first one in the family to graduate college had a good husband and good kid and another on the way and Gina all the years stayed on the second floor paying her utilities but I never took any rent from her even after Ma died she did good and her daughter Maria was in this national honor society at school and was going to be a teacher we didn't hear much from Peter unless he was causing trouble at home and Teresa would call they mostly kept to themselves his daughter and Teresa never left each other's sides except when Anna was in school they mostly stayed in the house and had no friends and sometimes Peter showed up at our house drunk pulling his routine about poor me life sucks I got tired of it and angry with him but the poor fuck never had a chance in the first place so what could I do but be a brother Ma made me promise before she died that I would take care of everybody and I could still see her in the window it's funny 'cause Ma always seemed old to me when I think about that time she lived with us on Broadway she was blind for at least ten years she spent her days at the window even though she couldn't see so if you walked by the house there was Ma looking out the second-floor window but she couldn't see you I wish she could have lived long enough for little Tony's graduation from high school Audry and me were worried about little Tony he didn't have good enough grades to get into college he didn't want to go anyway and once when he was a senior and I found out he was playing pool after I told him I wanted him to stay out of the pool halls I went down the pool hall and I took the stick out of his hand and broke it on the table and dragged him out by his ear then I found out Audry knew he was playing pool and I went even crazier she said she didn't tell me 'cause she knew if she did I would do exactly what I did which was go crazy and act like an idiot and that as long as she knew he was there and he wasn't playing for money she was glad that he told her the truth about where he was spending his time and I was the one who always said that you got to give the kids space and let them enjoy being young so I got little Tony a job at the store on the loading dock when he graduated high school he was doing ok out there and learning a little about the value of a dollar I told him as long as he lived at home he wouldn't have to pay any board or nothing but he did have to save part of his money I think Audry was

159

glad when I got little Tony into the store she figured that it was a good way to make sure that I wasn't doing anything I shouldn't be doing she was always suspicious about the store and all the chicks thinking that I was trying to do one of them and when I was having this thing with Craig she never even got suspicious so it kind of started to go on and on but after about six months he got worse and seemed to be more drugged out every time I saw him he was always asking for money and I was always giving it to him then once he showed up at the store and it really shook me up I was on the point and there he was coming down the escalator looking at me in that girlish way he did fortunately it was a morning so there were only two of us on and Faith was on her coffee break so I headed him off and told him he couldn't come here he said he knew but I was his last resort and I told him to go out in the parking lot I would meet him there in a few minutes Faith came back I told her I was taking a coffee break and went out to the lot he said he needed a car could he borrow mine it would only be for a couple of hours I told him when he brought it back to leave it unlocked with the keys in the glove box and not come back into the store at lunch I went out he still hadn't brought the car back and afternoon coffee break it was the same I was getting real nervous 'cause if he didn't have the car back when I got out of work I'd have to make up something to tell Audry about what happened to the car when I got out of work he was just pulling up and he had this look on his face like something was wrong then I looked at the side of the car where it was sideswiped he said he had the car parked in a lot and when he got back he found it that way he was sorry and would pay for the repair because the reason he needed the car in the first place was that he spent the day on job interviews he thought he had a job and the first thing he was going to do was pay me back I could tell he was high and drove him into town he wanted me to leave him off at

The Other Side so I did but I made my mind up on the way there that it had to stop and I told him so whatever it was that was going on between us had to stop it wasn't that I cared about the money or anything it was him I cared about I told him so and I wasn't doing anything good for him by giving him money 'cause there's only one thing he did with the money it wasn't a case anymore that I could help him but I couldn't help him until he was ready to help himself it wasn't like there was anything in the future for us it was all crazy he still had his future ahead of him he shouldn't waste it you're so sweet and nobody ever cared for me like you do he said with his sad blue eyes looking at me but I wouldn't kiss him I told him no matter what he shouldn't call me and if some day he got straight and his life was squared away I would like to hear about how he ended up but if he continued on the road he was on he was only going to end up dead or in jail and he would never find anyone who really cared about him and could give him the kind of love a person needs unless he was into a better lifestyle and off drugs he said you're so sweet and touched my nose with his finger and off he went into the bar and that's the last I saw of him for about six months I stopped going out to look at businesses and was getting real crabby around the house Audry and me were fighting a lot then once in a while in the middle of a fight we'd end up in bed having some wild fucking how do you figure and I got to hand it to Audry she kept her shape over the years she didn't gain more than five pounds in all the years together and still looked as good in a pair of jeans as she did when I first laid my eyes on her ass in the marking room all those years before sometimes I thought of Craig and wondered where he was there were days when I had all I could do to hold myself back from going downtown to find him but then it would go away I'd be ok for a while then Audry went down to North Carolina for a week and the boys wanted to go too 'cause her mother wasn't doing too good she had lung cancer and only had about a year to go Audry said Tony under the circumstances I think you should think about going down with us but in twenty years all that mother and the sisters ever did was make my life miserable plotting at every chance they could to figure out ways to get Audry to leave me and move back to North Carolina but at this point in time I knew Audry would never leave unless something really bad happened and when her mother died she wouldn't want to go back to North Carolina as far as I was concerned the bitch couldn't die soon enough but I didn't tell Audry that I just said there was no way I was going down there her mother never showed me one bit of respect or acknowledged even that I had done a lot and given Audry a good home and family Audry never had to want for nothing but that old crust thought that her daughters should be all living in mansions or something that's why she never kept a husband she either buried them or left them 'cause they couldn't give her the kind of lifestyle she expected if I wanted to work she said I would have stayed single the fucking bitch grew up in a trailer park and she thought she should be sleeping in satin sheets so even though Audry said it might be the last chance to see her mother alive in some ways out of respect I knew she was right but there was no way I was going and the first couple of nights she was away I thought about trying to find Craig and over the past few months Angela Rizzio who worked part-time in jewelry was nosing around and I knew that she and Phil Burns from automotive were having a thing for a while Angela and her friend Tricia both worked at the store part-time and since they'd been there which was a year or so they had a bit of a reputation Tricia was already fooling around with Mr. Sarcia the controller he was married with kids she was divorced and had a teenage daughter who was a looker too and one day Jimmy Wilson on maintenance walked into a supply closet and Tricia was on her knees giving Mr. Sarcia a blow job Angela was married and her husband had a television repair business in Arlington she had two beautiful kids and a nice house everything a person wants but she still had that itch and she wasn't like Tricia 'cause Tricia only fooled around with guys in the store who had some pull and she was already in line for a big-ticket job even though she had only been working part-time for a year but Angela she fooled around 'cause she liked it she already had the things she wanted she just wanted a good time and one night after work when Audry was away a few of the guys and Angela and Tricia were going out for drinks so I went along over the years I drank less and less so I got drunk pretty easy and once I felt it there was no stopping me so I was feeling good and talking a lot about sex it was the seventies and during the seventies it seems a lot of people were talking about sex we all got drunk and I was picking up on Angela's vibes she was cute a few years younger than me short dirty blond hair and one of those tight small bodies she still looked great even though she had a couple of kids and was about thirty-five and she always dressed real nice and wore make-up and had this beauty mark on the lower left side of her cheek that drove me crazy a few times at the store when I did some flirting with her she seemed to respond and flirt a little back I never thought nothing of it 'til that night sitting there I realized I wanted her so bad and as it got later we ended up sitting next to each other at the table getting out of the general conversation she said it was rare to see me out with people from the store I told her my wife was away one thing led to another and we were in my car in the parking lot making out she jerked me off and blew me I fingered her and she fingered herself and we both came it was incredible and then she asked me did I want to smoke I told her I didn't she said no pot I was already drunk so I took a few puffs and man I was really high and we started making out and

163

getting into it again the pot made me feel real weird and I
thought I was getting sick then there was a bang on the window
and I almost jumped through the roof of the car it was a cop
who said that we had to move on and so we kissed goodnight
she went off in her car to her house and family in Arlington
and I went home to the empty apartment in Somerville I wasn't
there five minutes when Audry called and I was pretty high
from the pot and bourbon and cokes so I had a hard time con-
centrating on what I said she asked me where I had been all
night I told her I was out with some people from work and she
asked who and I made the mistake of mentioning Angela and
Tricia Audry got really uptight and said that her mother was
dying and I was out having a party with the store sluts I told
her I wasn't going to listen to that shit hung up and left the
phone off the hook then I passed out that was the only time
Angela and me ever did anything besides flirt it's not that I
wouldn't if I had the chance I thought she was real hot and for
the first couple of weeks after that night I was hornier than I'd
been in a long time then I found out she was fooling around
with one of the younger part-timers I thought to myself why
would she want me shit I was overweight and bald when she
still had her looks I was lucky and I thought of that night a lot
when I jerked off there was something about her not just her
looks but about how she was with sex like she could just hop in
my car and get it on with me and do herself like that without no
hang-ups it's kind of the way I felt but I didn't fool around for
so many years by the time I did I couldn't help but feel a little
guilty she could just go home to her family and still be a good
mother and wife why not it was so different from Audry who
was real suspicious when she got back from North Carolina
that's one of the reasons why even if I could have got something going with Angela at the time I wouldn't have been able I
had to stay close to home Audry was watching me like a hawk

every time Audry got back from North Carolina she looked real good like either her hair was different or she got a little sun but she always knew how to fill a pair of jeans and me being so horny at the time we started getting it on a little but as usual most of the time Audry was just doing it to satisfy me and I could tell if she was blowing me or jerking me off or something she was doing it out of duty if I made a move to go down on her she would say no why don't you just come inside I don't think she came too often mostly she would work on getting me off so she could get it over with then sometimes I wondered to myself does Audry not like sex or does she not like sex with me I asked her is it me and she said no but she had to be having some sex I asked her did she do herself sometimes she said you know I don't like to talk about those things and so it went on for a while I started to dread going to work and that was such a change from years before when I used to look forward to it and charge into the major appliances at the beginning of my day like I was going to conquer the world now I went through the motions since I had it down so good I still made pretty good money but I took coffee breaks and long lunches things I never used to do I flirted a lot those were wild times with sex and drugs some of the young chicks they hired were really crazy flirted a lot but they were mostly interested in the younger guys I would have left the store but the economy was so bad and the stocks were low my profit sharing was only about half of what it was two years before then when Audry's mother died I wasn't going to go to North Carolina with her we had a big fight screaming at each other actually I did most of the screaming Audry cried and said I was never there for her when she needed me right after she left I got this real strange feeling like I fucked up bad so without even getting any clothes or anything I got a cab and went to the airport and ran around from different desks trying to find out Audry's flight and made it on the plane at the very last minute she didn't talk to me all the way down the boys were sad 'cause she was the only grand-parent they had left she was always good to them and they loved her but I only stayed for two days that was long enough with all the cold shoulders I was getting from her bitch sisters they're all crying and acting sad and I know them cunts they couldn't wait to get their hands on the old lady's money 'cause each time she buried or divorced a husband she had more of it and I know that at least one of Audry's sisters couldn't stand the mother Audry told me everybody knew but she played the good daughter through the whole thing of the mother being sick with cancer and all 'cause she knew some of that money was going to her and the mother left all of it to the girls includ-ing the big house she owned which the sisters had on the mar-ket before the poor old bitch was cold in the grave Audry got one fourth of it and I told her she could do whatever she want-ed with it we didn't need it I didn't want her family's money anyway but I went right back home and Audry stayed for a while to help settle things and Johnny stayed there with Audry 'cause he was on summer vacation and little Tony came back with me 'cause he quit his job at Pratt's and was working in a sporting goods warehouse outside of Union Square and being around Audry's family after her mother died got me thinking about Ma and her funeral since she was gone I thought less and less of my past 'cause when Ma was around every day there she was to remind me and say things like remember when we were in New York and ate the hard bread with the watery hot cocoa and remember when you got back from Korea and we all were at the airport waiting for you to get off the plane that after-noon seeing them all lined up there even Frank Ma Peter Gina Josie but with Ma gone I remembered things from when I was younger when I least expected like out of nowhere I would think of my father crawling up the stairs calling for Ma to put

166

on the water and no matter what she was doing or what time of day Ma would drop what she was doing put the water on and make Pa a dish of macaroni even when he ate he kept drinking he would cause a scene over something or other I never knew the Pa in the picture Ma kept on her mantle she said I looked like him and I guess I did he was kind of short and stocky too with the pointed nose and no chin and even at twenty he was half bald he looked sober in that picture and had a smile I never saw him with who would have thought that man in the photo was capable of some of the shit that Pa pulled over the years Ma used to say in the end it was good he died it was a chance for Ma to have a real life and have some peace 'cause even after she got back from New York and her sister helped her get the paper that said Pa could never go near Ma again Ma was always afraid 'cause Pa always said he'd kill her if she ever left him and she used to say that as long as he was alive she had to look over her shoulder and she believed that's why she went blind having to strain to keep an eye out for Pa but Ma Pa's been dead for years I had to tell her maybe no she said maybe no it was sad to think how much she had to go through trying to keep the family together without a real husband around and how no matter how little there was to eat she made it go around so we didn't go hungry she always had a story about when she was a girl in Italy and her first boyfriend who she kissed in the olive grove but her family made her marry my father who she wouldn't have married if she had to choose there were a few times at Christmas there was just no money Ma was able to come up with enough to put a good meal together I still remember homemade macaroni and meatballs and it was the first time we ate meat in a month and she knew we were sad 'cause we didn't get toys and she made us bundle up and we went on the bus and subway to some place downtown where people didn't have homes it was a shelter she said it was bad for us but not as bad as it was for others that always stuck with me and that's why from the time I got back from the Marines every year on Christmas I volunteered my mornings at a shelter helping prepare the Christmas meal actually I was never much of a cook I used to peel potatoes and wash the pots and pans out and one time I brought Audry and the boys there and made them eat Christmas dinner but they said it wasn't fair that they should have to eat their Christmas dinner there just 'cause I wanted to and Audry said she wouldn't do it again so after that I went alone for the early part of the day before we had Christmas dinner at home but I forgot it was my mother sent me to that place every year being a kid and realizing people had it even worse than us I never forgot it Audry called and said she was going to take another week and maybe even longer 'cause things were pretty screwed up with her mother's estate and Johnny was having a good time with some of his cousins her sisters all had kids with different guys who could keep track of them and except that when Audry was away I had to do my own clothes and shoes and cooking so I just ate out or got subs I kind of liked being on my own and little Tony came and went on his own and worked hard at his job he still liked to play pool but I figured at least I knew where he was at night for a while he liked this girl from work and went on a diet and lost about thirty pounds then something happened she started dating some other dude he put the weight right back on then one of those nights before Audry got back from North Carolina I was working the late shift at the store and after we closed at nine-thirty out of nowhere I felt this urge to go see Craig I didn't talk to him or see him for a long time and really didn't think of him much that day but between walking out of the store and getting into my car in the parking lot I made up my mind I was going to look for him so I drove down the South End and went to The Other Side but he wasn't around I had a drink with one

of his friends who said that Craig wasn't doing good but he
hadn't seen him for a few days I had another bourbon and coke
and started to feel good and left The Other Side and down to
the Zone to one of the strip clubs and when I got there a beautiful young chick was wiggling her ass at guys sitting in the
front stools to the tune of the song 'Cut the Cake' and I ordered a double bourbon and coke and drank it down real fast
ordered another one then a pretty black chick with incredible
long legs was dancing and started yelling up at her to do it baby
do it funny how a few drinks and the company how easy everything else could get turned off except for the energy of the
booze and sex driving me and I kept pounding those doubles
down and didn't realize how drunk I was getting I was hollering
up the strippers and cheering them on every now and then one
of them would bend over and shake her ass in front of my face
there were girls working the tables I spent about a hundred dollars talking to one of them as long as the drinks kept coming
she kept talking until finally it was her turn to dance and then I
left and staggered to one of the all-night porn shops browsed
through magazines and looked at all the vibrators and double-
ended dildos there was this huge dildo that had to be a foot
long and five inches around man people use those things like
what the fuck but whatever turns you on then I decided to walk
to Chinatown and get some food and when I was walking
down Washington Street I came closer to a couple who were
making out up against a lamppost looked like a hooker with a
fat middle-aged guy in a suit who was pretty drunk and slurring
his words the hooker was rubbing his crotch and pulling down
his zipper with her other hand she was reaching up inside his
suit pocket and in a second she had his wallet pushed him aside
and ran down an alley the guy was so drunk he fell over when
the hooker pushed him it all happened so fast that by the time
the hooker had the guy's wallet out I had walked past them and

turned around to see it finish and the hooker had to run right by me even in those heels she could fly and she didn't bother to look up and see me but I got a pretty good look at her before she ran down the alley that's when I ran down the alley after her she must have thought I was the guy chasing her and threw off her shoes and started running faster I shouted out Craig don't run it's me Tony and it took a second or two for it to sink in for him then he stopped in his tracks I took him to Chinatown and ordered a big meal I kept drinking bourbon and cokes trying to get him to eat something but he would only poke his finger at the food on his plate and I urged him to just try a little rice or one spare rib I was real drunk by then past the point of no return it was only luck that Audry was away I told him he could have called me if he needed money and he was going to end up in jail or hurt real bad but he was high and he had about eighty bucks that he stole from the guy and told me to take it as part payment for the money he owed me 'cause he was going to pay me back every penny it's funny how when you really love someone it's like family and people's faults you just have to live with I mean with all Frank's problems over the years I guess a lot of other guys would have thrown him out on his ass and some of the guys at work always said Luongo you're a fool you're not helping your brother letting him leech off you and I should throw him out and leave him to his own downfall but he was my brother and if you haven't got family you haven't got nothing and with Craig it was like family I remember that night as drunk as I was talking to him like he was one of my children and I was the father it's strange 'cause in the middle of telling him he needed to change his life he was worth more than what he was doing it hit me that I was already older than my father was when he died and I started to cry in the middle of the restaurant I guess it was the booze but I couldn't control myself Craig came over sat close to me in the booth

170

and put his arm around me and I told him I love you and I
don't want to see you die he said he wasn't going to die and we
left the Chinese place he wanted to go to The Other Side so I
drove to the South End it was after hours and the place was
supposed to be closed but there were a lot of regulars hanging
around and drinking most of the lights were out and music was
real low everyone in there seemed high or drunk by that hour
of the night the place had this odd kind of quiet about it like
one of the boys' rooms right after I used to put one of them to
sleep and in the nightlight light they were still awake Craig and
me sat at our usual table and he rubbed his hand through my
hair we kissed but I don't know if it was 'cause I was so drunk
or I just was feeling different but I felt like it wasn't right so I
pulled away and told him I went looking that night to see him
to say hello and find out how things were turning out not to
start things up with him again but I was afraid now that he was
going to keep doing what he was doing no matter what he
winked at me and smiled we talked a little more and the drinks
kept coming and got stronger until around four in the morning
he passed out I couldn't wake him and the bartender said that
we had to get out of there he had to lock up so I picked him up
and carried him out he still didn't have any shoes on and the
bottom of his nylons were worn through his feet were dirty his
dress was coming off him and his make-up all runny and
smeared he felt so light in my arms then I put him in the front
seat and strapped him in with the seat belt and figured I would
take him to a motel somewhere at least get him a bed for the
night I got my bearings crossed I was drunker than I realized
and I ended up heading out south of town instead of back into
the city so I turned to a side street so I could make a u-turn and
head the other way but it looked like I could drive to the end
and head back out in a direction that I thought I recognized
'cause I was in a part of Roxbury where the old factories and

warehouses used to be and at the end of the side street it looked like I had to drive down an alley to get out the other side and when I made it through the alley I was in the open but everything got all bumpy like and the car bounced up in the air and then I was stuck I tried going forward and back but the wheels were off the ground so I got out to look and the car was hung up on railroad tracks and the rear end of the car was caught on one of the rails one look I knew there was no way I was going to get the car off without a tow truck then I started to panic what if a train came but this was old tracks I was pretty sure and didn't get used no more for a few minutes I ran around the car confused then I opened the other door to wake Craig he was pretty groggy and then suddenly my worst fear was happening I could feel a little tremble under my feet and it got bigger I knew a train was coming so I pulled Craig out and dragged him to the side of the tracks and in a matter of a few moments I could see the train's headlight coming down the track and the ground rumbling louder and louder just then there was a huge fucking shriek when the engineer pulled on the whistle I could hear all this hissing squealing and screeching of the train as the engineer hit the brakes and that engine ran into the car and straight through like it was made of paper cut it right in half by the time the train stopped full the last car was a hundred yards off nearly out of sight of the car my car was burning in two squished half pieces one each side of the track I heard voices people running down the track from the train I picked Craig up put him on my shoulders and walked back towards where I thought Mass. Ave. was I could hear sirens coming from different directions fire trucks ambulances police and by the time I got back to Mass. Ave. I could hardly walk any more so I put Craig down on the steps of a vacant building he was still out of it I was afraid if a cop should come by he might get suspicious then I thought of the car and figured the only thing I could do at that point was to report it stolen there was a phone booth a block away so I called the police to say the car was stolen some time during the night in the South End then back to the steps Craig was still dozing with his head straight down frozen like a statue there in his beat-up dress no shoes stockings runny and torn I sat beside him for a few minutes it was quiet almost no cars on the avenue and no people out walking over towards the harbor the sky was changing color getting lighter I didn't know what the fuck I was going to do with Craig it was one of the times in my life I felt like I left time and the world completely outside of it all maybe what they said the LSD shit was or something I can't really describe that light but somehow being just a shade different not like sex 'cause with sex it always seemed just the moment of having an orgasm you leave your body for this ultimate rush but this was slower the light in the sky was changing the closer to the harbor the lighter it was but it wasn't like I could actually see it change I could only see the effects of the change like it lasted for minutes until the silence was broken when a bus went by then a few cars and more cars it got lighter out and people were out walking to bus stops and I had to be in work at nine in the morning myself but I was stuck there I just didn't know what to do by then Craig was starting to wake up I went across the street to a little breakfast place got some muffins and coffee and back over on the steps I made him take some coffee and food I guzzled down my coffee and was feeling dizzy starting to sober up moving into a hangover feeling at the same time I knew I had to get home Audry already probably called twenty times I had to put a good story together if I was going to get out of this one with the car being wrecked and me being out all night but the funny thing was that usually in a situation like that I would feel real bad and guilty and anxious but this time I was so relaxed it wasn't like me something felt different inside like the knot I usually felt inside my stomach was untied I knew that I had to get home as soon as possible and Craig was awake enough starting to get a little sick and shivering I was a little scared he said not to worry it's what always happened until he got something to get better I asked him where did he want to go and waved down a cab we drove him to a little park off Columbus Ave. I left him sitting on a bench he said his friend lived nearby later in the morning he could clean up and change there I gave him all the money I had which was about fifty bucks and kept enough to pay for my cab home I took my suit coat off wrapped it over him and when we drove away I looked back he already had his feet up on the bench and was asleep when the cab pulled up in front of the house the sun was up so was little Tony who was getting ready for work he didn't say much but looked at me kind of funny since I was without my suit coat and my clothes were messy from all the stuff with the car and carrying Craig he said Ma's been calling all night and the cops called too something about the car and when he left for work I took the phone off the hook to give myself some time to clean up I had to wear a wrinkled shirt and linty suit and none of my shoes had been shined since Audry's mother died so I put an outfit together best I could I always prided myself on having good clothes one of the things I used to think about a lot when I was in display was how good the salesmen got to dress and I knew that if I ever got to be a big-ticket salesman I was going to be known as the best-dressed salesman in the store and since we got discounts I was always buying new suits and shirts and made sure I was the sharpest looking one out on the floor when we were kids we had no clothes and I remember one summer living in a pair of shorts that were Frank's for the whole summer I wore them every day with the same shirt and if it got dirty Ma washed it and hung it out overnight to dry and poor Peter was taller than me and Frank

174

the hand-me-downs fit him real bad and the girls shared what they had Ma I always will remember wore the same dark blue dress and apron every day with stockings and her black shoes and I wanted bad to have nice clothes in high school it kind of worked out that I went to the Voke 'cause in shop we wore overalls and I didn't have to worry I didn't have enough clothes and had to wear the same things every day and before I got into the shower that morning I stripped down and remember having a great shit it was one of those times when sitting on the toilet can be as good as anything and I mean sex too I didn't understand the new kind of sense of relief I was feeling inside then I flushed and stood in front of the mirror to shave my thick stubs showing through when I had a dark beard shadow my extra chins made my face look even fatter and my belly and tits were hanging and my hair was all gone except for the sides which I combed back and I was staring into the mirror trying to figure out who I was and the sight of my ageing body made me kind of disgusted it seemed like yesterday I got out of the Marines bulky and hard and I raised my arms up flexed at least my biceps and arms were still in shape and I showered dressed and got myself into work on time the first thing I felt when I got there even though I kind of felt it before but it was never as strong soon as I put my foot inside the door I didn't want to be there I didn't want to spend another day of my life there and that was the longest day I watched the clock minute by minute for the first time in years I went blank I didn't make one sale everybody said that I should go home I looked real sick the guys used to say that I was going to die out on the sales floor 'cause I never called in sick there was a time I think they were right when I was top salesman and digging the job going in with my new suits and shoes and I thought I would stay at Pratt's until I retired but people change and years pass by quicker than you think suddenly you feel different than when you were ten or twenty years younger I knew there had to be a way for me to get out of there part of my feeling so bad was I was working through a hangover it really got to me a couple of times during the morning I got sick and threw up in the men's room leaning over the toilet bowl thinking about Audry what she was going to say I still hadn't talked to her and as the day went on I kept changing my story where I was all night what happened to the car and when she called the store from North Carolina she seemed calm I thought by then she'd want to have my balls she said she was real worried and stayed up all night worrying but she didn't want to talk about it on the phone she would be home the next day we would talk then she was real matter-of-fact and when I tried to say a few things to feel her out she only said that she didn't want to talk any more until she was home and hung up I passed out when I got home that night then woke up around one in the morning and I couldn't get back to sleep so I was going to go out for a drive until I re-membered that the car was wrecked so I dressed and went out for a walk down Broadway to the Sullivan Square Station the subway cars and buses were shut down but the Schrafts Candy Company building was all lit up and its parking lot full with cars of night-shift employees there were rumors that the company was closing down and if they did I don't know what Peter would do he was there a lot of years and he'd be lost trying to find a decent job with the economy being bad when he first started working there he used to bring home boxes of candy all the time and we would sit around and eat candy until we almost got sick Ma too she loved those chocolate covered cherries and Peter always brought plenty for her but then after a while the idea of those chocolates made us sick Peter said it was the same working in there after a while you couldn't even stand the smell it was a sweet smell like fruit when it's just ready to rot in the air that night coming from the factory I turned around near the

176

Charlestown line and walked back up Broadway to the house still not sure what I was going to say to Audry the next day but somehow feeling like no matter what I said or what she believed something inside me was different something had changed I couldn't quite describe it 'cause it was going on for a while I first noticed it when I fooled around and realized that I could still look Audry in the eye and even love her after all she was the mother of my kids and we were together all those years no one got me any hotter than she did in those early days it was summer and there were some incredible sweaty afternoons sex juices and sweat and sheets soaked body and hair soaked shit you can't keep that spark going for twenty years we're only human I think maybe I loved Craig but not the way I loved Audry I loved Craig more like a son and in the time we were getting closer we had a lot less sex and the sex stopped feeling as good as it did when we were first together but I must have been like a kid in a candy store after all those years with just Audry and then to have him like that but the sex got less interesting the more I cared and worried about him Angela really opened my eyes about how you could just get it on she was always fooling around with someone in the store and could go from that to being a Brownie leader with her daughters so some people don't have all them hang-ups Frank always said he didn't believe in love and he said as far as he was concerned women were all cunts and the only thing they were good for was fucking or having babies and he never met one that wasn't a cunt and the worse he treated them the better they liked it but Frank always picked certain kinds of girlfriends if all you look for is a chick who likes to get shit on that's all you'll find but I always believed in love I could never love anyone the way I loved Audry it didn't mean that we could spend the rest of our life together and everything would be just fine 'cause as years went on most of the time things seemed like they weren't fine but then just when you think you can't take it any more somehow I would see her in a new way like be able to step back and see her with fresh eyes then I knew that I still thought she was sexy and more I knew that I loved the person she was Audry was really a good person she never asked for much for herself she was a great mother and wife but it was hard year in and year out with Audry being afraid to go out too much and me having to do everything on the house and the errands she didn't want to do she was fine in her own element like at home with her regiment of chores and watching her soaps in the afternoon and calling her mother or her mother calling her and staying on the phone for an hour and having supper ready for me and knowing how I felt she hardly never said no when it came to sex and before you know it twenty years pass I finished the house and it was like it needed to be fixed up all over again the boys were almost on their own Johnny was in his last year in high school looking into different colleges I was hoping he would stay in Boston Audry wanted him to go to college in North Carolina he could be near her family we knew he'd get into a good college 'cause his grades were straight A it was a matter of what school he would choose I told him he could go anywhere he wanted and I would help him all I could with paying the tuition and helping with his expenses for books and living the idea that my son was going to college was unbelievable to me I was the first one in the family to even graduate high school Josie graduated college and now Johnny was going to go I only wished Ma was still alive she would have been proud of Johnny sometimes I fantasized what it would be like if Audry and me broke up how I might live what I would do the boys would be on their own there was enough money so that Audry and me would come out of it without too much trouble over that kind of thing maybe she would be happier on her own in North Carolina I could survive I wanted to keep the house maybe buy her share out or I could sell the house and travel or open the business with my part of the money all that stuff ran through my mind that long day at the store the police believed my story about the car being stolen and called to say it was found but totaled when hit by a train when Audry got back she was a lot cooler than I figured she'd be she didn't say much at first and put her things away the boys and me got pizza she had a slice and smoked a cigarette and kept looking at me nodding her head a little I didn't know what she meant by it but it was making me feel uncomfortable the boys went out by then little Tony had his own car he bought with money from his job and they took rides down to Revere Beach to look at girls and when they left and the front door slammed downstairs I was sitting at the kitchen table with her it was the quietest I ever remember any time being for only a few seconds it felt like forever then she asked me really calm so what happened to the car and I told her I went out for a drink with a couple of the guys from work then I wasn't tired so I took a drive up to New Hampshire then took the back road all the way home 'cause it was such a beautiful summer night and by the time I got back to the city it was late and I was hungry so I went to Chinatown ate some Chinese food at one of the all-night places and when I was finished I went back to the car and it was gone at first I thought maybe I parked it in a different place than I remembered so I walked up and down a couple of streets before I realized it was stolen and by then I spent all the cash I had buying some rounds of drinks at the bar and the Chinese food so I didn't have enough for a cab it was starting to get light I thought of calling little Tony and asking him to come down for me but I knew he'd be sleeping I was all worked up 'cause of the car getting stolen so I thought I'd walk home it really isn't that far you know from Chinatown to here if you take the backstreets it only took me about an hour maybe a little more

179

and when I got home little Tony was getting up he said Ma's been calling and I knew you would be automatically thinking the worst then I had to go off to work it was the worst day I ever had on the floor the first time I went blank and I looked at her and looked at her right in the eyes and said the police called today they found the car someone left it on the railroad tracks a train drove through it and split it in half she stared back at me into my eyes said you know Tony it hasn't been easy for me losing my mother you know how much she meant to me this is the hardest thing I've ever had to go through and if I find out that you've been lying to me I'm telling you right now you are going to be the sorriest mother-fucker that ever lived Audry sometimes swore but she hardly never said fuck and I knew she meant business and I told her I knew how hard it was losing your mother I still thought of mine and it still hurt that she was gone it never goes away she put her face in her hands and started to cry it wasn't that I felt guilty about what I did or anything I felt guilty about lying to her I tried to comfort her as much as she would let me and for a while later she was real fragile like that and would break out crying in the middle of the day or in bed a night I felt bad even though I couldn't stand her mother I knew how much she meant to Audry and since Audry never knew her father her mother must have been all that much more important I know that's how I felt even though I did know my father a little it wasn't like he was a real father I kind of see it as I was raised by my mother and that's where the real connection was my father was a far away thing like when years passed we even started to joke about him Ma would tell stories about some of the things he used to do like fall asleep on the sidewalk in front of the house it was strange he could make it all the way home then instead of coming in he slept out on the sidewalk those kinds of things aren't funny when they're happening to a family but when you look back on it after years somehow it's
180

easier to see it and laugh one time when I was about six or seven it was getting near dark and my mother thought my father was in the bar across the street she was just about to strain the spaghetti and she said for me to run across the street and tell Pa to come home for supper when I got to the bar the bartender said he thought my father was at Jon's Place which was a few blocks away so I decided to walk down to Jon's Place when I got there I couldn't find him but one of his friends said he just left and was going to another bar which was a few more blocks away so I walked down to that bar and my father wasn't there there was nobody I recognized so I left and on the way home I took a shortcut through an alley I was a little nervous 'cause it was getting darker I didn't know the neighborhood and I started running but the alley was a dead end so when I got to the end I turned around to go back out and when I did I noticed there was someone over in the corner and it was a guy and he was jerking himself off he couldn't see me he was facing the other way so I took off running and looked back over my shoulder and he was still jerking off never even noticed me and there was light about half way down the alley and a little bit of it reflected back there enough so that I noticed the guy was bald and I could see a little shine off the top of his head and in that moment I knew it was him and I ran all the way home Ma was all worried and everybody already ate the spaghetti I told Ma I couldn't find Pa and she saved me a dish of spaghetti but I couldn't eat I stayed up that whole night thinking about Pa and what he was doing out there it wasn't that I didn't know what he was doing because Frank had already been doing it and told me what it was but Pa doing it and outside like that it was the first time I had serious trouble shitting and I remember then my mother took me to the doctor 'cause I didn't go for a week and they gave me some stuff to take when I got older Ma said even when I was real little I had trouble that way and I was the hardest one of the kids to potty train and I was afraid to shit into the potty and would hold it and the doctor would have to give me enemas and stuff I guess I understood a little better about how fucked up Pa must have been and I kind of pity him more than I hate him or anything I don't know much about Pa or his family I met his brother a few times he was a drunk too and he died from drinking he had some kids but we never kept in touch with them but who knows how it was between Ma and Pa I mean she had five kids and lost three others during pregnancy he must have been at her a lot I always got the feeling from what Ma said that it wasn't something she was all that fond of she saw it more as a duty as a wife than something she was supposed to enjoy besides she said to me more than once when she married my father he was a good looking man she knew he drank but it didn't seem like it was such a problem but in a few years he changed so much that she asked God how could such things happen but she was always more relieved if he got home and passed out after supper than if he kept drinking 'cause if he kept drinking he got to raising hell and would end up hitting her or forcing himself on her she said he was like a different man all sweaty and unshaven with the booze on his breath poor Ma it was strange how that incident seeing my father that night had an effect on me even if he was in a good mood and wanting to be playful which sometimes he could I couldn't look him in the eye and sometimes I would lay awake at night and see him with his back to me and then I started to have dreams about it and when I got older the dreams changed and sometimes I dreamed I was jerking off somewhere and Audry and the boys saw me and stuff like that I went through a period where I doubted what I saw and figured it wasn't Pa that night but someone who looked like Pa and I buried it for a long time as I grew older except for dreams I kind of forgot all about it and only once in the greatest while it might be a year or more when I least expected it out of nowhere like bang there it would be like I was right there that moment running out of the alley seeing him as I looked over my shoulder when I couldn't go to the bathroom Ma would make boiled prunes and I had to eat them when Ma brought me to Dr. Campiglia who was an old Italian doctor with an office on the second floor above Tony the Butcher's in the North End where when Ma did have some extra cash she gathered us up on the bus to the North End and bought ground meat for meatballs and Tony's hot sausages and Ma brought me to the doctor a couple of times he could never find anything wrong with me he spoke only Italian so he talked with Ma I understood a little too and I remember Ma saying something about why they couldn't figure out what was wrong with my stomach and Dr. Campiglia in Italian said the problem is not in his stomach it's in his head pointing to his head and Ma said she didn't understand what he meant I didn't neither but when I grew up I understood what he meant when I was blocked up it was never just constipation where you drink some stuff and you shit your brains out that stuff had no effect on me when my system got blocked up it didn't go until it was ready when Audry got back from North Carolina I had a bout then ten days until I was able to go there was something about the way Audry was acting those first few days I expected her to be more pissed and giving me the third degree every time I made a move but she wasn't saying much of anything one day Frank said did I know I was being watched I didn't know what he was talking about and he said by a dick a private dick it was when Frank had his fall at the restaurant he slipped in the kitchen did some damage to his back and was out on workman's compensation the restaurant was fighting him over it he had some kind of trial and his doctor went to court to say how Frank wouldn't be able to work again 'cause of the damage done to his back in the fall and Frank would need a permanent disability at the time the insurance company was investigating Frank and making sure his claim wasn't fake it was hard to figure with Frank he had us all convinced the way he carried himself real slow around and was walking with a cane but the insurance company was checking him out and Frank said sometimes they had private dicks watch you and try to get pictures and evidence that you weren't really hurt so he was on the lookout and noticed someone in a car half way down the block then he noticed him there the next day so he was watching from behind his window on the first floor when I went downstairs and got in my car to drive away and that's when the guy started up his car and took off following me then it all made sense about Audry being nonchalant about things since she was back she hired a private detective to watch me I didn't say anything to her at first I played it real cool I was being real cool anyway since she got back staying close to home getting the insurance stuff taken care of over the car and then I went out and bought a new car I don't know why but I knew somewhere in the back of my mind that something was going to change soon I was going to leave Pratt's I was to a point that whenever I walked into the front door I felt like I was being strangled the days were longer and longer and my sales were getting so low that the month Audry's mother died I was low man in the department in all my years selling I was never low man it just didn't bother me 'cause I didn't care no more that's the way I was if I cared about something I could do anything but if I didn't it was like it could fall off the world as far as I was concerned I let the dick follow me once Frank pointed him out it was pretty obvious and thought that's what I should do be a private dick this guy wasn't too good at it and when Audry told me what she paid the guy for what he did I figured it had to be one of the best rackets going but after about a week of letting the guy follow me around I was real pissed at Audry and scared too 'cause if the guy was following me for a while he might have something on me but then I figured out that Audry must have hired him when she got back from North Carolina and if that was so then the guy had nothing on me I didn't know exactly what to do angry as I was that Audry would go behind my back and all but I was thankful that she didn't do it earlier 'cause she would have had me and with that kind of stuff against me she could have a pretty good case in divorce court and one thing I knew all along was that if something ever happened between Audry and me she wouldn't get any more than what she had coming I waited then one day I told Audry that I found out about the detective that she didn't trust me no more and would stoop to hire a detective to follow me she wanted to know how I found out and I told her it wasn't too hard and I don't know what she was paying him but he wasn't worth much 'cause I was on to him from the first day I only waited until I could figure out who he was and what he was doing the last thing I would have thought was she would pull something like that so I didn't expect he was someone Audry hired I told her if she didn't trust me how could we even stay together I always trusted her and never gave a second thought that she would do something behind my back she sat down and said that she had some things she wanted to say that's the way Audry was she could keep things inside for a long time and I'd know that something was wrong even from the way she might be keeping to herself and all but she'd stay quiet and calm and finally she would say Tony I have some things I need to say to you and she could sit down calmly and tell me what was on her mind that was the opposite of me I wish I could stay calm and keep things inside instead I feel like I got to explode all the time but that's the way I was and no matter if I tried to stay calm and talk steady I just couldn't so Audry lit a cigarette at the kitchen table and I sat down at one of the chairs and at that moment I still didn't

know what to expect 'cause I still wasn't sure that the dick was-
n't following me before Audry got back if he was and knew
about the night with Craig and me losing the car Audry was
going to put it to me and it would mean the end she said Tony
it's been so hard losing my mother and feeling like I didn't get
any support from you all the years I stood beside you through
everything and took on your family as my own and lived with
them through all the bullshit I've had to deal with and that
whole time you never gave a tiny bit of that back to me where
my family was concerned you always had this attitude that
there's something wrong with my family and my mother and
sisters and maybe so we're all a little fucked up but Jesus Christ
Tony take a look at your family they're not the Brady Bunch
either you know and you come off like you're so much above
my family and not only that Tony I know you and I know you
can't not be thinking about fucking around and I don't believe
you when you tell me you were out with the guys for a drink or
took a drive to New Hampshire what is there to not make me
think that maybe even once out of all those times you weren't
where you said and you were with someone you didn't want me
to know about there was a lot I had to deal with when I got
back from North Carolina Tony I was already thinking I could
never forgive you for being so fucking cold when my mother
was dying and the way you came right back after two days and
I'm calling from down there and you're out all night what the
fuck did you expect me to do Tony how much more can I take
I had to get a handle on a few things and a long time ago when
I suspected something my sisters said I should have you followed and I never did but when I got back from North Carolina I felt so alone and helpless I didn't know where else to turn
Tony I'm telling you I was at the end of my rope and closer
than I've ever been to just leaving you you know everybody
loves you and you're the guy who people always say will do
186

anything for anybody but for Christ's sake Tony the person
who needs you more than anyone needed you more than ever
and you weren't there for me Tony you weren't there even
when you were in North Carolina your mind was miles away
and I wasn't the only one who noticed it you don't think my
sisters didn't pick up on it 'cause they did and to be honest if I
was seeing it from where they are I'd be thinking that my sister
is married to a shit just like they were probably thinking not to
say they were never married to shits but they had the good
sense to get out while the getting was good sometimes I feel
that except for the boys I can't think of why I stayed here over
twenty years I've done everything you ever asked me to do Tony and you always said that you had no complaints about me as
a wife sure you could say you weren't getting enough as you
wished you were but who the fuck is Tony the grass is always
greener next door you know but maybe next door they think
your grass is greener it's all in your mind I don't understand sex
Tony and I wish it was better between us but I thought we had
other things going between us than just that and then when you
can be so insensitive like you were when my mother died I just
couldn't believe it I felt like I was living a fool's life for twenty
years and one of the few times I ever really needed you you let
me down when have I let you down Tony when and by now
Audry had gone from this real calm and cool talking to tears
and I sat there looking at my hands on the table feeling like the
biggest piece of shit ever I always said my family came first my
whole life I did nothing but sacrifice for my family but I guess
you just can't spread yourself out like that someone is going to
not get theirs and Audry was right for the most part when I
think of it I always took her for granted and never gave it a second thought how she took care of the boys and the house and
me and my clothes and did a lot for my mother in those late
years when Gina was working and I was always doing for Frank

or Peter or Ma or the boys and never for Audry but Audry
never asked and always was quiet and if it seemed like something was bothering her and I asked her what was wrong she
would say nothing everything's fine so what was I to do but she
was right I don't know what it was that made me so stubborn
about being there more when her mother was dying even if I
did hate the old bitch the way I did I could have helped out at
least for Audry's sake there's nothing worse than that feeling
when you think so much one way and suddenly you find out
that things might not be exactly the way you thought and you
have this idea of yourself and bang like out of nowhere the
whole thing comes crashing down it wasn't like I thought myself perfect or anything but I always thought Audry had everything she needed as a wife and sure I was old fashioned about
things and a husband's place and a wife's place in the home but
Audry was old fashioned too she liked it the way things were
she didn't want to be one of those modern women but the
hardest thing for me to swallow was the fact that Audry didn't
have everything she needed and what she needed the most I
could have given to her and worse I was more likely to be there
for a stranger and that really hurt but maybe there was some
truth to what she said 'cause as long as I could remember I was
known as a guy who would do anything for you and even at
work over the years I would go out of my way for customers
and drive to their houses on the way home if they were having
trouble with their new vacuum or washer and help them out
and all the guys at work would say I was crazy to do things like
that but it just seemed like the thing to do it wasn't like I actually thought in my head I'm trying to be a good guy or anything
but if someone needed a ride home and it was in the opposite
direction from where I lived who cares you drive them home or
if there's an old person at the supermarket waiting for a cab and
it's cold or raining or even if it's not you smile and offer them a

ride what always was strange to me was how many people would not take the ride and rather stand in the cold and pay for a cab I guess I learned all that stuff from Ma she was always having me do for people like go to the market with old Mrs. Tedesco who lived downstairs from us and help her carry her bags home and run down to the square and do errands for someone in the neighborhood and when it snowed I shoveled our house and the houses next door and across the street Ma would never let me take money or anything it was what you did she said I used to go to the church and help with the chores like raking leaves in the fall and spring cleaning Ma never asked she would just say in Italian Saturday morning you go to the church at nine to help out I liked church the best when there wasn't a mass going on there was something that got to me about the quiet if there were only a few people in there the way the footsteps would echo and everyone acting real holy like they were in God's presence as soon as they walked through that big door touched their fingers into the holy water and made the sign of the cross when I was a boy and wanted to be a priest I would sit in the church some mornings trying to take it all in and find the true holy feeling and I would talk to God and ask him please make a sign to me so I can be sure he was really there I never did see a sign but Father Gian Carlo always said you could never really be sure God didn't give those kind of signs it was a matter of having faith that God was there I guess the older I got it was harder for me to keep my faith but even Einstein said there was a God and when I was an altar boy there were always things we would volunteer for like to go to sing Christmas songs to the old people in the nursing home or do a food drive and collect canned food and whatever else for the poor or sell raffle tickets to benefit the sisters who lived at a convent in New Hampshire where they made the communion wafers we took on Sundays there was always something to do

and I was always doing and Ma said everywhere she went people said to her that Tony is the nicest boy and I think that was
important for Ma 'cause everyone knew Pa was a drunk and
when Frank started getting into trouble she must have felt it
was a reflection of who she was so I tried to make Ma proud
and it wasn't really that it was that hard or anything I liked people and being around them and doing things they liked me for
hey it bothered me too knowing about Pa and how everybody
in the neighborhood would hear him going on in the middle of
the night and banging things up and then Frank's teachers
sending notes home from school when he got into trouble and
the principal wanting to talk with poor Ma not even able to
speak English crying how she was doing everything she could
do to raise a good family so I did what I could to make it a little
easier for her it was Audry's saying everything she said to me
that night that made me aware maybe I should have been doing
some of that stuff for Audry too what hurt most was to think
how long Audry had felt these things and not said much oh
maybe once in a great while but mostly Audry was the kind of
person that everything was ok when you asked her and suddenly I was this mean bastard who cared more about strangers than
his own family I wondered how many times a day or a week or
a month I might have let her down like the time I did some
carpentry work for Bonnie Wheeler the store cashier and it
took me three or four of my days off and I wouldn't take any
money that was ten years before and Audry was jealous 'cause
she thought I had the hots for Bonnie I guess I did I had the
hots for everyone but that's not why I did things for people the
time when Peggy LaRonga our neighbor's car broke down I
drove her to Providence to see her sister who was dying in the
hospital Peggy was seventy years old I just did it 'cause that's
what I do but Audry said all those times I was off doing things
for other people did I ever once think that she might need me

to do something for her or maybe the boys needed me to do something for them I lost it at that moment 'cause suddenly after all the years of living and working for my family it was like I never did a fucking thing and I picked up one of the kitchen chairs and smashed it to pieces screaming to her what the fuck is it she wanted from me Audry cried she said that's just what I mean Tony some things never change I tore out of the house in a rage and drove but I didn't want to drive to New Hampshire so I drove up to the north shore and ended up in Gloucester at one of the beaches with a little footbridge it was getting dark there were only a few people walking on the beach I was never a strong swimmer the tide was going out I knew if I really wanted I could jump in swim out as far as I could and I would never make it back but I was too scared and I had this feeling like I would explode there was no place for all my anger and rage to go like I could just smash my head on a wall just to relieve myself I walked down the beach toward some rocks and on top of this big hill of rocks was a mansion and the lights were just coming on I wondered if the same fucking stuff went on in those places and what were they eating how did they fuck and don't tell me the lady of the house in her quietest hours didn't use her God-given fingers and think about getting the living shit fucked out of her by her Greek gardener and what the fuck did they do with all that space I thought about Craig the night when I last saw him I was already driving my brand new Toyota and he was probably high or giving someone a blow job so he could buy drugs and I thought of Ma and Audry and the boys all these different scenes from my past were racing in my mind like on a movie screen I loved Audry so much and the thought that I could hurt her so much made me feel like I was a complete failure and the biggest piece of shit on earth just like Pa was and all this stuff was whirling around in my head so fast I thought if it didn't stop I would go

crazy it was hard for me to accept that maybe I wasn't the father and husband I thought I was and what Audry said was it
was more than just working and paying bills and looking good
to the neighbors I knew that but it was her words that everything always had to be my way that really stabbed me too like
all the years we were together it was ok with her that what I
said goes it wasn't like I never asked her for her opinion no
matter what we were planning I always asked her what she
thought and listened then went right ahead and did exactly
what I wanted when it wasn't always the best for everybody I
made choices that were sometimes the best for me like insisting
Johnny go to Boston College so he can live at home instead of
New York University where he wanted to go Johnny got into a
bunch of schools but I thought if he could get into a local college it would be best so he could live at home and that way we
could save on the tuition and we'd all be closer and Audry
asked did it ever cross my mind that maybe Johnny wanted to
live away from us for a while why would he want to live away
from us I couldn't understand and beside he was too young to
be living in some place like New York City and Audry said that
Johnny was almost the same age I was when I joined the Marines and went off to Korea no matter how old your kids get I
guess you always see them like children and when I got to the
end of the beach there was a big sign that said private property
keep out where the grounds of the mansion started and some
lights were lit up bright from the windows of the place I was
tempted to climb up the rocks and have a peek in but I figured
they had dogs or something Frank always liked the voyeur
thing when we were kids a few times he took me down the
street and we hid in the bushes where a lady who lived alone
kept her shades up while she did chores around the house naked Frank beat off but I was too scared and even when Frank
was older he always kept a pair of binoculars right by his win-

dow 'cause he liked checking out windows at night and said it wasn't watching them have sex that he liked most but what he liked more than anything was to watch a naked chick clean her apartment they say the rich folks can get pretty wild and I started to imagine some kinky orgy going on up there but I knew that sooner or later I had to go back home and face Audry and when I got home she was in the bedroom watching television with the door closed the apartment was dark except for the television light coming out between the door and the frame I tripped in the kitchen 'cause the broken chair pieces were still on the floor and that wasn't like Audry in the past she would have picked them up like the time I got mad and threw a pot of boiling spaghetti on the kitchen wall and she spent an hour scraping it all up and Gina found out what happened she heard the noise downstairs and she said sometimes I was just like Pa I tapped on the bedroom door before I went in and called her name she was watching the screen on her side of the bed with her back to me I sat on the edge of the bed and called her name again only quieter in the months after that when I was at work I tried to get back that enthusiasm that I had when I was number one I couldn't there were days when I knew if I really applied myself I could be tops in the department again I could still sell double and triple service policies and hardly never sold advertised merchandise all the guys had their own methods of trading up some just made it seem like that cheap washer was the biggest piece of shit going others like Mike Cordano would take the order right away and only at the very last second when he was ready to ring the sale up he would stop and say to his customers hang on one second and go into the back room for a smoke and come out and say that he just called the warehouse and they had a couple of discontinued washers there that were far superior to the one they were purchasing and for a few dollars more he could make sure they got one if they ordered to-

193

day one of the guys would take the order for the advertised washer then write the order form on top of the top-of-the-line washer and not say a thing and nine out of ten by the time he was done writing up the sale the customer would ask some kind of question about the top-of-the-line like how much does this one cost and he would roll up the form place it in his pocket and then go into his pitch I always told the customer everything they wanted to know about the advertised machine and said what a great deal it was and how happy I would be to take an order for one but would they allow me just a few minutes to show them what a real top-of-the-line machine can do and it was how you got them over there and then convinced them that if I was going to purchase a machine for myself this is the one I wanted not everyone went for it and sometimes you might start to trade them down to a less expensive machine but in my day I sold more top-of-the-line than anyone but some-how I wasn't satisfied any more I felt that I was still young enough that I wanted a new challenge the stocks had reached the bottom and some people said they might even start to come back a little if Ronald Reagan was elected president so my profit sharing could get better it would be a good time to look around for my business again Audry was all for it though she said she didn't want me to risk all the profit sharing and savings I'd worked too hard to lose it all if something should happen but if the stocks would only come up a little I'd still stand to make some money and I'd use that for the business and still keep the savings which was a good amount though Johnny's college was going to take a chunk of it Johnny and Audry got their way and Johnny was in college at New York University he got some of it on scholarship 'cause he was a good student but I was paying the rest and his spending money down there but I was real proud and one of the happiest days of my life was the first check I had to write for his tuition no matter how hard I
194

tried I couldn't get him to go to Boston College I would have put my foot down and insisted that's where he go but Audry and me were trying to work things out between us and one of the things that always bothered her most was when I got to pulling my weight around and having things my way that night I got back from the drive to the beach and sat down on the edge of the bed we talked for hours it was like when we were first together there was always something deep between us sometimes you can just lose touch with that and she cried in my arms and I cried we talked about the old days when we met at the store and how fast time goes by how some things seemed better than either one of us hoped but in some ways they were worse and I promised her I would try to change and that sometimes it was hard for me too us being different 'cause I was the kind of guy who liked to be sociable and Audry liked to keep to herself and didn't like being with people besides her family she knew I was always into sex and over the years it got kind of hard for me 'cause she had her own hang-ups being shy about certain things as parents at least we were both proud of the boys they were good kids never got into any serious trouble and Johnny going to college we must have been doing something right it was a long time since we had sex but that night when our hugging started getting a little heavy we started kissing and did it real good for the first time in a long time it was our usual way it seemed like no matter how you might think you want something different when we got into it with each other it was exactly the same way we kissed a while and I played with her titties I licked them then she laid me back on the bed and jerked me off and did me a little then I turned her over opened her legs and ate her starting nice and easy and building up then she said to me come inside her and I slid in we kissed and went at it for a while kissing hard me playing with her tits I always tried to wait for her to come before I did sometimes it

195

was hard 'cause I would be ready and she wouldn't be so I would hold off by trying to get my mind outside of what we were doing for a few seconds think about work or something and that would give me the break I needed to go a few more minutes Audry had real spastic loud orgasms but over the years she kind of started to do this heavy but quiet breathing groan instead 'cause she was afraid of the boys hearing her and there were times when I wondered if she ever faked it and I asked her and all she said was that I shouldn't ask her things like that it made her uncomfortable in the old days we could do it out in the living room or kitchen I used to bend her over the kitchen table and once I even got her out into the hallway in the middle of the night and we did it on the stairs of my old apartment she was really turned on she kept asking what if somebody comes but she was hotter than I ever seen her but that night of the big scene when we did it even though it was our usual way we had done it time and time again something was a little different and when Audry came she had these long shivers like the night she came all those years ago on the steps in the hallway and when we finished we slept really deep it was the longest sleep I had in years and in the morning it was quiet but it was like somehow a lot of the tension that had been in the air and building and building wasn't there anymore and so after that things just went on for me and Audry I knew how close she was to leaving me and the more I thought about it the more scared I got but me making threats that I would do something crazy or anything like that wouldn't work it was like I was fighting for my life to keep her and we didn't do it for a while after that but we were closer than we were in a long time and started doing more touching we went to New York City to help get Johnny started at school Audry cried when we were driving home since little Tony was still living with us Johnny was the first one to leave home little Tony wasn't going anywhere they loved him at the

196

sporting goods warehouse and he got a couple of raises and he bought himself a used Caddie I thought it was too much car for him but that's what he wanted this big white four door Caddie and the first month he had it he got into an accident he said it wasn't his fault but he was cited for reckless driving I told him as long as he was living with us he still had to live under my rules and if he got into any more trouble with the car he was going to have to sell it it was hard for me to discipline little Tony I felt bad for him being so big and in the time he was out of high school he got even bigger and he didn't seem to have a lot of friends and the ones he had only hung out with him 'cause he had the big car they could drive around the only thing he seemed interested in outside of work was pool and he played pool almost every day I didn't know anything about the game but I heard he was real good at it so I couldn't stop him from doing one of the only things he was good at doing it made him feel good about himself knowing people thought he was a good pool player he wasn't home very much and most of the time he was working or at the pool hall or driving around with a friend looking for chicks we let him come and go as he pleased and with Johnny off at college in New York suddenly the house was so different and quiet with just me and Audry it forced us to be more in touch with each other 'cause without the boys there were no distractions it was just the two of us face to face Audry had dinner ready when I got home from work and we had breakfast together in the morning she still didn't like to go out much so I did the shopping and ran the errands when I was working she talked to her sisters on the phone and watched the soaps months went by and I had a hard time trying to understand how fast the time had gone with just the two of us alone again in some ways it was like the old days we started talking about more deeper things than the weather or what the boys needed or taking my mother to the doctor what was the news

how much business I wrote at the store and what was the store
gossip but we were talking about things like death and love and
life it wasn't like when we were first together when we talked
about all those things back then I don't think we really knew
what we were talking about so we had this great excitement like
we were going to take on the world together then before you
know it the boys need shoes again or Teresa took Anna and left
'cause my brother Peter was hitting her again years go by with a
bunch of these kinds of things happening but now with Ma
dead and Audry's mother dead twenty years of struggling to
keep our marriage together and raising the boys it was like we
were in our twenties again 'cause we still didn't know anything
about all the big things in life but it was like we knew we didn't
know and weren't going to be able to figure it out that made it
easier we often found ourselves looking at each other and
shrugging our shoulders thinking who knows at the exact same
time I never saw Craig again after that last time when the car
got wrecked he never called and I never went out looking for
him there were days when I felt like it all never happened then
there were days when it was too real like it happened yesterday
and it was going to come back to haunt me and it did when
everybody started talking about the Aids thing this new sex disease that made herpes look like a runny nose it was getting
passed around mostly by queers and people were dying and
then I started to get scared for him and then scared for me then
they said there was a way you could get tested to see if you had
it it was a strange thing the way you didn't just die from it but
you could catch a cold and die from that I didn't want to get
tested I didn't want to know and then I thought about Audry
'cause me and her had been getting on during the time I was
with Craig and they said it wasn't just sex between two guys sex
between anyone and you could catch it and people who used
drugs and needles were getting it too it was kind of like this
198

wrath of God was coming down on everything or something and one day at the store when I saw Angela then I remembered her and we didn't go all the way but we sure were swapping some spit and I thought about how if you got it everyone you got it on with after that might get it and pass it on to everyone they got it on with when I thought about all the guys he was with and that he used needles for shooting drugs I figured he was a prime person to get the fucking disease and then after all the times we did it there was a good chance I had it it was never that I was afraid of dying or anything but who would ever think you could die from fucking though when I was talking about Aids with the guys at work one of them said people used to die from the clap all the time and I never thought of that but at first I was as worried about Audry and the boys finding out as I was about dying then people were getting it from blood donations and stuff and it was like a black death who would have known after how far mankind had come sex would be killing people off the older I got I was less religious it's not that I stopped believing in God but I stopped going to church every week but during that time there were some Sunday mornings I got up and went to mass and Audry didn't know what was up with me and kept asking was I all right but I was going to church and praying a lot and asking God not to let me get Aids like with all the fucking problems in the world he would listen to me and stop me from getting it but I was so afraid I didn't know what else to do I couldn't go to the doctor 'cause he was our family doctor and I heard there were these clinics where you could go and they didn't take your name just gave you a number and you call back a few days later but then I realized that I didn't want to know if I had it I had it and I might have even given it to my own wife like think of it killing your own wife by making love to her it was all too fucking much so I went to church and prayed for Craig and hoped he didn't have

it and that maybe he got himself straight and went back to
school like he said he would but for months I couldn't think of
anything but the fact that I could have Aids and I might be dying and maybe Audry and Angela too I knew I should get myself tested 'cause if I did have the disease I owed it to them to
tell them but how could I I wondered even if I did have it
could I go to them and tell them Audry especially how so I got
all the information I could and called numbers where you could
ask questions and I had to do it all on the sly so no one would
know and they still weren't sure how it worked but it took a
while before you even showed it in your body so I could have it
and it wouldn't show if I got tested any-way one of the first
signs was that you lose weight so I started forcing myself to eat
and drink things like milkshakes and doing exercises again it
was the first time in maybe fifteen years I had done any exercises I could only do a few push-ups and sit-ups at a time I came a
long way from my days in the Marines when I could do fifty
push-ups like nothing I started walking when I was feeling
stressed instead of taking rides since I had a car I took rides and
when I drove around I used to get something to eat at some
point during the ride like donuts or a hamburger but then I
started walking and I stopped eating 'cause it was harder to eat
while I was out walking then when I was in my car whether it
was in the day or the middle of the night if I was worried about
things I did my best to keep it from Audry but sometimes she
would say to me what's wrong Tony you seem like your mind is
a thousand miles away one time when I was out walking I
thought about Craig and without a second thought I walked up
to a phone booth and took out my wallet 'cause I still had the
number of his friend where he used to crash it wasn't that I
wanted to see him I just wanted to know was he ok and maybe
his friend knew but the number was no longer in service I got
this cold chill over me walked for hours it wasn't that what I

did was wrong or that I felt bad about it it was that others would think it was wrong and what a way for everyone to find out to have me and maybe Audry die because I cheated what a crazy fucking life I just couldn't understand how one thing could lead to another in such a huge way but that's the way things were people were sick and dying all over the country I'm sure there were guys out there who already passed it on to their wives and I wouldn't be the first one like I always said nothing you could think of hasn't already been done and after about a year went by it was hard not to think about what happened between me and Craig 'cause day to day it was in the news and everyone was talking about it they said straight people were passing it along too and almost overnight people who used to fool around a lot started getting scared I could see it around the store how all the people single or married it didn't make no difference were changing their habits and had to be thinking to themselves about who they'd been fucking and who that person had been fucking and when I think of it there was a lot of fucking going on in the seventies not to say there's not always a lot of fucking going on but it was much more open at least 'cause while there was always some shifty stuff going on at the store when I started working there it was in the seventies when all the guys were letting their hair down and the chicks wearing those hot pants and what else one week Bill Nardella fucked four different chicks from the store and even he was saying it was time to be more careful he was using rubbers again even if the chicks were on birth control that last year at the store I had one of my best years of earnings ever but a lot of it was 'cause the prices on all the merchandise had gone up when there was a price increase there was an increase in my commissions but I daydreamed my shifts away thinking about when I would be out of there it was like a slow hum life then going to work coming home having dinner with Audry watching television going

to bed early and when I couldn't sleep I took a walk the worst part of the night was always around four in the morning I didn't mind being up at five or three or one but four was the time I dreaded the most it was when my mind was the least in control and my thoughts would race and it was so dark and quiet like it wouldn't end then in the fall the guy who owned the storefront across the street put it up for sale again he had been renting to a woman who started a beauty salon but she went out of business at first he wanted too much money it wasn't that I didn't have it I didn't think it was worth what he was asking and I told him what I was willing to pay and said if he called me within a month I'd take it after that my next offer might be less and three weeks later he called and said he would take my offer and suddenly this new fear took hold of me like it was really going to happen after all the years of thinking about it and wishing it I was going to start my own business I went into the store the very next day and gave my notice all the guys said I was crazy to leave now after all the years I built up and I should not forget all those before me who tried to leave for something better and were sorry I was too old now to be risking everything I had what if it didn't work out I'd lose all my profit sharing my savings even my house and in some ways they had a point I thought about all those things but in other ways they were just jealous 'cause over the years one thing was certain that they were all as unhappy as me there some of them were miserable and hated Pratt's and all of them smoked too much and had ulcers and took stuff for their stomachs they were under so much pressure to sell and selling just came so natural for me it never was that stressful from where I was I just got bored with it and a lot of them would have left if they could and Tony Deluca always talked about opening a horse stable and giving riding lessons and Nick Luciano always talked about buying a bigger boat and taking people out on fishing
202

trips but they always just talked any of them could have done it if they wanted but they were afraid that if it didn't work out they'd be stuck without jobs to make enough for their lifestyle and all their savings gone maybe their houses too but look how miserable you all are I said but secretly they were glad I was going even though I wasn't top salesman any more they always had it against me the way I came in like I did and outsold them all year after year and I told Ms. Clarkson the new personnel manager I didn't want any kind of party or anything 'cause anyone who worked at the store as long as I did would automatically get a party of some kind she said people would want to throw me a party I had a lot of friends in the store but I told her flat out that I wouldn't come so she would be best to discourage it I was keeping real close to home I only went out for walks or to run errands otherwise I was home with Audry or working it was a long time since I'd last been with Craig and I was feeling good and lost some of my extra weight from all my walking and push-ups and sit-ups and was hoping that if nothing happened to me by then it probably wasn't going to happen though they said it could stay inside you for longer before it showed up and started doing things I wondered about Craig sometimes where he was how he ended up and I still sometimes thought of him when I jerked off but it was strange no matter how hard I tried I couldn't remember exactly what he looked like once in a great while his face would come flashing by in my mind when I didn't expect it like when I'd be in the middle of talking to a customer or taking a turn while I was driving in the car but if I tried to remember his face I couldn't only little things like his light skin or his blond hair or his blue eyes or the earrings he wore when he was dressed up or how he could bat his eyelashes when he had all that stuff on them and I always remembered how skinny he was like when I put my arms around his waist he used to wear boys-size blue jeans and even they would hang off him but it's that way with people you know in the past even people you loved and slept with unless you saw them or had photographs to remind you there was no way you could remember them perfectly I still used to think of Laura great love of my life besides Audry and maybe in her own way more important than Audry and couldn't remember everything about her only her freckles or her curly hair little things like that I couldn't picture her completely in my mind so it was strange to jerk off thinking about somebody in the past 'cause if I didn't remember how they looked you kind of had to imagine it and so it's not like jerking off to that person but jerking off to who I imagine is that person with Craig and me the first few times we did it it was animalistic 'cause after I saw him a while it changed and the sex was never like it was those first few times my feeling about jerking off was always it doesn't matter what you fantasize about it's only in your head and even though me and Audry had practically stopped doing it I still liked jerking off as much as when I was a kid I could do it all day if I had the chance got to the point with Audry and me we spent our time together and I kissed her when I went off to work and when I got home and we put our arms around each other at night in bed but that's about as far as it went it bothered me that we lost that part of our marriage but as I got older I felt less and less shitty that I wasn't able to fuck all the time Frank never let up no matter what he always had a new girlfriend it was always the same too he kept them around for a year or maybe two then started cheating on them until they found out and eventually they'd leave and the new girlfriend move in but sometimes it took longer than you would think I could never believe how women could cling to Frank one of his girlfriends even told him that she didn't care if he cheated she loved him and would be there for him when he got home he had to throw her out by force and then there were the two that got into a fist fight at the bar at the tavern and they had to call the cops in Frank loved it especially since his new girlfriend beat up his old girlfriend and when I left the store to start the ice cream business he wanted to be part of the business and did every different kind of pleading and begging but I stayed firm I knew him better than he knew himself he already had been running a book business on the side since he was officially given a disability from his fall at the restaurant he walked around with a cane and a little bit of a limp which I was never sure he faked or was real but he was running his own little racket making plenty and collecting a monthly disability check but he still didn't have no money he offered to have his monthly disability check signed over to me if I took him in as a partner I told him in twenty years you never paid me a nickel in rent while you live in my house now you want me to take you in as a business partner it was so easy for me to do all the money business over buying the property the lawyer I hired said it was all just moving paper around and he was right one day we showed up and signed a bunch of things and it was over I signed a bunch of forms at the store to transfer my retirement and my profit sharing money and suddenly I owned this property across the street from the house I paid cash and still had some profit sharing left over to buy all the things I would need to fix the place up it needed a lot of work and I planned to spend the winter doing all of the work myself and then have a grand opening in the spring so I left the store after twenty-five years just like that I worked right up to my last day and in twenty-five years I never called in sick and some people thought it wasn't the right thing to do to say you didn't want a party 'cause everyone who worked there as long as I did got a party but on my last day Mr. Kelly the new manager called a meeting in the furniture department before the store opened and made this nice speech about me and what kind of employee I was all the years and handed me this giant card everyone in the store signed and some just said good luck other people wrote some nice things about how much they liked me and all that the guys in the department said that they finally drove me out like they said they would when I started in sales and Angela wrote how much she'll remember that one time we worked inventory day together inventory day was when they close the store down once a year and everyone had to do inventory for a day with a partner but Angela and me never did inventory day together as partners I knew what she meant thank God Audry didn't 'cause she read the card but that made me feel real good 'cause I often wondered did she ever think of me any more like I knew she had a few more flings in the store but after Aids I think she started keeping it close to home like a lot of people but I still thought of her and that night in the car her doing herself and doing me I went home that night finished my last shift after all those years getting to know so many people many of them were working at the store when I started in display I said good- night to everyone on my way out and I never once went back it wasn't on purpose I told everyone I was nearby and I wouldn't be going nowhere and I'd come in and say hi but I never did and before long it's too long and not long ago they closed the old Central Square store down it was the oldest Pratt's store in the country and they closed it down to put a mall in there with all these little stores inside so I never saw anybody again and in all the time none of them ever came by the ice cream store like they said they would but that's the way things go I left my last shift on a Saturday the very next Sunday morning I was across the street at the store and for the next seven months worked morning noon and night by myself seven days a week getting the place in working condition everything needed repair from floor to windows and walls I stripped banged and painted it was almost like building the place from the ground up after

206

Christmas that year I started to talk with people about franchises who had soft ice cream who had homemade the money was in soft 'cause you whipped it up so much but I decided that I didn't want to franchise who needed them I bought all the necessary freezers and equipment and opened my own place without any debt to anybody else and called it Tony's Ice Cream and I bought my ice cream from who I wanted to buy it from and I sold soft ice cream and regular ice cream and I had a company in Rhode Island do this great sign for me and it came just in time for when we opened I was still putting the finishing touches on the outside paint and I needed at least one more big freezer but I figured I could make it through the first season I didn't want to overextend myself so that if something went wrong I'd be screwed and I knew if I sold a lot of ice cream I'd go buy some somewhere quick if I couldn't keep enough in the freezers I already had I could buy supermarket ice cream if I needed and scoop it into a cup and make good return then after all the planning and building I did I decided people didn't hang out much inside ice cream places so I took out the big front picture window boarded it up put two take-out windows there and the city said it would be ok to put some tables and chairs out front for people and Audry thought I was crazy out there at midnight keeping the neighborhood awake with my sawing and banging but I had my mind made up to open on May first and nothing was going to stop me after months of work and trips to the lumber yard and the hardware store then trying to buy all the equipment I went around looking to buy used but most of it was all overpriced fucking junk so I bought all brand new stuff it cost me a fortune and I had to go into my savings which I didn't want to do but I used up all my profit sharing and retirement money faster than I thought I would then at twelve o'clock in the afternoon on the first of May we opened I took out an advertisement in the *Som-*

erville Journal for the four weeks in a row announcing our opening and we had big balloons and on Memorial Day I rented one
of those search-lights that shoots into the sky and that was the
first weekend I did any business up to that time there were days
when it was cold and rainy I was there from twelve to ten and
didn't sell one ice cream it was real scary for a while and I was
afraid if any of the guys from the store ever dropped by and
saw that I was doing no business I would be embarrassed I
knew I had to hang in there but I was tapping into the savings
heavier than I wanted to Audry told me that I shouldn't do
things like rent the big light which was expensive but I always
felt that you had to spend money to make money and that
summer I worked seven days a week from twelve when I
opened to ten at night closing time and Audry helped out a lot
or just hung around 'cause she was across the street she would
bring me my supper every night work the counter while I ate I
didn't really do much business that first year I started to think
that I fucked up and would be sorry just like the guys at work
told me would happen but what I remember most was how
good I felt to be sitting there every day in my own building
running my own business and having nobody to answer to it
was the best feeling and I knew that the first year would be a
rocky one then that summer Johnny didn't come home from
school in the spring he was going to stay in the city and get a
job for the summer I was pissed 'cause I was counting on him
to come home and help work the business with me since I was
paying for his college and I threatened that if he didn't come
home I wouldn't pay for his school the next year and he said to
me over the phone like he was talking to a stranger instead of
his father if you want to do that Dad it's your right but I'll stay
here anyway and take out student loans for school I couldn't
believe he could fucking talk to me that way it's not like he
talked to me disrespectful or anything it was like he was his

own boss and he didn't need me and it hurt real bad Audry talked me into giving in she always hit me with the same line that when I was his age I was across the world in Korea think how my mother must have felt and it was just that no one was around anymore Gina finally married this older guy who was divorced and had two kids in college but he seemed like a nice guy and he had some money from a business he owned installing air conditioners in cars and they bought a house on the south shore and I was lucky if I saw her more than once a month but we talked on the phone a lot and her daughter missed Somerville and all her friends at first but then she started to like the new place and Peter's wife threw him out finally after she couldn't take his shit and he was giving his daughter a hard time too when she divorced him she had so much evidence against him from all the restraining orders and police files that she got the house and most of the money Peter had and he moved back in the second floor after Gina moved out and he was kind of down and out drinking a bit feeling bad for himself and saying that she got all his money and I let him stay there free and he paid his utilities little Tony finally got married and lived in New Hampshire he worked for the highway department 'cause his wife's family had connections up there and they had two kids right away and it was really the thing that made me realize how fast time goes by when you see your kids with their own kids before you know it another chunk of years goes by like you didn't even notice and who would have figured little Tony the kid from the city moving to New Hampshire but Manchester was like the city anyway and he still played pool a few nights a weeks the ice cream store turned out better than I ever hoped and once I figured all the ins and outs of running the place I opened from Memorial Day at the end of May to Columbus Day in October every year and made enough money to take the rest of the year off mostly Audry and me just stayed home we didn't do much she usually went down to North Carolina for a month during the winter and I went down for a couple of weeks that was as much as I could stand her sister Sue had broken the family record and was on her fourth husband and I said being the youngest she'd probably break her own record more than once Johnny finished college then got a master degree and became a math teacher in New York City he loved it there and he never said anything but Audry and me didn't neither he was a good looking guy and he never had a girlfriend so we kind of knew it wasn't that it bothered me 'cause it didn't long as you're a good person I don't care who you sleep with what kind of bothered me was that he couldn't tell us or at least felt that he couldn't he never did I thought of telling him I knew and didn't care but the few times I saw him it didn't seem like the thing to do I worried about Aids too but Johnny was a smart kid and I figured he knew how to be careful we didn't see him much maybe once or twice a year on holidays we saw little Tony and his family a lot they would come down on Sundays for dinner and Audry made macaroni and gravy little Tony got bigger and bigger and the doctor told him he would die young if he didn't stop eating so much but he wouldn't listen his kids were beautiful he had a boy and girl and I feel lucky in a way 'cause looking back to when I was a kid being on welfare and my family never having nothing and then me doing as good as I did and the house all paid for and the store property all paid for and suddenly after all the years they stopped rent control in Cambridge and overnight the property values in Somerville started to go up higher and higher who would have known and all these real estate agents started getting in touch telling me how much property was worth and I had a small fortune on my hands and that's what this country is about that a guy like me could start with nothing and later be leaning on the counter of his own business on his own property looking across the street at his own house and my brother Frank sitting out at one of the tables on the sidewalk with his notebook and beeper and cane he's probably worth more than me though his goes right back out fast as it comes in there was no way to stop Frank from doing what he wants to do when I told him I was worried about the cops he said every cop that drove by knew what he was doing that's the way things went when was I going to smarten up and quit working so hard and I did think that if the real estate prices were going to keep going up at some point I would sell it all and maybe me and Audry move down to someplace warm like Arizona or something and buy a nice house with a pool and big television for her and just live out our days I got to hand it to Audry even in her fifties she looked good and kept her figure me I let it all go and after the ice cream store was doing good I started shaving my head I don't know why but one morning I woke and got this urge and shaved my head there was really only the sides to shave the top was bald already Audry said I looked kind of scary to people but I got into it and the customers got used to it and the kids liked it and every morning I got up and shaved my head before I showered and sometimes I still looked close in the mirror to see if any bugs might he crawling around somewhere even though I knew there's no place for them to crawl and the one thing that never did change is that I never stopped thinking of sex even though me and Audry only did it maybe once a year I still jerked off every chance I could I never stopped Frank was in his glory sitting out there all day and night he said what better way to watch chicks than at the ice cream store with all the young moms coming down their summer clothes and those bored wandering eyes checking out the young dudes and the little girls so young I don't want to know in their short shorts and little tit tops the older I get the better they look I know what they mean by dirty old man now that I'm there I don't feel

211

guilty one bit getting off on a twelve-year-old girl licking the top of a vanilla cone I mean what the fuck

My Ground

Joseph Torra

For Jonathan Strong

One

I slept three hours. I dreamed of Harry. It was the summer-vacation class annual show. We pantomimed to the Chipmunks. Harry was Alvin. Her brother Eddie was the director. It was exactly like our performance, except in the dream we wore black plastic wrap-around glasses.

I never experience a full night's sleep. After years of sleepless nights a slight nap's a full night's rest. Over time I tried everything to find a way to sleep. Drugs and alcohol. Meditation and yoga. Sex. Suddenly, I turned forty and started sleeping in two and three-hour bursts. Four in the morning is the worst time, when I am most vulnerable to the racing thoughts and despicable anxiety, when I can levitate to a shaky hover.

I light a cigarette in the dark. My cup is empty. At first light I will rise and steep more green tea. The heater blows invariably more than I need and I sleep in a sleeveless t-shirt with a sheet over me. Outside the temperature is below zero. Wind whistles through metal gutter pipes and rattles every creaky joint in the house. I rub my belly and test my flabby breasts to see if I want to masturbate. I rub my hair with my hand and smell my fingers. My dandruff is worse during the winter because of the excessive heat and dryness in my room. Mrs. Hale has a habit of brushing the dandruff off my shoulder when she is speaking to me.

I snub out the cool menthol cigarette. All the different brands in nearly thirty years of smoking, I come back to the same brand Harry offered me behind the Curtis School when I smoked my first. It lifted me, and made me dizzy when I in-

215

haled the way she showed me. Grandmother smelled smoke the moment I walked through the door. I told her some of the kids I played with were smoking. Denise said that was a lie and she saw me smoking with Harry and Billy Donovan.

I don't know how long it's been since Denise's last call. There's no way her new marriage will turn out better than any other, though this time she might get some money out of it. He left his wife, children and grandchildren. What kind of man would do that? At her age Denise is pushing it, there's no time left to be marketing herself as a young dish. She says he's sixty but thinks he's twenty-one.

They called Jim, Denise's father, Sully. He was attractive, in his own strange way, with blond hair and a beer belly. Sully was the dumbest of all Mother's men. He couldn't help me with sixth-grade arithmetic. No wonder he couldn't manage his business. Sully sells seashells by the seashore. Don't say that. Just did. Mother got rid of him after he lost his plumbing and heating business. He grabbed me. I slapped his face and he smiled. I told my mother she said don't be silly. Sully had an ex-wife and three other kids. I remember holidays when all the kids had to be together. I didn't like his children. I hid. He would find me and order me down to play with all my brothers and sisters. They're not my brothers and sisters.

Although I remain the Hales' house cleaner, after all these years, as Mrs. Hale says, I'm like family. I've always felt some kind of barrier between me and Mrs. Hale. Despite her ever-friendly gestures, she speaks to me in talk-down clips. The assumption is that I am her servant and couldn't possibly know as much as she does about anything. Dr. Hale is all business, the good father and hard-working man of medicine.

I lost the rest of my customers during the last bout. The Hales remained supportive and welcomed me back. This stems in part from Mrs. Hale's fear that she won't be able to replace

216

me with another white person. I expect a call from Denise now that Grandmother is dead. As soon as she finds out, she'll want to know why nothing was left for her. It's really not much money, or a lot of money, depending on how I look at it. It's more than I've ever had at one time.

I'm glad I saw Grandmother in the end. I visited her a week before she died and she looked healthy as ever. She made beef stew. I helped her clean up the dishes. There was so much stew left she sent me home with it. I tried to tell her I didn't have a refrigerator only a tiny one-burner plate in my room. She said it would keep until the next day I should eat it then.

Harry said with no fear that God was in people's minds. I see her spitting after she utters those words, then dragging on a cigarette. We roamed the neighborhood streets playing this way and that on our bikes. Harry showed me this way and that, a bike-riding game where you rode anywhere you wanted not paying attention to street signs until you ultimately found yourself outside the neighborhood in unfamiliar territory.

The day we rode to the Bear Hill Reservation out on the edge of town's when Harry told me about sex. I knew what she was going to say. Mother didn't make it a secret. But Harry told me the more important things, the girl things, and taught me about myself and my genitals and what was inside me. She already had done it with guys. She said she masturbated too. She told me what masturbation was and we pushed our bikes up Bear Hill and I had an idea what she was talking about because I was already having some of those feelings. When we were nearly to the top, we wheeled our bikes off the path for a cigarette. Harry started talking about sex again and what an orgasm was and did I ever have one? She fondled my breasts and then my vagina. Then she got on the ground and told me to get on top of her which I did, wrapping my legs around one of her legs as she pushed it up into me hard. I rode it looking out at cars below on Route 133, and the lights coming on in Wilton, a few of the old factories that were still making shoes lit-up.

We moved in with Grandmother when my father and mother broke up and they sold the house. He was the best she ever had, and caught her red-handed with another man. Mother got nothing out of the settlement but support for me because he never had as much as my mother suspected. My father was a hard-working man with a small construction company of his own. He specialized in reliable additions, roof repairs, fixing doors. No job too small. He loved her deeply, he told me so one day in tears when he picked me up and took me out for an ice cream. The divorce crushed him. In those days she was the kind of beauty that men stop dead on the street and stare at.

I met Harry the September I started in the Wilton schools. Mother said it was humiliating to have to move back to this shitty town. Everywhere she went people were talking. She started dating other men immediately. I don't remember any of them from that time. One day Harry and I were playing this way and that, we were over near Salem Street where there were a lot of bars and I saw Mother in a car in-between two guys in the front seat and they both had their arms around her. She didn't see me and I never said anything about it.

Mother wasn't around much and she was never awake in the morning before I left for school. My grandmother woke me and cooked eggs and toast or oatmeal which she called oakmeal. I don't remember Grandfather much. He was in the hospital when we moved back stricken with cancer he died shortly thereafter. Before she was divorced my mother hardly brought us to visit, so my recollections of him are few. They lived in a two-story, single-family, tar-shingled, factory-worker house on Foster Street. It was one of the older neighborhoods, though when I was younger there was a small wooded area at the end of Foster where people dumped things. If I remember anything about my grandfather, it was his warning me to stay away from the woods because there were bad men living there.

In time, I saw my father less and less. It wasn't because he didn't want to see me, but Mother made it very difficult for him. If he was going to come and pick me up she would take me out at the same time and later tell him he got the day wrong. Once he called the social services department to report her. They contacted my mother and she told them he was a drunk and she was afraid to let me get in the car with him. He tried to fight her but she just made things more tangled until he eventually moved away. But he never once missed a support payment for me. And he would call at night from Arkansas at prearranged times when we knew my mother would be out. Otherwise she would hang up on him.

In Arkansas he married another woman who Grandmother said was just like Mother. And he got divorced again, this time with a son, whom I never knew. He moved to California — in the country somewhere where he could fish. We lost touch for years. Then he died from a heart attack. It was during the first time I was away. I didn't find out until I was released one month later. I wanted to fly out to California to visit his grave. I was in no condition.

The first time Harry and I skipped school we took the train to Boston. Harry knew the subway system. She was afraid of us getting separated in the crowds, so she brought a pair of handcuffs and handcuffed us together. She showed me how to sneak into the subway under the turnstile when the man wasn't looking and we took the underground subway and aboveground trolley around various parts of the city and didn't get back home until late afternoon. The principal had phoned and spoke with my grandmother. She said she would not tell my mother this time. But I must promise her I wouldn't skip school again. It was one of many promises I never kept with

219

her. Many a time she came between me and Mother who never was rational under any circumstances. Mother just screamed and threw things and hit me with a broomstick.

For many years she worked as a cocktail waitress, and I've heard other things too. She slept until noon and by the time I was arriving home from school she was readying to leave for work. If she had any free time she spent it with one of her boy-friends. She had no female friends to speak of. I helped Grandmother with the chores. I did laundry, cleaned floors and windows, changed bed linen. Grandmother told me stories about her life in Ireland and how hard a man my grandfather was to live with.

I follow the exact system of cleaning I learned from Grandmother. It's much more efficient for me if Mrs. Hale is out but once the cold weather sets in she's home permanently unless they take a ski vacation or fly to some place warm during the winter. When she's not there I can do the entire job inside of two hours by throwing a load of laundry in, starting down-stairs in the kitchen and working my way out to the library, din-ing room, first-floor bathroom. Second floor is a huge family room with a big screen television. There's a guest bedroom, another bathroom and Mrs. Hale's study which has some books and a computer she never uses. Third floor consists of the bed-rooms, another bathroom and a master bathroom off the mas-ter bedroom. I vacuum, bed-change, back downstairs to throw the laundry in the dryer, back up to finish scrubbing the mas-ter-bedroom bowl.

Grandmother said those old things like clean house clean mind. A watched pot never boils. It's a great life if you don't weaken. As long as you've got your health. She scrubbed and cleaned. She washed her walls and counters down with alcohol. When you hang a carpet out and give it a good beating you clean the carpet and clean out all the bad energy in your body. I never saw Mother make a bed. During the times she was married she had house cleaners or beds went unmade and unchanged.

Recently the Hales started a new cook. It's always the same. We love your food. Cook anything you like. That lasts about two weeks. They'll drive him out and be wanting me to fill in until they hire another one. It's not bad money to spend one day a week in the kitchen and put all this food up in the refrigerator and freezer. I can't really cook but I know what they want. I want out. I don't know what to do with Grandmother's money, but Dr. Hale says it shouldn't be in a savings account where it is now and he can put me in touch with people and I can buy something called a Certificate of Deposit or mutual funds. I can do what I want now. Go to college again. Learn a trade. Anything but clean houses. I sit in the dark after a few hours' sleep and listen to the heat blow on and off.

Harry lived in one of the new side-by-side two-family houses which were called duplexes. They were built in the woods at the end of Foster Street. What was a mysterious forest when I was a child was barely enough area to contain the three duplexes with tiny back yards. The new homes looked out of place on Foster Street with its tar-shingled old factory-worker houses cramped every which way.

I was only inside Harry's house two or three times in all those years. I recall a startling quiet, and a clean that would have made Grandmother proud. Harry's parents were church goers and active with various parish activities at Saint Ann's. Mr. Harrington worked for the post office and Harry's older brother Eddie was known as a sissy. He had girlie mannerisms and didn't go in for sports like the other boys. Eddie looked a lot like Harry with his overbite and freckles. Though his hair was black and Harry's dirty blond.

They called her a tomboy. She was cute enough that the

boys went for her. It frustrated them that she often made the best play of a baseball game or ran for the winning touchdown in tag-football. After we started hanging out together I never went to church again. Her parents went to the eight o'clock mass and we met for the ten-fifteen. In the good weather we rode our bikes around; in the bad weather we hung out in a laundromat and smoked.

My mother never went to church and slept through Sunday morning. Grandmother never missed one week of confession or mass. She said she didn't have many rules around the house except that Denise and I go to confession, mass and receive holy communion each week. Denise continued to attend mass. She said in confession she told the priests about all this made-up sex stuff. And she enjoyed mass because there were lots of boys to check out; she sat up front and flirted with the altar boys. When Mother was waitressing she worked Saturday nights. She said she was too wound up to just come home after her shift and stayed at the lounge for a drink or two. Sometimes on Sunday morning she wouldn't arrive home until after the sun had come up.

Denise got Mother's looks and body. Tall, thin, leggy and busty all in one. I had the great body for about two years when I least understood it. Or, to put it another way, I had great breasts before any of the other girls had them. All the boys were friendly for a while and after one thing. Tits drive boys crazy Harry said. How do you figure they're just milk sacks. Mother said I was fat and I would be fat all my life if I didn't do something about it when I was young. Grandmother said I was plump and had a large frame, there was nothing I could do with it, mine was an athletic body and that's the way some girls were born.

<u>Two</u>

Harry was a year older than I but she was kept back, so we were in the same grade. If she was in the mood she would go with a boy and let him have his way, although she said she liked playing sports with boys more than making out with them. Sometimes I let a boy feel me up. I humped Billy Donovan's leg and had an orgasm like I did the time with Harry.

Our make-out place was under the Route 133 overpass. We climbed a steep concrete-block grade and perched under the road in the steel rafters. The rumble of cars and trucks above resounding through the tunnel, and the occasional swish of cars from the rotary below, made us feel like we were in some out-of-this-world place. Sammy Carbone was the sweetest of all the boys. He liked to cuddle. We held each other close, gave each other soft kisses on the lips and he never tried to feel me up.

Harry went through the ice at Meadow Pond and people said any other girl would be dead. We all skated on Meadow Pond, and it froze solid each winter except at the far end where Corser Brook flowed in and the ice thinned out. Harry knew it, but she skated farther out than any of the kids, in black boys' hockey skates doing her foot-over-foot stride, dribbling a puck back and forth at the end of her stick, sound of blades carving the ice, splash and she's gone.

The Hale kids skate at a private skating club on an inside rink. One of Mrs. Hale's chores is take the kids to their after-school activities. Sometimes she can't even do that and I've seen her put them in a taxi. Caroline takes cello lessons and plays soccer. Justin Jr. plays football, baseball and basketball.

Every hour after school is accounted for. Weekends it's the same. They plan family activities weeks, months, and years ahead, sitting around the table with a planner like they're running a business. When she's at home and functioning, Mrs. Hale still checks my work when I'm finished, as if after all these years she'll catch me not cleaning one of the bathrooms, failing to vacuum a rug or leaving a load of laundry unfolded.

It's good to be home. To brew tea and open a can of soup. It's remarkably quiet down here and hard to tell that I'm in the city. These streets of Winterhill are so congested with two and three-family homes, and most lots with large yards have long since been split up for rear dwellings. This house is an exception. In the summer I can walk back into the yard to look at the rows of flowers, vegetables and fruit trees that my landlords tend. My apartment is illegal. The Portuguese family who own the house finished off a room in the basement with a kitchenette and bathroom. I pay them cash every month. They speak little English and I no Portuguese, it makes it easy. The grandmother has a huge voice and shouts everything she says in rapid-fire action. They fight once or twice a day but the nights are quiet.

There are seldom phone messages, except maybe the Hales asking me to do something for them like pick up one of the kids or stop at the store on my way in tomorrow. Sometimes the phone rings but no one leaves a message. Mrs. Hale said those calls are pesky salespeople. One man left a message. He was from a securities or financial office and said he needed to speak to me about my recent loss and the financial implications. It sounded official until I phoned and he was a financial advisor who wanted me to give him Grandmother's money to invest. He said he had some ideas that he knew would be beneficial to me and my family and when would be a convenient time to come out and discuss them with me. There are letters from insurance salesmen. And car salesmen. They read the obituaries for future clients. There is no good time.

I'd been without sleep for weeks when they finally admitted me the first time. It got to a point that when I slept, the night-mares were so bad it was as if my body was defending itself against itself and wouldn't allow me to sleep. But then the nightmares were coming while I was awake. Grandmother had no choice but to get help. She was a simple woman and didn't understand. It was Father Foley from Saint Ann's who told her to call the doctor. She thought maybe I needed to be exorcised. They said the ECT would help me forget. Grandmother came every day to the hospital. She brought me books, magazines and flowers. I didn't even know who she was at first. I'm your grandmother.

She tried her best to teach me things about a woman's cycle and sex but she got embarrassed. She repeated something about a man has to plant the seed, and a woman is the earth. It was impossible to believe that she was my mother's mother they were so different. Harry told me everything. She had peri-ods before I did. She made it sound like no big a deal except for the mess. Even now, there's something I like about the cramps and when they begin, I welcome them, as if my insides are telling me I am alive.

Harry passed out from sniffing glue and I thought she died. All the other kids ran. We were on the fire escape of the Curtis School on the top tier. I stayed with her and kept opening her eyelids and telling her not to die. It was just getting dark. Billy Donovan and the others ran out through the entrance at the far end of the schoolyard. I thought maybe I should run too but I couldn't leave her.

Mostly I sit in bed. I have no television or radio. As a child, I remember watching shows like *Leave it to Beaver* wondering where those families were and Denise said California that's

225

where she was going to go some day and she did. Her first husband was a hotshot hair dresser with a string of hair salons whom she met at a party. She moved to the West Coast two weeks later and married him. She'd done the suicide thing before, so it didn't surprise me all the shit she pulled when he ran off with someone else after he lost his salons. There never was a string, only two. Theirs was an open marriage, and the two of them were swapping partners. I don't know what she expected.

The cramps are getting worse. I'm about to start flowing any minute. My periods are more intense as I get older. I light a cigarette and finish my cup of tea. The woman upstairs is shouting at her granddaughter. It's four of them living there. I don't know where the child's father is. I've never seen him.

My mother grudgingly ate Sunday dinner with us. Grandmother insisted that on Sunday anyone in her home must sit down and eat. She called upstairs several times for Mother, who might be getting out of bed into the shower, we're waiting and dinner's getting cold. Even when she was there, it was as if she were not, though she was always charming, calling us her sweet things or dear ones and patting us on the head. Before dinner was finished she lit a cigarette, made phone calls, and shortly thereafter she disappeared for the day and that was the most we saw of her in a week.

Grandmother lost four pregnancies after she gave birth to Mother. She said that if Mother wasn't an only child she might have grown up to be a different person. After my mother divorced Denise's father we moved back in with Grandmother again. My mother didn't spend much time in Wilton. Most of her waitress jobs were in Brockton and for a while she drove all the way to Boston every night. Grandmother forbade her to smoke pot in the house but she paid her no mind and sometimes if I woke to go to the bathroom after she got home I could smell it coming from her room. Grandmother got up after mother fell asleep to look and see she didn't leave a cigarette burning on the bed.

The furnace is directly next to my room. First there is click and the sound of the machine firing-up. Then a pause. Then the blower kicks in. Even with my vent closed I get too much heat because it has so little area to travel. It's so dry my scalp flakes. I rub my head and smell it with other people around but mostly I have that under control. I rarely do the blinking thing with my eyes any more. The heat blows. Upstairs is quiet they must be in bed. Because my heating vent is closed the air forcing through it whistles.

We attended vacation school at Saint Ann's during the month of July. It was a chance for the nuns and priests to indoctrinate public school kids. There were snacks and games, an annual talent show and a trip to Washburn Lake Amusement Park. Mostly we read catechism, sang religious songs, listened to the nuns and priests tell us about Christ and original sin. They showed us movies and slide movies. I remember spikes through his hands, how he was made to hang there.

One year at Washburn Lake Harry and I rode the roller coaster all day. As soon as we finished a run, we went straight back into the line, the longest line in the park. By the end of the day we rode that coaster sixteen times, front car, back car, middle car. Every single ride Harry held her hands over her head and never touched the safety bar. I got sick on the bus ride home and was forced to ride with my head between my legs, throwing up into a bag. All the while Harry sat next to me and rubbed my back and neck.

Her real name was Kathleen Harrington. She blew great smoke rings and freely talked about sex, or her vagina and its workings, like it was perfectly natural. Grandmother referred to her as that Harrington girl. Though Grandmother rarely spoke ill of anyone, in the early days she frequently hinted that I might do well to associate with other kinds of girls too. Regarding Denise Grandmother would only say that she never had a chance like I did. What she meant was that at least I had Grandmother. Denise really never had anyone. She could have had Grandmother; instead, she saw her as the enemy.

That's the way it is with Denise. You are either with her or against her. Her great ally or her enemy. No middle ground. I've been on both sides. Denise hated Harry. She made up stories about her and spread them around. She made fun of Harry's brother Eddie and called him Edwina the Ballerina. By the time she was ten she had boys fighting over her. If the attention on her waned, she created a crisis and everyone came running. Mother indulged her when she was around. Grandmother ignored her. I often did a little of both. But the older we grew I tended to side with Grandmother.

I call up a dream while I am awake. It's as if I dreamed that very dream last sleep. But the more I examine the dream, my vivid recollection dissolves into variations of a dream I've dreamed hundreds of times. Or maybe just once. There's a house and Harry and I are cleaning. We're climbing stairs. Harry is talking. She's talking fast jumping from one subject to the next, as she could, ahead of me on the stairs. She reaches the fourth level and says oh my this is what always happens I told them we hadn't cleaned yet. I reach the top floor. Mr. and Mrs. Hale, Caroline, the baby and Junior. Blood's splattered everywhere. Harry picks up one of those medieval handles with the spiked ball on the end which has been sitting on the floor. Now I know where this is. She begins to clean as if everything's normal. The Hales are strewn all about the room their faces and skulls bashed in. The carpets, floors, walls and ceiling are soaked with blood. Harry what are you doing? Harry?

A thin beam of light seeps in from outside. The streetlamp light streams from the head of the driveway, down through the narrow space between the closed window shade and the window casing, and into my room. Without that light there would be a fainter light from somewhere. Without the furnace there would be sound from elsewhere. There is always light somewhere. There are always sounds.

Three

Summers we swam in Corser Brook. There was a small beach at Meadow Pond but we walked a woods path to where the railroad bridge crossed over a deep pool. We jumped off the bridge. Harry and I swam by moonlight. She took off all her clothes but I was afraid the police might come and I might be seen naked. I jumped feet first but Harry dove straight off, even at night she plunged to the pool's depths and came up with a rock to prove she'd been to the bottom. She'd play tricks and swim underwater to the other side of the bridge and, while I stood overhead screaming, she'd sneak up on me from behind with a boo.

I weighed one hundred and eighty-five pounds by the time I was twenty. I wore potato-sack dresses or overalls. I hated looking at myself in the mirror and had none in my room. I cut off all my hair like a boy so I could just let it dry after showering and not have to tend to it. Grandmother said it was a shame because my full wavy hair was one of my best features. I ate lots of food. I wasn't partial to anything special. Cakes, chips, pizza, French fries, peanut butter and jelly sandwiches. I'd eat until I passed out then the dreams would start. Grandmother could only indulge me. She baked pies and cooked big dinners and brought things to my room and tried to make conversation. I didn't go out or see anyone.

In terms of age, Grandmother could pass for my mother. She gave birth to my mother when she was seventeen. My mother had me when she was sixteen. Grandmother was fond of singing, and I remember the first time we moved in with her and she sensed that I was scared she baked special cookies and sang me to sleep. It was a song about fish having to swim and birds having to fly. When I was twenty she was only fifty-three.

A message came in at midnight. It's Denise, clueless to the time difference between here and California. She says hi it's me we need to talk about some things give me a call. With all the money that's been through her fingers she's after Grandmother's paltry savings even with her current husband who owns a private plane. I'll give her the money. I'm sure she has no idea what a nominal amount it is. Neither did Grandmother. You'll get it all, she often said with a tone that made it sound like she was leaving me a huge estate. It's not that I'm ungrateful. Between working, welfare and Medicaid, I've done all right over the years and never taken from her except for a place to stay when I couldn't keep one myself. The house needed a lot of work and property in Wilton isn't exactly prime. She had a life insurance policy she paid month in month out, going back to the days when the insurance man would come to the door and collect the money. The policy barely covered the cost of her funeral. I buried her next to Grandfather at the Wilton Memorial.

It's been years since I shaved any part of my body. I twirl the hair under my left armpit with my right fingers. My fingers smell of my body. I rub my scalp with my right hand, hard so that it almost hurts, flakes fly up in a dust storm around me. I twirl my hair again. My fingers smell of the earth. I place my right pinkie finger into my right ear and rotate it around. Earth and potatoes. My left hand is for cigarettes. Between my first and second finger there's a brown stain. The smell of burned tobacco never goes away even when I wash my hands. My left hand is smoke. My right hand is my body. I sit up and rub my hands over my belly. I squeeze the belly fat hard between both

231

of my hands.

I never went back to the Urich house after the incident over the missing money. Four years of service and the first sign that some cash was missing they blamed me. Professor Urich, the big lecturer at Harvard and author of a famous book, the great humanitarian, groveling on the phone to me how sorry he and his wife were, how badly they felt about their mistake and how much they liked me and wanted to keep me on as their cleaner.

Sully always had beer on his breath. He and my mother were nearly broke up when he cornered me those few times. It was kind of pitiful. I was never afraid of him. Wild fights erupted between them at any time. Sometimes they would continue for hours, especially if they were both drunk. Mother would scream through the night at the top of her lungs. Get the fuck out of here. I hate your fucking guts. She slammed doors and threw things. All the neighbors could hear. Sully never got loud or violent, he responded in a quiet voice. I'm not going anywhere. I'm staying right here. And he sat in his recliner silent drinking beer which was his way of taunting her. Sometimes she would jump on him, scratch and punch in order to provoke a response. The most he would do was stand up, wrap his arms around her waist, lift her up and carry her to the bedroom. He'd put her down and walk out closing the door behind him. She followed him out and immediately started over again.

When neighbors called the police, Mother claimed that Sully was beating her up and she wanted him out. Sully remained inert in his recliner. I haven't touched her ask the kid. I had to stay in my bedroom but I could hear everything. The police would remain a few minutes and talk with each of them separately, then together. After they left Mother and Sully would wander off to bed and I would sit in the dark and listen to them. First the giggling, then the laughing, then Sully groaning a low slow oh yeah and mother screeching her high-pitched ahhhhh, their bed rocking the house until they eventually passed out and everything went quiet.

The tide is going out. Harry is swimming hard and fast with those determined strokes of hers and her head turning in time, her feet paddling like a machine. Harry don't go out too far. It's rainy and cold, not beach weather. She stops now, treading water way out there. She raises one of her arms up in the air and shouts but I can't hear her over the sound of the surf and the wind. She rolls over and begins to swim again, farther out with the tide. Harry cut it out and come back. Farther out. Harry cut it out.

Four

First there is bright light. Second there is a shadow. Third there is a sound.

Then there is absolute blankness.

Then, slowly, a terror of not knowing who I am or what is happening overcomes me.

The shadow gradually takes on features. The sound develops into a voice which slowly clarifies from an electronic muddle to words.

You are Laurel Bell. You are at the South Shore Mental Health Center. You have just had a treatment.

I am confused and scared.

Do you understand what I am saying? You are Laurel Bell. You are at the South Shore Mental Health Center. You have just had a treatment.

Gradually the fragmented associations click in. I am told my name again. Where I am again. What is going on again. Why I am here again.

They have always been good to me the nurses and doctors. It's rough in there. People get hurt and it's more likely to be a staff member than a patient. I wonder what they think when they see those of us they recognize, the ones who return dependable as the seasons.

There are so many varieties of green tea I have yet to sample them all. The furnace is blowing. I snub out a cigarette. I am horny. I'm afraid that's not a good sign. I'm afraid when I begin to feel. The thinking part I can cope with; the feeling

234

part's where I find myself adrift.

Harry said waking after passing out from glue was the same as waking the time she went unconscious going through the ice. On glue she was only out for a minute or two. No sooner did the wave of panic sweep over me, she was coming to and trying to lift her head up. But when she went through the ice they had to resuscitate her, and if she was under the water any longer, they say she could have suffered brain damage.

First she said was light. Then shadows. Then voices. Then confusion. The confusion might last for days. I'm clumsy. Every action feels awkward to perform. I knock things over. Even walking is difficult. My short-term memory is practically non-existent. I could wander off the unit so they watch me and follow me around. Then, just as the particles begin to settle, another session. And it begins all over again. Three per week. Three weeks in a row. It helps me forget.

My mother used all her various last names as it convenienced her. She was Lisa Clark. Lisa Bell. Lisa Sullivan. Baby Jennifer was said to be a La Valley but it was never proven. Mother never married Ray but she used his last name for a while too. Lisa La Valley she said has a lot of class. Denise, like mother, has a string of last names. She was born Denise Sullivan. Then she married Bobby her first husband and became Del Grecco. Her second husband was a Peterson and now her third Grassfield. There was nearly a fourth marriage wedged somewhere in there. It was called off after some kind of crisis that Denise caused. I don't remember the details; she was in California and I was in the hospital.

It took me by surprise when I phoned her and she didn't mention anything about Grandmother's money going to her. She said she was glad I had something of my own and she didn't have to worry about me now. Her pregnancy was the big news. I love him, I really love him. Her new house was huge and from her kitchen window she had a view of the mountains. I've never been so happy. The previous day they flew in his plane and watched the sunset from the air. Isn't that the most romantic thing you ever heard? And she went on like that for fifteen minutes completely uninterrupted, talking away, going through a list of the most minute details of the day-to-day things she and her new husband had been doing. And what a tiger in bed. You'd never know he's sixty. Her pregnancy can only mean this guy's got more money than she ever dreamed. I listened. I congratulated her. I must listen. If she asks me a question, by the time I'm half way through with an answer, she interrupts to talk about herself again.

A sleepless night isn't worrisome to me any longer. I seldom have two in a row. Lying still in the dark, even without sleep, allows the body some rest. I don't find Dr. Hale attractive, but his passivity and boyishness can be appealing. I imagine him a rambunctious lover, a kid jumping into a haystack, though from what I gather from Mrs. Hale there's not much going on between them at this time. Once I was in the basement and heard Mrs. Hale confiding to her sister on the phone that she was never able to enjoy it, not the way you do she said. Sully tried to be a good father to Denise, stepfather to me and father to his other children. One afternoon he gathered all of us in the back of his truck and drove us to where he rented a pony for the afternoon. He led each of us around on the pony, then took us for hamburgers. Another time we took a hike up Bear Hill. When we got to the top, he pulled a can of beer from his pocket and drank it down in a few gulps. Mother never came along on such adventures. When she and Sully went to Bermuda for a week they left me and Denise with Grandmother. Mother never took us on any of her tropical vacations. What kind of vacation would it be with the two of you tagging along.

236

Sully's company contracted with the town of Brockton. He had plenty of work and employed a crew of men. Then there was a scandal concurring bribes and politicians. Sully was somehow involved and he lost his contracts. Instead of going out and generating new business, Sully laid off most of his crew. Then he sold all the vans with the fancy lettering Sully's Plumbing and Heating except one. He started drinking more and working less. The fights got worse and my mother was trying to get him to move out of the house but he wouldn't budge. She had a sense that the money was running out. She also had a growing fear that Sully was draining his company of money, and diverting it so that she wouldn't be able to get at it legally. Sully never did pay mother child support for Denise. At least none that Mother admitted to.

I remember my father took me to his place for the weekend. I got sick at his apartment and threw up all over myself. I was four or five. I was terrified because I had no control over my bodily functions. Father kept cleaning me up and carrying me to the bath wrapped in a towel to wash me off with warm water. Everything's going to be OK. Everything's going to be OK. He had an old cushiony chair and we spent most of the weekend snuggled in it watching television, Father with his arms wrapped around me.

Billy Donovan was the cutest kid in the neighborhood. Even if he was a little short. He had blond hair, blue eyes, a sincere and spontaneous smile. I didn't let on to Harry at the time, but it crushed me when she told me. Billy seemed so innocent and Harry said he was until she got hold of him. He had eleven brothers and sisters. His parents came from Ireland and I had a hard time understanding either of them when they spoke. Grandmother said they came from a different part of Ireland than her parents did. I never openly flirted, but I tried to be near him whenever I could. Sometimes we walked home

237

together. His house was directly behind ours and he liked to cut through our backyard.

I'm at my mother's apartment and it's me and Denise, Harry, Mother, baby Jennifer and a man who I can't identify, though in the dream I'm familiar enough to converse with him. We hear giggling from the porch. I rush to the window and look out. Someone is out there. The man runs out and catches Billy Donovan and several of his brothers spying in the window. He drags them into the apartment by the necks of their shirts. Billy says they have gifts they wanted to bring and he pulls out a gift-wrapped box and hands it to me. I undo several layers of wrapping down to a cardboard box. Inside the box is a blue glass bell. I lift the bell out of the box. It has no ringer. Billy says ringers are bad luck and can turn glass to blood.

Billy made out with me. I let him feel me up and he let me hump his leg but for a long time I was afraid to do anything more. I liked Billy more than any other boy. Harry said I wanted someone with a little experience, otherwise you might not know if it's right or wrong. I understood where he was going to put it, but I was horrified that it might hurt and I would bleed everywhere. You have to be relaxed about it otherwise you won't be able to enjoy it she said.

Mrs. Serge reminds me of Grandmother. Physically they are much different. Mrs. Serge is tall, muscular and worldly. During the late summer she knows which of the mushrooms growing on the Hales' lawn are safe to eat. She knows about poetry and politics, art and music. The Hales won't eat any of the mushrooms so she fills up her basket before she leaves for home. She's great with the children, especially Eliza. Mrs. Hale says the other two combined were easier than Eliza.

I don't understand how someone like Mrs. Serge, who in her homeland was a music professor, would have to take work as a babysitter here in this country. It's her passion for living and for people I envy. When neither of the Hales are home she sits at the piano and plays. She knows hundreds of pieces by memory. I sit in the living room and listen. She enjoys the audience. There's something about the way the notes can cut right through me. Without words. The pitch and fall of sound.

Five

For several years you never saw one of us without the other. We didn't have to make phone calls or prearrange meetings. I knew where Harry would be at a given time or she knew where I would be. We shared everything; and Harry not only knew about sex, but she could talk about places in the world as if she'd been there herself. Tropical countries. Frozen continents. Far away cities. I thought she made things up, the way she would come out of nowhere in the middle of a conversation about cats she'd say in China they eat cats. Are you making that up? You're making that up. I'm not making it up it's true.

Sleety-snow whips against the windows and vinyl siding hard enough to be heard over the furnace. The room brightens up for an instant as I flick the lighter and the flame ignites the tip of my cigarette. Dark again. A long drag on the cigarette. A soft red glow over the white bed sheet. I keep the clock turned around on the dresser. It doesn't matter what time it is. The habit began years ago when I couldn't sleep. It helps not knowing what time it is. Sometimes when I get up for a bathroom run I'll turn it around and peek. The tea makes me pee. Sometimes it's within a minute or two of my guess. Other times I'm hours off.

A light. A shadow. A voice. The gradual awakening back into some kind of conscious being. Memory lifts off. Particles rustle and get caught up in the air currents. Clouds form and turn in and out on themselves, amorphous, but gathering energy and force as they go. Something has to give. Blank sky and

240

no footing.

Betsy Milmoe said something about Harry. Harry said something about Betsy Milmoe. For a week everybody said there was going to be a fight. Betsy was bigger and older than Harry. She was crass and loud, always pushing girls and boys around. It was a hot summer afternoon. I saw Betsy walking through the entrance of Dilboy Park. Harry looked up and saw her too. She took one last drag on her cigarette, threw it on the ground and stamped it out hard with her sneaker.

Betsy had five or six kids with her. We had about the same. Betsy said I hear you've been saying some things about me, Harrington. Harry said maybe I have but what goes around comes around. Betsy said if you're not ready to say you're sorry you better be ready to get your ass kicked. Harry said I don't want to fight you Betsy, but if I have to I will. Hit her Betsy her friends shouted. Harry's brother Eddie broke in and told Betsy nobody wanted any trouble. Betsy said fuck off you sissy. Eddie said fuck you Betsy and got ready to stand his ground but Harry pushed him out of the way and told him she could handle her own battles.

When Billy Donovan fought Charley Dunn bloody, it bothered me a lot, but I figured that's what boys did. But to see Harry and Betsy in the ninety-degree heat, swapping punches, wrestling each other to the ground, clawing, biting, kicking. I couldn't get it out of my mind for days. Harry was much quicker and each time she punched Betsy in the face, a bruise rose on Betsy's cheek or forehead or chin. Betsy pulled out a handful of Harry's hair. Kids were yelling and worked up into a fury. I was horrified and became sick to my stomach. As much as I hated Betsy Milmoe, I felt for her every time Harry bought a fresh welt to her face. Finally, a man pulled over and got out of his car, took one look at the two girls and got between them. By then they were so exhausted they gratefully accommodated the man's demand to break it up immediately. Betsy's friends said it was a draw. Considering Harry was smaller and younger, we figured she got the best of it. Her face and arms were scratched and bleeding. There was a white mark on her scalp where Betsy pulled the hair out.

Grandmother told me by the time my mother was thirteen she had no control over her, just like with Denise. Mother came and went as she pleased. There were nights that she didn't come home. Grandfather was of the old school and did things like lock her out. Mother told me that he used to hit her too. Grandmother was drawn into the middle having to protect my mother, while knowing at the same time that my mother needed some kind of limits set on her.

The first time my mother got pregnant she was fifteen. She had an abortion. Grandfather never knew. Grandmother gave her the money behind his back and assisted in finding a safe place to have the procedure performed. Grandmother didn't believe in abortion. But she was afraid for mother who refused to disclose the identity of the baby's father. She feared my grandfather and his reaction. When he lost control he was capable of crazy behavior. Mother told us Grandfather used to beat Grandmother. Grandmother said she only remembered a slap once or twice. Briefly, Grandmother contemplated sending Mother off somewhere to give the baby to a Catholic organization. Mother told her there was no way she would have the baby and then give it up. Wilton was a smaller place back then Grandmother said. One year later Mother was pregnant again but she miscarried.

Mrs. Hale had a breakdown after Eliza was born. It looked like a breakdown except Mrs. Hale remained home instead of being hospitalized. There were private nurses around the clock, taking care of her and the baby. Dr. Margolis, an old family friend, looked in on Mrs. Hale once a day and had her heavily medicated.

Every reference of Mrs. Hale to Eliza is couched in her animosity. Everything was fine until Eliza came. I never got sick during pregnancy until Eliza. Things have not been the same between James and I since Eliza. It's strange how people will say most anything in front of servants, as if they're not there. Mrs. Hale has a way of softly purring and pawing her way around, doing very little while at the same time appearing to be the perfectly competent doctor's wife, vulnerable, mousy and nonthreatening.

The Hales produce so much dirty laundry that the washer and dryer run continually while I am there. The last thing I do before I am finished for the day is fold the clean clothes and pile them high in baskets on the basement floor. There are dozens of pairs of socks to sort and match. Mr. and Mrs. Hale's underwear. Sports uniforms. The kids' clothes. Jeans and slacks. Sweaters, shirts, baby clothes, bibs, table-cloths, napkins, towels, bed sheets, bedspreads, pillowcases. Mrs. Hale's blouses and skirts with her special washing instructions so that I have to do them all separately. Sweatshirts, sweat pants, Dr. Hale's golf and tennis clothes.

When I learned to do laundry with Grandmother, we washed by hand in her big oversized sink using a washboard and brush. Even after she got an electric washer, she never wanted a dryer. Everything was hung out on the long clothesline that extended from her back door high to a big oak tree that stood in the rear of the yard. The pulleys were rusted and let out metallic squeals as she ran another strip of wet hanging clothes over the yard. In the winter she had rope lines in the basement near the furnace where the clothes dried quickly and shriveled.

As the days grow longer more light seeps in through the narrow basement window. The shade is drawn but light emanates around the edges so by daybreak, various objects in the room gather out of the darkness. My dresser. A pile of clothes on the floor. Grandmother's chest at the foot of my bed, the top of which resembles the rounded top of a gravestone. The telephone on the little table. The corner chair. It must have snowed even though spring is near. The landlord is shoveling and his shovel-blade is scooping and scraping outside the window. Upstairs the little girl is jumping around from room to room. Her grandmother is shouting at her. Then the girl's mother begins arguing with her mother in Portuguese. Grandmother shouts her down.

Six

Schoolwork came easy for me. My grades were good and my efforts minimal. Reading and writing I liked most, and competing in a spelling Bee I was a finalist every time. When I took the exam for my high school general equivalency test I passed effortlessly. Grandmother encouraged me to go to college. You're a smart girl. There's no reason you can't do anything you want to do.

I don't read. I don't write. I don't like to add up how many hours I worked for the Hales. I'd be unaware if they try to beat me for an hour or two each week. I don't want to clean the Hales' house any longer. I don't want to change baby Eliza for Mrs. Hale when Mrs. Serge is not around. It's always the same with Mrs. Hale. Can you do me a quick favor and change the baby I've got to run upstairs and do something? Grandmother took us to the hospital when Jennifer was born. Because the birth was premature they put Jennifer in an incubator. She was a tiny, wrinkly thing and resembled a laboratory specimen under glass. Mother looked great with her face made-up and her hair brushed out. She kept sneaking into the bathroom to smoke.

Grandmother and I mostly took care of Jennifer. Mother worked late, slept late, held the baby for about five minutes over her cup of black coffee and the day's first cigarette. She bounced Jennifer on her knee until the first sign of any discomfort on Jennifer's part then she handed her off to me or Grandmother. Denise wanted nothing to do with Jennifer.

245

Suddenly, Denise was no longer the baby. I fed Jennifer, changed her, held her when she cried and listened to Grandmother for tips on what to do and what not to do like make sure you clean her thoroughly inside her private area, as Grandmother called it. In the first days I watched her eyes start to focus. Then she was able to hold her head up. She made near-silent coos, sighs. In the middle of the night, she cried so fearfully Grandmother's touch was the only one that brought her relief.

I didn't fit in with the kids at school. The popular boys and girls walked to school with crowds around them. If I wasn't walking with Harry I walked alone, or if I felt particularly brave, on the outskirts of one of the circles. Billy Donovan could hang out with the most popular group and then hang out with me and Harry. I didn't have the cheerleader glow like a lot of girls; and I resented them for it. In high school Harry and I were in different classes. We met in the third-floor girls' room after second period for a cigarette, and also in the courtyard after fifth period. I can see her standing outside the Building C door, drenched without a hat or rain jacket, smoking a Salem.

The first time I tried pot with her was on the hill behind the high school. Harry said she liked it better than glue or beer. She showed me how to hold the joint and draw in the smoke. It made me choke and I coughed wildly but nothing happened. The second time I tried was on the same hill during the winter. We shared a joint and I was still convinced that nothing happened. Walking down the hill, I began to feel powerful rushes swelling up through my body and I could almost hear them as they swished out through my ears. I was confused and my heart was beating fast. I slipped on the snow and slid all the way down the hill, by the time I got to the bottom I was laughing so uncontrollably my nose was running down my face. At home Grandmother wanted to know what was wrong with my eyes because they were red. I don't remember what I told her, but I ate voraciously then went directly to bed.

That was the last time I smoked pot until I was older when I found it made me paranoid, more depressed, and hungry. Harry said smoking relaxed her and made her feel part of everything. Mother said that too. I should have known why people were showing up at the house for quick visits. And all the phone calls, younger neighborhood kids too — including Harry.

With her bathroom cabinet overflowing with pill bottles, Mrs. Hale goes on tirades about drugs. She says if they could just get rid of drugs there would be so much less trouble in the world. Sometimes, just when I start to feel better is when I play with the dosages, or stop taking my medications. But after all these years I've learned that the longer I manage to stay on the proper dosage, the longer I go without major trouble. Denise started doing cocaine when she was young. It's the reason her first husband lost his hair salons.

I've missed so many years. There were treatments. I was in and out of the hospital and recovering at Grandmother's. I don't know how she managed during that time. Grandmother kept things inside. She never voluntarily spoke about anything unless I brought it up first. We must put it behind us so we can heal. Nothing we say can change a thing.

A light. A shadow. A voice. The heater switches off. It must be midday and sunny judging by the amount of light stealing in. Shouts of school children from the nearby elementary school. The regular bang of metal to metal from somewhere. Every few minutes a plane taking off or landing from the Boston Airport. They say when the wind blows a certain way they route the planes over Winterhill. Then the song of birds.

The first time Harry ran away from home she lived in the loft of a barn in Bobby Burke's back yard. At dark she came out to hang with us behind the Curtis School. Another time she ran she hitchhiked to Boston and we didn't hear anything for a week until the authorities found her and she was returned. Her reasons for running were vague. If I asked her why she ran she said oh I'm just not going to put up with their crap anymore and dismiss it with a hand gesture. She never suggested anything wrong was going on at home and she seemed to have more freedom than any other kid, coming and going as she pleased. I never got to talk with Eddie about anything after it happened. We never spoke another word to each other before the Harringtons sold their house and moved away.

No sooner I was getting into boys, Harry was losing interest in them. Billy Donovan was sensational, for about a minute. Before I even figured out what was going on it was over. We made out, rolled around in Bobby Burke's loft, and I knew it was time. I liked how our touching made me feel. And I liked Billy. He tried to unsnap my jeans but he couldn't. I was self-conscious that I was too fat and my jeans too tight so I slipped over and unfastened them myself. Billy lifted my legs in the air and pulled my jeans over them. I forgot about my sneakers, so Billy just pulled them off without unlacing them. He said he had a rubber and removed one from his pants' pocket. Then he dropped his pants and underwear at the same time and Billy looked at my legs and I thought he must think they're too fat. He got down beside me and we tried to pick up where we left off but this time he was in a hurry to get the rubber on and get inside me. I wanted him to kiss me, but he sucked on one of my breasts so hard I told him to go easy it hurt. Then it was over.

I didn't know what to make of it. If that was it, then why did everyone act like it was such a big deal? Harry said that's the way it was with boys. She asked me did I have an orgasm and I didn't. She kissed me on the cheek and hugged me. Said she

248

loved me, I was her best friend ever. There were other feelings she had for me too. Harry I said I'm not like that.

Seven

I've had two relationships that lasted longer than one month. Aaron and I made it six months, though it was doomed from the beginning since he was my therapist. Nancy and I were together for eight months. It might have been longer but she left me. Who wants to spend their life with someone who mopes around depressed all of the time. She knew about me when we moved in together, but she thought she could change me. I want to make it better for you she said. Nancy did make life better for me. But she wanted to make it better for me on her terms.

Aaron drank. After we became involved, he suggested I get a new therapist, which I did. Ours wasn't as much a physical relationship, though we had good sex the first month; but Aaron wanted someone who needed him, and wouldn't mind when he came home late from drinking after a long day of his sorting through other people's dirty laundry. I needed someone who wouldn't mind if they found me in the evening the same way they left me in the morning, in bed. Aaron understood me more than any other person I've known, including my grandmother. He came home slurring his words and tottering, dropped his clothes beside the bed and jumped in like an overgrown boy with a wide smile. I was awake and we embraced. Tell me how you are. And I told him how I was feeling while he stared at me with his blue eyes flaming red, nodding his head compassionately to my every word. When I finished, we shut the light, held each other in the dark until he began to snore loudly and I kept my arms wrapped tight around him.

Mrs. Hale says I could be an attractive woman if I lost a little weight and did something with my hair and dress. She refers to my outfits as work clothes although by now she knows the corduroys, jeans, sweatshirts and t-shirts I wear in work or out. She loves shoes. Shoes are always on sale and there is always a good reason to buy a new pair. There is a closet off the master bedroom just for her shoes. Her dresses, like her shoes, demonstrate no individual taste. Dozens of slight variations on the same theme. Old-time standard patterns and colors. Plaids, florals, pastels. Her evening dresses, like her expensive blouses and skirts, are dry-cleaned. I handle that too, making sure the cleaners follow Mrs. Hale's specific instructions and seeing to her list of what night she'll need which outfit. Dr. Hale is always giving or receiving some kind of award or attending a dinner with a board member from the hospital. The Hales even dine with the cardinal himself once a year, their social schedule is filled months in advance.

Grandmother wore the same blue knee-length dress every day. Once a week she washed it out and hung it to dry overnight. She wore simple black shoes and a blue and white check apron from the time she dressed in the morning until she undressed at night. Mother said it was a waste of money trying to buy nice clothes for me because I wouldn't wear them; and even if I did, I wouldn't look good in them. One of the few times I remember being dressed up was when I made my first holy communion in a white bridal-like dress with a veil. I had my picture taken holding an open a catechism and the rosary beads in my hands. The photographer touched up the photo so I had this unnatural rosy glow about my cheeks. Grandmother brought me to Flora the hairdresser and she put my hair up in big rollers and I sat under the dryer. When Flora took out the rollers my hair was fluffier and curlier than usual for the entire afternoon.

In a city like Winterhill it's easy to remain anonymous because it is so congested with recent immigrants, students, and blue-collar families. I continued to live in Wilton for years. After everything happened I had tried going back to the high school. But the eyes were upon me everywhere I went. In school, on the street, in the supermarket. In time, the event diminished in the public's consciousness. At first there were newspaper articles and news spots, one year ago today, five years ago today; but there are too many other stories, even in a place like Wilton.

After I found my way out of Wilton, I began to understand what it was like to walk down the street or into a store or coffee shop without anyone having a clue about my past. To be able to look into the eyes of a clerk or a waitress, stand at a bus stop or in line at the supermarket without the whispers and glares was completely new to me. It was the first taste of freedom I knew in my adult life.

For a long time I had no choice but to remain in Wilton. If I didn't have Grandmother's house, I wouldn't have been able to take care of myself. Grandmother said she would never sell the house. She spent her entire life in Wilton, and she was going to die there. She didn't care that people talked. She didn't care what they said. As time went on I came and went. If I was able to manage on my own, I lived in Brockton, or Fall River, and eventually, north to Winterhill. If things got bad and I was hospitalized, I found myself back at Grandmother's until I was able to get back on my feet.

Going back to Wilton after being away I noticed the changes more readily. The old storefronts are fast-food and market chains. Factory Row is lined with discount malls and condominiums. The farms around the edge of town have all been developed into suburbs. Now that Grandmother is gone and the house is sold, I can't imagine any reason to return to Wilton ever again. When I went there to sign the last of the papers, I had to strain to see people I recognized as I drove through town. I saw one of the Donovan brothers with his wife and their kids coming out of a pizza shop. Mike Kelly, who sniffed glue with Harry and later bought pot from my mother, who went to jail for breaking and entering, was wandering down Main Street, bloated and gray. Caroline La Farge, the head cheerleader, still looked wholesome and fit, walking into a bank dressed in preppy clothes with her two perfect-looking children.

I drove through the old neighborhood, down Foster Street, past Grandmother's house, down to the dead end and the duplexes where Harry lived. Harry's blue house was brown. I turned around, took a left on to Fulton and a right on to Clark Street. The six-apartment tenement was no longer dark gray but an ugly purple. There were windows open in Mother's corner apartment. I could see children jumping around and playing. I heard a woman's voice shouting go outside if you're not going to play nice I'm in no fucking mood for your shit.

I'm cleaning a house which is made up of a one-story series of long narrow connecting rooms. The building is windowless and I quickly lose track of the entrance. Room to room I clean asking various family members I encounter where the door is. Suddenly the mother of the house confronts me with an order to re-clean one of the rooms. You could at least say please. We have words back and forth over who is in charge. The next thing I know I'm in one of the rooms and the family members are all lying around the floor with blood pouring out from gashes and I have a knife in my hand thinking that I will be blamed even though I know that I didn't do it. The mother comes out from nowhere and attacks me. In self-defense I stab her continually. I hear and feel the blade tearing into flesh until

253

she falls dead.

I had my most intense sex with Nancy. I never liked cocaine. It has the opposite effect on me than it has on most people. I get more withdrawn and paranoid. But when Nancy put a little on my clitoris and did the things she did, it was something I'd never experienced. The problem was Nancy wanted to be my savior. I should be in college. I should do this or that. She bought me books, magazines, a portable television on my birthday because she couldn't stand the fact that I spent my free time sitting in the easy chair staring off into space. The harder she tried to change me, the more frustrated she became until she began to be mean. I didn't mind the intense sex, but sometimes I wanted to be softer and gentle but the rougher the better she said. I knew she went out on me. Everyone was after her. Men too. She was an Italian beauty with dark curly hair, green eyes, olive skin and the kind of body women kill for, with oversize breasts, a thin waist and long legs.

Aaron didn't mind what I did or didn't do, as long as I didn't bother him about staying out late and drinking. He was gentle and patient. I felt safe with him and trusted him. Aaron was fond of sailing and owned small boat that he docked at the harbor. Several occasions he packed a picnic lunch and we sailed around Boston harbor. I can see him sitting at the back steering with a can of beer in his hand, looking out in every direction with a content smile. Aaron didn't talk much and talked less out on the boat. Those were some of the most peaceful times I've ever known. We sailed, gazed at the skyline, and waved to other boaters passing by. When we were hungry Aaron dropped anchor and we ate in silence in some out-of-the-way island cove. As the day wore on Aaron became drunk but he steadfastly kept control over the boat and got us back home as it was darkening.

No one would be interested in me now. It's not that I overeat any longer. In fact, I eat less than I ever did. I've never been able to lose much weight. I don't exercise. I see people out running in the streets or working out on treadmills and bike machines in the window of the fitness center. I see Harry doing a flying leap to make a game-winning catch. Everyone surrounds her; the boys lift her up on their shoulders and carry her off the field. Harry with her right arm up in her air, fist clenched.

<u>Eight</u>

Mother sometimes claimed they ran off one night and eloped. He lived with her off and on at the Clark Street apartment. Ray looked right through you as if you weren't there. He was dark and muscular with a thick head of black hair that he greased back. In the summer, he went around shirtless and his arms and chest were tattooed. He wore a bushy mustache, chain-smoked, his next cigarette always placed behind his right ear, and when he lit that one he replaced it with another from his pack. It was difficult to understand him because his manner of speech was a low mumble. On Monday nights Mother and Ray played cards with friends, drinking and smoking until early morning. Ray would get into fights over the games and once punched my mother's friend's boyfriend from across the table. Ray's first wife divorced him before they had kids. He had two children with his second wife, who lived out of state. He owned a junkyard near Fall River and Mother met him on her waitress job. It wasn't until later we found out about his past. Mother was fond of borrowing his white Cadillac convertible and driving around Wilton. Grandmother put her out when Mother was beginning to see him. It wasn't because of Ray. Grandmother gave Mother several warnings, but Mother wouldn't stop selling pot out of Grandmother's house. There was no room for us at the Clark Street apartment, so Denise and I remained with Grandmother. At first, Ray was there all the time. Then they started fighting and police were frequently called by neighbors until eventually he was barred.

In less than five minutes I can clean my one room with its minuscule kitchenette and a tinier bathroom. I have one dresser half full of clothes and a small closet with room to spare. I own a pair of sneakers and construction boots. Food no longer carries the importance it once did for me, and I heat soup out of the can or make toast. I failed when I first tried to move away from Grandmother's and make it on my own. But it was only until I moved far enough away from Wilton I was able to stay away. There had to be enough space so that it made it that much harder for me to go back. Roommates I vaguely remember, various apartments, jobs, hospitalizations. Sometimes Grandmother took the train to Boston to visit me in the hospital. When I was well enough I would take the train to visit her. However, I found that the longer I was away from Wilton, the more painful my infrequent visits were on me. Grandmother said she understood if I found it impossible to return. She found it impossible to leave.

I started the cleaning business on my own. I placed notices up around neighborhoods and in the local papers. It took a while, but, eventually, I got a call. It was the Hales. They were my first clients. If I liked clothes, I could buy anything I wanted now. I could buy a new car. My old Datsun has been out in the street buried in a snow bank since the second big snowstorm of the season and the registration has expired. I take public transportation and walk the last stretch to the Hales'. Since they are my only clients, I leave all my cleaning equipment there. Mrs. Hale always questions my bills, how much window cleaner or floor wax I use and how they're only responsible for what supplies I use in their house. I remind her that they are my only clients, everything I buy I use in her home, and she signs the check as if she's doing it under protest.

There was a time when I was reading much and I had designs on going to college and studying psychiatry. After receiving my high school equivalency, I took some courses at the local community college. I was working days cleaning house, and going to school part-time evenings. That was after Aaron and before Nancy. One of the longest periods I've gone making progress. But then I got sick again and fell behind in schoolwork. I tried to catch up later, but I couldn't and I never went back. Nancy brought home the forms so I could register again and went so far as fill them out for me. All you have to do is sign them. I wouldn't.

Harry paid school no attention. She made cheat sheets and slipped them up her sleeve or under her dress. Even in elementary school, where there was no way you could skip school without getting caught, Harry would skip. She took the train to Boston, or the bus to Fall River, and suffered the consequences. Standard punishment at home was a strapping at the hands of her father. Harry dropped her pants or lifted her skirt to display the strap welts on her thighs. It really isn't that bad and it's over in a few seconds.

Grandmother never put a hand on me or Denise, though there were times Denise warranted it with her swearing and being disrespectful to Grandmother. Mother broke a wooden spoon over my head when she was on the phone and trying to talk. I was in the kitchen fighting with Denise. It was the closest thing she could grab but it didn't hurt. Mother would throw things, or swing at you. But it never really hurt. She yelled and blew off steam then it was over.

Mother told me lies about my father. He did send money. She said he abandoned us both without any thought. Grandmother told me that one time my father sent a ticket to fly me to California and visit him. Mother sold the ticket. Grandmother kept much of this from me when I was young. She said she just wanted to protect me. At Christmas there were gifts, at least in the early years. A box of candy. Another time he sent a

258

small wooden house with tiny carved people and furniture to put inside.

My dreams come right back upon wakening. Or later in the day one might surface from the depths and seize me. I'm never certain if I dreamed the dream the night before, or just remembered a version of it. On the seventy-seven bus I'm suddenly walking with Harry. We've skipped school, though it is night. We are in a part of town we don't recognize, near the highway, the backside of one of the old factories. We come out from an alley, around a corner, and walk into a small lot that is a dead end. At the far end of the lot is a car full of men. We see them just as they see us. Harry says turn around and keep walking like everything's fine. There's the roar of an engine then tires squealing. They're coming right for us. Run Harry says run.

Because I take the same bus at the same time every day, I recognize people who regularly ride the seventy-seven. There's a smart-looking young couple too cool for anyone who giggle and whisper to each other; the guy who gets on at Warren Street is a little slow and has something wrong with his eyes, it's like they only open half-way; an elderly Portuguese man in some kind of green work uniform always studies any of the young girls aboard; and a large Haitian woman is already sitting at the very front of the bus when I get on.

I read the ads on the bus over and over. They change every two months. I can go to school evenings, learn one of a hundred languages, electronics or broadcasting. Am I tired and bored with my present job? I've never considered a career in the navy. There are so many ways to invest my money, how do I know my investor has my best interest in mind? How will I know? And I will not leave the Hales' until I have something to do. It's not that I need the money. It's what to do with my time.

The Hales live in one of the most expensive neighborhoods around. It's an area wedged in the backside of Harvard Square

259

in Cambridge. Big, beautiful old houses owned by beautiful old families adorn large tree and lawn-lined streets. When my cleaning business was going at its height, I was cleaning six different homes in the Quad. I made a lot of money. I just put it in the bank. I did it because six of houses kept me busy six days a week ten hours a day. But it wasn't enough. I crashed. And came back. And crashed again. Now it's just the Hales. If Mr. Hale wasn't a psychiatrist, and Mrs. Hale so afraid of hiring a new cleaner, they would have let me go too.

Nine

Grandmother said although Grandfather was capable of being a mean man, inside he was a good man. In the beginning, he seemed like a nice Irish boy and her family liked him; but as the years went on, his family's problems became more apparent, as did my grandfather's. It wasn't easy for him growing up she said. She could be forgiving like that. If she didn't have much good to say about a person, Grandmother said little. If I knew the family Grandfather came from she told me, I would understand his actions better.

When Mother moved out her reason for getting a small apartment was money. She said when she had more, she'd get a bigger place and we could go with her. At least the Clark Street apartment was close by and she could be near her girls. Mornings on the way to school I'd see Ray's convertible parked out front. One night Harry and I were coming back from the movies and the police were in front of Mother's place because she and Ray had a fight. Ray was enraged, swearing out in the middle of the street while the police were trying to control him. Another officer was sitting with my mother on the apartment steps. She had her face in her hands, crying. Ray kept calling her a fucking slut. There were many people gathered around the scene who knew me and my family. The cops made Ray drive away and helped Mother back into the apartment. Then people were beginning to stare at me and I hurried off embarrassed.

Under my arms the smell changes over the course of days.

261

Same with my scalp, vagina and my feet. From the clean-soap smell after a shower to the first hints of sweat and fluids. After several days the various bodily odors take on fouler essences. The direct rankness of my armpits. The earthy potato smell of my ear wax. The fishy urine smell of my vagina. The sweaty sneaker-sock smell of my feet. The muddy smell of my scalp. All of them at the tips of my fingers.

During a treatment they put a breathing bag over my mouth. Someone stands next to me throughout the procedure, squeezing air into my lungs so that I don't stop breathing. I'm a blank sheet of paper when I leave the hospital. What is clear are the simple, concrete things. I walk. I see. I sip tea. I smoke a cigarette. The day is gray or blue. I sleep an hour or two. I keep everything away or I think I do because in actuality I have no control. A light. A shadow. A voice. Enough time passes, probes into my memory. A fleeting look into a dream. A song on a passing car radio. Brings something back.

We were her angels, darlings, sweet things. But never her children. Never I love you. She seemed to be broke every time Christmas or a birthday came around so Grandmother bought gifts and planned parties that Mother failed to attend. Denise wanted the big birthday parties with two dozen kids and presents and all the attention on her. I hated parties. I only wanted my favorite orange spice cake which Grandmother made for me. When I fought with Denise she used situations like this to be hurtful. You don't even have any friends to invite to a party. Denise leaves two messages in a day. Then one the following day. I return her call. How am I she was worried sick when I didn't call right back. Take a trip out to visit in California. Dan wants to meet her family, he'll pay for my first-class ticket round trip. I'll love it out there. Wait until I see her house and the pool and take a drive in Dan's refinished Corvette. I can come now, or later when the baby comes. She'll probably need some help then. Can I believe the way it's worked out for her after all these years.

Every time something new comes along, usually a man, it's the right one and this is what she's been waiting for all her life. Now is not a good time. There's much I have to take care of here. Maybe later after the baby comes. I say these words to Denise but I don't believe them. I don't want to see her. I don't want to see her baby when it is born. I don't want to go to California, except to find my father's grave. Denise will suck me in and suck me dry.

There have been at least two abortions with her past men. Dan's the oldest of all her men at sixty. But I'm glad she has Dan. If she were without a man right now, I wouldn't have one peaceful moment until she had what she saw as her rightful share to Grandmother's money. She plays people like marbles Harry said. I know she's your sister, but don't trust her. Harry could talk with a kid for a few minutes and come away with an astute assessment. That kid's got a lot of problems. That girl thinks every boy is in love with her.

Harry said she knew about her brother Eddie. What was the big deal? I tried it again with Harry, after I went all the way with Billy Donovan and Brian Walsh who I went steady with for two weeks. It didn't seem right. It wasn't like the time years before on Bear Hill. I just kept thinking that this was my friend Harry I was kissing. I let Harry have her way a little with me and helped her to an orgasm. But after that I avoided that kind of stuff with her and we started to see less of each other.

I learned that my mother was pregnant with Jennifer from Harry. I told Grandmother who turned bright red, then completely pale. Mother said she intended to surprise us with the news. We assumed that Ray was the father. It hurt me that Harry knew more about my mother's personal life than me. I didn't see Mother much then. Once a week maybe, except for a wave

263

hello if she drove by and I was out around the neighborhood. Harry was at the Clark Street apartment a lot, buying pot, hanging around when the weather was cold. Now whenever I saw Harry she was high or wanted to get high.

It wasn't as if I was losing my mother. She was never mine to lose. Harry was my savior. Outside of my grandmother she was all I had and she got me through. Now, even when I saw her, she was growing distant and withdrawn as she smoked more. Somewhere around that time Harry's brother Eddie was arrested for breaking into houses. Eddie hung around Dad's Variety. Dad was a heavy old man who chewed stubby cigars. In addition to cigarettes, milk and bread, Dad sold small appliances like radios and toasters. Harry said that the merchandise was stolen. I don't know what else Dad did, but Eddie was one of a regular group of older boys, most of them who quit school and used Dad's as a kind of home away from home.

Eddie had to go to the reform school in Plymouth for three months because it was the second time he was arrested. I don't know why, but when Eddie was at Plymouth, Harry ran away again. I wasn't even aware she was on the run until I called on her one day and her folks acted uneasy and said Kathleen wasn't there and started asking me when was the last time I'd seen her. Billy Donovan told me Harry was hiding out in the woods at Bear Hill Reservation during the day and at night she was sneaking into town and staying at my mother's apartment on Clark Street. I ran over to my mother's apartment. There were two people there who Mother said worked with her at the bar. They didn't stay long and after they left I confronted my mother about Harry. It wasn't true and she didn't know where I got my information from but she hadn't seen Harry in days.

I hurried home to fetch my bike. I peddled furiously towards Bear Hill Reservation. There were miles of woods and Harry could be anywhere but I didn't care. Fate, I assumed, would direct me to her. I negotiated the rotary around Route 133 and started in on one of the woods roads. My body had worked up a sweat from my ride, and now that I was in the woods it was cooler and there was a breeze that said autumn was around the corner. The forest was still in late-summer green, but tinges of red and yellow could be detected on leaf tips. There were people walking dogs and a bunch of stoned laughing boys. I asked all of them if they'd seen a girl about my age with blond hair. None of them had, though one of the stoned boys said he wished he had and the others all broke up laughing.

I knew Harry's spots in the woods, places she'd taken me to over the years. I buried my bike in some brambles and went ahead on foot to Gone Place which was right behind Meadow Pond. Gone Place was so close to the pond where everyone picnicked and swam during the summertime you could hear all the shrieks and life-guard whistles, but you were completely alone and sealed off from the crowd. Harry first showed me the footpath. It was only a short walk up through thick underbrush to a small clearing. Under pine trees and years and years of fallen pine needles lay the softest natural bed. She wasn't there.

She wasn't at Indian Ground either, the place where kids went to party. The spot was marked by large, dead and burned-out trees which lent the area a strange and forbidding air. It was nestled on the backside of Little Bear Hill and you could see miles of woods spreading out towards Brockton. Indian Ground, Harry said, was sacred and kids should be respectful when they party there.

My last chance was My Ground. Harry said nobody knew about it except her, until she took me there. There were no trails. It was just a spot. Nothing special about it. You'd walk right past it without a notice. Harry knew exactly where the spot of My Ground was. She said she came upon it by accident one day, but as soon as she found herself there, she had a peculiar feeling and knew it would be her own sacred place. She never approached the place the same way twice so she never wore a footpath there. I only knew it was between Corser Brook and what we called the Old Mine Road although there was never any evidence of an old mine. I started walking a crisscross pattern between the brook and the road. I knew she had to be at My Ground. It was the only spot where Harry could go when she absolutely wanted to be alone. I called out her name. I called out her name again. Harry, it's me Laurel.

Ten

One day the temperature is in single digits. The next day it's fifty degrees. Yesterday was blizzard-like snows. Today is spring rain. Water drips off four sides of the house, tapping ceaselessly in irregular rhythms.

There was a windy day in March, after a long cold spell suddenly one day was seventy-five degrees and Dilboy Park overflowing with kids. Dad's Variety sold out of ten-cent kite kits, by mid-afternoon most of them lay in hundreds of pieces on the park floor. Harry's brother Eddie bought a one-dollar kite at a hobby shop in Brockton and he and Harry flew that kite so high we could barely see it. Harry and Eddie stood ground below, taking turns holding the wooden handle with the kite string wrapped around it, eyes to the heavens, serious in their communication with each other — let a little out, take a little in — intent on keeping that kite up there as high and for as long as they were able.

I don't know what I would do without cigarettes. The medications come three times a day. It's not like I notice them in a way that I feel high, but everything's held at a distance so that I'm able to move safely, if only inside my head. The joy of cigarettes is endless with each deep breath, smoke and fire, hand to mouth.

Grandmother didn't drive so after Grandfather died she sold his car. Once or twice during each summer, however, she took us by bus to Singing Sands Beach near Plymouth. She packed sandwiches, cookies, fruit and soda into a big basket

267

and Denise and I took along whatever beach toys we could find. As we grew older, I enjoyed these ocean-side excursions less and less. I was becoming more self-conscious about my body and embarrassed by my exaggerated roundness. I sat on the blanket wearing cut-offs, a t-shirt and big hat while Denise pranced around in her bikini entertaining all the males in the immediate vicinity. A few times Harry came along. She always wore a one-piece suit, even though she had a better figure than Denise. The boys checked out Harry too, but Harry didn't care and she never flaunted it. I never liked the smell of the ocean. High tide was bearable and had a certain crispness, but low tide turned my stomach sour.

Some green teas are low in caffeine, others higher. Some are laced with various herbs. I used milk and sugar. Then honey. And now just black. It doesn't matter how high or low in caffeine my sleep is never affected. The part of a cup I like least is when I get near the bottom and it's had time to cool, the bottom-of-the-cup sediments turn bitter. I drink it, sediment and all, listening to my stomach gurgle deep and long.

My late twenties I call my suicide period. I never directly attempted to take my own life, though many times I seriously contemplated it. I was drinking very heavily, taking the drugs my doctors prescribed as well as cocaine and pills that I could buy. Grandmother was horrified but helpless to do anything. In one of my stays in the hospital I met a guy who was getting ECT for his crazy behavior. When I was released he asked me if he could call me when he got better and I never thought when I gave him my number he actually would. Vanity can come out of nowhere and suddenly I was derailed. He was a small and thin guy, but handsome. The idea that someone so attractive could be interested in me was enough.

I began to hang around with his friends. They were mostly my age, a few were from Wilton but many were from the outly-

ing small towns and places like New Bedford. They were drug-
gies who always had a little money but never seemed to work. I
had a crazy affair with Teddy. It was a party day and night.
Then we broke up and I started sleeping with a friend of his. I
wouldn't go home at night. I woke up drank and drugged myself into obliteration until I woke again. I slept with anyone
who had a bed. It was mostly with guys, though several of the
women in the group were topless dancers who were more interested in other women off hours. For a brief period I became
involved with one named Sunny, but she had more problems
than I did and we were doomed from the start. Once I woke up
in a bathtub full of ice water because I passed out from drinking too much Jack Daniel's and taking too many pills. Another
time I had to be rushed to the hospital and had my stomach
pumped. It didn't last long, that period of my life. A year, two
at the most. Then I was back in the hospital for treatments and
when Grandmother got me home she managed to keep me
away from those people.

If I fly to California to see Denise I can visit my father's
grave. They are in completely different parts of the state. I
don't want to see her; and I don't know for sure if I want to see
his grave. Hold on tight he said when I rode him like a horse
and he pranced around the living room of our old house on all
fours making horse sounds. Another game of ours was I'll get
you, where he chased me around saying I'll get you I'll get you.
I ran excitedly ahead, and he allowed me to remain just out of
reach until I finally ran out of breath and he caught me, raised
me up over his shoulders, and played me like a trombone as he
marched around the living room.

Except for Harry, my closest friends in school were two
teachers. Mrs. Macken was my home economics teacher, and
Miss Wilkins my seventh-grade English teacher. Miss Wilkins
was from the South and spoke with an accent. She was pretty,

and youthful. She was born with some kind of birth defect and had no fingers on her left hand. When we had to write stories or reports, she often read mine aloud to the class as an example. Sometimes after school I wandered into her room and sat in the front row while she readied to leave and we chatted about how she ended up in Wilton coming from Virginia and what was college like in Boston. I told her about my home life, she said my grandmother sounded like a fine woman. Then one day she announced that she was leaving to get married. The following Monday morning she was gone. Mrs. Hill, a mean, tired-of-teaching older woman who banged the top of her desk with her fist and yelled damn damn damn this class, took over. I never saw Miss Wilkins after that.

The warm spell melts all the snow. My car has been fitted with a locked boot on the wheel and was sideswiped while it was buried under the snow during the winter. At the traffic office I pay the money to have the boot removed. The car won't start and needs repairs. It's fifteen years old and I don't have the energy to deal with it. I dial a number in the phone book. The ad that says highest money paid for your junk car turns out to be a guy saying it will cost me fifty dollars to have him come and take it away. I don't really need a car. I only had one because when the cleaning business was going I had to have means to get my equipment and supplies around. I pay the man the fifty and watch him tow the car away. It is cold and getting colder. This week will be a blue moon.

I don't know where I will be three or four or six months from now. There are so many people in this city it is easy just to wash out. No one notices anything. I've had several treatments while living in this space, and the people directly above me haven't a clue. I tell them I've been visiting a relative or away on vacation. Since most of them don't understand English it's not difficult.

270

In my life there are two places where I have felt grounded. The first house, with my father and mother, though I was so young I vaguely remember any concrete details, and those that I do recall might be only in my imagination. The second place is Grandmother's house, although later it became like a slow torture chamber, despite her support and love. I couldn't get out of the loop there. A light. A shadow. A voice. When the weather improves I'll purchase one of those train passes and go around the country stopping at different cities. I'll see places I've never seen and experience different landscapes and people. Perhaps in some far off city, town, or state I could never have imagined, I'll find a place where I want to stay.

<u>Eleven</u>

I see my therapist every other week now. She is an American-raised Japanese woman, petite, attractive, shiny black hair, skin like porcelain, brilliant mind. I fantasize about her.

As I get older doctors and therapists look younger. She is younger than me by ten years. My experiences with therapists have been anything from total failures to an occasional breakthrough. There was a brutish old man who took an impatient attitude with me and somehow implied that my problems were all brought on by me. There was a woman who sat and stared. She never said a word during my entire session. She sat and stared at me, visit after visit. Dr. Isu is the best yet, though I guess she's only been out of school a few years. She can listen, respond, and be supportive. She knows everything there is to know about me. It's as if she's a best friend except I pay her.

She was the one who suggested we meet every other week. I was afraid that the longer I am away, the easier it is to slide into my old thought patterns; the easier it is to think I don't need a therapist and see my therapist as part of my problem; the easier it is to play with the doses of my medication, come apart and wind up in treatment again. If you don't do something about it yourself, you'll continue the same pattern for the rest of your life the old brute therapist barked at me.

I'm walking through the park, it's late at night and the light at the basketball court is shut off. I'm halfway across the park, directly in the center, where no light from streetlights is able to reach. Harry appears from shadows and startles me. She says

272

that everything's all right. She smiles and begins one of her silly free-form dances. Where have you been Harry? Stop it Harry. Tell me where you have been.

When I do the Hales' hardwood floors with oil soap it takes me the exact number of mop strokes every week. I clean the same four-foot square sections at a time. In one hour I can do the wooden floors on all levels. The new cook is already complaining to me how the Hales only want to pay him from the time he shows up at the house, while, at the same time, they expect him to stop at the grocery store on his drive in. I've heard it all before. He's a strange, large man perhaps my age. He has a look in his eye, the look I've seen before, like he's seeing something else in addition to what's in his field of vision. He talks to himself in the kitchen. I'll punch you in the fucking face. Listen motherfucker I'll rip your heart out. He was a musician and his cousin was someone famous who I never heard of. Person to person, he has a sweet, gentle demeanor. The Hales love his cooking and he likes the kids.

Once my mother had a dog. It was a birthday gift from a boyfriend, a fluffy white thing about the size of a cat. Her name was Ginger. She peed and shat all over Grandmother's house and since mother was never around Grandmother and I cleaned up and made sure the dog got fed, watered and walked. No matter how many times I walked her, Ginger preferred to relieve herself in the house. When Mother was around, she paid more attention to Ginger than she did to me or Denise. She would fuss over her, pet her, kiss her and talk to her like a little child. Then one day Ginger got out of the house. Harry and I went all over the place on our bikes looking for her. The next morning a police car pulled up, the officers had Ginger's collar. She was hit by a car and killed on Main Street. I ran to my room and cried hard. I felt like it was my fault she was loose in the first place. Grandmother said it was no one's fault, we

273

couldn't watch Ginger twenty-four hours a day. Mother cried hysterically, trying to blame us for not watching the dog closer. Grandmother told her it wasn't our dog and Mother was lucky we did what we had done for Ginger.

I never liked pets after that. Cats I especially don't trust. And I can't stand the smell of those odor boxes. Denise's second husband owned a horse farm on the Wilton-Townsend line. She had an expensive black horse while she was married and spent a small fortune on equipment, clothes and private riding lessons. Then she had a fall and broke her wrist and never rode again. She and her husband lived in a big farmhouse that was remodeled. There was a pool and many acres of land. Everything was going so well and the next thing she cut her wrists again. He was a monster she couldn't live with. There were stories about physical and mental abuse. Even though she's my sister, I'm never sure what to believe. Since I can remember, Denise has never been able to distinguish between truth and lies.

The woman upstairs does chores any hour of the day or night. Hers are the heaviest footsteps. They are all overweight, but she is the heaviest, square jaw, square shoulders, square frame, black square cut dress, dark square-cut hair. I hear her footsteps back and forth in the kitchen, up and down the cellar stairs where she has a load of laundry going. I hear her footsteps ascend the creaky stairs between the two floors of her apartment. She blows her nose loud and long. I cannot let go of a vivid memory I have of her, the first summer I lived here. One afternoon I walked down the driveway, I paused looking for the keys to my basement door. I heard the back door close and she came down the stairs in all her abundant squareness, holding a large round platter overflowing with raw red meat she intended to grill. In one hand she had a long two-pronged fork, in the other she carried the platter, full of rings of orange sausage, bloody steaks and fleshy pink chops. There was enough meat to feed a dozen people but there are only three adults. They always cook like that. She smiled a wide gold-capped smile and said the only word she knows in English, a long drawn out hiiiii.

Mother was miserable when she was pregnant with baby Jennifer. She was fighting a lot with Ray. Then they were going to be married. Ray was the love of her life. And he was going to be the father of her baby. She continued to smoke and drink and work nights at the lounge, and she was impossible to be around. Her outbursts, which she could always take to extreme limits, became more frequent and irrational. Grandmother was worried that she might lose the baby, and urged her to move back into the house with us. Mother insisted that once she and Ray were married, they were going to buy a big house outside of town, then she could take us and Grandmother wouldn't have to be put out one more day. Mother could be cruel to Grandmother and say things like I know you don't want me or my kids here.

For several weeks Mother planned a wedding and spent her free hours making arrangements. She scheduled a justice of the peace, planned a party at a local hall and hired a band. The next thing the wedding was off and they broke up again. Harry alluded to the fact that Ray was never sure if the baby was his. Harry also told me that on several occasions Ray had hit my mother. It was nothing that I ever noticed in terms of bruises, but he slapped her face and pushed her around when things got heated between them. Harry said that she didn't like Ray, there was something about him she couldn't trust but my mother was blinded by love. I don't think my mother ever knew what love was; Ray was the most available guy with the most money.

Until I was in therapy, I always thought Grandmother was perfect. She was my savior. But in trying to be perfect, one makes mistakes. Sometimes I feel that Denise might have turned out better if Grandmother gave her the same kind of attention that she gave me. And Grandmother always said that I was the good one, and she didn't know what happened with Denise. In a way she was right. But Denise always said that Grandmother loved me and not her and Mother didn't love either of us. Looking back Grandmother made it very clear that she favored me.

In therapy, I started to see things differently. You get shaken up that way and all the usual defense mechanisms get eaten away. You think yourself innocent and realize no one is. You think someone perfect and realize you only want them to be perfect so you see them accordingly. You think you acted one way for one reason, only to find the opposite to be true.

Twelve

There are two dozen various cleaners in the box where I store my supplies. Glass cleaners, floor cleaners, floor waxes, hardwood floor oils, disinfectants, bowl and tile cleaners, grease cutters, stove cleaners, laundry detergents, bleaches. By the time I am finished with my work, the Hales' house reeks of the disparate chemicals. It's a seductive bouquet, and I find myself breathing deep and slow through my nostrils. I smell Grandmother's house. I see her glistening kitchen floor and the waxy sheen of the red pine floorboards in the humble living room; the glistening tiled bathroom; clean folded stacks of laundry I could bury my face in and smell fresh air.

Nancy ate a strict vegetarian diet. Drugs were fine but meat wasn't. She wouldn't take any dairy, to my dismay, since, at the time, ice cream was big in my diet. It's all chemicals she said. Our bodies are made up of nothing but chemicals, like the universe. She was like that. She frequently waxed philosophical. She usually quoted from something she'd recently read in one of the books she was always trying to get me to read. You need to overcome your dominant paradigm she said to me after reading one.

Sometimes when I am finished cleaning at the Hales', I open the windows to let in fresh air. Grandmother called it airing out the house. In the middle of winter, several times a week after her house cleaning was finished she opened every window in the house, regardless of the temperature, to let the bad air out and the good air in. A practice I continue with my cleaning, though Mrs. Hale disapproves of wasting heat in winter or the central air conditioning in summer. Grandmother had no spray

277

bottles and miracle cleaners. She mixed her one cleaner with water, varying the cleaner-to-water ratio with each job. She scrubbed standing, she scrubbed on her hands and knees, toting around with rubber-gloved hands her blue bucket filled with soapy warm water.

Mother's Clark Street apartment was filthy. She hated natural light and the shades were drawn day or night. It was because of how she looked. You see all the lines in daylight she said. As beautiful as she still was, in those days she lived on Clark Street, in the morning her face lines and shaky hands showed a woman five or ten years older. It got so bad there a fetid smell overwhelmed you when you walked through the door, a combination of stale beer, cigarette and pot smoke, dust and beefy grease. Ray was fond of frying hamburgers and the dishes and pans stacked up in the sink. There was no way Grandmother wanted Mother to take baby Jennifer, but Grandmother had no choice. She couldn't turn her only daughter in. And Clark Street was close enough so we had Jennifer most of the time anyway. Mother was trying to get back at Ray. Somehow she thought having the baby living with her would help.

Every day Grandmother or I went to Mother's to bring Jennifer back. Many nights Jennifer slept over with us. Other nights Mother hired a baby-sitter, one of her co-workers' teenage daughters, or one of the girls to whom she sold pot. Grandmother and I never trusted any of them and dropped in unexpectedly so the sitters knew we were close by and keeping an eye out. One time Caroline Mason was watching Jennifer and when we dropped in she was in the middle of having a party. There were a dozen kids there, all of them I knew from the neighborhood or school. They were drinking beer, smoking pot and cigarettes, and Grandmother threw them all out. We took Jennifer home with us and the next morning Mother showed up at the house screaming at Grandmother she had no right to do what she did. Grandmother threatened she could report her to the social services department.

Everybody knew my business, and in some cases, more of it than I did. After the night when Grandmother and I found Caroline Mason partying with the kids, I couldn't look at any of them in the eye and felt ashamed, as if it was my fault. I was estranged from part of my family and the kids in the neighborhood. Denise had no problem. She acted as if nothing out of ordinary was going on. If she was mad at Mother, Mother was the enemy and she went on campaigns to undermine her. When she was getting along well with Mother, she used her whenever she could for things like money or a ride somewhere.

It's easy for me to lose track of the day of the week or time of the day. I'm only at the Hales' three or four hours a day, three days a week, and the rest of the time I'm here. I am never completely alone. There are sounds coming from upstairs or outside. I am never completely in the dark because, day or night, some semblance of light slips in from somewhere. Days and nights are a continuum. I lay on the bed. I sip green tea. I smoke. My short stints of sleep may come any time and the moments of waking are most confusing as it may take as much as a minute for me to retrace my steps back to where I am at the moment.

They keep the television on very loud upstairs. Often it's tuned to the Portuguese station. At night the little girl watches the same American shows I hear the Hale kids talking about. The grandfather listens to soccer games on the radio, the rise and fall of the announcer's voice and roar of the crowds fill my room, especially in the summer when he sits in the yard at the picnic table, sipping his red wine with the transistor radio next to him. Mother always had the television or the radio turned on loud. She never turned it down when I asked, so I often had to lay awake at night waiting for her to fall asleep so I could get up

279

and turn it off. She'd come home from a shift late at night and watch reruns of old black and white movies. If she wasn't completely asleep when I entered her room to shut off the television, she'd bark out leave it alone I'm still watching it.

I have no television or radio. I don't read the newspapers or magazines. But there's no way to cut myself off from any of it. On buses, in markets, at the Hales', people talk about what's on television and what's in the news. The most recent murder. The big game. The terrible parents who were shooting their children with drugs and having sex with them. There's no way to avoid it. Someone on the bus has a newspaper or magazine open and my eye is drawn to a headline. The Hales have a television running on every floor sometimes. Television journalists prying their way into the face of some grieving woman whose child has just been found raped and strangled. There's a country somewhere that we are bombing. People are starving. Prep School Prof. Kept Kiddie Porn. Having spent so much time in institutions, I've learned to recognize certain characteristics in people. Denise, for example, is like other women I've met, who cut themselves like some people get haircuts. They act out. They stalk. They cling. They claw. It started with her at an early age and really escalated once she hit puberty. Fact and fiction are one. When she told me about what happened with Ray I didn't believe it, at first. Then I thought back to those times. She was twelve or thirteen. The backyard cookouts at Grandmother's. Ray with his shirt off and Denise with her short shorts and tight tops sitting on his knee. They never went all the way. She said they mostly made out when they had a minute or two alone. Ray would feel her up some, but that's as far as it went. When mother was pregnant and crazy to be around, she said she and Ray got into it more often, right up through the time that baby Jennifer was born. The one who forced her against her will was Al. I hardly remember Al, he was before

Ray and it only lasted a month or two.

One night Denise took her bike to the lounge where my mother worked to bring Mother something she'd forgotten, most probably pot. This guy Al was hanging out at the bar and offered to put Denise's bike in the back of his pickup truck and drive her home. Mother thought it a great idea. On the way home the guy pulled off Route 133 into the woods where he raped her. Denise said he told her if she ever breathed a word about it to anyone, he would claim she was a liar and that everyone already knew her reputation and they would believe him. I didn't know these things at the time. I learned them from Denise in bits and pieces. But sometimes her stories changed.

With someone like Dr. Isu, I might consider having a relationship with a woman again. She wears no ring. But that doesn't mean anything. Her mannerisms don't offer the slightest clue as to her sexual preference. It's not her looks, which I do find attractive, but something that comes from deep inside her. She's gentle, wise, sensitive; and has no mean spirit. At least none that I can detect. But I only see her forty-five minutes at a time the same time every other week. And it's her job to be gentle, wise and sensitive. Who knows what she's like on a bad day wearing her darkest suit?

Dr. Hale has all of these traits. In public, he is celebrated for his humanistic achievements loved and respected by his peers and the public. But he is not the same person at home where he is controlling. This is easily disguised as an over caring virtue in public; but in private it is potent and stings. On the surface is the jolly we're-all-in-this-together family personality; but, in a passive way, things go his way or no way. The piano lessons. The voice lessons. The sports the kids choose. The vacations or family days out. How Mrs. Hale wears her hair. Everything is centered around what he wants, needs, and thinks is best.

281

So some people have different personalities, depending on the situation. I have been the same person for too long. As much as I sometimes think otherwise, a relationship is not going to change that. I've learned that already. It's not that I prefer women. I would love the love of a man. But most of them are so simplistic. No one would want me. I'd have to lose weight. Fix my hair. Go out. I can't imagine having someone lying next to me here, interrupting my space, seeing my naked body. I would have to bath every day. They would have to know everything. They would want to know everything. They would want to put their hands on my flabby body and smell my smells and I would have to believe.

Thirteen

I try to imagine Grandmother's life and what it was like for her those last years alone in the house. The frequency of my visits coincided with my stability; but even when I was able, I visited less frequently in time. She grew frail as the years chipped away, although her mind remained sharp and clear.

On my visits she reported how she spent her days cleaning and preparing meals for herself. She had some spinach left over and broiled up a small steak. She washed the stairs going down to the basement, a task that was long overdue. Yesterday she made a nice chicken soup and she'll eat it through the week. She liked to preface her food descriptions with the word nice. On her soap opera a long lost twin brother of one of the main characters appeared out of nowhere, impersonating his brother. And the man came out the other day to look at the roof. It only needed to be patched in a few spots. She rarely went out. Even her groceries were delivered.

Eventually she stopped lobbying for me to move back with her. She wanted me there, but she knew that I had to make a life somewhere beyond Wilton. I'm glad she didn't suffer and went in her sleep, although she was dead in her bed all those days. Her heart was the last thing I suspected would give out. She previously requested a funeral service in the church, and I buried her alongside Grandfather. I was the only family member at the service. The only other attendees were several old widows in black who attend mass daily. They sat in the back clutching their rosary beads. Until the week of her death,

Grandmother attended church every Sunday morning. But she made no friends or contacts. God's enough to get me through the day. I sat in the front row at Grandmother's funeral, the priest's words echoing empty through the church, empty in my ears. I desperately wished what Grandmother believed in were true. In that event she might have peace in another world.

Harry can't hold herself up and falls off the Bear Hill tower. That's when I wake up. What really happened was she terrorized me for several seconds. We were hanging out at the tower, smoking cigarettes and hoping the boys we'd seen on our way up would follow. They did, and judging by the way they coughed when Harry lit them up, they never smoked before. We usually avoided going inside the tower because of the strong urine smell. It was built of fieldstone three stories high. That day we decided to walk up the spiral stairs to the lookout platform and see if the boys were coming. You could see the ocean way off in the distance on one side, and the forest stretching out to Brockton on the other.

Harry whispered in my ear they're virgins. On the top deck, the conversation was awkward. Harry asked them if either of them had ever kissed a girl before. They both said sure. Harry said I don't believe you prove it. The boys got nervous and looked at each other and down at their shoes. Just at that instant, without any warning, Harry climbed over the railing and held herself up by her hands on the stone ledge. The drop was enough to seriously injure, if not kill her, and the two boys and I gasped. Harry was always capable of daredevil antics, but this was the most dangerous thing I'd ever seen her do. I screamed at her Harry what the fuck are you doing? The boys looked at each other and ran down the stairs in a panic. By the time I made any gesture to help, Harry was already pulling herself back over the ledge and back in again grinning the entire time. She jumped down on to the platform and brushed herself off.

Scared the shit out of them she said as we watched those boys run down the trail and out of our sight. My heart was pounding. I grabbed her hard don't ever do that again.

When I was a child, Grandmother's house seemed big. But after I finally moved out and continued to visit her, the house grew wearily small. I didn't want to have to go back in there; but someone had to get Grandmother's things out of the house. Most of her possessions were old and there was nothing of value. The furniture. The curtains. The dishes, glasses, pots and pans. Every single object in that place oozed with some kind of flash memory. It was too much, and I had all I could do to have someone come in and haul it all away. A lifetime of her accumulations, cellar to attic, gone in a matter of a few hours.

I was forced to spend considerable time in Wilton after Grandmother died. First I had to make her funeral arrangements. Then the house needed to be cleared out and sold. It was over a decade since I left. The neighborhood changed. New families occupied the houses. Now I could drive through Wilton to Grandmother's and not see anyone I recognized. Though at any particular time the sight of a certain street corner, fire escape, park bench, strip of fence, stretch of road, kids playing baseball or riding bikes, group of teenagers hanging out, or that lone girl bringing a cigarette to her lips like she owns the world, I saw Harry.

There were some personal items of Grandmother's and I knew where they were, including a few pieces of jewelry, a box with photos dating back from her wedding and following up through my mother's first wedding and various family gatherings on holidays, birthdays, my first holy communion. The newspaper clippings. I put everything in one big chest which sits at the foot of my bed. I don't want what's inside; I don't care to look in there. I owe it to her to keep these things. Her house didn't sell for as much as she would have thought. One

285

is hard pressed to find a reason to be attracted to Wilton these days. And clean as it was on the inside, all those years of structural neglect left the house in need of serious repairs. I experienced a tremendous sense of relief the day I finally had no reason ever to return to Wilton.

Radio stations, television stations, newspapers. The headlines, photographs and film-clips. Triple-murder-suicide, black-and-white photos of victims, uniformed men carrying a body bag on a stretcher down a flight of stairs. Her chest sits at the foot of the bed. I must make a clean break. I can't move. My body is wrapped in gauze. A light. A shadow. A voice. Do you understand me? You are Laurel Bell. You have had a treatment. You are in . . .

Upstairs they fight. The little girl's mother and grandmother work during the day. The grandfather works through the night as a baker and sleeps through the morning and afternoon. This is fine when the little girl is at school, but during the summer when she is home, there's always a ruckus going on because she's not allowed outside of the yard. I never see her with friends and when I leave my apartment and she's out in the yard playing alone, she follows me to the end of the driveway asking where I am going when I'll be back. She says they never let me go anywhere. I can't leave the yard. When she gets bored in the yard she goes in the house and disrupts the grandfather's sleep and he yells and sometimes hits her. Recently she had a black eye and said she fell.

I fear the unknown as much as I fear what I know. Stillness. Quiet. Dark. Green tea and cigarettes. The heater clicks on. Dust rises and settles. Upstairs dishes are placed on the table. Lunch. Dinner. Breakfast. The grandmother shouts. They eat fast and voraciously, breaking bread with their hands in large chunks. I've seen them in the yard under the grape arbor. Germs gather in the minutest crevices. Smell of fatty sausage grease, cigarette smoke, and my scalp. Sound of voices raised in a language foreign to me, conspiring to undermine the trajectory of my memory.

Denise says once I come out to California I won't want to return to Massachusetts. And there's absolutely no reason to with Grandmother gone. Mrs. Hale's been trying to be closer and more sociable since she knows I no longer need the work. I don't understand how Denise will be able to parent. It's not as much selfishness but her nature. It's the only way she can be. She won't accept the competition.

I wonder which ones they are. I am walking down the street, sitting on the bus, shopping at the market. How do they get on? What kind of marriages? What kind of parents? What kind of work? What kind of sleep? What kind of dreams? They are out there as close as the next seat.

I have met many over the years. Names and faces I forget. I remember the stories. The girl who watched her father murder her mother when she was five. The two sisters who were continually raped by their stepfather for years while their mother knew. The girl who used to set fires. Even in the hospital she set fires. No matter how closely they watched her she managed to smuggle matches and get a fire going somewhere. Once she jammed her door shut and lit her bed and curtains on fire and they had to break down the door. The girl who counted her cuts which numbered in the hundreds. I've never once ran into one on the outside. At least anyone that I recognized. But we all go back out. We all have to go somewhere when they tell us we are ready.

Fourteen

Harry first showed me how to shoot a can of beer behind the Curtis School. First you puncture a hole in the lower side of the can then flip the ring-top hold the can upright and the beer shoots out the lower hole. Harry sucked the contents of a can down in seconds. When I tried, beer went all over my face and I gagged. I had to sneak into the house so Grandmother didn't catch me with the smell of beer. Harry loved beer, when she was drunk, she got even funnier, performing one-person shows or saying the most inappropriate things. She started to drink a lot, and as she got drunker, she became less able to carry on a coherent conversation and her physical agility gave way to a stumbling, falling kid who would pass out in the bushes behind the school. Unable to wake her, I left her to sleep it off.

She didn't tell me she was on the run that last time. I found out from Billy Donovan, who also informed me that Harry was living at my mother's apartment. I saw her there frequently when I picked up baby Jennifer or dropped her off; I thought nothing of it at the time. Ray wasn't living in the apartment because there were ugly fights and the police took Ray away in handcuffs and warned him to stay away. If Mother didn't need baby Jennifer as a pawn in her war with Ray, she would have let Jennifer just stay with us all the time.

Sister Agnes opens her arms with her palms flat-out towards the class, she tilts her head back, rolls her eyeballs up into the back of their sockets and says they nailed him to the cross. For several long seconds she stands there with her arms outstretched and her eyes rolled back. Then she speaks again. Imagine the spikes straight through his hands and feet, shaking her palms when she says the words *spikes straight through his hands and feet*. And he hung there, blood oozing out of his wounds. Imagine what it must feel like to have spikes hammered through your hands and feet and to hang by those spikes. *He suffered and he died for you*. And she looks through us with piercing gray eyes, flat face, oversized lips, pasty skin. Then she looks up at the large carved crucifix hanging above the blackboard with glossy globs of red paint around the hand and foot wounds. *And he hung there for you*.

Harry could do a great imitation of Sister Agnes. Over the years, the phrase *he hung there for you* became a catchall funny line which we used on each other, and as an in joke on others. Sometimes, out of nowhere, Harry would walk up to one of the neighborhood kids or a complete stranger on the street and say *he hung there for you*. And it always cracked me up. What I remember most about summer-vacation school, besides the time Harry and me, her brother and Billy Donovan did Alvin in the talent show, was the image of the crucifix. Everywhere I looked, in the classroom, the dining hall, the church, the rectory, were larger than life carved images of Christ nailed to the cross with bloody globs of blood at his wounds. *And he hung there for you*. We came in second in the talent show. We should have won, but Angela Valarelli's father was in the army and was fighting in Vietnam. She came out and sang the words 'My father left for Vietnam/He'll be gone/for three whole years' to the tune of 'Greensleeves'. So she took first place even though we were the best act.

Dr. Hale loves opera, especially Italian opera. He has thousands of records, tapes and CDs. There is no longer good opera in Boston he says so he goes to New York. One of the highlights of the many highlights of his year is when Dr. Hale goes to New York City for the opera. For days after his return he is in a euphoric state, walking around the house as if on air, humming and singing to himself. I know nothing of opera. My music interests stopped abruptly when I was a teenager. Over the years, having heard various operas that Dr. Hale has played on his stereo, and though I speak no Italian or German, one thing is for certain: the same things that happened to people then, happen to people now. I can tell by the highs and lows of the songs. Dr. Hale says this is where they fall in love or this is where someone has been killed and I already know that from the music.

Days that Mrs. Hale is particularly annoying, I am anxious to give my notice. I am afraid to let it go. I feel that I need something I can cling to. A series of memories to form a skeleton on which no dead flesh hangs. Clean folded laundry. Lemon-shiny wooden floors. Oil-soaped mahogany railings and buffed brass door knobs. A glass pane so clean you could put your fist through. Fresh linens and perfectly made beds that others sleep in. Scrubbed sparkling sink bowls bath tile and tubs. Disinfected toilets. New shelf linings and neat coffee tables. A burning whiff of ammonia.

A clean house isn't everything Harry said. We were talking about our mothers. I couldn't understand why she could think I was lucky to have my mother. But she said I was. Harry always liked my mother. I never gave it a second thought when she was around Mother more and more. I noticed it in a marked way after Mother moved out to her Clark Street place. Up until then, I imagined that one of the reasons she was at our house was me. But when Mother moved, Harry never came around Grandmother's house. She already quit school, and I was with Harry at school or I was with no one. The popular crowd, those blessed with the right looks and skills, the cheerleaders, the pom-pom girls and the boys they hung around with horri-
290

fied me. I never felt so self-conscious as when I had to walk through the dining hall, alone, past rows of tables seated with the popular kids.

Nonetheless, I managed to do well in school, despite my math and science deficiencies. As I finished the tenth grade, the guidance councilor suggested that I switch over from the business course to the college course. I never had thought of going to college up until that time. I was lost, as any girl my age, still trying to figure out what was going on with my body, and imagining I would meet a nice boy and get married and have a family like girls from Wilton always did. Young as I was perhaps I still believed I could right all that Mother made wrong. College was a way to one-up my mother in a way she could never accept. I started taking French class in the eleventh grade and whenever I was around her, I spoke French words and phrases much to her dishevelment. Speak English who wants to hear that crap no one can understand.

My father loved to fish. One of the few times he managed to get around Mother and take me somewhere we drove out on Route 133 where he parked his car on the side of the road. His fishing gear was in the trunk and we gathered it up and walked a winding woods path to a little pond. All the way to the pond he pointed out various things, like the difference between a hardwood forest and a softwood forest. How some kinds of trees grow leaves and shed them in the fall and other trees stay green all year long. I remember how the evergreen forest smelled like pine, different from the hardwoods which had a nutty aroma. Around the shallow edges of a cove, where the sun beat down on the muddy shore, a film of petroleum settled reflecting silvery blue and smelling like excrement. Father showed me how if the sun is out and you keep mind of your position to it, you can walk in a straight direction without a compass and you never have to worry about getting lost. He

291

pointed to various kinds of birds, squirrels and chipmunks; and he knew the names of all the fish in the pond and what they ate. I felt sorry for the worm when it wriggled as he spiked it with the hook. But when my plastic red and white float started bobbing just like he said it would, I counted to five when it went under and set the hook. I was so excited I nearly fell in the water. Somewhere in the trunk at the foot of the bed there's a photo he took of me holding my first and only bass. When we got back to his car that day, we discovered that someone threw a rock through the windshield. He brushed the broken glass off the seat very calmly and cleaned up the mess. While driving home he said it was unfortunate that there were some very mixed-up people in the world. But he assured me that mostly people were good, and he held my knee firmly in his right hand while driving with his left. Father didn't leave right after that. It may have been months or more. But that afternoon fishing is the last solid memory I have of being with him.

I wake and doze for several hours. A steady rain falls. Water rushes down the drainpipe from the roof to the spout outside my window and splashes on to the driveway. The heater is running less and less now. As spring approaches, as in fall, my room gets damp. I switch over from my panties and men's sleeveless white t-shirt to a sweatshirt and sweatpants. So I won't wake anyone in the middle of night with a whistling teapot, I boil my water in a tiny pan. Water spats scald against the inside of the pan. I steep the tea for a long time. I light a cigarette and draw deep. The menthol cuts cool into my lungs and I hold the smoke a second. Light hurts my eyes. During the daytime I wear sunglasses when I'm outside, I'm so frightened of making eye contact with anyone. I can do anything around the room in the dark like a blind person. I have no need to turn on the lights. Moreover, the stove pilot, electric digits on the clock, the red dot on the telephone machine and outside light spraying in around the drawn window shade deliver more than enough light for my eyes.

Fifteen

The tiny red light blinks fast. Her voice sounds desperate. Between sobs Denise says call me, you're the only person who I can talk to.

It could be anything with Denise. She loved to gather everyone around her hospital bed. Mother, Sully, Grandmother, me, her various boyfriends. When Mother was with Ray and they were going to take a trip to Las Vegas and leave us behind, Denise couldn't stand the thought of being left behind. I could see it coming and knew she was getting ready to cut. What she didn't expect was Mother would run off on vacation anyway. In the hospital, Denise acted out so badly they transferred her to a special unit at Bridgewater.

An orderly wheels me from my room to the room where they administer the ECT. It is often the same orderly who wheels me back, although at that particular moment, I'm unable to remember. The new combination of medications has completely eliminated my sexual urges. It's not that I'm active with anyone but myself. I feel like my feelings are filtered and slightly out of reach. Some of the drugs have a more distinct effect than others. I still find people attractive. Dr. Isu. Dr. Hale, though it took me years to see him that way. And there is a professional man about my age who is always on the seventy-seven bus dressed smartly, reading a *Wall Street Journal.* He wears no wedding ring and I sit so I can watch him out the corner of my eye. The orderlies follow me around for days until my next treatment, making sure I don't wander off the unit. Maybe that man on the bus can advise me what to do with my money.

Sometimes when I lay in the dark I hear Mrs. Serge's piano notes. She plays many of the same pieces over again, and certain passages have become familiar to me. I don't know titles. Most of the authors have Russian names. She complains to me about the cook's radio which he keeps tuned loudly to a rock station, and when she plays the piano, he turns up the radio. She spoke to Mrs. Hale about him and how he talks to himself; but Mrs. Hale didn't seem to care.

Harry put up a fight. She clawed his face good. He had bite marks and several broken fingers. By the time the details got around Wilton, the citizens had twisted and inflated any factual detail. Nothing I heard would have surprised me. It was even said that she was the one who pulled the trigger to kill him with her last dying breath. Just take a little time off again, and just go out there again. Walk down the streets of the neighborhood. Go to school. Have normal conversations with other kids. Denise later moved to Brockton and in with a boyfriend when she turned sixteen. A year later she left for California. In all those years since, I've only seen her once, and that was a time in between husbands, when she returned and lived briefly with me and Grandmother. Not long after that, she wound up in the hospital after another cutting incident. When she was released she moved back out west. It's been more than half a lifetime since she was regularly part of my life; it seems like yesterday, and she's as close as blood and a phone call.

All babies are beautiful one way or another Jennifer was the most beautiful baby I'd ever seen. More beautiful than Denise was as a baby. Jennifer got all of mother's looks. The blond hair. Turned up nose. Big round blue eyes so radiant it was hard to believe they were real. She was a gentle baby. Coos and caws when I comforted her. Happy little sighs. She always situated herself the same way when I fed her, with her delicate legs stretched out and crossed at the ankles, head back, gripping the bottle with her tiny hands, and, sometimes, I would let go just to see if she could hold it herself and it would tumble over out of her mouth. Before she crawled forward she crawled backwards, scampering around on Grandmother's living-room floor bumping into things. It never seemed to bother her being shuffled around from Mother's to Grandmother's and back. I wheeled her in the carriage and she smiled wide, the queen of the neighborhood.

In the new dream that I haven't dreamt yet, I'm standing on my father's grave somewhere in the hills of northern California. I don't know the name of the town. The sun is shining and the sky is clear and blue enough to scoop. The foliage is green, lush, the clean air smells of wild herbs and spices. I'm looking down at his grave, conversing with him. I still feel your hand on my knee. I'm sorry I didn't come sooner. My blood and my bones.

If you think something hard enough before you fall off to sleep you can shape your own dreams. When I was a girl, near Christmas, or the night before we went to Washburn Lake Park, I would think of nothing but Christmas morning, or riding the roller coaster with Harry. Sure enough during sleep that night I would dream of such events, though the dreams never turned out the way I'd hoped and I would miss the bus for the amusement park or Santa brought strange unusable gifts.

Denise had Mother's looks except for the black hair. Black Irish. My looks came from my father's family. Mother said they were all rolly-polly and flat-footed. Once a month I cut my own hair. I've figured out a system using mirrors, holding one behind me and one in front of me. Nothing fancy, but I keep it short. Mrs. Hale once asked me who cut my hair. I told her I cut it myself and she said oh. In my wilder days I grew it out full and long. Women said it was the kind of hair they would die for because it was so naturally thick and wavy. When the grays started coming, I dyed my hair various shades of red, brown, and even jet-black. I tried jogging, working out at the gym, swimming. Once, for three months straight, I counted every single calorie and gram of fat I put in my body each day.

Harry broke her ankle playing basketball. Her leg was in a cast from the knee down for six weeks. She wore the first cast out in three weeks. Crutches she discarded the first day, they were too cumbersome and she found it easier hobbling on the stump at the bottom of the cast. Her wound couldn't slow her down. She played basketball, rode her bike and ran about with all her usual reckless energy. The doctor left her without a stump on the second cast. This forced her back on to the crutches because the break would never heal unless she gave it a chance. Even on crutches, Harry beat most boys at a game of twenty-one on the basketball court.

The heater clicks on. It's only two or three times a night now. Soon I'll be sliding open the little window if I want some circulation. They grow everything in the yard. Tomatoes, greens, beans. There's a peach tree, a pear tree, and the grape arbor. Where they eat their ravenous meals, including the little girl who is only six or seven. She has beautiful long blond hair and blue eyes. It must have come from her father, because everyone on her mother's side is square-jawed and dark. They sit at the red and white check table clothed picnic table to platters piled with grilled red meat, oversize salads, crusty bread and red wine by the gallon jug. On towards the end of summer and into early fall, the grapes ripen and air takes on a rich grape juice smell until the first frosts.

My mother always looked remarkable. I never saw her do anything close to exercising, though she always said eight hours running around serving drinks was all the exercise she needed. She drank, smoked, loved chocolate. I remember her sitting in

297

bed, cigarette in one hand and a chocolate bar in the other, watching television. Her figure never changed.

I am walking out on the ice unsure of my footing. It is frigid, shades of gray. She is out there ahead, waving me on, far enough away that I can't see her face, only the slice of a figure and a waving arm. In her other arm baby Jennifer is wrapped in layers of blankets Mother continues to walk, cautious of the slippery ice despite my pleas for her to slow down and wait. The wind is blowing against me and my words go unheard. She is slipping and sliding as I am, she turns and waves me on again. Farther out on to the frozen lake she heads into a hard wind. My face and the edges around my ears are numbing over. The ice is beginning to swell, surge, and crack. Great blocks are separating from the main body of the frozen lake top. Mother and baby Jennifer become imprisoned on a floating block drifting rapidly away.

Sixteen

There are two calls from the same man waiting on the machine. This is a message for Laurel Bell. I am Dan Grassfield your sister's husband. Please call me as soon as possible. There's been an emergency. The second message is exactly the same, except his voice sounds more grave.

The answering machine is on when I phone. I leave a message. I am Laurel Bell. I am returning your call. I brew tea, open a can of soup. Odor of fried fish. They cook fish every Friday. My soup is bland. I eat because I need nutrition. I smoke. I drink more tea. Eventually I slip from the tiny kitchenette chair and settle into bed with a fresh cup and pack of cigarettes but before doing so, I turn the ringer back on the telephone in case he should call.

I'm startled, and I jump when the telephone rings, spilling tea on to the bed and losing my cigarette on the bed sheets. I recover my cigarette and answer the phone. It is Dan Grassfield. He hates to have to meet over the phone this way, and with such hard news. Denise lost the baby. The grief was so painful that she tried to kill herself. Judging by how he tells me the story, he knows nothing of Denise's history and as far as he knows, this is the first time. I wonder how you can be married to someone and not know the most basic things about them. But what can you learn when you marry someone you've only known for six weeks? Despite the fact that he dropped a wife and family for her, I almost pity him for his ignorance. He wants me to take a trip out there to try to help. He offers to pay

299

for my flight. I assure him there's nothing I can do if I should fly out there; I am in a difficult situation of my own at the present time, and it would be nearly impossible for me to fly to California. He leaves me a phone number where I can reach her in the hospital. Please call her there. I know she wants to hear from you.

Several neighbors said they heard quick pops in the night. Other than that, no one heard anything. The newspapers and television stations keyed in on the same image. A black body bag being lifted down the stairs on a stretcher. I was never sure whose body was in the bag. The alienation in the eyes of the four uniformed men who carried it down the stairs said it all. It was one of those photos, as soon as it became clear in the dark room, the photographer knew it was payday.

It's not too late for me to have a child. These days women regularly give birth right through their forties. I don't need a partner. At the sperm bank I could choose a donor from any background I wish. I'd select Mediterranean. Italian or Greek. Someone with some skills in the math and sciences to round things out. Maybe someone with a thin frame, small-boned. Perhaps it's for the best about Denise. Not that she cut again. That she lost the pregnancy. This is the first time I am aware that she's cut in several years. And what did she tell him about all her scars on her arms and legs. Those thin arms carrying her traumas in thin slivered marks from inside above her palms all the way up. And when she didn't cut she took pills while managing to phone someone at the last minute so she'd be rescued in the nick of time. How could he make love to her and not see the scars and not know what they meant.

I was jealous of how close Harry was getting with baby Jennifer. Whenever I went to pick Jennifer up, Harry was there playing with her. If Mother was supposed to come to Grandmother's for Jennifer, she sent Harry. Your mom's busy Harry said I'll take her back. However, somehow, I felt more at ease knowing that Jennifer was under the watchful eye of Harry rather than my mother.

Close the door and put the quarter in Harry says. I close the round glass door and the metal rim snaps shut. I hesitate. Put the quarter in she yells from inside the clothes dryer. Her voice is muffled and sounds like metal. I slip the coin through the slot and turn the little knob. The machine rolls into motion and Harry rolled up inside rotates around in three hundred and sixty degree turns. A wide grin's spread on her face as the machine twirls her at a dizzying pace. She tries to persuade me to try but I won't. I use all of our quarters to keep her spinning around in the dryer the entire length of the ten-fifteen mass.

I don't believe he meant to hurt anyone that night. The pistol was out in the truck. He only went out for it later. There was an hour's time in between. Apparently he sat down and poured himself a drink. The baby never woke up. They say he drugged her. They say he drugged them all. They say that he drugged himself too. But he did have an hour, maybe as much as two. He sat there in the living-room chair with a drink. His face was scratched and bleeding and several of his fingers were broken.

The summer before I went into the eleventh grade's when factory row burned. It was a tremendous fire that went on for twenty-four hours. Flames and smoke were seen from as far away as New Bedford, Fall River and Rhode Island. Arson was suspected but there was never any conclusive finding. Every one of the old factories either burned to the ground or was gutted. Most of the buildings had long since been vacant; by the time I was a girl Wilton's shoe industry was a thing of the past. After the fire, police and firemen ribboned off most of the area which comprised of a dozen square blocks. Some of the old red brick walls were standing on makeshift staging and braces.

It was one of the rare days Harry and I were together that summer. She was working at a dry cleaner's and recently quit or was fired. Things weren't going well at home so she was threatening to run again. We were too cool for riding bikes by that age, though neither of us drove, and we were hanging out in the center of town just walking from corner to corner. It was hot out and we debated whether we should spend the money for a bus home to get our swimsuits, and then go to Meadow Pond for a swim. Suddenly, she said I know let's go down and see the factories. What was there to see? I asked her. Besides, no one was allowed down there it was dangerous.

Several weeks had passed since the fire. A lot of the publicity had waned. There was still a police officer on each end of the street which was now road-blocked. To avoid the officers we walked down a side street, cut up through an alley slipped under some yellow ribbon and we were inside the ruins. I was afraid and the entire area looked like it had been bombed. I couldn't find any sure footing underneath me and when I saw the brick walls leaning over into the braces I told Harry I wasn't going any farther. C'mon she said you'll never know what we might find, and she made her way around kicking through the rubble. I knew her well enough to know that the more I begged her to come back, the deeper out into the danger zone she would go, so I kept quiet, walked back behind the ribbon and watched her. At one point she held up some shriveled and burned pairs of old shoes. What's your size? I said nothing with my heart beating fast, expecting a wall at any moment to tumble and take Harry down with it.

Seventeen

I suddenly blank out. It seldom lasts longer than a few seconds and when I come around I'm not aware I've gone out. Like being woken up sharply from sleep, I open my eyes but my consciousness hasn't caught up with them yet.

It's happened while I'm riding on the bus. I miss a block and, on occasion, my stop. One time at the Hales' Mrs. Hale brought me out of a blackout while I was standing in the middle of the living room with the vacuum cleaner in my hand, completely unaware of who or where I was. My biggest fear is that I will be outside and walk out into a car. Months can pass without such incidents; or it might happen twice in a week. It was a good reason to stop driving.

An absolute whiteness until references in the environment slowly paint colors on to my blank memory. Your name is Laurel Bell. You are at the South Shore Medical Center and you have just had a treatment. Do you understand what I am saying?

The birds are returning. I hear them outside the window. They move through the yard at first light. Except for the few parks, trees are scarce in the city. But for some particular reason the backyards that come together at this point in the neighborhood are heavily treed and populated with birds. Now they are the tiny ones, chirping in a swarming chorus. The heat clicks on. There's still snow melting on the ground. I reach down and rub between the layers of fat on my belly. I bring my fingers to my nose and inhale the sweat.

Warm air reaches up to my toes, in soft currents it works its way up to my legs, midsection, face and head. The tea is room temperature. I light a cigarette and draw. Two days since sleep. In air pockets knotty stomach-stuff festers. Dust swirls and re-settles according to the air-stream. Quivering shadows swim in exhaling smoke, elements of me in what is around me. Smoke returns in warm drafts. The heater abruptly stops. Birds again. Components of me settle in millions of particles. When I walk through the door and down the hall they follow me. They follow me into the bathroom. They follow me into the dining room. They check on me in the smoking lounge. The earth is wet brown. The snow clings in shaded clumps, dirty white with black mascara.

Baby Jennifer should have slept at Grandmother's house. For some reason, at the last moment, Mother picked her up, insisting that she wanted a quiet evening off with the baby. Usually on her nights off she didn't want Jennifer because she had something going on at the apartment or she and Ray went out. At that time there was some kind of court order for Ray to stay away. Thinking back, Harry was always there when I was picking up or dropping Jennifer off, but I surmise she must have remained out of sight in one of the rooms. Grandmother was just putting dinner on the table. It was winter, Christmas vacation from school. I was in the eleventh grade. The tree was still up and all the new clothes and toys we bought for Jennifer sat underneath the dying, sagging branches. We sat down for dinner, me, Denise and Grandmother. Baby Jennifer was in the high chair. Mother stormed in and said that she was going to take Jennifer for the night after all.

Big crows move in as the morning passes, chasing smaller birds away. They crow loud and long. The entrance to my apartment door is a half-door and I must stoop down. There is no hallway or entrance area, I step directly down three wooden steps into the room. Forms come together, images and shapes correspond to each other. Then I take too much for granted, let my guard down and the lines and boundaries shift until there are gaps I can't account for. I lick it all and place it under my nose. Colors stain my tongue rancid purple-green. The crows are crowing. Mother walks ahead of me, blanket- wrapped Jennifer in her arms. Wind is blowing hard across the open ice. There's not one surface of the place without blood on it. Water cannot wash it away. My ears are numb from the cold. I want the heater to come on but it is too warm. Blood spots the ice and snow drifts. The contents of my nostrils freeze and melt.

Eliza is a sickly child. Her nose runs continually and every week she has some kind of stomach virus or cold flu. She keeps Mrs. Serge very busy between visits to the doctor's office and tending to her every need at home. Mrs. Hale is around most of the time, but she takes no physical part of the day-to-day duties. Someone does the cooking. Someone does the cleaning. Someone takes care of her children. Regarding the children, Mrs. Serge reports to Mrs. Hale. If Mrs. Serge isn't exactly clear, or didn't ask the doctor about a particular detail that Mrs. Hale has deemed important, Mrs. Hale shows great impatience with Mrs. Serge. The same way she does with the cooks. The same way she does with me. Eliza is just beginning to stand and walk around holding herself up. The first time she did it, we called Mrs. Hale into the room so that she could see but she was unresponsive.

Since she had Eliza, Mrs. Hale spends more and more time sitting in the family room big chair watching television. She likes news shows, especially world news, and while watching, she invariably wears a panic-stricken look on her face. Whenever I pass by the room or come within earshot of her, she retells

305

grim details of reports from the four corners of the earth. I don't know what this world is coming to is one of her favorite phrases. Then she spews out one sweeping statement like if they would only stop doing this or start doing that then the problem would immediately go away. When she's not sitting in the big chair, she sleeps. The kids are off to school with the help of Mrs. Serge. Mrs. Hale rises mid-morning and takes Eliza until noon before her coffee and some toast. If time allows she naps in the afternoon. She's very shy about socializing even though Dr. Hale has such a busy social calendar. I've frequently heard arguments between the two of them. Usually Mrs. Hale is attempting to get out of an engagement at the last minute, one of her migraines or a sore throat. Just tell them I'm ill you're the one they want to see anyway.

In the paper it said that she'd once been arrested for prostitution. I didn't believe it. Grandmother wouldn't admit or deny it. She said only that it was years in the past and no one ever knew the truth about it except my mother. She did try to settle down with my father, and with Sully. She quit waitressing for a time during each marriage. She was never a housekeeper and was clueless to the ins and outs of running a household. She mixed whites and darks in the laundry, couldn't get a vacuum to work because she never changed the bag, cooked out of cans or we ate frozen dinners.

There was always plenty of beer. My father didn't drink more than a beer or two. It got to be another wedge between them when he learned that my mother often drank beer through the afternoon while watching television or sitting out by the pool. Even at work she drank and was fond of making jokes about her special cups of coffee. One too many gin and tonics her chin dropped and she began repeating herself in slurred words. Then she would instigate an argument with him and start getting rough. Once she punched him in the face. Another time she scratched his arms. He would just cover himself up to defend himself the best he could. For Christ's sake he said what about Laurel.

Eighteen

I walk up a long steep rocky slope. Rocks crumble under my feet. A wind blows from behind and lifts me with it. Mother's words echo in the air.

Laurel, don't let . . .

And then it trails off. Where are you? I cannot see her. There are clouds and mist blowing overhead.

Laurel, don't let . . .

And then it begins to drizzle drops of blood. Steadily it falls, harder and until the ground is blanketed and the air a red sheet. I hear Mother and call her. The blood is soaking my hair, seeping into my eyes, my clothes, down my neck and back. I continue to climb, my feet unsteady on the slippery ground. The slope becomes steeper until I am forced to use my hands to pull myself up. My palms are cutting on the sharp rocks. I am calling her. My blood is mixing with the raining blood.

Mother was a shoplifter fond of changing price tags. I was always frightened to death when she took me shopping. While waiting in line I wondered fearfully if her scam would be detected and we'd get arrested in front of everybody in the store. For years she bought clothes and groceries with her own markdown system. When I needed a new dress for junior high graduation dance, we went to Lake's Department Store and found the beautiful dress that I wanted. Mother thought the dress too expensive and switched tags with another dress marked down ridiculously low. When the cashier rang the dress she stopped and said she thought it was a mistake. They called the manager who said the dress was the higher price and someone must have changed the tag. Mother argued with him, the law said that the customer only had to pay what the merchandise was marked. In the end, the manager won. I think he knew that Mother changed the tag and, if it came to it, Mother would have to back down rather than stand accused. She turned to me at that point and said that's a lot of money do you still want the dress? Everything went quiet, all eyes were upon me, the manager, the cashier, Mother's, the other customers who were behind us in line. I looked at the dress, and I looked at Mother, who was waiting for an answer. Yes, I said, I do. Outside the store she acted as if the incident never happened and I doubt she gave it another thought. I wore the dress and went to the dance without a date. Harry was supposed to meet me and we would go together. But she appeared at the dance an hour late, very drunk. I walked home alone and was in bed by nine. I never wore the dress again.

Another one of her tricks was to have us eat candy bars and drink soda in the market while she was shopping. Denise became a rampant shoplifter for a while. She was caught twice. The first time she was young and they let her go. Later she practiced mother's switching tags technique. If she needed money she returned the merchandise claiming it was given to her for a gift without a sales slip, and received full price back. She did this at various stores around Wilton, then Brockton. And when they caught her she was prosecuted but pulled a suicide attempt before the trial date and ended up in the hospital. Eventually the incident was dismissed because of her mental health.

I called Mother's early the next morning. I wasn't expected to pick Jennifer up until around noon but knew if Mother and Ray were up late, Jennifer might need some tending. There was no answer. I waited a little while. There was no answer again.

309

Sometimes Mother slept very soundly and I had to let the phone ring for a minute or more. Even if the ringer woke her up she could fall right back to sleep. I was afraid they were passed out and imagined baby Jennifer in her crib with a soiled diaper, hungry and crying.

It was a cold Saturday morning and there were tiny snowflakes spitting in the air. Foster Street was quiet. None of the kids were out yet. Cars were sitting quiet in driveways collecting snow. The wind whipped the trees and rattled the loose drainpipes and gutters on the rickety houses. Snowflakes blew harder, making a tick sound against my jacket. I turned down Curtis Street. In my head I was singing 'California Dreaming' which at that time was Denise's favorite song. She bought the record and played it over and over again. *On such a winter's day.*

Everywhere outside things are clanging and banging. Trash cans are overturned and rolling around on the ground. Loose windows are shaking in their frames. Screen doors are whipping open and snapping back. The rain has stopped and the wind is fierce. It is March. At first I gave myself until April and then moved it to May. To force myself into some other kind of situation. For two days it rained and now the wind. There have been no birds. I don't know where they go when it's windy and rains.

I smell fish. I hear screaming and banging. The grandmother shouts out the little one's name then yaps in rapid sentences. The mother gets involved with her own verbal assault which I can't be sure is aimed at her daughter, or mother but she ends up crying. Finally the grandfather enters with his own   brand of shouting and then it sounds like objects are being thrown.

Every hospital smells the same. That unmistakable sterility. One tiny whiff of it and I can be thrown into the cauldron. Spotless. Shiny. White. Shiny. Spotless and white. Bland food. Friendly orderlies. Nurses you get to know and forget. You call them by their names, and the next day you can't remember. They wheel me down an elevator through a series of corridors into a room.

A light. A shadow. A voice.

I smoke in a room where they let the patients smoke and orderly watches us through a window.

In order that I forget. In order that certain parts of my memory are temporarily burned out. In order that I start fresh. In order that I can be Laurel Bell. In order that I can be at the South Shore Medical Center. In order that I have just had a treatment. In order that I am meeting my orderly, or nurse, or another patient, for the first time. In order that they can follow me around in case I should wander off the unit. In order that I met him yesterday. In order that she was here last night but I don't remember.

It's been harder without Grandmother. She always knew when it was time. I no longer slept or got out of bed. I stopped eating and bathing and couldn't get up to go to the bathroom. She hated to do it. She would call and they would come and take me and I would go without word, Grandmother by my side in the ambulance. Every time I came back she tried her hardest to help. Let's make that the last time. You can do it if you really want.

All the kids stared and talked. Some walked right up to me what was it really like in there? Teachers acted as if they were afraid of me. I was on medication. They gave me and Denise tranquilizers to get us through the wake and funeral. The doctor and Grandmother thought we should stay on them for a little while. Denise wouldn't go back to school. She cut herself within days of the funeral said she didn't want to live either.

It was more than the pot and drinking that came between me and Harry. I think it disappointed her that I wasn't that way. The trouble with you is you won't let yourself go. That's what

311

she said the time we tried to do it and I got so uncomfortable. If you'd only let yourself go you might like it. And Harry started hanging around with Annie Smith who was also known as a tomboy and for a while they were inseparable and I saw very little of Harry. Without Harry my only friend was Billy Donovan who I only saw if I went down the Curtis School where he hung out. He always tried to get me to go out more, and invited me to beer parties out in Bear Hill Reservation.

Nineteen

Ray's truck was parked in front. Mother smashed up the Cadillac. I don't know whose baby Jennifer was if she wasn't Ray's.

The snow was falling harder and everything was quiet. A car rolled slowly down the street. I could see headlights before I could hear tires rubbing over the newly fallen snow. It was Mr. Harrington. He saw me and pulled over to the curb. Rolling down the window, he said hi Laurel in his squirrely manner of speaking. He barely moved his lips when he talked, so it made it difficult to understand him. He raised his head and looked me straight in the eyes. Seen her? Have you seen her? I hadn't in days. He rolled up the window and drove on, the sound of his tires crunching the snow.

There have been no calls from Denise or her husband. Anything could have happened by now. He's flown her off to Paris for a second honeymoon. Or the marriage has been annulled. It isn't flying that scares me. You just give yourself over to it I imagine. When I was little and I flew to Florida, I was too excited to be scared. I'd have to buy tickets. Pack. I don't even own a suitcase. Get to the airport and find out where the plane is then be on a plane in close quarters with all those people only to land on the other side of the country in a city I've never seen before.

I knew about Harry and Peggy Rotondi. She was the park instructor. Every summer for the month of August, the city gave jobs to older kids, some of them in college. One boy and

313

one girl per park. They came five days a week armed with bats, balls, basketballs and volleyballs purchased by the city. They stayed at the park from nine to four and organized games. In our park things were more crossed over than other parks, and the games were coed. Peggy and Martin were the coaches on each side and while the teams changed daily, Harry always ended up on Peggy's team. I thought when I saw them, close that way, touching and laughing with everyone else around, there was nothing to think. Then Harry began going off to lunch with her in the Mustang convertible that Peggy's father, who was a town selectman, bought her when she graduated high school. Peggy was pretty and wore make-up and didn't look like a tomboy. Lots of the boys had crushes on her. She was going to Bridgewater State College in the fall. I saw her and Harry on the grass. It was innocent enough. Harry was flat on her back and Peggy was leaning over her, tickling Harry's stomach and Harry was laughing helplessly.

Harry defended herself to the end. She fought him with every last trick. She bit, clawed, punched, kicked, gouged and pulled hair. But he managed to nail her with a decisive blow. They say he never meant to do it. His friends said he went there to make amends and one last effort to win mother back. They followed me around. Some kids did. They said horrible things. Best we put all of that behind us. The police gave her information. About Ray. About my mother. They follow me around. I wander away. Sometimes the cramps can double me over.

I tried hard to stay off the medication during my natural period. I read books about herbs and nutrition. I took yoga classes and meditation. For nearly two years, I didn't eat meat, fish, bleached white flour or processed sugar. I refused any help from Western medicine. I took myself off my meds and stopped seeing my doctor who was prescribing them and the

314

shock treatments. I began reading about Taoism and Buddhism. They were so contrary to everything I'd learned from Catholicism. There was no blood. No suffering on the cross. Only suffering through existence. And for a while I believed I found a way. I wore certain colors like purple and orange because I believed in their special powers.

Nancy could be cruel. We'd be having a nice moment, just hanging out together. Stop rubbing your scalp she'd bark out. Or worse, you're sniffing again. She had a way of constantly reminding me of all my shortcomings. All the things that made me so self-conscious. If we were going out somewhere with her friends, I never had any, she often reminded me, she made sure to say don't touch your scalp and don't blink. Blinking is another habit I picked up over the years. I can sit for hours, alone, and blink obsessively. You're a freak, she said in the end. Who would want to live with you?

The Harringtons eventually sold their house and moved. I tried living life again. I ran errands for Grandmother. I went to the movies and waited in lines next to everyone I know who knew. This is my home Grandmother said. I needed her; and in some ways, the more of a burden I was to her, the more it became obvious how much she needed me. Her house was so small when I went back. After the men came and hauled a lifetime of accumulations away, the empty rooms seemed cloying, especially my bedroom, the room of helpless years in bed, smaller than my tiny basement studio.

They say I wandered around in the snowstorm for hours. It snowed heavier through the day. The biggest storm of the winter. Billy Donovan saw me in Wilton Center, and when he approached me I had a completely blank look in my eyes and wouldn't talk to him, it was as if I didn't know who he was. My hands were frozen, and he shook me and asked what was wrong. My first memory of Billy that day is sitting in the Pewter

Pot Muffin Shop. We were at a booth and Billy ordered me coffee and I had already sipped half a cup. Still disconcerted, it was another half an hour before I was able to speak, and even then, the words only came one or two at a time and I couldn't complete a sentence. I don't think Billy believed me at first. He thought maybe I'd taken LSD and was freaking out. Eventually, as pieces of my story began to connect, he left me under the watch of the waitress and ran the two miles through the storm to Clark Street.

I rub my scalp, put my fingers to my nostrils and smell. Each part of my body, every tiny crevice, has its own particular smell. My scalp. The inside of my ears. My armpits. My feet, between my toes. My anus and my vagina. The inside corners of my eyes. So many smells. Aaron called it compulsive behavior. Under the circumstances, it wasn't unusual at all. We had as much control as we had no control over our actions he said. It was all right to be human. When he woke in the morning his eyes were bloodshot, he sat on the edge of the bed groaning, trying to keep from being sick. If he couldn't, he ran into the bathroom and vomited in the toilet. Aaron had a way of kneeling over the toilet like he was praying, groaning long, painful groans in between. Then he would put some brandy in his coffee and go off to a twelve-hour workday at his practice.

Even my stomach has its own smell. Burning, acidic, decomposing. It's on my breath. I cup my hands over my mouth and nose, breathing out with my mouth and in with my nose. As the day goes on light forces its way through every possible crack. Every object in the room clarifies. A young girl was found dead on the side of the road. Her breasts were cut out. Her vagina was badly bruised. The corpse lay by a fence. Minute particles rise from my skin. I breath them back in. Some things can crumble in your hand. The tissue. The rioting of bitter tastes and smells. You look like the face on a coin, that's

316

what a sweet crazy man I once met in the hospital said every time he saw me. I lose the light and assume the body of another, and become that other. She was sexually violated in every hole. The sound of crows now. Unrelenting. Losing my footing. The ice beneath me cracks and she is no longer in front of me. I mustn't remain in bed. I need sleep. I am white and sterile. My hands and fingers tingle. I wriggle them to motion. Smoke a cigarette. They have great black wings. You cannot fall off the world only through the ice.

Twenty

There are three messages. The first is another from Dr. Hale. Laurel I'm beginning to grow concerned please phone me. Second is Denise's husband, call at my next possible convenience. Third is Dr. Isu's voice inquiring about my missed appointment. I unplug the machine and the red light goes out.

Upstairs the little girl is crying. The adults are yelling. I don't know what day it is but it's dark. I didn't know what to make of it, what they said about Harry and Mother. They say he never went there to do anything but when he found them that way he went crazy. There is no reason to bathe. There is no reason to change my clothes or the bed sheets. Sometimes when the grandmother is downstairs in the basement doing laundry, she pauses by my door and listens. She knows I'm in here, but I am silent. She must smell the smoke. She stands there listening.

Black and minute glints of white. In California there are many colors. They told the story in the most sensational manner. Newspapers. Radio. Television. The same photo in the Wilton paper as in the Boston newspaper's front page. Those men carrying the body bag down the stairs on a stretcher, and on the television those few long seconds making their way down the stairs. Over and over for days. And the side stories and reporters calling and showing up at our door. Until the next catastrophe. And he hung for you. And they put spikes through his hands. A girl was found dead on the side of the road. Her breasts were cut out. Her vagina was badly bruised.

318

And the photo of the rest area out on Route 133 where the body was dumped.

I try to eat soup but it tastes of metal. The door was slightly ajar but I didn't think anything of it. Bright Christmas colors. The first thing was the Christmas tree fell. Bulbs broken all over the floor in the front room, strings of lights strewn everywhere still lit. Clean house clean mind. A watched pot never boils. Stay away from the woods there are bad men living there. Days go by I won't look directly at my skin. The dim shape of the telephone or glint of faucet over the sink. Hours count off second by second in my forehead. They said he was driven to madness by love. I experience abrupt pains in my skull, striking through to various nerve centers. I could be an attractive woman if I only lost a little weight and did something with my hair and dress.

She stands by my door and listens. She grills meats and sausages by the plateful. In spring she turns the soil in the garden herself, working the pick like a man, swinging it over her head, the blade cuts into the ground at intervals I can clock. The sound of hard metal strikes into soil and small rocks. I don't know what she expects to hear, what she conjectures that I do in here. There. He hit her. Now they're all screaming again. She was found naked. Her clothes were nowhere around. The men in the woods who could harm me. And they built Harry's house there. The men must have moved. Even with the windows shut I can smell the fat burning on the grill. Sister Agnes spread her hands out, tilted her head back, rolled her eyeballs into the upper sockets and stood there. But it's fish I smell. My earwax. I don't remember myself. Her breasts were cut out. They said it was some kind of Satan worship group. Sully said c'mon Laurel you know you want it. Sully sells seashells by the seashore. Don't say that. Just did. Not getting out of bed to go to the bathroom's when I know it's time Grandmother said. A light. A shadow. A voice. Darlings. Angels. Dear ones. The cramps are easing up. I am flowing.

She was living under the bulkhead. How long have you been there Harry she was cooking on a portable stove. Macaroni and cheese. Ray beat up his teacher in junior high. She had to go to the hospital. They sent him to reform school. They told my grandmother. She told me later. Before he moved here Ray beat up a policeman with a baseball bat and they sent him to jail. Ray sat at the table in the yard, shirt off, his muscular dark arms always at a slight flex even while holding a hand of cards. Denise bouncing on his knee. She lived under the bulkhead for sixteen years until the police came. Sixteen days. I am wet. I light a cigarette. My teacup is empty. The police brought her to Fall River. Or Brockton. The lights were still blinking all over the rug and the fallen tree. She's in California I haven't seen her. Wrapped wrists.

Harry knocked over the tree then passed out in the middle room. It was absolute quiet. She was on her stomach. You can smell it coming through the walls. And she carries it on big platters. Her eyes rolled up into the sockets. Breaking bulbs under my feet. The sound of them grinding into the rug. Blood dripping out from where the spikes were driven in. They never found her breasts. Or her clothes. They showed her mother and father on television. Harry what the fuck. She has no face. I turn her over she has no face. It's a mask but she has no face. I walked right past Ray on the floor in the front room next to the tree. I am wet. My hands are bloody. There is blood everywhere. All over Harry. All over the rugs and walls and the sofa. There is a crowbar next to Harry. It is coated with blood. I'm throwing up all over Harry. I see the crib and rise slowly like in a dream. Baby Jennifer is sound asleep. She has a hole in the middle of her forehead and her hands curled up above her shoulders.

The bedroom door is open. Mother's long legs are stretched out. They are covered in blood. The bed sheets are soaked in blood. Mother has no face either. I am sick again. I throw up on the floor. The smell of my vomit and the blood and the dead flesh and fish. It's coming through the cracks of the doors and windows. My hair is knotted from all the rubbing. The smell of my scalp is dried meat. I run out. Down the sidewalk my boot soles leave red tracks in the white snow. I stop to fill my hands with snow and rub them red raw.

Made in the USA
Lexington, KY
28 June 2014